IRRESISTIBLE?

The Things We Do For Love...

Ellie Sutherland will do anything
to get a date—including offering herself up
as a guinea pig in a study on sexual attraction.
But once the study's over, will men still find her...

Irresistible?

Jo Montgomery will do anything to land an account—
including playing "mommy" to her newest client's
three little monsters. She quickly learns that...

Kids Is a 4-Letter Word

Pamela Kaminski will do anything to land the man of her
dreams—including following him on his honeymoon!
Her mission? To change his belief that...

Wife Is a 4-Letter Word

When these women go looking for love,
nothing is going to stand in their way....

Relive the romance

Three complete novels by one of your favorite authors

Dear Reader,

You're bumping along in life, minding your own business and *wham!* Out of the blue, love strikes you like a bolt of lightning—and leaves you nearly as fried! In the spirit of the unexpected zigzag that true love brings to a person's life, Harlequin has assembled the first three romantic comedies I wrote into this madcap collection:

In *Irresistible?* a woman enrolls in a scientific study on human pheromones, and she meets the perfect man. But when the pheromone pills are gone, will he still find her irresistible? This story introduces Manny, the much-loved character who appears in several of my subsequent books.

In *Kids Is a 4-Letter Word*, an interior designer who knows nothing about children pretends to be mother to a widowed architect's three little charmers in order to land the account of a day-care chain. Only, she quickly discovers their hunky father is more trouble than the children....

In *Wife Is a 4-Letter Word*, a jilted groom takes his maid of honor on his defunct honeymoon—just as a friend. But the calamity-prone siren soon lands him in more physical and emotional trouble than he could have dreamed!

I'm so thrilled to see these linked books reissued together, especially since so many of you have contacted me asking where you can find my out-of-print titles. Here they are, beautifully and conveniently packaged for your uninterrupted reading pleasure. I hope these favorite stories of mine bring you many hours of laughs. So, don't simply *fall* in love—get *Lovestruck!*

Until we meet again,

Stephanie Bond

Stephanie Bond

Lovestruck

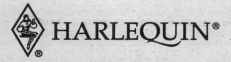

HARLEQUIN®

TORONTO • NEW YORK • LONDON
AMSTERDAM • PARIS • SYDNEY • HAMBURG
STOCKHOLM • ATHENS • TOKYO • MILAN • MADRID
PRAGUE • WARSAW • BUDAPEST • AUCKLAND

HARLEQUIN BOOKS

by Request—LOVESTRUCK

Copyright © 2003 by Harlequin Books S.A.

ISBN 0-373-18518-9

The publisher acknowledges the copyright holder of the individual works as follows:
IRRESISTIBLE?
Copyright © 1997 by Stephanie Hauck
KIDS IS A 4-LETTER WORD
Copyright © 1998 by Stephanie Hauck
WIFE IS A 4-LETTER WORD
Copyright © 1998 by Stephanie Hauck

This edition published by arrangement with Harlequin Books S.A.

CONTENTS

*Falling in love's easy
when you're under the influence…*

1

ELLIE SUTHERLAND opened her mouth to speak, but the sound that emerged was more like a croak. "I'm fired?"

Her supervisor, Joan Wright, coughed lightly, then leaned forward to rest her elbows on the desk. "Not fired. With the new budget cuts, I'm afraid we have no choice but to let you go. In one week," she added sorrowfully. "Please don't take it personally."

"I don't believe this," Ellie mumbled, shaking her head. *How am I going to make the rent?*

"Ellie, yours is not exactly a dream job."

"Oh, great. I'm fired from a job that sucks, and that's supposed to make me feel better." *Credit cards. Food.*

"You know what I mean, Ellie. You're overqualified to be a gofer in a dumpy little federally funded arts center. You're too talented."

"Yeah, that's why gallery owners are beating down my apartment door." *Utilities. Painting supplies.*

"You'll get your break. Just hang in there. You know as well as I do it takes talent, luck and perseverance to make it in the art industry. And since you have incredible talent, you only need one of the other two qualities."

Tears pricked the back of Ellie's eyelids. "I had a

feeling when I woke up this morning I should just stay in bed.'' She sighed. ''I'd hoped to make some contacts at this job.''

Joan brightened. ''You did—me. I'll see what I can do about throwing some commissions your way.''

Ellie raised her head to look over at the woman who'd become a friend in the short time they'd worked together. She could tell Joan felt bad about the turn of events. Ellie summoned her best what-the-hell smile, rose to her feet and said, ''I'd appreciate it.''

''Let me buy you lunch,'' Joan offered, glancing at her watch.

Ellie shook her head. ''Thanks, but I'll be poring over the want ads.'' She trudged toward her tiny cubicle and grabbed her purse. She couldn't afford it, but she'd go out for lunch today and save the bagged egg-salad sandwich for dinner. Right now she needed the time to think.

She walked half a block to her favorite gourmet deli, then admired the handsome order taker as she waited her turn. The hunky guy in the apron was no small part of the reason this was her preferred lunch stop. When she stepped up to the counter, she took her time ordering a salad. The guy scribbled her order on a pad, then studied her intently. Ellie smiled demurely, enjoying the unexpected attention.

''You've been in here before,'' he said.

''Several times,'' Ellie confirmed, sucking in her stomach and turning at a more flattering angle. She saw his nostrils flare as he leaned toward her slightly and inhaled.

''May I ask what kind of perfume you're wearing?''

Ellie fought to suppress the smirk that teased the

corners of her mouth. Maybe this day wouldn't be a total loss, after all. "It's my own special blend. I worked on it for months to get it just right."

The attractive man smiled wryly and scratched his temple. "I just realized I get a migraine every time you come in here. I figure it must be the perfume."

She stood stock-still, her eyes darting sideways to see how many people were privy to the remark. Several customers snorted to cover their laughter and the buxom blonde behind her looked downright triumphant.

Ellie paid for the salad as quickly as possible and slunk to a table by the door. *Will this day ever end?*

She sighed as she sipped her diet cola and skimmed the wedding announcements. Starting with the lifestyle section had seemed like a good way to cushion her journey to the classifieds. But rather than enjoy the snippets about impending weddings, Ellie miserably counted off the handsome men with straight teeth who were now officially out of circulation in the city of Atlanta. She conceded the pictures also proved a little less female competition existed, but a new crop of co-eds graduated every spring to catch the eyes of marriageable men. And spring commencements were upon the city.

She winced. Twenty-nine and dating wasn't so bad. But twenty-nine without a prospect in sight was downright depressing.

The bell on the door tinkled, announcing another customer. A stiff gust of unusually warm May air rushed over Ellie's table, lifted the page she'd been reading and wrapped it around her head. She clawed at the sheet with her hands, battling the breeze. After a few seconds of flailing, she tore her way clear, sneaking a glimpse at the person who'd just entered.

Her pulse jumped in appreciation of his profile. His dark head was down, alternately consulting his watch and an electronic organizer as he joined the long line snaking toward the counter. Ellie frowned at the expensive drape of the olive-colored Italian suit and turned back to her mangled paper.

Why do the cute ones always look as if they were just stamped out with a Donald Trump cookie cutter? Give me a great-looking guy who doesn't own a beeper and I'll give him lots of imperfect little kids. Where are all the good men, anyway?

A sudden jolt to Ellie's elbow sent her cola flying, dousing the paper, her salad and her lap. The icy liquid sluiced down her legs, stealing her breath. Ellie raised her arms, helplessly watching bubbly pools gather and run over the sides of the tiny café table to plip-plop onto the white tile floor. She squeezed her eyes shut and mourned the short life of the white linen skirt she'd scrimped for two months to buy. Then she stood and furiously spun to face the klutz who had ruined her lunch and her outfit.

Mr. Italian Suit had wedged himself between her table and another one, presumably to take a cell phone call in peace, away from the din at the counter. He held one finger to his ear and stood with his back to Ellie. The big palooka hadn't even noticed his errant rump had wreaked so much havoc. Or worse, he didn't care.

"Hey!" Ellie yelled, reaching up to poke the man none too gently on his shoulder blade.

The man was just ending the call and turned toward her, his chocolate-colored eyebrows lifted in question.

Ellie caught her breath. *Mamma mia*. He was gorgeous. Light brown hair, with green eyes framed by those wonderful dark, dark eyebrows and lashes.

"Yes?" he asked, apparently still unaware of the soda puddling around Ellie's shoes.

Ellie opened her mouth to speak, and the phone started ringing again. The man muttered, "Excuse me," then flipped down the mouthpiece and said, "Hello? Yeah, Ray, what's up?" He glanced at Ellie and shrugged apologetically. Ellie stood, arms akimbo, and glared.

A few diners around her tittered and shook their heads. The hunky guy in the apron cast worried glances toward the spill. Well, Armani-man had picked the wrong day to mess with Ellie Sutherland.

She marched around to face him and jerked the phone from his unsuspecting hand. "Ray," Ellie spoke into the phone, "he'll have to call you back, sweetie." She snapped the mouthpiece closed, but held the phone out of reach when the red-faced man lunged for it.

"What are you, some kind of lunatic?" he thundered. "That was my boss—give me my phone!"

"No," Ellie said sweetly. "Not until you pay me for damages."

"Damages?" Confusion cluttered his handsome face. "What on earth are you talking about?"

Ellie swept her arm down dramatically to indicate her skirt.

The man stared blankly. "You're saying I did that?"

"That's right." Ellie smiled tightly. "And I have witnesses," she added, gesturing to the diners close by.

The man looked flustered, then sighed, withdrew a

gold business-card holder, flicked out a card and extended it to her. "Send me the cleaning bill."

Ellie pushed his hand away. "No cleaning bill, mister. A new skirt. You can't get cola out of white linen."

The man looked briefly at her skirt and made a sound as if he didn't deem the garment worth saving. He ran his fingers through his hair, obviously out of his element dealing with a pint-size irate woman. "How much?" he asked finally, taking out his money clip.

Ellie couldn't help doing a double take at the wad of bills stacked there. "Geez, mister, what are you doing carrying that much cash around? You got a mugging fantasy?"

Every eye in the diner turned to the money in his hand. The man looked around, then shook his head and leaned forward. "Why don't you go out and tell everyone on the sidewalk, too?"

Ellie balked. "Sorry."

"How much?" he asked through clenched teeth.

"Let's see..." Ellie frowned. "The skirt was brand-new. This is the first time I've worn it."

"How much?" he demanded, counting off bills. "Fifty?"

"Well, then there's my salad and drink."

"Sixty?"

"And my panty hose are sticky."

The man inhaled a mighty breath and expelled it noisily. "Here's seventy-five, and we're even, okay?"

"Okay." She took the money, grinning. "Thanks."

"Do you think I could possibly have my phone back now?"

"Oh, sure," she conceded with a generous smile, handing him the unit.

He snatched the phone out of her hand and gave her a final glare, then strode out of the deli without ordering. Immediately, he began punching numbers as he walked by the window and out of sight.

"Yuppie scum," Ellie murmured, counting the bills. "What a waste of good looks," she continued to herself, stuffing the bills into her wallet. She mopped up the table and herself as much as possible, ordered another soda, then begrudgingly turned to the want ads.

Jobs were plentiful on the north side of town, in Alpharetta. But Ellie didn't own a car and public transportation hadn't yet caught up with the economic explosion in that area. She narrowed her job search to the few-mile radius surrounding her Little Five Points apartment. She could ride her bike if necessary, or take the train. The pickings were slim, and the artistic opportunities were nil. She had resigned herself to the waitressing section, when a blocked ad caught her eye.

Wanted: Single women of any age with no current romantic attachments to take part in a four-week clinical study. Minimal time commitment. Above-average compensation. Must be willing to keep daily journal.

Ellie frowned. No current romantic attachment. She scanned the bottom of the ad to see if she was mentioned specifically by name. No, but it looked, sounded and smelled like her. She wondered briefly if it could be a scam to target unsuspecting women, but she recognized the address as a reputable clinic. Shrugging, she circled the ad with a red felt-tip pen. It was worth a phone call. A glance at her watch told her she'd be better off to make the call from her desk.

The rest of the afternoon passed mercifully fast. Everyone had heard Ellie would be leaving, so in between expressing their heartfelt regret, co-workers piled last-minute remedial tasks on her desk. Somehow between photocopying, filing, and delivering mail, she managed to call the clinic to obtain a few vague details about the study.

The woman who answered prescreened her with several lengthy general questions. Ellie had to interrupt the interviewer twice to answer other calls. After paging Joan over the intercom, Ellie feverishly punched a button to retrieve the woman she'd been talking to.

"Sorry—I'm back. Now, where were we?"

"Are you heterosexual, bisexual or homosexual?"

"Hetero."

"And are you currently romantically involved with anyone?"

"No."

"When was the last time you had sexual relations with a man?"

Ellie coughed. "Um, about a year."

"Can you be more specific?"

Ellie sighed. "Fourteen months, five days, and—" she checked her watch "—two hours."

"Very good?"

"No, it wasn't very good."

"That wasn't a question, ma'am," the bored screener replied.

Her cheeks burned. "Oh."

"There will be an information meeting tomorrow

evening.'' The woman gave her the time and place, and the compensation rate.

Impressed, Ellie counted the days on her fingers until her rent was due, then asked, ''When will the study begin?''

''As soon as enough participants register,'' the woman told her. ''And you're the most ideally suited caller we've had today.''

Ellie's eyes rolled. ''I'm thrilled for us both,'' she said, then slammed down the phone just as Joan walked around the corner.

''We're thrilled for you too, Ellie,'' she said, fighting a grin.

''How much of that did you hear?''

Joan started to respond, but was interrupted by a yell from John, the accountant who sat two cubicles over from Ellie. ''No more than anyone else, Miss Fourteen Months, Five Days and Two Hours.'' Choruses of hoots and cheers all over the department backed up his belly laugh.

Her eyes darted to Joan. ''The intercom?''

Joan bit her lower lip and nodded sympathetically.

DESPITE THE FRIGHTFUL DAY, Ellie's spirits rose on the walk home. Yes, it was incredibly expensive to live in downtown Atlanta. Yes, traffic was a nightmare. And yes, in summer the humidity was unbearable. But it was worth every inconvenience to be part of the supercharged atmosphere. Ellie loved the outdoor cafés, the street musicians, the colorful murals, the unique shops. People-watching was one of her favorite pastimes, and the eclectic mix of residents that made up the artistic and somewhat affluent area of Little Five

Points always provided a treat for the eyes. Atlanta was a wonderful place to live. Now if she could just find a decent job.

Ellie pulled her keys from her purse as she walked down the hall to her apartment. When a motion in front of the door caught her eye, she gasped. "Esmerelda, what are you doing outside?"

The tabby meowed an indignant reply, and Ellie scooped her up, hurriedly glancing down the hall. Her landlord would probably evict her if he discovered she was breaking the no-pet rule.

"It's me," Ellie yelled as she walked in. She could hear Manny in the kitchen. Dumping the cat on the couch, she said, "Esmerelda must have gotten out when I left this morning." She headed in the direction of enticing aromas, her pet pouncing off the sofa to follow her.

"Naughty puss," Manny chided, shaking a long finger at the cat. "Bad day?" he asked when Ellie flung her purse on the table.

Ellie suddenly felt close to tears. "Would being fired and having my new skirt ruined qualify?"

Her roommate clucked and came over to give her a hug. "You'll find another job," he said soothingly. "And that skirt—" he examined it with a thoughtful eye "—we'll dye it black and no one will ever know."

Ellie laughed. "You're an incurable optimist. Can't you let me be depressed for even a little while?"

He shook his blond head. "No. Now go change. I'm trying something new for dinner."

Ellie stopped long enough to unwrap her uneaten egg-salad sandwich for Esmerelda, then walked the few steps through the living room and down the hall to her bedroom. Manny Oliver was a gem. They'd been friends for three years—in fact, his friendship with Joan Wright had landed Ellie the job at the arts center in the first place.

He made his living doing cabaret shows in drag. Ellie had seen him perform many times, and stood in awe of his singing, dancing and his killer legs. Her male roommate looked better in stockings and heels than she did. And if that wasn't bad enough, the man could cook, too.

After Ellie had changed, and joined Manny in the kitchen, she recounted her day over a scrumptious meal of Italian potato dumplings.

"Men are dogs," he supplied when she described the deli disaster.

"He gave me seventy-five bucks."

"But rich dogs can be housebroken," he amended, and they both laughed. "Was he divine?"

She nodded, the image of the man's face forming in her mind. "Definite model material."

"Nice dresser?"

"Immaculate."

"Straight?"

Ellie shrugged. "I think so, but who knows these days?"

"*Tell* me you got his name."

"No, he offered me his card, but I smacked it away."

He shook his head. "Ellie, how many times do I have to remind you, the game is *hard* to get, not *impossible.*"

She laughed. "He wasn't my type at all, Manny. A

real stuffed shirt. I'll bet you couldn't get a toothpick up his—''

''Ellie!''

''Well, you know what I mean. Except for his obviously better taste in suits, he reminded me of the way my dad used to be—a corporate robot.''

''People change, Ellie. Look at your dad. The man sees more naked people than a doctor.''

''Yeah,'' she said with a short laugh. ''Imagine my mom and dad retiring next to a nudist colony. It *was* by accident, you know.''

''Oh, sure, Ellie, what would you expect them to tell their daughter? If they didn't know about the nudist colony when they moved there, why haven't they posted a For Sale sign in the two years since?''

''I don't want to think about it. The whole situation brings to mind pictures I'd rather not see.''

''The point is, your dad finally mellowed out.''

Ellie snorted. ''After thirty years of missing family dinners and undergoing two bypass surgeries.'' She stabbed another dumpling. ''My mom should have left him decades ago.''

''He's a good man, Ellie, you said so yourself.''

''He neglected his family.''

''But your mom was always there for you.''

Angry tears welled in her eyes. ''But who was there for her?''

Manny reached over and laid a hand on her shoulder, giving her a light shake. ''They're happy now, Ellie. Save it for your therapist.'' He took a sip of wine, then asked, ''So what are you going to do about rent money?''

Leave it to Manny not to mince words. ''I called

about an ad for participants in a clinical study. The money sounds good—I'm going to find out more about it tomorrow night.'' She told him about her conversation with the screener. Manny laughed and agreed it sounded promising.

''You've got a guardian angel on your shoulder, Ellie. How else can you explain losing a job, then finding a want ad for desperate women on the same day? A toast!'' He lifted his wineglass to hers.

Ellie stuck out her tongue at him, then good-naturedly clinked her glass to his.

THE MEETING ROOM WAS more crowded than Ellie had expected. Based on the cramped accommodations, the crowd had apparently surpassed the clinic's expectations, as well. The room resembled a college classroom: no windows except the tiny one in the door, fairly new, dense low-grade carpet in a speckled gray, and filled with more folding chairs than the fire marshal would probably care to know about. A large blackboard covered the entire front wall. The side walls were adorned with various-size corkboards bearing dozens of multicolored sheets on topics ranging from sleep disorders to impotence.

Ellie lowered her dark glasses and, as inconspicuously as possible, peered at the other women in the room. She judged her appearance to be somewhat better than the room's average, and the observation depressed her even more. She pulled down her floppy hat and slumped in the hard metal chair.

Opening her pocket sketchbook, Ellie flipped through to find a clean page, always ready to draw the face of the person nearest her for a few minutes' practice. Her hands stilled at the page where she had sketched a caricature last night. Mr. Italian Suit with the gooey dark eyebrows smirked back at her, a cellular phone clutched in his cartoon hand. His athletic body strained at the savvy suit, miniature in comparison to his big, good-looking head. Ellie studied the rendition of his eyebrows and nose and wondered how close she'd come to capturing his true expression. If she remembered when she got home, she'd add a smudge of green to highlight those brooding eyes.

At that moment, a bespectacled, lab-coated woman walked to the front of the room and raised her arms to hush the chatter.

"My name is Dr. Cheryl Larkin. I'm a medical doctor, and a professor of human behavior, and it is my privilege to oversee this clinical study. Each of you has been prescreened to a certain extent to qualify for a four-week experiment using pheromones, chemicals produced in animals which attract other animals of the same species."

Ellie sat up. Her own experiments in perfume making had overlapped into the area of aromatherapy. She had become intrigued with the idea that certain scents could be aphrodisiacs. Supposedly, pheromones went even further.

The doctor continued. "Pheromones are subtle but powerful secretions. Some people say they explain the elusive chemistry that attracts a specific man to a specific woman, and vice versa. The objective of this study is to see what effect, if any, oral pheromones have on your ability to attract and meet a romantic interest."

Ellie glanced around and saw that Dr. Larkin had the undivided attention of every woman in the room. Hope shimmered in the eyes of the shy, the overweight, the very short and the very tall. She swallowed because she knew her own baby blues reflected the same emotion.

"It will be necessary for participants to answer a lengthy and somewhat personal questionnaire, and to keep a daily journal detailing encounters, or absence of encounters, for each day." A spirited buzz broke out in the room as applicants whispered excitedly to strangers next to them. Ellie ignored the gleeful exclamation of the middle-aged woman beside her.

"The dosage is two pills first thing in the morning, around midday, and again at bedtime. Besides the aforementioned hypothesis," the doctor said, finally smiling, "there are no proven side effects with this particular formula. We will ask, however, that participants be especially aware of and record any changes in your energy level or in your eating and sleeping patterns."

An arm shot up near the front. "Let's say I take these pills and meet a great guy. You're telling me after four weeks the rug gets jerked out from under me?" Everyone laughed and the doctor joined in, then raised her hands defensively.

"Wait a minute—we can't guarantee you'll meet even one eligible man during the course of this study. If that were true, we wouldn't need the experiment at all."

Intrigued, Ellie nodded. This could be fun. After the doctor had finished her talk, Ellie stayed to fill out the necessary paperwork and wait for a counselor to administer the dreaded questionnaire. Three hours later, she emerged with a week's worth of pills and a small

blank journal in her purse, feeling as if she'd just been
to confession. But she noticed a new spring in her step.
She believed in the powers of aroma. Pulling off the
hat and dark glasses, she tossed her short blond locks.

Unsuspecting men of Atlanta, beware!

"WELL, Marcus, if you're not going to get married,
you're going to have to learn to cook," Gloria admonished her son as she held a dripping whisk.

Mark Blackwell plucked a green olive from the tray
on the kitchen counter and popped it into his mouth,
smiling. "I like to eat out."

The plump woman turned back to her bubbling red
sauce. "It's beyond me how, out of all those women
you've dated, not one of them could find her way
around a kitchen."

"I don't—" he walked over and took the whisk
from her hand "—date women for their culinary
skills." He flashed a grin in his mother's direction.

"Oh, you." She rapped him playfully on the arm.
Then her tone grew more threatening. "If you're not
careful, you're going to grow old all by yourself."

"I'll hire a comely young nurse," he teased. "Besides, you'd be bored if you couldn't fret over my state
of bachelorhood all day."

"Not if I had grandchildren," she replied with a
twinkle in her eye.

Mark didn't miss a beat in the familiar exchange.
"You're much too young to be a grandmother."

"And you're much too young to be working yourself
to death in that law firm."

Mark grabbed two plates and settled them onto his
arm, waiter-style. "That's what I came to talk to you

about,'' he said, smiling. He dished up a hearty helping of lasagne for each of them, and spooned on the rich homemade sauce. When he set the laden plates on the table, he struck a cocky pose and said, ''Say hello to the newest partner of Ivan, Grant, Beecham, and... Blackwell.'' He bowed slightly, rewarded with enthusiastic applause from his seated mother.

''How wonderful, Marcus!'' She beamed and brought his hand to her mouth for a long kiss. ''I'm so proud of you, son. I wish your father were here.'' Tears sprang to her eyes immediately, but she blinked them away.

Mark swallowed the lump of emotion that lodged in his throat. He knew his father would be proud of him at this moment, even if Mark *had* ''caved to the corporate philosophy,'' as his flighty father was fond of saying. Ever the softheart, his dad had been struck by a car three years ago when he'd stopped to help a stranded motorist. Mark patted his mother's hand. ''I wish he were here, too,'' he said simply, then smiled. ''Now, let's eat.''

During dinner, they chatted about his long-awaited promotion, but Mark had a feeling he wouldn't escape without at least one more lecture on the importance of finding a good woman. Especially now that he'd made partner. He was right. As he helped his mother clean the dishes, she said in an innocent voice, ''You know, the family reunion is this weekend. Are you coming?''

''Yes,'' he said patiently. ''Don't I always?''

''Hmm,'' she agreed, then asked, ''Are you bringing a date? Your cousin Albert will be there with his new bride and baby. And Claire with her newborn—this is her third, you know. Her husband is such a dear man.''

"I can't wait," Mark said, inwardly wincing. He considered these get-togethers his penance for bucking the long family tradition of having a houseful of kids before having a house. He would endure one whole day of shaking hands and exchanging cheek kisses with new family members. And dutifully praising and holding everyone else's kids while his mother drank wine in a corner and her sisters tsk-tsked over her woeful lack of grandchildren.

"So, are you bringing a date?" she asked hopefully.

"I'm definitely bringing a change of clothes in case Mickey's little one has the runs again."

Gloria covered her mouth and shook with laughter. "The video he took of you two is just precious."

Mark rolled his eyes heavenward. "I'm awaiting my debut on one of those home-video shows."

"Stop changing the subject. Are you bringing a date or not?"

His thoughts shifted to Shelia, the woman who'd last graced his bed. She hadn't struck him as a woman who'd appreciate the rural pleasures of pitching horseshoes and doing the hokey-pokey. Neither did Vicki, Connie or Valerie, come to think of it. "I'll see what I can do," he said. It was as close to a promise as he could make. Suddenly, a vision of short blond hair and flashing blue eyes came to mind, and he frowned. "I'm not really seeing anyone right now."

Gloria clasped her hands together gleefully. "Stella's niece is in town for the Sunday-school teachers' convention—shall I give her a call?"

"No," Mark said quickly, then recovered. "I have a lot to do at work this week, you know, rearranging my office and all that. I'll be working late every night."

His mother shrugged, clearly disappointed. "Suit yourself."

Later, Mark squashed down guilty feelings which threatened to surface as he drove home. He knew his mother wanted to see him properly settled with a nice, quiet girl, but he truly liked being single. He'd sacrificed his social life during law school and the first few years after joining his firm in order to get a foothold. Now at thirty-six and established in his career, he was enjoying his unattached status. Life was good.

He almost managed to drive by the interstate exit to his office, but he merged onto the ramp at the last second. Just a few minutes to go over some paperwork, he told himself.

After he unlocked the office suite, he walked across the glossy inlaid wood floor not without a measure of pride. He considered the law office tastefully furnished, with just the right amount of opulence. His new office space had been achieved by removing a supply room adjacent to his existing office. He had been asked to select additional furniture, and he was pleased with his pecan wood and cream marble choices.

The Piedmont Park painting had been hung, and he approved of the location. One of his favorite pieces of art in the law office, he'd requested it for his own work area when the move began. He flipped on a floor lamp near his desk, and settled into his familiar tan leather chair to shuffle through the stack of papers on his desk.

Congratulatory memos comprised the top layer of paper. A box of cigars and an expensive leather-covered pen set were gifts from thoughtful colleagues. He smiled in satisfaction. Everything he'd worked for had finally been realized. He would never have to struggle like his father just to make ends meet. Clasping his hands behind his head, he leaned back in the swivel chair to prop his feet on the corner of his desk, basking for a moment in the recognition of his hard-won achievement.

Partner.

At a sound from the doorway, Mark turned his head. Patrick Beecham stood there, holding the hand of Patrick, Junior. ''Hi, Mark,'' Patrick said, his voice full of surprise. ''Pretty late to be working.''

Mark rearranged himself into a position more appropriate for talking. ''I could say the same,'' he said to his partner with a smile.

''I just stopped by to get a fax,'' Patrick said. The small boy pulled on his father's pant leg. ''This is Pat, Junior,'' he added.

''I remember,'' Mark said. ''He's growing like a weed. How're you doing, buddy?''

''Okay,'' the child ventured, half hiding behind his father.

''Say, Mark,'' Patrick said, ''Lucy and I would love to have you over for dinner sometime. Do you have a lady friend?''

''You sound like my mother,'' Mark said. ''Are you two in on a conspiracy to get me settled down?''

Patrick laughed. ''No, but I must admit it helps to have someone presentable when socializing with the other partners and clients. I'll warn you—Ivan kind of expects it.''

Mark felt a sudden swell of anger that anything would be expected of him other than top-notch work. ''I like being unattached.''

''So did I,'' Patrick admitted. ''But there comes a

time when we all have to grow up. Luckily for me, Lucy was there when I came to my senses.'' He swung the little boy into his arms. ''Just food for thought, friend,'' he said absently, tickling the little boy until he squealed. ''Don't work all night, and let me know about dinner, okay?''

''Sure,'' Mark said. ''Sounds great.''

Mark listened to the footsteps fading down the hall, and pounded his fist lightly on his desk in frustration. What idiot had said behind every successful man was a good woman? He'd made it this far on his own, and he wasn't about to share the fruits of his labor with some money-hungry man-eater. He'd seen the way women's eyes lit up when they discovered he practiced law. He'd seen them peruse every stick of furniture in his home as if assessing its worth. He bought nice things because it made him happy, not to impress women. And he resented the females who thought he'd be all too eager to turn over his possessions to their care. Demanding, all of them. Take that little chiseler in the deli the other day—seventy-five bucks for a scrap of fabric!

Where could he find a woman who'd settle for a no-strings-attached arrangement to be his escort, in return for a few nights on the town and an occasional romp? Oh, sure, they all said they weren't looking for a com-mitment, but after a few dates, whammo! Feminine toi-letries and articles of clothing started to appear in his house, and every jewelry commercial seemed too clever for her to let pass without a remark. Where was it written every man was supposed to settle down with one woman and be content for the remainder of his days?

He resumed his propped position and nodded his head in silent determination. *Bully for the poor schmucks who fall for it, but count me out.*

2

"WHAT DO YOU THINK?" Ellie asked, peering at the two shell-pink tablets in her palm.

Manny leaned forward, sniffed at the pills, then said, "I think if these little pills can make you irresistible to men, then I want in on the action."

Ellie scoffed. Manny was tall and slim, with a handsome face. On more than one occasion, female acquaintances of Ellie's had offered to try to "convert" him. "Manny, you've got more dates now than you know what to do with."

"But none of them are keepers," he said, sighing dramatically.

"What do you consider a keeper?"

"Anything below eight inches gets thrown back," he declared, making an over-the-shoulder motion.

Ellie shook her head, grinning, and pulled a clean glass from the dishwasher.

Manny's forehead knitted. "This is what—the fourth day you've been taking those things?"

"Uh-huh," she said, tossing the pills into her mouth and downing them with a swallow of fruit juice.

"Shouldn't something be happening by now?" he asked, watching her face carefully. Suddenly his eyes widened, and he covered his mouth to muffle a scream.

"What?" Ellie yelled, shoving past him to run to the hall mirror.

"Gotcha," he called, doubled over laughing.

"Oh, very funny," she said after a reassuring glance in the mirror. "You're a regular comedian, Manny."

"Gotta run," he said, heading for the door. "Good luck on your last day at the Smithsonian."

Ellie pantomimed a drumroll. "Ba-dump-bum."

Friday at last. When she walked to her overflowing closet, she toyed with the thought of wearing something ratty—what did it matter? Then she spotted her pink-and-black-checked mini. Why not go out with a bang instead?

With renewed vigor, she pulled on black hose, clunky-heeled pumps and a long, white knit cardigan. She buttoned up the lightweight sweater so she could omit a blouse, then added large earrings, funky bangles and a handful of gold chains around her neck. She slicked back her pale hair with gel, then traded her regular beat-up canvas bag for a soft shoulder-strap briefcase and a small silver purse. At the last second, she remembered to skip perfume, lest it interfere with the pheromones. When she stopped in front of the mirror on the way out, she nodded. Not bad for a gal down on her luck.

She held her head higher than usual when she stepped onto the sidewalk. Not quite seven o'clock on a beautiful May morning, and suited pedestrians already clogged the walkways. A few well-trained individuals even read the morning paper while their feet moved and stopped automatically at crosswalks. Ellie shook her head in determination. She would never get caught up in a seven-to-seven job like a lot of people she knew, like her father.

It had taken two bypasses to convince him to change his workaholic ways. He'd wasted so much of his life cranking out numbers for an accounting firm. If not for her mother's patience and virtue, their marriage would never have survived. And less than a year of the bureaucracy at the hole-in-the-wall arts center where Ellie worked convinced her she wanted no part of a rigid office setting on a long-term basis. Still, the regular, if small, paycheck had paid her rent.

An oncoming dark-suited banker type lowered his stock quotes long enough to admire Ellie's legs and whistle. Her spirits rose and she shrugged guiltily. Okay, it didn't hurt her feelings to be *appreciated* by the well-heeled.

With the money from the study to tide her over for a few weeks, she planned to spend her free time updating her portfolio, and pestering gallery managers to take a peek. Being fired might turn out to be the best career move she'd ever made.

The aroma of bagels and cream cheese reached her, prompting her to dig in her bag for loose change. "Ellie!" old Mr. Pompano exclaimed. "You look good enough to have for breakfast, yourself. Did you get a promotion?"

"No," she said smugly to the popular street vendor, pointing to a chocolate bagel. "I got fired."

"Well, it suits you." He smiled, handing her the dark bread. "You are especially—" he made a corkscrew gesture in the air "—appealing today."

"Why, thank you, kind sir who wants my money." She curtsied.

He grinned and bowed slightly, then patted his right knee. "Something good will happen to you today—I can feel it in my gimp leg."

Ellie winked. "Can your bursitis tell me if he'll be a blonde, a brunette or a redhead?"

"The way you look today, *Cara,* you might get all three."

Ellie flipped him a quarter tip, and munched her bagel the rest of the walk to the musty office building where she worked. Several men's heads turned, eyes lingering, and she felt her body unconsciously adjust to the attention. Her short stride lengthened to show off her legs. She thrust her shoulders back and her small breasts out, and clenched her buttocks with each step to add a powerful sway to her back view. It worked. She'd heard two wolf whistles by the time she reached her office, where a handsome co-worker, Steve Willis, who'd never even glanced her way before, held the door open.

"Ellie, isn't it?" he asked, his pale eyebrows arching attractively over his tortoiseshell-rimmed glasses.

"Yes, but I'm afraid I don't know your name," she lied.

"Steve," he said, straightening the knot of his tie. "Steve Willis. I was thinking, maybe I could call you sometime?"

"Sure," she said nonchalantly over her shoulder.

"What's your number?" he called behind her.

Ellie turned to eye the man who'd gone out of his way to ignore her when she'd delivered his mail every day for the past year. She almost felt sorry for him— he didn't stand a chance against the pheromones. "I'm in the book," she said simply, and left him standing.

Once she got around the corner, she brought her fist to her chest in a triumphant gesture. "Yes!" There was something to these pills, after all.

The flowers on her desk were a nice surprise. She knew they were from Joan even before she opened the card. But before she had a chance to thank her boss, the phones started ringing, and the day began.

Later, a few co-workers took her to lunch, and Steve Willis appeared out of nowhere to sit beside her. He even managed to knee her a couple of times under the table. Feeling generous, Ellie humored him with a smile. He really wasn't bad. Maybe Mr. Pompano's gimpy prediction had been right.

Joan stopped by Ellie's desk an hour before closing. Ellie smiled, gesturing to the flowers. "I meant to swing by to say thank you."

"You're welcome. I wanted to talk to you before you left."

Ellie turned her swivel chair toward Joan. "What's up?"

"A commission, if you're interested." Joan leaned against the cubicle wall.

Ellie nodded enthusiastically. "Sure."

"It's a corporate portrait for a law firm—pretty boring stuff, but good money."

"Suit-and-tie picture?"

"Yeah."

"How did you hear about it?"

"I know the wife of one of the partners. I've acquired a few paintings and a couple of sculptures for their office. It's the same company that bought your Piedmont Park scene, by the way."

Landscapes were Ellie's forte. Although she enjoyed

painting portraits, as well, she preferred a little creativity with the subject's presentation. Still, it was a job. She smiled and nodded to Joan. "Sounds great."

Joan handed her a card. "Here's the name of the firm and the address. I've written the agreed fee on the back."

Ellie turned over the card and her eyes bulged. "I get to keep this?"

"Less the ten percent cut for the center, yeah," Joan said. "Consider it a severance bonus."

"Gee, thanks."

Joan glanced at her watch. "If you leave now, you can get over there before they close."

The women said their goodbyes and Ellie promised to let Joan know how the commissioned painting progressed. Stopping by the apartment, she dropped off a box of accumulated desk junk and her briefcase. After taking a few minutes to freshen up, she walked to the street to hail a taxi.

"Where to?" the heavyset man yelled, looking her up and down with appreciation.

Ellie told him the address and climbed into the back seat. During the ride, the talkative driver hinted at his single status. Ellie, enjoying the attention but not wanting to encourage the man, simply smiled and said, "That's nice."

He screeched to a halt in front of the building, and she got out. He leaned out the window and said, "Miss, do you mind telling me what kind of perfume you're wearing?"

Ellie rolled her eyes. "Let me guess—it gives you a migraine?"

The man looked confused. "No, I'm serious."

Ellie opened her mouth to tell him about her own special blend, then stopped short. "I'm not wearing any," she said, suddenly remembering.

"Yeah, sure, lady," he said. "Whatever it is, I hope my date is wearing it tonight when I pick her up." The man tipped his hat, waved away her fare and drove off.

Ellie stood on the sidewalk, perplexed. She raised her wrist to her nose and sniffed. Nothing, just skin. She shrugged, glanced up at the towering building, then walked in.

When she exited the elevator onto the appropriate floor, Marcus Blackwell's name was being gilded onto the double glass doors. The graphic artist seemed to be having a heck of a time repositioning the firm's name on the door to work in all the letters. If they added another partner in the future, they'd have to install a third door, she thought wryly.

Ellie sighed, wondering how much money would be squandered by the firm to herald the addition of Mr. Blackwell. A new sign, new company stationery, an expensive portrait. Must be nice.

His secretary was beautiful. More like gorgeous, really. The woman's nameplate said Monica Reems.

"May I help you?" she asked.

Ellie frowned. Nice, too—how despicable. "I'm Ellie Sutherland. I'm here to see Marcus Blackwell about painting his business portrait."

"Is he expecting you?"

"No, I'm sorry, he isn't. I received the assignment only a half hour ago and I was hoping to catch him before he left for the day."

The woman smiled, displaying—what else?—model teeth. "He's in a meeting, but he should be out any minute. Have a seat and I'll make sure he knows you're here as soon as he gets back.''

Ellie sat down and studied her surroundings. Ivan, Grant and Beecham were doing very well for themselves. And of course, Mr. Blackwell, the latest rising star of the firm. She tried to picture him—early fifties, salt-and-pepper hair. Eyeglasses, probably, which were always a pain to paint because of the glare and because they made the eyes seem flat. Dark suit, no doubt. Small gray teeth. Or bright white dentures. And one or two prestigious rings—Harvard perhaps, or Michigan. Very ho-hum, but relatively easy.

Begrudgingly, she conceded the office decor was impeccable. A little stodgy, but first-class leather furniture and textured wallpaper. And honest-to-goodness artwork. Ellie wondered where they'd hung her Piedmont Park painting, and prayed it wasn't in the men's room. She'd heard those things happened. From her position, she could see the door to the men's room at the end of the hall. As minutes clicked by and boredom threatened to settle in, she became convinced her painting adorned the wall. Over the urinals.

She sneaked a peek at Monica, who had her back turned and the phone crooked between her shoulder and ear. It would take only a few seconds to check, and she hadn't seen anyone go in the entire time she'd been seated. After one last glance at the busy secretary, Ellie sidled down the hall, then pushed open the heavy door, straining to hear voices or other sounds of activity. Silence. She stepped inside.

The outer room was a lounge of sorts with inappropriately elegant furniture. Ellie began a hurried search of the walls. There were several framed prints, most of them architectural, but she didn't see her painting. She sighed in satisfaction. An arched doorway led into a tiled room of more predictable sterile-looking gray Formica stalls. Three individual urinals lined an adjacent wall, and Ellie eyed them curiously. "I've always wondered," she muttered. Her voice echoed, and she jumped. Then another sound reached her, approaching footsteps from the outside hall. Sweat broke out on her upper lip.

Searching frantically for cover, Ellie dived into a stall and slammed the door behind her. Then she realized her pump-clad feet would be a dead giveaway because the door didn't extend all the way to the floor. She jumped up and straddled the black seat of the commode, crouching so her head couldn't be seen.

The man who entered whistled tunelessly, probably celebrating the forthcoming weekend. When he stopped in front of her stall, Ellie held her breath. She could see the shadows of his feet and legs. At last, he walked away from her hiding place and stopped near the urinals, she deduced. Sure enough, she heard the slide of a zipper and the sound of urine splashing against porcelain. Ellie grimaced and prayed he had a small bladder.

What if someone else came in? What if a whole crowd came in at once? She'd be trapped listening to a herd of men relieving themselves!

The man peed. And peed. Ellie rolled her eyes. This guy belonged in the record books. And just when she thought he'd stopped, he started again with the same gusto. Her arms began to ache from balancing herself between the slick walls. She repositioned herself slightly forward to relieve her shoulder pain, and caught a glimpse of the marathoner's back through a tiny slit in the closed door. Her hand slipped and she caught herself, thumping lightly against the stall. She jerked back and held her breath, then relaxed. He seemed to be conjuring up a grand finale, too occupied to hear her.

Finally, the man zipped his pants and flushed the urinal. Ellie listened as he washed his hands slowly and seemed to dry them just as slowly. He walked by her stall on the way out, and she grew weak with relief.

Then she dropped her purse.

Most of the contents were emptied on the first bounce, then the silver bag rolled out of sight. Makeup, coupons, pens and miscellaneous items scattered everywhere. She watched a tampon slide until it stopped by a leg of the stall. She closed her eyes and waited.

At first there was no sound at all. Then the man took three slow steps back to stand in front of her door. And he knocked.

Ellie swallowed. "Y-yes?" she managed to get out.

"The ladies' room is down the hall." His voice vibrated deep, distorted with echoes.

"I, uh, I didn't know this was the men's room," she improvised.

"Are you standing on the toilet?"

She carefully stepped down and straightened her shoulders, then addressed the man through the closed door. "No," she said, and bent to retrieve the strewn articles within her reach.

He'd bent to pick up the purse and the items laying outside the stall. He wore nice shoes, soft black leather loafers with perfect tight little tassels. On feet big enough to make Manny salivate.

After a few seconds, he asked, "Are you coming out?"

"I'd rather not."

"Okay," he said, his voice booming. He sounded close to laughter. "I'll put your purse on the counter and leave."

Ellie waited several seconds after the outer door closed before she moved. She opened the door and scooped up her purse, quickly checking the floor for wayward keys or coins. Then, praying fervently the man wasn't waiting outside, she swung the door open and stuck her head out.

No one in sight. Uttering her thanks, she trotted down the hall and reclaimed her seat near the still-distracted Monica. When the secretary ended her phone call, Ellie stood and asked, "Has Mr. Blackwell returned?"

Monica shook her head. "Any minute now, I'm positive." The phone rang again and she answered it quickly.

Ellie sighed. Then, hearing someone approach, she turned, and inhaled sharply. Mr. Italian Suit. The yuppie who'd ruined her skirt! What was *he* doing here?

Still several feet away, the man slowed, his head tilted in question. Suddenly, his eyes widened in recognition, and he strode toward her, his forehead knitted. "Look," he said, making chopping gestures in the air, "I don't know how you found me, but I'm not giving you another red cent for that overpriced skirt you said I damaged."

Ellie drew herself up to her full height of five foot two inches and leaned toward the fool, ready to… to…muss his hair. "For your information, you big klutz, I have no idea who you are and I haven't been looking for you." She lowered her voice to a hiss. "I'm here to see a client and I hope you scram before he gets here because I'd like to make a good impression."

Blue eyes blazed into green ones as the silence mounted. Behind them, Monica hung up the phone and coughed politely. "Excuse me, Mr. Blackwell."

Ellie felt the blood drain from her face. "You?" she whispered.

"Me, what?" he asked impatiently.

"You're Marcus Blackwell?"

"Mark Blackwell," he corrected. Turning to Monica, he asked, "What's going on here?"

"This is Ellie Sutherland, sir. She's here about your portrait."

He frowned and threw up his hands in a gesture of frustration. "I'm lost."

"Didn't Mr. Ivan tell you? Your portrait will go up in the boardroom beside the other partners'."

Mark Blackwell glanced from Ellie to his secretary. Ellie relaxed her stance and offered him an exaggerated shrug.

"I'm not prepared for this," he said finally, in a guarded tone.

Ellie gave him a shaky smile. "This isn't litigation— there's nothing to prepare for."

He looked at her, chewing his lip. Obviously Mark Blackwell stood in unfamiliar territory, and didn't like it one bit. His eyes narrowed. "And how, may I ask, did you get involved?"

Ellie smiled brightly. "I'm an artist."

Mark rolled his eyes and sighed mightily. "Why doesn't that surprise me?"

She glared. "What's that supposed to mean?"

He waved dismissively. "Forget it, um—what did you say your name was?"

"Ellie," she said with growing impatience. "Ellie Sutherland."

He ran his fingers through his hair, a gesture she recognized from the deli incident. "Well, Ms. Sutherland, perhaps we can discuss this, er, project in my office." He swept his arm toward a door a few steps away and motioned for Ellie to precede him.

She stood her ground. "After you."

He pursed his lips, then turned and walked toward the door.

Ellie noticed the painting as soon as she entered the huge masculine room. She walked over to it, soaking up the familiar shapes and colors. An afternoon in the park. A cliché, really, but her first truly good piece. There had been others since, additional impressionistic renditions of city landmarks, but she had been especially proud of Piedmont Park and the price it had brought. She lifted a finger, and almost touched the canvas. "Nice picture," she murmured.

"Nice purse."

Ellie's hand flew to her bag as her eyes swung across the room to his feet. They were big feet, wearing nice black leather loafers with tight little tassels.

"Do you make a practice of skulking in men's washrooms, Ms. Sutherland?"

She felt a blush start at her knees and work its way up. She raised her scorching chin indignantly. "Certainly not. I told you, I didn't know it was the men's room.''

He smiled a disbelieving smile, then leaned on the front of his desk. "Now then, what do you need from me?"

Ellie turned and took a step toward him. Their eyes locked. And just like that, something passed between them. At least she felt it.

A shiver ran up her back, and a low hum sounded in her ears. Looking at him, she realized she'd done a shamefully good job of capturing his features for the caricature. His eyes reminded her of a length of dark green velvet she'd once bought just because she liked it. She'd hesitated to cut it, to tamper with the natural drape of the lush fabric. She'd ended up folding it across the footboard of her bed, unhemmed. Now every night when she went to bed, she'd be thinking about Mark Blackwell's eyes.

"Hmm?" she asked, completely oblivious to the reason she'd come here.

Mark shook his head, as if to clear it. "Um, I asked, what do you need from me?"

This time, his words were slow and coated with fresh meaning. Need from him? A hundred images galloped through Ellie's mind, and Mark Blackwell loomed naked in all of them. She could see the surprise in his eyes, the slight confusion lurking there. Then she remembered. Of course, the pheromones.

For an instant, disappointment fluttered in her chest. Then she recovered and walked closer to his desk, conjuring up a natural smile. "Just a few hours of your time, really." She paused for a moment, then said, "Do you have a favorite suit?"

"I never thought about it," he answered slowly.

"One you reach for when you have a very important meeting?" she coaxed.

He pondered for a few seconds, seeming embarrassed. "My olive one, I suppose."

"I've seen it," Ellie said, nodding her approval. "It's a good choice."

"Is this a new look?" he asked, eyeing her avant-garde hair and outfit.

Ellie recognized a diversionary tactic when she saw it. She looked down at her trendy, chic clothes. "Don't get out much, do you?"

His left eyebrow rose a fraction of an inch.

She blinked purposely and continued. "Wear the olive suit to the first sitting. Bring both a solid white shirt and an off-white shirt. And a handful of ties."

"First sitting? I'm afraid this is all new to me."

"I'll need you to sit for me for a total of about fifteen hours."

His eyes widened. "Fifteen hours?"

Ellie laughed and raised her hands in defense. "Not all at once. One or two hours at a time—whatever you feel up to. I'll take photographs to work from at home."

He scowled and folded his arms. "I'm not comfortable with this."

The toothpick remark she'd made to Manny came to her lips, but she bit it back. Instead, she said, "Just relax—I'm not painting you in your mallard-print boxers."

Mark studied her for a minute, the tiniest hint of a smile lifting the corners of his mouth. "I don't wear mallard-print boxers, but then I thought you'd know from your earlier vantage point in the men's room.''

Ellie swallowed. Maybe he wasn't as uptight as she'd thought. ''Briefs, then.''

He shook his head. ''Wrong again.''

''Bikinis?'' she squeaked.

Mark extended a finger and beckoned her to come closer. Ellie did, and leaned forward for him to whisper in her ear. ''Bare-assed.''

Ellie jerked up and took a step back before she realized he was laughing at her. ''That wasn't very nice.''

''You fished for it.''

''Where were we?'' she asked, trying to reassume a professional stance.

''I was sitting for you.''

''Shall we do it here in your office?''

His eyes raked over her body. ''It would be a first, but sure.''

Her pulse leaped. The image of them vibrating his desk across the room came to mind, but she stifled it. The chemicals she emitted triggered his reaction and she'd do well to remember that. She forced a serious face, refusing to verbally acknowledge his innuendo. ''Fine. When?''

He still smiled, his eyes dancing. ''Tomorrow morning at nine?''

''I'll be here with my camera,'' she said, already walking toward the door.

''You bring your equipment,'' he called to her. ''And I'll bring mine.''

Mark caught the flash of her silver purse being slung over her shoulder as she closed the door. Where had that idiotic comment come from? He jumped up and clutched his head with both hands, pacing. He'd never made suggestive comments to women he'd worked with. Willing women were plentiful, he'd never had to worry about mixing business with pleasure and risking a ruinous outcome. He cursed, rubbed his eyes, and walked the length of his office to his liquor cabinet. Appraising the newly stocked shelves, he selected a fine Kentucky bourbon, and poured himself a shot.

Tomorrow he'd conduct himself like the professional he was. He'd refuse to rise to her bait, no matter how enticing. The last thing he needed was for a nut like Ellie Sutherland to complicate his life.

3

"YOU'RE JOKING," Manny said, his eyes wide.

"Nope," Ellie declared, swallowing a bite of cheese omelette. "It was him, in the flesh."

"Was he as dreamy as you remembered?"

She nodded enthusiastically. "Absolutely."

"And single?"

Ellie frowned. "I didn't notice a wedding ring, and he was kind of...flirtatious. But that doesn't mean anything these days."

"You said it, girlfriend."

"He's too stuffy, and way out of my league. He probably has a black book full of women named Muffy and Phoebe."

Manny touched her forearm. "You're probably right." Then he grinned. "So why don't you introduce him to *me?*"

"Sorry," Ellie said, and pulled a sympathetic face, "but I don't think Mark Blackwell is your type, either."

"I can put on a skirt if he insists."

"I'll see if I can work it into the conversation today," she offered sarcastically.

Manny lifted a sausage link to his mouth and bit off an end suggestively.

"You're a kook," she said, laughing.

"Me?" he asked. "Who's the one who sneaked into the men's room and listened to him pee?"

"I didn't see anything."

"Oh, so you did look?"

"No!" She grinned sheepishly. "Okay, I peeked, but I only saw a sliver of his back. Cut the wisecracks for a minute. I have to tell you the strange things that happened yesterday."

"I'm all ears."

Ellie told him about the incidents with men on the street, with Steve Willis, her co-worker, the taxi driver and some of the things Mark Blackwell had said to her. "And when I got home, Steve Willis had left a message on my machine. I haven't had *that* many men flirt with me in my lifetime," she asserted, reaching for the bottle of pink tablets. "It has to be these pheromones working."

"Well, aren't you glad they're working? What's the name of the manufacturer? I'm buying stock." He reached down to stroke Esmerelda's ears.

"Do you think I'm imagining things?"

"I think you're horny. You haven't had a relationship since…Drew, wasn't it? That was ages ago. I've forgotten, why did you end it?"

"His penis had attention deficit disorder."

"Oh, yeah, right." Manny nodded. "Well, if you want to see if the pheromones are causing all the hullabaloo, don't doll up today and see if you get the same results."

Ellie snapped her fingers. "Good idea."

THE LAW OFFICES of Ivan, Grant, Beecham and Blackwell were several blocks away, but easily accessible by bicycle. Ellie pulled on a neon green helmet that matched her bike, strapped on her backpack of supplies and jumped on to begin pedaling away her breakfast calories. No man could possibly flirt with her at this speed.

It was another beautiful day, too nice to be cooped up inside. She figured she'd be through with Mark Blackwell by noon, then she could spend the day sketching crowds at Underground Atlanta in preparation for her next portfolio painting. She stopped at a traffic light and waited for a police officer to wave her through the dense jam.

The police officer was within touching distance. And, she noticed, cute beneath his half helmet. He waved the traffic by on the side street, but his eyes stayed on Ellie the entire time, a whistle clasped between white teeth. She smiled at him and he smiled back. He waved through more traffic and studied her legs. She smiled. He waved through more traffic and winked at her. She winked back. Suddenly horns began to sound behind her from commuters impatient with the lengthy amount of attention the officer paid to the cars on the side street. Finally, he pulled his eyes away from Ellie and blew his whistle to halt the line of cars whizzing by. When she pedaled by, he lifted his hand to his helmet in a friendly gesture. Definitely the pheromones, she thought.

When she reached Mark's building, she took the elevator to his floor. The law offices were much quieter than the previous day, but still busier than Ellie imagined they would be for a weekend. On the other hand, Mark Blackwell probably worked Saturday, Sunday and holidays. To her surprise, more than one set of male eyebrows raised appreciatively when she made eye contact in the halls. Of course, she did look a little out of place wearing her cycling togs.

Monica's station sat neat and unoccupied, so Ellie stepped to Mark's office door and knocked.

"Come in," he called.

He sat at his desk, pen in hand. He glanced at his watch and said, "I was getting ready to check the men's room."

"Sorry," she said. "I had a flat this morning." She patted her bike, walked it over to the side wall and lowered the kickstand.

She pulled off her gloves and realized he was staring quizzically at the bike. "No place to chain it up out front," she said cheerfully. "I can't afford to have it stolen."

He pointed to the bags of dried herbs she'd picked up from a street vendor on the way. "I hope you don't plan to smoke that stuff."

Ellie glanced at the ingredients she'd purchased for a new perfume recipe. "Not here," she said, grinning wryly.

"Is that your night gear?" he asked, smirking, and indicated her neon clothing.

Ellie looked down at her pink bike shorts and bright yellow tank top. She had certainly dressed down today, complete with running shoes. She pulled off her helmet and ran a hand through her short waves. "You can't be too safe in this traffic."

He stood, tossing the pen on a stack of documents, and tugged gently at his waistband. Ellie caught her breath. Mark Blackwell looked deadly in pleated olive slacks and an off-white shirt, open at the collar and revealing a shadow of dark hair. *Easy, girl. This is just a job.* His jacket hung from a light-colored wooden valet in the corner behind his desk. Several ties hung there, as well as a white shirt, still under the dry cleaner's plastic.

"I see you brought the things I suggested," she said, nodding her approval.

His eyes locked with hers. "I'm nothing if not obedient," he said in a tone which indicated that wasn't the case at all.

The undigested omelette flipped over in her stomach. "Well," Ellie said nervously, "let's get started, shall we?" She unstrapped her backpack and pulled out a folder. "I've taken the liberty of drawing up an employment contract."

Mark poked his tongue in his cheek as if he was amused, but said nothing.

"Pretty simple stuffy, really," she continued. "It mentions the materials used, the fee and the delivery time frame of the portrait."

Mark reached for the document and read it quickly. His eyes swung up to her. "I would never have imagined painting to be so lucrative."

Ellie set her jaw and took two deep breaths. "It isn't. Jobs like this are few and far between. And I'm buying all the supplies, which includes framing the finished portrait."

"Still, it's a lot of money. You must be very good." He sounded doubtful.

Ellie bit her tongue, tempted to mention the Piedmont Park scene hanging ten feet from her, but the thought suddenly struck her that maybe he didn't even like the picture and had merely inherited it with the office. Instead of leaving herself open, she raised her chin, gave him a small smile and said, "I am *very* good."

Mark Blackwell chewed on his tongue for a moment. Then cleared his throat. "What is a 'kill fee'?" he said, looking back to the document.

Ellie shrugged. "My protection. I do freelance photography for magazines, and I've been burned on last-minute publishing cancellations. This protects me if you—" She stopped and bit her bottom lip.

"If I'm run down by a beer truck?" he finished.

"You could say that, although I doubt if the term has ever been applied quite so literally."

"What if I don't like the painting?" he asked, laying aside the contract and folding his arms.

Ellie opened her pack and pulled out miscellaneous supplies, including a camera. "Satisfaction guaranteed," she said, smiling wryly.

He opened his mouth to speak, but a knock on the door stopped him. "Yes?" he called.

The door opened and a handsome, wiry, black-haired man stepped in. "Blackwell, about the Morrison deal—" He stopped when he spied Ellie, a blatant admiring look crossing his face. Glancing back to Mark, he said, "Maybe we can discuss this some other time."

Mark's face hardened. "After our conversation yesterday, Specklemeyer, I thought there was nothing left to discuss."

The tension between the two men hung in the air, almost palpable. "Perhaps I should wait outside," Ellie offered, starting for the door.

Mark stopped her, holding up his hand. "No." He glared at the younger man. "This won't take long."

Specklemeyer's shoulders went back and anger diffused his smooth skin. "Morrison is my client, and I intend to do what the man asked me to do."

Mark's voice hummed low and deadly. "You work for this firm, and you will do what you're instructed to do. If not, there won't be anyone here to cover you when the IRS comes calling for you."

"Being partner has gone to your head already, hasn't it, Blackwell? Last week you were just a flunky like the rest of us, and now you think you have veto power."

"You're wrong," Mark said calmly, refolding his arms. "I *know* I have veto power."

The other man's eyes narrowed, his fists balling at his sides. Convinced they were going to fight, Ellie moved her supplies back a few feet to the perimeter of the office, but when she glanced up, the younger man was stalking toward the door. He closed it with a resounding slam.

"Sorry for the interruption," Mark said into the ensuing silence. "Tell me how this works," he said, waving an arm to encompass Ellie and her things.

"First I need to see the other portraits yours will be displayed with so I can maintain the corporate mood, so to speak. Your secretary mentioned it will be hung in the boardroom—is it close by?"

"Right this way." He led her out of his office and down a wide hallway. The boardroom sat dim and deserted this weekend morning. It reeked of old books. The overhead lights did little to brighten the dark paneled room, so Ellie opened all the blinds. Then she walked around the room, perusing the five large somber portraits adorning the walls. Two partners had apparently retired—or worse.

"Pretty standard stuff," she acknowledged, pulling a tape measure from her pocket and recording the size of the canvasses and frames. She glanced at the towering man beside her. "Wouldn't you at least like to smile in your portrait? Remember, it'll be your legacy."

Mark frowned. "My legacy will not be a vanity painting on a wall."

His vehemence surprised Ellie. "You have children?" It hurt more than a little to know he was married, after all.

The frown deepened. "No, I don't have any children—yet."

"But you're married?"

"No," he said, a bit flustered, then added, "not yet."

"Engaged?"

"Not yet."

"Oh, you're one of *those*," she said knowingly, then turned her eyes back to the painting in front of her, immensely relieved.

"One of those what?" he said defensively.

"You're a Peter Pan man. No wonder green suits you," she said, indicating his slacks.

His mouth opened, then closed. Pointing with his index finger, he said, "I don't believe this—*you* are psychoanalyzing *me?* And what is all this Peter Pan nonsense? Let me guess—*Cosmo*'s feature this month, right?"

"There have been volumes written on men like you," she said, sashaying past him into the hall.

He caught up with her in a few seconds. She thought he'd be angry, but surprisingly, he seemed to concede defeat. "Do you by chance know my mother?" he asked. "Gloria Blackwell sent you here to torment me, didn't she?"

Ellie laughed as she reentered his office. "No, I don't know her, but I know someone just like her in Florida—Gladys Sutherland." She shrugged. "It's universal. It's what mothers *do*."

The last woman my mother set me up with brought a book along to read."

Ellie threw her head back and laughed. "The last guy my mom set me up with informed me over a fast-food dinner that women were getting way out of hand and needed to be put in their place."

"Oooh," he said. "A real charmer." Their laughter peaked, then petered out as they looked at each other and realized they'd just shared a friendly moment.

"Well." Ellie cleared her throat, and moved toward her supplies. "I guess I'd better get to work."

"Just tell me where you want me," he said, hands on hips.

Ellie looked up and saw the implication in his eyes. He was tempting, all right. She measured her response. "How about in that straight-back chair by the table?" *Which has always been a personal fantasy of mine.*

"Suits me," he drawled.

To her horror, a stab of desire knifed through her as she watched him swing his coat on, grab a tie and walk to the chair. She stood mesmerized as he efficiently tied a tiny knot at his throat. Watching his nimble fingers move was suddenly the most sensual thing she'd ever seen. Ellie moistened her lips with the tip of her shaking tongue. Few men could be this sexy *putting on* clothes.

The celibacy was making her behave this way. She'd gone too long without a man's body next to hers. And now, the first time a man with the physique of an exotic dancer came along, she fell to pieces. She wiped beads of perspiration from her forehead. "Turn the chair sideways, and have a seat." She picked up the camera and busied herself attaching the lens, willing her pulse to slow.

At this rate, she'd be jumping his bones by lunch.

Mark eased into the chair and exhaled deeply. She was doing it again, throwing him sexual crumbs—and he was gobbling them up like a starved man. He clenched a fist to steady his nerves, but his traitorous eyes sought her out. How was it possible this woman could turn screwing on a camera lens into foreplay?

He had steeled himself against her this morning, but he hadn't counted on her wearing skintight elastic neon clothes. And little white crew socks with pom-poms on the heels. And for her hair to be so…mussed. He groaned.

"Are you okay?" Ellie asked, walking toward him, concern on her pert little face.

"Uh, sure," he said, sitting straighter.

"First I'm going to rape you."

Lights burst behind his eyes. "Excuse me?"

"Drape you," she repeated. "I'm going to drape you." She held several different-colored cloths over her arm and, picking up a navy one, shook it in front of him for emphasis. "See? I need to decide what color background would be the most flattering."

Disappointment shot through him and he fingered his

collar a fraction looser. "Whatever you say." *Get a grip, man.*

Using small, capable-looking hands, she placed the navy fabric over his right shoulder. Her fingernails lightly nipped the back of his neck, and a gray swatch suddenly appeared over his left shoulder. Ellie stepped back to observe him, stepped forward to adjust the drapes, and back again, studying. She reached for her camera and snapped five or six pictures at lightning speed.

With eyes narrowed, she walked toward him and leaned forward. Suddenly her face was mere inches from his. He could see a freckle centered perfectly on the end of her nose, and for one crazy second, he thought she might kiss him. He parted his lips and waited. She grabbed his chin and adjusted his head, sharply, to the right. "Don't move," she ordered, then started snapping more pictures.

"I can't," he said testily. "I have whiplash."

If she heard him, she didn't acknowledge it. If fact, her next adjustment to his head was even more severe than the first. "Ow!" But she was busy focusing and clicking. More drapes appeared, this time red and burgundy, then dark green and gold. To pass the time, he'd been halfheartedly keeping track of the number of rolls of film she'd used. But as she draped him in a deep plum color, he'd gotten a chinful of soft breast, and the blood rushed from his brain to more urgent parts of his body. She reloaded. Did that make twelve rolls? Or twenty-one?

Ellie Sutherland turned into a different person when she worked. She was a study in concentration, utterly efficient.

"Smile," she ordered.

And she was devastatingly beautiful. He could imagine sliding those bike pants off and pulling her onto his lap, her straddling him wearing those delightful pom-pom socks.

"There's a good smile," she said. Click, click. "Whatever it is you're thinking, keep thinking it." Click, click, click.

He could reach under that ridiculous yellow tank top and push it up to expose her to him. She'd have great tan lines, her breasts outlined perfectly, surrounded by sun-kissed skin. And her nipples—

"Hey," she said, lowering the camera. "The lurid grin suits you, but I don't think it's what you want for posterity, is it?"

Mark recovered with a start, and reined in his wayward thoughts. "Are you almost finished?"

"Just a few more," she said, bending down on one knee for a different angle. When she stood up a few seconds later, Mark breathed a sigh of relief. Finished at last, he hoped. Then she would leave. Out of sight, out of mind.

Ellie, however, reloaded again. "Now, let's try the white shirt and a different tie," she said without looking up.

Mark gritted his teeth. How much longer was he going to have to put up with her incessant teasing? He stood and walked past her to the valet, loosening his tie along the way. With his back to her, he unbuttoned his cuffs, then the front, and slid the shirt off his shoulders. As he lifted the plastic from the white shirt, he distinctly heard the camera go off. He swung his head, but Ellie was wrestling with the camera, pointing it at the floor. Her head was down.

Mark turned back to his new shirt, and heard two more clicks. Again he swung around and her face looked downward, contorted from her strenuous efforts with the suddenly temperamental camera. This time, when he resumed his task of removing the shirt from the hanger, he kept her in his vision in a mirror to his right. While he appeared to be absorbed in undoing buttons, she glanced at him over her shoulder, then turned, focused on his naked back and snapped two quick pictures.

Why the little voyeur! Then a thought occurred to him, and he grinned to himself. "Don't turn around," he said over his shoulder, rehanging the new shirt. "I must have sat down in talcum powder before I left this morning. Give me a minute to remove my pants and dust them off." In the mirror, he saw the back of her head jerk up. He unzipped his pants and made other noises of undressing, but left his slacks buttoned. Her head moved slightly side to side as if she was contemplating her next move. Just as she raised the camera and turned, so did he.

He heard two clicks before Ellie realized she'd been had. She straightened, her face flushing to a most becoming shade of deep rose.

"Are these for your personal collection?" he asked, crossing his arms over his bare chest.

Busted taking pictures of the man changing clothes! Ellie's mind raced faster than the heat growing in her cheeks.

Mark Blackwell stood completely still, except for a muscle that twitched beneath his left pec. God, the man was gorgeous. His shoulders were broad, his arms athletically defined, but not overly so. A tangle of dark hair covered his chest, his dark nipples slanted on firmly uplifted muscle. His waist was sectioned in flat planes of taut skin, which narrowed into his waistband. Ellie felt a single drop of sweat trickle between her breasts as she moistened her dry lips.

With an effort, she shrugged into a relaxed posture, then threw one arm up in what she hoped resembled a casual gesture. "It's not what you're thinking. Some people are more relaxed when they don't know their picture's being taken," she said in her most authoritative voice, bobbing her head for emphasis.

Seconds passed. Then a full minute. She willed her head to stop bobbing, but it jerked up and down of its own volition.

"If you'd gotten the picture you wanted," he said quietly, "you'd know just how *un*relaxed I am at the moment."

"Can we get on with this, please? I do have other plans for today."

He eyed her for a few seconds longer, then a strange look came over his face. Reaching to tug on the white shirt, he said, "Sure." His face once again melded into a serious, professional mask.

Ellie frowned while he concentrated on his buttons. No wonder this guy was still single. Who wants a moody man? Up then down, hot then cold in a matter of a few seconds.

Then it hit her and she almost slapped her forehead in revelation. She kept forgetting about the pheromones. The poor guy didn't know what was going on.

It all made sense now—his early teasing, and now suddenly pulling back, as if he'd just regained his senses.

She busied her hands with the camera, but kept one eye on him. His hands were slow on his buttons, and he seemed almost thoughtful. So intent was she on analyzing his silence, his voice startled her.

"Do you mind telling me what kind of perfume you're wearing?"

Bingo! "I'm not wearing perfume."

Mark looked up and frowned slightly. "Scented lotion? Shampoo?"

Ellie shook her head.

"Are you sure, because I could swear…" His voice trailed off, and he shook his head in uncertainty.

"What does it smell like?" she asked. She could record his observations in her journal. The counselor stressed the importance of noting details.

"I don't know," he said. "It's hard to explain. Like…fresh air." He glanced at her, seeming embarrassed.

Ellie grinned nervously. "In downtown Atlanta? Your schnoz must be playing tricks on you."

"Right," he said, sliding on a tie and stepping to the mirror to complete the knot.

His phone trilled, causing Ellie to jump. Mark strode to his desk, glanced at the tiny number-display screen, then groaned.

"What?" Ellie asked.

"It's my mother," he explained, picking up the receiver. "Hi, Mom…yes, I saw your number come up on the screen." He looked at Ellie and smiled. "Yes, it's an expensive feature, but all the office phones have it…no, I don't know how much it costs, but it's worth it…yes, if I think of it, I'll ask Monica…yes, I promise.''

Ellie giggled and motioned she was leaving to give him privacy. Mark shook his head and waved her toward a chair, holding up a finger to indicate he'd wind up the call in a minute or so.

''Yes, the name of the person calling appears…uh-huh…no, it wouldn't be possible for you to know if Stella was calling from Gert's house, Gert's name and number would still appear.'' He rubbed his eyes with index finger and thumb, clearly trying to remain patient.

Ellie enjoyed eavesdropping on his conversation. Even a senior partner could be reduced to childlike politeness around his mother.

''Mom, did you call just to talk about my telephone?'' He frowned. ''Oh. Sure you can ride with me and my date.'' He turned slightly away from Ellie and she couldn't see his face.

Ellie felt a tiny pang of jealousy. Which was ridiculous, she thought. It was only reasonable to assume a man like Mark Blackwell dated, whenever his hectic schedule allowed, that is.

''No, you don't know her…uh, a couple of weeks now…yes, she's nice…no, no children…no, I don't think she's ever been married, but the subject hasn't really come up…yes, I agree that's very important, but it just hasn't come up…you'll meet her tomorrow, okay? Look, I've got someone in my office, so I'll call you later, okay? I love you, too, Mom. Bye.''

He hung up the phone with a heavy sigh, then turned a wry grin toward Ellie. ''That was the infamous Gloria Blackwell.''

"She sounds persistent."

"The IRS should hire her," Mark agreed. Suddenly his face brightened. "Hey, are you busy tomorrow?"

Ellie's heart skipped a beat. A date? In an instant she remembered the woman in the clinic who had asked about the chances of meeting a great guy and then having the rug pulled out from under her when the pills wore off. It would be too easy to lose her heart to Mark Blackwell. Plus, she wasn't about to get involved with a man whose arteries were probably already clogged with stress. And he'd only made the offer because he was under the influence of the pheromones. Self-preservation kicked in. "I'm busy every Sunday."

"Working or playing?" he asked in a teasing voice.

"A little of both," she admitted. "I usually go to Underground and set up an easel to draw caricatures." Gathering courage, she stood and attempted to clarify the situation. "Look," she said earnestly, "you're not exactly my type and I'm probably not yours, either, so—"

"Whoa," he said, raising his hands. "It's just a family picnic. I'm in a bind and I really need a date."

"And I really need the money I'll earn at the mall," she said sincerely. *And you scare me to death.*

He leaned against his desk and drummed his index finger against his chin. "How about a business proposition?"

"What do you have in mind?" Ellie ventured cautiously.

"How much money will you make drawing at Underground?"

Ellie averaged her earnings from the last few times

she'd worked there and added twenty percent. "About two hundred fifty dollars."

Mark whistled. "Two fifty? Okay, I'll give you three hundred to go to the picnic with me."

"Why?" Ellie asked, suddenly suspicious. "You could probably get a date just by picking up the phone."

"How good an actress are you?" he asked, smiling.

"I made a pretty convincing artichoke in my fifth-grade play. Why?"

"Because," Mark said, now grinning broadly, "I want you to be the epitome of my mother's worst nightmare."

Hurt speared through Ellie. "Excuse me?"

He stood up and walked toward her. "Don't take this wrong. But if we could convince my mom you're my new girlfriend and that we're completely wrong for each other, she might ease up a little and realize my being a bachelor isn't so bad, after all. Come on, it'll be fun."

Ellie balked. "I'm not sure if I'm flattered or insulted."

Mark took a step toward her with his arms extended. "You said yourself I'm not your type. Think about it. We seem to get along okay—"

Ellie snorted.

"Sort of, plus, I need a date with no strings attached, and you need the money," he finished triumphantly.

Ellie frowned. "I'm not for sale."

"Three hundred fifty."

"Shall I bring baked beans or potato salad?"

"UNBELIEVABLE! This man is actually paying you to go out with him?" Manny exclaimed, counting the bills

Ellie handed him. "Do you realize two out of the three times you've seen this man, he's handed you a fistful of cash?"

"Oh, for heaven's sake, Manny, you make it sound sordid," Ellie said. "It's a simple business arrangement, that's all."

"Sure. And I guess you're naive enough to think this man is going to shell out money like this and be satisfied with a peck on the cheek at the end of the day?"

Ellie frowned. It hadn't occurred to her that Mark would expect anything other than a convincing performance.

"Ellie," Manny continued in her silence, "you already think this man and several other strangers you've encountered are affected by those pills you're taking. Did you ever think it might be dangerous if the pheromones push someone to, you know, take liberties with you?"

"I can take care of myself, Manny," Ellie countered, then she softened. "But I appreciate the concern."

Her roommate touched her arm, his face serious. "I want to meet this guy, to check him out and see if he's safe, okay?"

"You just want to check him out, period." Ellie poked a finger in his side, lightening the mood. "I told you, he's not your type."

Later, when she picked up the developed film from the photo shoot with Mark, Manny's warning of Mark's physical interest resurfaced to send Ellie's heart pounding. She flipped through dozens of photos of his handsome face, and groaned. Not only was the man good-looking, but photogenic, too.

Her breathing became shallow when she came to the photo of Mark shirtless, arms crossed, his eyes haughty from tricking her. Recalling their light, fussy banter, Ellie realized uneasily she could get used to his company. But the memory of the deal they'd struck sobered her immediately. He needed someone his mother would object to, and he'd chosen her for the part. How much clearer could he have made it that he would never be interested in her romantically?

4

"SPARE SOME CHANGE, buddy?" The ragged man's dead tone and tired eyes told Mark he fully expected to take no for an answer.

Mark hesitated outside Ellie's building, then withdrew a five-dollar bill from his wallet and placed it in the man's trembling hand. The man thanked him profusely, then trotted down the street. He wasn't in the habit of giving handouts, but he'd felt a stir when he'd looked into the man's lost eyes. Mark shook his head sadly. His old man had given away and loaned out enough money to save an entire generation. And look where it had gotten Rudy Blackwell.

Mark shook off the somber thoughts of his father and looked around the neat, trendy area. Panhandlers knew Little Five Points inhabitants were liberals, for the most part, with a social conscience and lots of spare change to back it up. Mark knew this because he'd rented an apartment not far from Ellie's building before he'd signed a hefty mortgage and moved north to Dunwoody.

At only eleven-thirty, the sun already hung high and scorching. He pulled a finger around the collar of his golf shirt and felt relieved he'd worn khaki shorts. He'd arrived at Ellie's a few minutes early, but his mother wanted to get to the picnic shelter at Stone Mountain before anyone else so she could prevent relatives from setting green-bean salad next to strawberry pie, or some similar unforgivable act. He chuckled, thinking about Ellie Sutherland and Gloria Blackwell mixing for an entire day. He couldn't imagine the surprises Ellie had in store. This might be the most fun he'd ever had at a family gathering. And it would very likely get his marriage-happy mother off his back.

As he climbed the steps to Ellie's second-floor apartment, Mark tried to ignore the anticipation he felt at seeing her again. Many times during the previous sleepless night he'd reminded himself she'd managed to extort a good chunk of cash from him in the one week he'd known her. She was just like the others, he told himself. So why had he tripped twice in his haste to get to her door?

He knocked twice before he heard footsteps approaching. When the door swung open, a tall, handsome blond man stood before him with a questioning look on his face.

"Excuse me," Mark said abruptly. "I must have the wrong apartment."

The man extended his hand in a firm grip. "You must be Mark," he said. "Ellie's almost ready. I'm Manny, Ellie's roommate. Come in."

Mark blinked. A ridiculous stab of jealousy jolted through him. Ellie hadn't mentioned she lived with a man—a very good-looking man, to boot. He followed her roommate through a shallow entryway and halted to stand on the black-and-white kitchen floor, grimacing at the screeching voice that reached his ears. Ellie stood at the stove with headphones on, her back to them, stirring a fragrant concoction in a saucepan

and belting out a horrid rendition of Patsy Cline's
"Crazy."

Manny turned to him and shrugged apologetically.
"It's country this week, next week—who knows?" He
walked over and tapped Ellie on the shoulder. She
jumped several inches, her hand to her chest, and the
shrieking stopped. She saw Mark and smiled, tearing
off the headphones.

"Hi," she said, picking up a towel to wipe her
hands.

"Hi, yourself," he said, annoyed at the rush of pleasure he felt. "Is that your contribution to the potluck?"
he asked, pointing to the gooey liquid in the pan.

Ellie laughed and reached around to untie her frilly
cotton apron. A vintage garment, he suspected, noting
the pleasantly faded fabric. "That," she said, nodding
to the pan, "is twenty-five thousand dollars."

"What?"

"I'm entering a homemade-perfume contest. The entry fee is one hundred dollars, which I'm working off
today." She smiled at him impishly. "Top prize is
twenty-five thousand, and I want it."

Intrigued, Mark walked over to the pot and sniffed.
A sultry blend of musk, fruit and flowers assailed his
nostrils. "Hmm," he said, nodding. "Very nice. I've
never smelled anything like it. A woman's fragrance,
I assume?"

"Of course."

"What's in it?"

"Oh, this and that. Chamomile, marjoram and juni-
per for relaxation, ylang-ylang as an aphrodi—" She
stopped and cleared her throat loudly. "Plus vanilla,
and a little cocoa."

"It's colorful," he said, noting the muddy brown hue.

"I haven't worked out all the kinks yet, but my idea is to launch a whole line of perfume products based on foods."

"Pizza perfume?" he asked, teasing.

She smiled. "More like orange marmalade or peach pie."

When she pulled the apron over her head, Mark inhaled sharply at the sight of her in a full-skirted, floral minidress and flat cloth tennis shoes. No bra either, which was not unbecoming. She looked all of sixteen. He swallowed. "What do you call the perfume?"

"I've decided to call it Irresistible You."

Bull's-eye. Mark nodded. "Very appropriate."

She turned off the flame and said, "I see you've met Manny. Let me grab a couple of things and we'll go." She swept by him in a cloud of homemade fragrance, the pom-poms on her socks bouncing up and down as she strode away.

Mark watched her, then turned when he felt Manny watching him. As the man waved him toward a purple-and-gold velour chair in the tiny living room, Mark again wondered about his relationship to Ellie. They were both blond, perhaps he was her brother. "Are you related to Ellie?" he asked when they were seated.

"No," Manny said, tapping a cigarette from a pack and rolling it between his fingers. "Ellie and I go way back."

His tone implied intimacy, and Mark didn't really want to delve further.

"She's a great gal," Manny continued. He lit the cigarette, inhaled deeply and turned his head to release a stream of white smoke from his mouth. His voice and bearing suggested a challenge.

Mark nodded his agreement, but said nothing. His nose itched ferociously, and he ran a knuckle over it.

"She has men falling all over her."

It seemed like a strange thing for her roommate to say, but Mark smiled amicably. A savage sneeze seized him, and he dragged a handkerchief from his back pocket. Wiping at watery eyes, he sniffed. "I can see why," he finally managed to say.

"Is the smoke bothering you?" Manny asked, cupping his hand over the cigarette.

Mark shook his head. "Smoke never bothers me." On cue, he sneezed into the handkerchief three times, each more powerful than the last. "I don't know what's wrong." Mark felt a sudden soft weight land in his lap, and he looked down into the green eyes of a very hairy orange cat. One inhale solved the mystery as Mark dissolved into a sneezing fit, which did nothing to spook the arrogant feline.

"Allergic, huh?" Manny said, stubbing out his cigarette in a nearby ashtray. "Come, Esmerelda." He removed the feline from Mark's knee and disappeared down the same hallway Ellie had taken.

By the time he returned, minus the cat, Mark felt much better.

"Sorry about that," Manny said unconvincingly. "Ellie loves the puss." When he sat down, Manny leaned forward in his chair. "Do you find yourself drawn to her?"

Mark frowned and drew his shoulders back a couple of inches. "Who?"

"Ellie."

"Drawn?"

"Yeah, you know." Manny toyed with another cigarette, but didn't light it. "Like *compelled* to be around her?"

Mark glanced from side to side. *Is this guy for real?* "I don't know if I'd use that word exactly," Mark said slowly, "but she does seem to have an effect on me."

Manny's sandy eyebrows shot up and he leaned back, nodding and contemplating. Mark glanced toward the hall. "Ellie?" he called, standing.

To his relief, she appeared with a huge canvas bag over her shoulder. A floppy denim hat nearly hid her cropped wavy hair and made her appear even younger. She smiled and shaved off another couple of years.

"Just how old are you?" he asked.

"Twenty-nine," she said cheerfully. "Did I go overboard?" she asked, looking down at her outfit. Silver earrings brushed the tops of her shoulders. "Your mom will hate it, won't she?" Concern pulled down the corners of her eyes and mouth.

Mark grinned. "Yes."

Ellie grinned, too. "Then let's go." She leaned forward to study his face, undoubtedly red from the sneezing. "Sorry about Esmerelda. She's a hairy thing, isn't she?"

He waved off the incident and reached for her bulging bag, then playfully buckled under its weight. "Let me guess—you brought books to read, didn't you?"

Ellie laughed. "No, just a few necessities for a picnic." She picked up a small bottle from the kitchen counter, shook two pink tablets into her palm and filled a glass with water from the tap.

"Headache?" Mark asked, suddenly concerned.

"Hmm?" Ellie asked. Apprehension crossed her face, then disappeared. "These are just, um... vitamins." She stuck the bottle into the weighted canvas bag. "I have to take them throughout the day," she explained. "Woman stuff," she added in a whisper.

Mark had figured as much and nodded curtly, and he hoped, sympathetically.

When Ellie pulled a huge chocolate layer cake from the fridge, he shot her a questioning look. The last thing he needed was for his mom to think he'd snared a domestic dream.

"Well, I can't go completely empty-handed," she said defensively.

"Okay," Mark relented. "But it'd better not taste *too* good." For a few seconds, he experienced misgivings. What if she did hit it off with his family? If they pestered him to bring her around again, his plan would backfire in his face.

"So TELL ME, what kind of woman does your mother expect you to marry?" Ellie hoped setting the stage for her performance would soothe her jangled nerves.

Mark pursed his lips and glanced back at the road in front of him. He looked relaxed and athletic in his casual clothes. The muscles in his legs bunched when he shifted gears, sending shocks of awareness through Ellie's body.

"Someone demure and domestic, I suppose. Like her." He smiled wryly. "She thinks I need someone to be a hostess in my home and help me entertain to further my career."

"And you don't?"

"No."

"Why not?"

He sighed. "Because I've seen too many of my friends get rooked into marriage only to find themselves digging out from under a divorce settlement within a couple of years. I worked my tail off to get where I am. I have no intention of starting over."

Ellie sat still, heat burning her neck and cheeks. Mark was convinced that women were fortune seekers. And she'd given him ammunition by lowering his bank account by more than four hundred dollars since she'd met him a week ago. "So," she said, trying to cover her embarrassment, "you've never been married?"

"Nope." Then he shot her a worried glance. "Have you?"

"No," she said quickly, not that it mattered to him anyway.

"Who's Manny?"

For a split second, Ellie felt pleased he even cared, but his concentration on the road and casual tone indicated he was just making conversation. "Just an old friend," she said and Mark nodded lazily, clearly uninterested. Her heart sank. "Is your mother a widow?"

"Yes," Mark said, frowning slightly. "Dad died three years ago."

"I'm sorry," Ellie said. "Were you close to him?"

"As close as you can be to someone with whom you have nothing in common."

Ellie felt a stirring of kinship. "My father was never around when I was growing up, either."

Mark's low laugh held no humor. "Mine was always around. Couldn't seem to keep a job. He was a great man, but a lousy provider."

"Where do you live?" Ellie asked, searching for firmer ground.

She thought she saw his lips tighten. "Dunwoody."

He didn't have to add "in a big, expensive home." The one word said it all. "Do you have a large yard?"

Mark glanced at her sideways. "I suppose so."

"Trees?"

"Uh-huh."

"What kinds of plants and flowers?"

Mark shrugged. "The usual stuff—azaleas, forsythia, a few bulb flowers and lots of ground cover. I might build a gazebo this fall."

"That sounds nice," Ellie said, and meant it. Room for a large herb garden was the only thing she yearned for that apartment living couldn't give her.

"I like it," Mark said, his voice tight.

From his manner, Ellie concluded he probably didn't want her discussing domestic things like gardens and homes with his mother.

"How exactly do you want me to act?" Ellie asked. "And what should I talk about?"

Mark smiled again, and she felt a rush of pleasure. "You've got a mom," he said. "You'll know what to say and how to act."

"Don't you feel guilty about lying to your mother?"

Mark shook his head. "I know my mom. It's only when I'm *not* seeing anyone that she panics and puts me on a guilt trip because she doesn't have grandchildren. The minute I *do* meet someone, she scolds me for neglecting my career and says I've got plenty of time to get married." He relaxed his hands lower on the wheel. "I'd rather not have to stage this little charade, but no one's getting hurt."

Ellie bit her tongue, and a little sliver of disappointment shook her heart. *Speak for yourself, Mark Blackwell.* She'd promised him a wacky performance for his money, but deep down she wished today could be different. It was easy to imagine herself as Mark's girlfriend, on her way to meet his family at a picnic. But, a deal was a deal, and today she'd be everything Mark Blackwell wouldn't want in a partner. The bad thing about it was, she wouldn't have to do much of an acting job. She realized, for the most part, just being herself would be suitably unsuitable.

Gloria Blackwell strutted out to the car exactly as Ellie had envisioned. Buxom and conservatively dressed in a shapeless jumper. Neat hair in a low bun. Plump elbows and arms full of pot holders and steaming casserole dishes.

Gloria gave Ellie's outfit a long glance, then offered a shaky smile. Introductions were cheery and forced. Gloria asked Ellie to move to the back seat of Mark's sedan, citing her perpetual car sickness as the reason she needed the front passenger seat. As Ellie moved to oblige, she heard the woman whisper to Mark, "Isn't she going to miss her prom?"

"Be nice," Mark whispered back.

Ellie smiled wryly. This would be the easiest money she'd ever made. The thought did not ease her conscience.

"Ellie, dear," Gloria asked when they were on their way, "what do you do for a living?"

Ellie hesitated a split second, then said, "I was laid off from a secretarial job a few days ago." She saw Mark frown at the news, then his face cleared, as if in understanding. He winked at Ellie in the mirror. He thought she was making it up to get under his mother's skin!

"So you're unemployed?" his mother asked, her disapproval thinly veiled.

Ellie ground her teeth, but maintained a sweet and pleasant voice. "Well, I'm really an artist, working on my portfolio and doing commissions on the side—like painting your son's portrait."

"An unemployed artist," Gloria chirped. "How interesting." She addressed Ellie by looking at her in the side-door mirror. "My late husband dabbled in paint—it never earned him a penny."

Ellie sat back in her seat, biting off a defensive retort. Gloria Blackwell had disliked her on sight. That fact might have bothered her if she thought this thing with Mark was going anywhere. But since he'd made it clear he wasn't interested in pursuing a relationship, she could relax. So what if his mother pooh-poohed her occupation and clothes? Mark said he wanted to go for shock value. For three hundred and fifty dollars, she'd be Madonna for a day.

"So how did you meet my son?"

"The first time we met, he dumped a cola in my lap and paid me off to avoid a scene."

"And...the next time?" Gloria ventured.

"In the men's room at his law office. Your son has an enormous—"

"I don't think—"

"—bladder," Ellie finished.

Gloria fanned herself. "Do your parents live in Atlanta?"

"No, Florida."

Mark's mother breathed an audible sigh of relief at finding a safe subject. "That's nice. Are they retired?"

"Semi-retired," Ellie said pleasantly. "They run a restaurant."

"How lovely!"

"At a nudist colony."

Gloria gasped and a sudden fit of coughing seized Mark.

Ellie bit back a wry smile.

For the rest of the drive, Gloria conversed with Mark, making general comments about the picnic and who would be there. Ellie guessed Mark's mother would not be directing any more questions her way, so she relaxed into the soft leather seat and listened to the woman's chatter.

"Did I tell you your uncle Jerome will be there? I know you're not fond of him, Marcus, but he *is* your grandmother's only brother. He's married again, did you know?"

Ellie smiled as Mark made a big show of counting off on his fingers. "Is this the fourth wife, or the fifth?"

"Fifth. You know the second Julia was really a gem—we all wish he'd kept her."

"I don't remember his second wife."

"No, I'm talking about Julia, his third wife. His second wife was also Julia, but we didn't care for her. She sniffed all her food before eating it. Always sniffing, it was very annoying. But his third wife, Julia—the second Julia, we always called her—now *there* was a nice girl. Real Southern manners, and a proper wife she was."

Ellie couldn't resist. "If she was such a proper wife, why did he get rid of her?"

Gloria jerked her head around quickly, as if she'd forgotten about their passenger. She adjusted the mirror so she could see Ellie. "I really wouldn't know," she said airily, as if gossiping was beneath her, then adjusted the mirror back with a snap.

"Here we are," Mark said cheerfully, shoving the gearshift into Park and turning off the ignition.

"How am I doing?" Ellie whispered as they walked to the back of the car.

"Great," he said, smiling. "I think she hates you."

Ellie frowned, then nodded agreeably. She was earning her pay, wasn't she?

She spied several shelters within walking distance, but a sign bearing the name "Blackwell" led them to one off to the right and up a small incline.

"I thought this was your mother's family," Ellie said to Mark as they unpacked the food.

He smiled. "It's both, really. Without getting too complicated, my dad and four of his brothers married mom and four of her sisters."

"Is that legal?"

This time he laughed. "It's legal, but sometimes I don't think it was very smart. All of their children are double first cousins. It makes for a pretty tight-knit group." He pulled a huge cooler from the trunk of his car, and led the way up the path. Gloria hurried ahead, visibly crestfallen that one of her sisters had beaten her to the punch and, having arrived first, was already spreading vinyl tablecloths over the ten or so picnic tables in the shelter.

Within a few minutes, several carloads had arrived, and Ellie's head spun from the names and faces she'd tried to commit to memory. Everyone, including Gloria, seemed impressed with the chocolate cake she'd made. "It's low-fat, too," she said to Gloria.

"Well," harrumphed Mark's mother, giving Ellie a sweeping glance, "not everyone was meant to look like a stick." The cake was thereby relegated to the lowly salad table, to occupy a spot beside a plate of unpopular celery and carrot sticks.

After an hour, Ellie decided to take a break from the adults and mix with Mark's young cousins. Delighted to discover several of them had brought in-line skates, she retrieved hers from her bag and joined them on the paved parking lot, ignoring disparaging looks from Mark's mother. She taught the more experienced skaters a few moves and was soon enjoying herself very much, laughing in spite of the sick feeling building in her stomach. She felt like a fraud, but it was equally disheartening to know that even when she was being herself, Mark's mother disapproved.

As unobtrusively as possible, Ellie watched Mark mix with the odd collection of relatives. The fussy aunts, the crying babies, the joke-telling men were so different from the stoic manner he put on. Ellie wondered how he'd metamorphosed into the polished, articulate executive he'd become. He was obviously everyone's favorite. It was gratifying to see he'd originated from homespun people—good, decent people with simple wants and needs whom he seemed to care about. This was a side of him she hadn't expected to discover, and it caused an unsettling shift in the characteristics she'd assigned to him.

It bothered her, too, that his family was so different from hers. He'd mentioned he was an only child, like Ellie, but Mark's extended family was large and varied, warm and comfortable around each other. She tried to conjure up images of long-forgotten aunts and uncles from faded photographs she'd seen in family albums. Both sets of grandparents had died before she was a toddler. Ellie's mother had been the youngest of her three siblings by nearly a generation—she wasn't close to them at all. Her father had one brother left, living somewhere on the West Coast, she recalled. She wondered how many unknown cousins she had all over the country, and made a mental note to pump her mother for more information the next time they talked on the phone.

She stole a glance at Mark, and felt a zing go through her at the sight of him, his head thrown back, laughing. She envied Mark Blackwell and his rowdy relatives. Ellie sighed. A big, close, loving family was all she'd ever wanted, and all she'd never gotten.

Mark slapped his cousin Mickey on the back, enjoying a shared joke. His gaze slid to Ellie, an annoying habit he'd adopted in the last hour, along with every male relative at the picnic over the age of ten. His smile died and his mouth went dry as she whirled on the skates, causing her skirt to billow alarmingly high.

"Where did you snag *her*?" Mickey whispered hoarsely, admiration tinting his voice.

Mark jerked his head around to find the eyes of his balding, chunky cousin riveted on Ellie. A strange feeling of possessiveness descended over him. "She's an artist and my office commissioned her to do a painting."

"An artist, huh? That explains it."

"That explains what?"

"Why she's not like every corporate female clone I've ever seen you with."

Mark frowned. "What's that supposed to mean?"

"Not that you haven't dated some beauties, cuz," Mickey hastened to add. "It's just that my tastes lean toward *warm*-blooded creatures." He exhaled heavily. "And that woman is hot."

Mark's frown deepened. He hadn't hired her to be hot. Guilt stabbed him in the gut when he remembered the money he'd paid her. The thought struck him that it might be nice if Ellie Sutherland had accompanied him of her own volition, instead of having to be bribed. Then she could have acted naturally and his family could have fallen in love with her...wait a minute— what was he thinking?

His cousin let out a low whistle through his small teeth. Mark joined him in holding his breath when a particularly risky move revealed every square inch of her rock-hard thighs and the barest glimpse of white cotton undies. Mark licked his lips nervously and Mickey dragged a handkerchief out of his back pocket to mop his forehead.

"I don't think she hit it off with Mom," Mark said carefully, attempting to plant a seed of dissent.

"That settles it," Mickey said, nodding confidently. "Marry her."

Someone rang a bell to signal the meal being served. Ellie removed her skates and rejoined the adults, dutifully giving disappointing, but true, answers to repeated questions from Gloria's sisters about what she did for a living and how she'd met Mark. Mark hovered close by, as if to verify she was doing what he'd asked of her. Every infant at the gathering squalled when she held them, and soon the new mothers were keeping their babies to themselves. Ellie slipped her camera from the bag and snapped two rolls of pictures, the women politely rigid when she focused on them, the men curiously hamming for the camera.

Indeed, it seemed the chilly reception extended to her by the Blackwell women wasn't a feeling shared by the Blackwell men. They buzzed around Ellie continually, laughing and flirting, elbowing appreciation to a silent Mark. Uncle Jerome, the marrying man, shadowed her every move, offering her lively, if suggestive, conversation throughout the afternoon. Even beating the men at horseshoes didn't banish their smiles and winks. When it looked as if the female relatives were about to descend on her with tar and feathers, she rejoined the children. This time, she pulled out her sketchbook and drew caricatures of the ones who could sit still long enough for her to render a pastel drawing. The children gleefully took the sketches to their parents, and before long, an audience had gathered.

The sudden attention made Ellie nervous and she noticed a frown on Mark's face. He wasn't paying her to make a favorable impression. She glanced at her tablet. "One sheet of paper left," she said. "Gloria, how about it?"

Mark's mother suddenly turned shy and blushing, but smiling, she nodded and sat before Ellie, striking a regal pose.

Ellie scanned the woman in front of her for a few seconds. The phrase *queen bee* kept going through her mind. Ellie looked at Mark, who gave her a slight nod. "Go ahead," he seemed to say. "One last nail in the coffin."

Hurriedly, Ellie sketched, hardly looking up. Once finished, she swallowed, amazed at how unkind the picture had turned out. With a bemused smile, Gloria reached for the drawing as everyone gathered around. Instantly her smile dissolved and her face reddened, then she handed it back to Ellie and huffed away amid choruses of laughter from her family.

Mark stepped forward to look at the sketch, a buxom insect with a tiara on her head, wielding a giant-size stinger. He pursed his lips. "Queen bee," he said, studying the drawing with a tight smile. "So true. You're very good."

Ellie watched people drift away to the dessert table and said, "It was hurtful to her, and I should apologize."

Mark shook his head. "You're doing just what I asked you to do," he said, handing the sketch back to her and looking into her eyes. "Everyone got a chuckle out of it. Mom's just not very good at laughing at herself."

"Still, I feel so mean," she said, biting her lower lip.

He extended his hand to her and pulled her up. "Let's get dessert." His first touch sent charges of electricity through her fingers. She quickly withdrew her hand once she got to her feet.

When everyone discovered Ellie's cake was low-fat, most of the women relented and served themselves portions ranging from polite to generous. Uncle Jerome even teased Gloria into having a chunk, pointing out it wouldn't hurt her to start counting her fat grams. Gloria begrudgingly ate every crumb. The men deferred to more fattening fare. Mark declined, saying he wasn't big on sweets, and Ellie declined as well so someone else could have the remaining piece. To her surprise, it was Gloria.

"Are you sure this is low in fat?" she asked Ellie, shoveling in the second piece. "It's surprisingly good."

Ellie beamed, glad she would leave with one redeeming mark. "The guy I live with gave me the recipe." When she saw Gloria's eyes widen in response to the remark about her roommate, Ellie hurried on, "This is the first time I've made it. I'm glad it's as good as he said it would be."

"You know," Gloria said thickly through a mouthful, "Marcus needs a good cook in his kitchen."

Ellie's smile froze, wondering if Mark had overheard the comment. She nodded woodenly, surprised at the concession his mother had made, but more surprised at how good the idea sounded, her cooking in Mark's kitchen. Of course, they'd have to eat chocolate cake every night since it was the first and only thing she'd ever made that had turned out well enough to actually serve. Avoiding Mark's eyes, Ellie enjoyed the slight lifting of her heart.

About halfway through the hokey-pokey, the Blackwell women started dropping like flies. Clutching their stomachs, they ran for the nearest bathroom, several yards away. Gloria seemed to be the most violently ill. When they emerged an hour later, wiping sweat from their clammy foreheads, they'd determined the culprit must be Ellie's cake since no one else had been afflicted.

White as a sheet and mad as a hornet, Gloria demanded, "What did you put in that cake?"

Ellie backed up a step and tried to keep the shakiness out of her voice. "The normal stuff—flour, eggs, cocoa, prune juice—"

"Prune juice?" Gloria screeched. "Who puts prune juice in chocolate cake?"

"It replaces the oil and m-makes the cake low f-fat," Ellie stammered.

"How much did you put in?" Gloria asked, her eyes bulging.

"A b-bottle of concentrated—" She stopped at the horrified looks around her. "A s-small bottle," she added weakly, holding up her thumb and index finger.

"A whole bottle? Lord, we'll be purging for a week—" Gloria stopped, grabbed her stomach and trotted back up the hill to the rest room, followed by six others.

Ellie closed her eyes and took a deep breath. When she opened them, Mark stood before her, a wry smile on his face. "That really wasn't necessary, Ellie—" he took her hand "—but it certainly cinched you a spot on my mother's least-likely-to-be-a-good-daughter-in-law list."

Her senses leaped when he touched her, her mouth instantly parched. She swallowed miserably. He'd never believe her if she told him none of it had been planned. Ellie fought back tears of frustration.

This day had proved one thing to her. She was inherently wrong for Mark Blackwell.

MARK SWUNG his glance from the road ahead to Ellie's profile and tried to guess what she was thinking. The day was an unqualified success as far as his original plan was concerned, but he hadn't counted on his feelings shifting somewhere between the time he'd picked her up and the time he dropped her off. Away from her, he seemed able to logically dismiss her. But once in her presence, some undefined feeling took control.

"Your pictures turned out well," she said, breaking the silence and, thankfully, his train of thought.

"Did they?"

"Yes." She still stared straight ahead, her voice unreadable. "I think the dark gold background will be the best, if that's okay with you."

"You're the artist."

"Yes, and I'm very proud of what I do," she said, a note of defensiveness in her voice.

"As well you should be," he said quickly, once again speaking to her profile. Suddenly he remembered the disparaging remark he'd made about her being an artist when she first came to his office. And, the raised eyebrows and rolling eyes of his mother and her sisters had not escaped him today. Apparently, they hadn't escaped Ellie, either. "I admire your talent," he said sincerely.

She didn't respond, but her head shifted slightly toward him.

"It was a nice day," he said lightly.

Ellie's dry laugh rang out. "Sure it was," she said miserably. "I gave enemas to your mother and all of your aunts."

"Most of them have been constipated all their lives." He chuckled, but at the look on Ellie's face, he bit his lip to stem his laughter. "It's okay—no one was hurt." Actually, he couldn't remember enjoying a family gathering more than he had today. His family's bout with diarrhea aside, he'd enjoyed watching Ellie skate and mix with his young cousins. And cut up with his uncles. And her drawing ability was truly special. She was a very unusual woman, and damned attractive, at that. Another peek at her in the semidarkness of the car revealed a long expanse of lean, tanned leg. His right hand itched to reach over and rub the smooth length of skin.

"When can you sit for your portrait again?" she asked.

"How about Saturday morning? That is," he added quickly, "if you don't mind spending another Saturday with me." He held his breath for her response. Could he wait another six days to see Ellie again?

"Saturday morning is fine," she said, finally swinging her head around to meet his gaze.

"Fine," he said, feeling the breath leave his lungs. God, she was beautiful. "Fine," he heard himself repeat. His groin tightened uncomfortably and he dragged his eyes away from hers. Her apartment building loomed ahead on the left.

"Thanks," Ellie said quickly, hopping out as soon as he pulled to a stop.

"Wait," he said to the closed door. He cut the ignition and jumped out of the car. "Wait," he called, and she turned back, struggling under the weight of that ridiculous bag. "I'll walk you to your door." He strode toward her, his knees suddenly rubbery. Would she let him kiss her? Would a kiss be appropriate under the circumstances? And when was the last time he had ever worried about whether or not to kiss a woman goodnight?

She waited until he'd caught up and taken her bag, but remained a couple of steps ahead of him, walking into the apartment building and up to her door on the second floor.

"Thanks," she said, sounding a little breathless.

"You did me the favor," he said, referring to the picnic.

She smiled. "I meant, thanks for walking up with me. It wasn't necessary, but nice."

He could barely see her eyes for the brim of her hat, which sat slightly askew. New freckles glowed across her cheeks from the afternoon's sunshine. Her lips held the frosty remnants of pink lipstick long since faded. She hadn't bothered to renew it. How refreshing to be with a woman who was content to be her natural self sometimes. He wet his lips. "Ellie?"

She raised wide, innocent eyes to his. "Yes?" She didn't have a clue he wanted to kiss her. And why should she? He'd hired her to go on a picnic with him. The whole arrangement seemed very impersonal at the moment. Did he dare?

"Ellie?"

"What is it, Mark?" she asked, her head slightly angled.

"This," he breathed, lowering his mouth to hers. Her lips were silken, parting to accept his fully, her tongue tentatively offered. Desire shot through his body. He dropped the canvas bag with a loud thud and took her into his arms to draw her deeper into the kiss. Suddenly, the apartment door swung open.

Mark and Ellie parted and turned their heads to see a questioning Manny, holding a half-eaten apple. "I heard a thump," he explained, leaning on the door frame and taking a large bite.

Mark straightened. *What is the deal with this room-mate man, anyway?*

Everyone stared at everyone else, the silence broken only by Manny's loud chewing. After a few seconds, Mark cleared his throat. "Well, I'd better be going."

Manny reached inside the door to retrieve a light jacket from a hook. "I was on my way out myself— just wanted to make sure you got home safely, El." He flashed her a tight smile. "I'll walk out with Mr. Blackwell." He took a last bite out of the apple for punctuation and tossed it into a trash can beside the door. Then he stepped squarely between them in the hall, struggling into his jacket with exaggerated movements that obstructed Mark's view of Ellie.

Mark frowned slightly, then said, "I'll see you Saturday, Ellie." He peeked around Manny's breadth as the man took his time pulling on the jacket. Ellie said nothing, but he saw— reproachfulness?—flicker in her eyes. Had his kiss been unwelcome? It hadn't seemed so, but then again she hadn't counted on her roommate/boyfriend/whatever catching them.

Mark walked side by side with Manny down the stairs and out into the dusk. They stopped on the sidewalk and Mark withdrew his car keys. "So," he said casually, "what's your relationship with Ellie?" He pressed a button on his key ring and his car interior light came on a few feet away. Mark swung his attention back to her roommate.

Manny stood with his hands in his jacket pockets, studying Mark silently with narrowed eyes. Finally, the tall blond man spoke quietly, "Ellie means more to me than anyone else in this world. Don't break her heart, mister.'' With that, he turned and walked away, pulling a cigarette from his pocket and poking it in his mouth.

Driving away, Mark decided it had been one of the most unsettling days of his life. The picnic had been unexpectedly enjoyable, and Ellie's good-night kiss unexpectedly flammable. Feelings nagged at him, annoying him like radio static. Just exactly what did Ellie Sutherland mean to him, other than a guaranteed end to his orderly life?

5

"YOU DIDN'T!" Manny looked horrified.

"I did." Ellie nodded solemnly, slathering jelly on a plain bagel. Breakfast was the first chance they'd had to talk. "You should have seen those big women running for the john. And we had to stop three times on the way home for his mom to go."

"I always said you were going to poison someone with your cooking one of these days," he chided. "You've got to remember, preparing food is not the same as whipping up one of your perfume batches."

Ellie brightened. "Which reminds me, I'm sending a vial of Irresistible You to the contest today." She pointed to a small bottle of reddish-brown liquid beside a gummy saucepan. The recipe I came up with yesterday turned out just right, after all."

Manny shook his head. "You can kiss that hundred-dollar entry fee goodbye. It's a scam, El."

"No, it isn't," she insisted. "I know someone whose cousin's girlfriend won the contest two years ago. And my proposal for a line of fragrances is a great idea."

"Who wants to go around smelling like food?"

"For your information, studies show men are more turned on by the smell of pumpkin pie than by most expensive store-bought fragrances."

"Makes you wonder what Betty Crocker wears under her apron, eh?"

"Go ahead, make fun, but I'll get the last laugh. That twenty-five grand is mine." She rubbed her thumb against her fingers to emphasize her quest for big money.

"You'd better hope so," he said. "It doesn't sound as if you're in danger of marrying into the Blackwell bank account."

Ellie stiffened. "Very funny."

"Hey," he said, laughing gently, "I was kidding, okay? Don't look so wounded. I thought you weren't impressed with this guy."

"I'm not." Ellie studied Esmerelda's paw, refusing to look at her roommate. "He's too much like my father, you know…corporate. I want a man who worships the ground I walk on, who isn't tied to his desk, who would play hooky just to spend the day with his kids. My mother never had that, but I intend to, one of these days."

Manny groaned. "Despite your wish list, you've fallen for him, haven't you?"

Ellie opened her mouth, but Manny held up his hands to ward off her protest. "Before you say anything, Ellie, let's look at this in black and white. The guy hired you to make a bad impression on his family—this is not the sign of a marrying man. Why on earth would you put yourself through the agony of going after someone who's made it perfectly clear he doesn't want to be caught?"

Ellie tried to speak, but once again he stopped her. "But," he said in a singsongy voice, "it's nothing to me." Manny stooped to pick up the cat. "Not to change the subject, but we have other problems more imminent than your love life. Have you noticed anything different about Esmerelda?''

"No," Ellie murmured, popping the pinks pills into her mouth with a grapefruit-juice chaser. "Why do you ask?"

"Here," he said, handing Ellie the furry package.

She abandoned her glass to juggle the struggling feline. "She's heavier," Ellie said immediately, shifting the cat slightly for confirmation. "We should have put you on a diet weeks ago," she said, snuggling the cat's face to her own.

"We should have put her on a *leash*," Manny amended, arms crossed and lips tight.

"What do you mean?"

"Esmerelda is knocked up."

Ellie's eyes widened. "Kittens? Are you sure?" She held the cat up to scrutinize her rounded tummy, grinning. "It must've happened on one of those days she escaped."

"Must have," Manny chirped. "You realize, don't you, this means your cat has a better sex life than you do?"

She shot him an exasperated look. "Oh, Manny, do you have to be so...so...''

"The word is *truthful*," he supplied. He plucked a piece of paper from the counter and waved it in front of her. "It gets worse. This was under our door when I got up this morning."

Ellie reached for the paper and gasped at the words in large print across the top of the page. "Eviction notice? Why?" She began reading the sheet in earnest, but Manny cut in.

"It's the cat, El. She got out one too many times and someone complained. According to the notice, we have one week to find a home for her or we'll have to find a new home for ourselves."

"I'll find someone to take her in," she said, gently setting Esmerelda on the floor, then reaching for the phone.

Two hours later Ellie had called every person in both her address book and Manny's, but no one could shelter her precious cat. She sighed, explaining to Manny, "Denise has a new baby, the Worths have a dog, and Robin just bought a bird. Everyone else already has too many cats or kids, or lives in a no-pet unit." Ellie pulled Esmerelda to her and relished the deep purr of the mother-to-be. "What am I going to do?"

"YOUR MOTHER CALLED TWICE," Monica said, handing Mark the message sheets. "She asked me to tell you to call her back as soon as you get a minute."

Mark nodded absently and laid the notes aside.

Looking over his shoulder, Monica asked, "What's so important about Saturday?"

Mark glanced up at her and frowned in confusion.

She pointed to his calendar. "It's circled. Do I need to add something to my schedule?"

Mark realized with a start he'd circled the day while thinking about Ellie. "No," he said quickly, then added, "just another sitting for the portrait."

Monica's left eyebrow rose a fraction and she smiled. "Oh, yes, the cute little painter. Are sparks still flying between the two of you?"

He feigned innocence. "What do you mean?"

Monica brought her steno pad to her chest and

crossed her arms. "What I mean is, when she came to meet you that first day, you were at each other's throats. I haven't mentioned it, but you two have got me curious."

Mark felt his neck grow moist beneath his collar. "A simple misunderstanding in a delicatessen, that's all."

His assistant leaned forward slightly, as if eager for more details, but Mark picked up a memo on his desk and began reading to signal an end to the subject. Monica took the hint and walked toward the door.

"Hey," his partner Patrick said as he strolled in after a perfunctory knock.

"Hey, yourself."

"Clear your calendar Friday evening."

"Okay. Mind telling me why?"

"Lucy's organizing a dinner party and my instructions are to make sure you come." He grinned at Mark apologetically. "Can you scrounge up a date? Ivan will be there, too," he added in explanation.

Ellie's face rose to float in Mark's mind, but he squashed down the image. "Is an escort mandatory?"

Patrick shrugged. "I have my orders." He turned to leave Mark's office and added over his shoulder, "Come stag at your own risk."

"It might be safer than the alternative," Mark muttered as Ellie's face stubbornly reappeared to taunt him. Absurdly happy for a reason to call her, his fingers itched to punch her number. Then, furious with himself, he deliberately dialed Valerie's work number instead. He'd managed to keep from getting emotionally involved with a woman for this long, and he wasn't about to start with someone who was obviously so wrong for him.

But when Valerie responded with such clinging enthusiasm at the sound of his voice, he winced and manufactured a vague excuse for calling. Within seconds of hanging up, his traitorous fingers dialed Ellie's number from memory. Instantly nervous, he wondered if he'd have to bribe her again, or if she'd go freely this time. Too late, the thought surfaced that she might feel obligated to buy a new dress. And he suspected she couldn't afford it.

"Hello." She sounded breathless, and he imagined her in her work apron, wiping her hands after working on some creative project.

"Hi, it's Mark," he said, then added, "Blackwell."

"Oh, hi," she said with a slight question in her voice.

Mark felt awkward and fished for conversation. "Are you busy?"

"As a matter of fact, I was preparing the canvas for your portrait." Animation exuded from her voice. He liked the musical quality of it, not throaty and superficial like most of the women he knew.

"I don't have a clue as to what that entails. Is it difficult?"

Ellie laughed lightly, a tinkling sound. "No, I tack canvas over a wooden frame, then paint over it with gesso, a white substance that makes the canvas stiff when it dries."

"Ah, I see," Mark murmured.

The silence stretched for thirty seconds, then they both started talking at once.

"What's up—"

"The reason I called—"

They both laughed and then Mark started again. "The reason I called is to see if you're busy Friday night. I'm in another bind—are you up for a dinner party at the home of one of my partners?"

Ellie's heart had just stopped thudding from the initial shock of hearing his voice. Now it began pounding anew, followed by a sharp barb of disappointment. Apparently, he needed another date for hire. Or maybe not. Maybe this would be a real date. "I, uh, that is...what did you have in mind?"

Mark hesitated for an instant. "Same terms as before?"

Ellie's heart sank, then she panicked. Oh, God, did he think she was trying to wangle a higher price? "Look," she said finally, "I'm caught up on all my bills, so thanks, but I really don't need... Wait a minute." Her mind raced furiously. "How about a business proposition?"

"Go on." This time, *he* sounded cautious.

"My cat needs a home for a few weeks."

"Impossible," he began. "I'm allergic—"

"And I'm desperate," Ellie interrupted, pleading. "She's pregnant and my landlord won't let me keep her—"

"I really can't—"

"Please? Just until the kittens are born and I find homes for them? That's only four or five weeks—eight at the most. Once Esmerelda's gone, he'll get off my back. Then I'll be able to sneak her in again later."

Mark exhaled heavily. "I really can't...believe I'm doing this," he finished, with wonder in his voice. "Okay, it's a deal."

Ellie grinned into the phone. "Great! I'll get a cab to your house Friday night and bring Esmerelda with me." She scribbled down the address. "What should I wear?"

"I'll have something sent over," he said, surprising her.

"I *do* have clothes, *Mr.* Blackwell."

"Why is everything an argument with you? Let me do this, okay?"

He obviously didn't trust her judgment. Or perhaps he wanted her to make another bad impression. Either way, the ball bounced in his court. "Okay," she agreed hesitantly.

"I'll see you Friday," he said, then hung up.

Ellie sat holding the phone and listened to the dial tone. Her scalp tingled. Every day it seemed her life became more enmeshed with Mark Blackwell's. The memory of his kiss had kept her up late last night. She felt warm now just remembering how she'd pulled the length of green velvet from the foot of her bed and slept with it cuddled against her cheek.

She touched her lips, her mouth watering at the thought of his taste. For a brief moment, he'd pulled her to him and she'd felt his arousal for her. Desire stabbed her even now and she allowed herself the luxury of wondering what it would be like to lie beneath him. She knew the pheromones were getting to him— he'd probably bed her willingly enough, she mused. But was her heart durable enough to withstand the letdown once the chemical reaction fizzled out?

The following day, Tuesday, marked exactly one week since Ellie had begun taking the pills. She dutifully collected her journal and walked the few blocks to the clinic.

The unadorned white two-story building squatted on Parish Street between a parking garage and a vintage clothing store. Ellie waited politely while two women entered the door in front of her, wrinkling her nose appreciatively when the smell of paint wafted out. The old structure was getting a face-lift.

Two giant stepladders flanked the wide entryway, supporting slow painters with big paint buckets and tiny brushes. Ellie tilted her head back to check their pace and progress. They'd be there at least a decade, she decided, then turned toward the empty waiting room, relieved she wouldn't have to wait.

A cold, slimy dollop of something plopped onto her head. Ellie closed her eyes and lifted her shoulders in a deep shrug, instinctively wanting to touch the stuff oozing down behind both ears, but already knowing it was off-white wall paint.

"Sorry," came a muffled voice many feet above her. "Nice buns, though."

"Thanks," Ellie mumbled without looking up.

Thirty minutes later she sourly joined a large cluster of people waiting to speak to the harried receptionist standing behind the tall white counter. The clinic was a busy little place. Apparently, a crowd had arrived during her attempt to remove most of the paint from her hair in the rusty old bathroom.

After a long wait, she was directed to one of the cracking vinyl-upholstered chairs lining the perimeter of the waiting room. Ellie passed the time leafing through an ancient copy of *Museum Art*, her hair dripping milky water on the curled pages.

At last her name was called, and she followed a gray-haired, stocky, somber-faced woman to a tiny closet of a room. "I'm Freda," the woman said defensively, as if Ellie was going to make something of it. She didn't. "Pleased to meet you."

Freda looked more like a prison guard than a clinical assistant. After a perfunctory glance over her chart, the woman snatched Ellie's journal and perused the contents with tight lips. After a few moments, her eyes swung up to meet Ellie's. "Impressive," the woman muttered. "All true?"

Ellie nodded patiently.

"Are you taking the pills exactly as directed?"

"Yes."

"Any physical symptoms? Changes in energy level or diet?"

Ellie thought for a moment. "My concentration seems diminished, and my appetite has been depressed." She grinned and patted her stomach. "I've lost two pounds."

"How about your exercise level?"

Ellie shook her head. "About average—no change."

The woman noted Ellie's answers on a form. "Have you become sexually active with any of the men you've mentioned in the journal?"

Ellie squirmed. "No."

"Have you developed an emotional attachment to any of them?" She skimmed the last journal page with her index finger. "I see the name Mark mentioned quite often." She peered over her glasses at Ellie.

Clearing her throat, Ellie said, "N-no. Well, maybe."

"I don't have a checkbox for 'maybe,'" said Freda. "Do you like the man or don't you?"

"Yes, I do."

"And do you have reason to think he likes you?"

"I'm not sure *like* is the right word. He looks at me in this certain way…"

"Do you feel the pheromone pills have in any way influenced this, er, watchfulness?"

"Yes, I do."

"In what way?"

Ellie hesitated, then tried to put the situation in words. "He seems to be attracted to me, but confused by it all—like he doesn't understand why he would be. I've seen him shake his head as if trying to clear it. He told my roommate I have 'an effect' on him. And, he and other men keep asking me what kind of perfume I'm wearing. I think I'm emitting some kind of scent."

Freda leaned toward her, sniffed mightily, then shrugged. "Hmm." She scribbled notes on the form and turned it over. "Keep omitting any commercial body fragrances like we instructed. Here's a new supply of pills, and your payment for the week." She pushed the items toward Ellie and resumed writing.

"I mean, it's nothing serious," Ellie rambled. "I wouldn't even call it a relationship, really. It would never work between us because he's allergic to my cat and his mother hates me. Of course, I did ruin her family reunion, but that was purely by accident. Besides, if he ever settles down, it'll be with some classy woman, not an unemployed artist. No, it would never work, not in a million years." Ellie frowned at the woman's silence. "Any advice?" she asked.

Freda didn't bother to look up. "Practice safe sex."

MANNY LET OUT a long whistle. "Damn, you look good, girl."

Ellie grinned and smoothed a hand over the short black crepe dress. "Think so?" A froth of pearl-studded cream chiffon floated around the low neckline and spilled over her shoulders. The formfitting dress would have been an impossibility two pounds ago.

"Fabulous," Manny said cloyingly, then he frowned. "If only we wore the same size."

"I'll let you borrow the earrings," she promised, fastening the dangling pearls.

"He must have spent a mint," he said, picking up the Parmond's garment bag.

Ellie nodded. "What are you doing tonight?"

"I have to do an early show, then Joan's picking me up. We're going to swing by a friend's house for cocktails, then downtown for some real fun. By the way, El, she feels terrible for having to let you go."

She shrugged. "It was just a job. So tell me, does Joan like men or women?"

"Neither, as far as I can tell—or maybe both. You know how outrageous Joan can be—I think she likes to keep everyone guessing."

"Well, tell her hello for me, and that the commission is going well. Will you help me gather Esmerelda's things? The cab should be here any minute."

The cabbie appeared daunted when he saw the cat and all her feline paraphernalia, but when Ellie smiled at him, he softened and began loading the trunk of the car.

"'Bye, Cinderella," Manny said to Ellie before she stepped into the back seat. "Have a good time at the party. But remember to take your pills or you'll turn into my cousin Betty at midnight.''

ELLIE HAD TRIED to visualize Mark's house, but two blocks away from his address, she realized his home would surpass all her expectations. The cabbie pulled up to a two-story, taupe-colored stucco house with elaborate arches and pale cornerstones. The sloping yard was a paradise, the lawn all but completely sacrificed to tall trees, enormous mulch beds and lush leafy plants. Mounds of blooms flowed downhill. A fountain of stacked stone bubbled a stream of water, which fed an aquamarine goldfish pond. Ellie had never seen a more beautiful sight.

''Are you sure this is the place?'' she breathed.

''Sure as shootin'.'' The driver nodded. ''Nice spread, eh? Friend of yours?''

''Yes,'' she said absently, unable to take her eyes from the house.

''Some guys have all the luck,'' he said dismally. ''But if you get bored with Richie Rich, my name's Cal, and I get off at ten.'' He swung out of the cab and opened her door before she had a chance to respond.

The front door of the house opened. Mark came out and descended the steps to the walkway. He wore dark slacks, a crisp off-white shirt and a mustard-colored tie. He looked absolutely devastating. Ellie alighted from the cab and smiled toward him. She could detect the clean scent of his cologne as he neared her. Esmerelda struggled for release to inspect the fish, but Ellie held on tight. ''Hi.''

''Hi.'' He smiled, and held his hands at his sides,

swinging them slightly as if not knowing what to do next.

"Nice house."

"Thanks. Nice dress."

"Thanks."

"Nice bill," the cabbie spoke up, motioning to Mark.

Mark reached for his wallet and counted off several bills, folded them, then handed them to the man.

The cabbie thanked him and opened the trunk. Mark's eyebrows shot up. "What's all this?"

Ellie stepped to the back of the car. "Esmerelda's things."

Mark passed a hand over his face. "You've got to be kidding."

"No," Ellie said, pointing. "Her bed, litter box, kitty litter, food bowl, water bowl, food, brush, play gym, scratch pole, toys, videos—"

"Videos?"

"Sure—one shows birds flying around, the other is of fish swimming and splashing. They keep her entertained for hours."

Mark nodded and pursed his lips. "I see."

The cabbie started pulling things out and setting them on the sidewalk.

"I wrote down her schedule for you." Ellie pulled a sheet of paper from her tiny evening bag. "She has a bladder infection right now, so you'll need to give her medication once a day." She looked up and recognized impatience on Mark's face. Suddenly he sneezed violently. "We can go over this later," she said with a weak smile, refolding the sheet.

While Mark made several trips to bring in the cat's

accessories, Ellie stood in the two-story slate foyer of his home and stretched her neck to see as much as possible from her vantage point. The open layout and cool colors stole her breath. A large living room stretched to her left, an expansive dining room to her right. His furniture was fairly traditional in design, but light fabrics and colors lifted and extended the rooms.

"Wow," Ellie said out loud. If she hadn't been sure before that she and Mark Blackwell existed in different worlds, she was convinced now.

Esmerelda yowled and jumped from Ellie's arms, bounding up the stairs. "Esmerelda!" she yelled, then took off after her.

When Mark entered the house with the last armload, he found the foyer empty. "Ellie," he called, setting the things down on the stairs. He sneezed, and pulled a handkerchief from his pocket to blow his nose. "This is unbelievable," he muttered. "Why did I agree to this?" An implausible answer skated across his mind, but he dismissed it.

When she didn't respond, he walked around the first floor, thinking she might have gone to the bathroom. When he found the door to the downstairs bath ajar, however, he assumed she'd gone upstairs to look around. One of the things that had impressed him the most when she'd asked about his home was that she'd seemed much more interested in his yard than in the grandeur of the house. Mark felt a slight pang of disappointment that she'd been so anxious to check out his digs that she'd helped herself to a tour.

He climbed the stairs, calling her name as he walked room to room. He heard a muffled sound coming from his bedroom and frowned. Not that he hadn't entertained ideas of Ellie seeing the inside of his bedroom, but her forwardness annoyed him slightly.

When he entered his bedroom, he covered his mouth to smother a chuckle, then decided she couldn't hear him, so he laughed out loud, anyway. Ellie Sutherland's very fine-looking rear end stuck straight up in the air, the points of her high heels following suit. He'd pictured her in his bed many times, but never under it. Her head and shoulders were hidden beneath the dust ruffle of his black bed, and she seemed to be saying something, he surmised, to the cat.

After enjoying a full minute of the delectable view, he spoke loudly. "Ellie?"

She raised her head quickly and he heard bone collide with metal. "Darnit!" she yelled, her voice still muffled by all the fabric surrounding her.

Mark laughed again, this time more quietly.

She inched her way backward, out from under the bed, and Mark felt his groin tighten as her hips tested the strength of the dress's seams. He couldn't remember when he'd ever found a woman more appealing than at that very moment.

Her head appeared, her hair wonderfully mussed. She dragged her fingers through it and stood awkwardly, brushing the front of her dress. "I'm sorry," she said. "Esmerelda jumped out of my arms and ran up here and under your bed. I didn't mean to snoop." She chewed on her bottom lip, her glorious blue eyes wide with worry. "I think she's scared."

Her beauty slammed into him with enough power to stagger his senses. *I think I know how the cat feels.* "I'll put her things in the guest room down the hall. Will she come out and look for her bed later?"

Ellie nodded. "Probably."

"Then leave her. How about a drink before we go?"

Ellie smiled at him and his breath caught. "Can I use your bathroom for some repair work first?"

"Sure." He pointed to the master bath. "I'll meet you downstairs."

Ellie took a few seconds to glance around his bedroom, impressed at the sheer size of the bed. King-size and sleekly modern, the elevated bed reigned over a huge room lit by a bay window encompassing an entire wall.

She walked into the spacious bathroom and flipped on the light. "Mmm," she murmured, taking in the tiled floor and large sunken tub. Gold fixtures winked at her from the long double vanity and porcelain sinks. The fragrance of his after-shave lingered. A razor drained on a folded hand towel. Frosted doors encased a shower large enough for a quartet. She could picture Mark showering, soap running down his slick body. She bit her bottom lip and shook her head at the image, then turned to fix her hair.

She gasped at her reflection. Besides her explosive hair, the expensive dress he'd bought her was covered with long cat hairs and carpet fibers. And her lipstick smeared down the corner of her mouth. She groaned, opening her purse and spilling its contents across the counter in her haste. Ellie tugged a brush through her hair, yelping when it skated over the lump fast forming from her encounter with the bed rail. Tears of frustration gathered in her eyes.

"Look at you," she said miserably. "You're a nobody going nowhere. What business do you have falling in love with Mark Blackwell?" Gasping at her own

words, Ellie covered her mouth with her hand. Taking
a shaky deep breath, she straightened her shoulders,
and set about making herself presentable again. All the
while, she hummed to herself, taking great pains not to
talk to the crazy woman in the mirror.

6

ELLIE FELT SPARKLY from the two rum drinks she'd downed to alleviate her nervousness before they left. Too late, she realized she should have had a nonalcoholic beer with Mark. She could feel her body pulling toward him in the darkness of the car. His cologne, the soothing music, the special dress, all of it combined to make her feel languid and sexy. A shiver of premonition traveled the nape of her neck and she trembled. Trying to shake the feeling, she turned to Mark as they exited the expressway and said, "Any last-minute instructions?"

Mark looked at her, eyebrows lifted. "Such as?"

Ellie shrugged. "Such as, is there anybody in particular I'm supposed to make dislike me?"

Mark stared at her for a moment, then quietly said, "No, just be yourself."

A pretty scary prospect in itself, she thought. "Will your partners be there?"

Mark nodded. "Ray Ivan will be the one with the pipe. His wife passed away a year ago, so I suspect he'll be alone. The other partners and their wives will be there, and various guests, I suppose."

When he maneuvered the sedan into a luxurious neighborhood, Ellie's shoulders tensed.

"Hey," he said, reaching over to cover her hand with his. "Relax. You look wonderful."

His touch electrified her hand. Ellie swelled under his praise. "Any woman would in this dress."

He pulled the car behind a long string of vehicles in a semidark driveway, then cut the engine. He unfastened his seat belt, turned toward her and leaned forward until his lips were mere inches from her face. "Not true," he said, then dipped his head to sweep a quick kiss on her jawbone. "Trust me." His voice reverberated in her ear, flaming her senses. Ellie swallowed hard at the rush of desire flooding her body.

Mark looked into her eyes. "We were rudely interrupted last weekend outside your door."

Ellie tried to smile. "Oh, that M-Manny. He's always looking out f-for me."

He smiled, his eyes crinkling at the corners. "You're not scared of me, are you?"

Terrified. "N-no, of course not. That's not what I meant—"

He silenced her words with his mouth, his lips hungrily descending upon hers. Her throat constricted for want of much-needed moisture and oxygen, then she finally remembered to breathe. His tongue parlayed hers in a sensual battle she gladly forfeited. He twined his hands firmly around her waist, she lifted her arms to his neck and wrested sideways to deepen the embrace.

Something restrained her, prevented her from meeting him fully. She reached down to fumble with the seat belt and it snapped loose, tangling in his arms, then hers as they struggled to free themselves. Gasping for breath, they dived at each other again. This time Mark lifted her, putting his hands beneath her hips to pull her up and against his chest. She could sense his mounting frustration at the awkward angle. Suddenly he pulled her over the low console to straddle his lap. Her hair brushed the ceiling of the car and the steering wheel pressed into her back as she settled around his arousal, her dress hiked up to expose the garter belt she wore. Somewhere along the way she'd lost her shoes, but she didn't care. All that mattered was Mark Blackwell touching her, wanting her.

Mark thought he might climax on the spot when his hands discovered the snaps of her garter belt. This woman was killing him. "Ellie," he whispered against her neck. She arched her breasts against his chin and he buried his face in her cleavage. She rained kisses over his forehead as she wrapped her arms around his head to pull him closer. He bit lightly at her hardened nipples through the fabric of her dress and bra. His hands rode her waist, pushing her down on his arousal. The blood pounded in his brain as it exited, rushing to his midsection. Her breathing rasped as ragged as his as she moaned her pleasure.

"Hey!" a voice shouted outside the window. Mark jerked his head up and panic seized him. One glance confirmed his worst fear. Ray Ivan stood there, crouched and peering into the window. "Blackwell? Is that you? Get a room, son!" Then his partner turned and walked toward their host's home.

They were still for a few seconds as the realization of their indiscretion sunk in. Mark laid his head back and groaned. His arousal wilted. He opened his eyes and looked into Ellie's, wide with concern.

"That was bad, wasn't it?" she asked, biting her lip.

Mark stared at her for a few seconds, then burst out laughing at the incongruity of the situation. And the more he laughed, the harder he laughed. Soon, Ellie joined him as she climbed from his lap and fell into her own seat.

Slapping her knee, Ellie laughed and laughed, until she realized Mark had fallen silent. Looking at his suddenly somber profile, she emitted a final, weak giggle, then cleared her throat.

"What is it about you?" he asked, still staring straight ahead. His rumpled hair and slack mouth were in startling contrast to his dressy attire and normally regal bearing.

Uneasiness crept over Ellie as she fished for her shoes under the seat. "What do you mean?"

He looked over at her with an exasperated expression. "I mean, you drive me to do crazy things like make out in the front seat of my car at a business dinner!"

Anger flashed through Ellie and she pointed her index finger at him. "I didn't exactly fly over there and land on your lap, buster!"

He turned back to stare ahead, then raised his hands in a questioning gesture. "I'm a normal, red-blooded guy, but I've never done anything this stupid before." He spoke quietly, as if to himself, his hands animated. "After all these years of busting my butt and keeping my nose clean, my partner now thinks I'm Mr. Happy Pants."

Ellie sat up, and snapped open her purse to retrieve a comb. The pheromone pills fell into her lap, and she froze. She straightened her dress and asked, "Are we still going in?"

"If you're up to it, I am. I'm sorry I put you in this situation—"

"It's all right, Mark," Ellie assured him guiltily. If not for those magic pills of hers, the whole incident would never have happened. "Let's just make the best of it."

"You're right," he said, adjusting his tie. "It'll look worse if we don't go in. Thanks for being a sport."

They spent a few minutes righting their clothes, then stepped out into the cool early-June night air. Ellie took several deep breaths to clear her head, and took the arm he offered her to walk up the steps.

Mark rang the doorbell, then smiled at her as they waited. "I'll have to admit," he said, turning back to stare straight ahead, "the garter belt was a nice surprise." He rocked back on his heels casually, confident.

Ellie couldn't resist knocking him off balance again. "Then I can't imagine what you would've thought of my tattoo." The look on his face was priceless as the front door swung open and a man who identified himself as Patrick pulled her into his home with a friendly handshake.

It appeared they were among the last of about seventy-five to arrive. Cocktails and finger food circulated the room. Laughter and spirited conversation buzzed around them.

"Ellie?" A familiar female voice spoke behind her, and Ellie turned to see her former boss, Joan Wright, walking toward her.

"Joan," Ellie said, delighted, stepping forward to hug the woman.

"How wonderful to see you!" the older woman said. "What brings you to the Beechams'?"

"I do," Mark said, stepping in to introduce himself.

Joan shot an amused glance at Ellie, then said, "Ah, you must be the new partner." She shook his hand, then frowned slightly. "Is something wrong with your forehead?"

Ellie's eyes and Mark's hand traveled upward. Lipstick kisses dotted his hairline. She made a frantic wiping motion with her hand, then turned to draw Joan into a conversation about the arts center.

"And the commission is going well?" Joan's eyes asked more questions than her lips.

Ellie nodded. "The preliminary work on the painting is done. I hope to get down to business tomorrow."

"I'll let you ladies talk," Mark said, inclining his just-cleaned head. "Excuse me." Ellie felt a curious sense of loss as he walked away. Darn, she was getting much too used to having this man around.

"Hi."

Ellie turned to see Mark's secretary, Monica, standing next to her and Joan. Ellie made the introductions.

"So," Monica said, her tone silky with innuendo, "how's it going with you and Mark?"

"Oh, we're just friends," Ellie assured her.

"Mark is quite a catch," she said.

Ellie smiled. "I'm not fishing," she said, then steered the conversation in a safer direction. "Joan, I thought you and Manny were going someplace tonight."

Joan's eyes twinkled mischievously, then she moved her head slightly to indicate someone across the room.

Ellie turned to look and nearly swallowed her tongue. Manny, looking feminine and elegant in a brunette wig and long navy dress, stood chatting with none other than Ray Ivan, senior partner. He glanced up and caught her eye, then gave her a tiny shrug of bewilderment. She beckoned him frantically, but even as Manny tried to break away, Ivan followed him with a hand at his elbow. A finger of fear nudged Ellie's stomach.

While Ray and Joan exchanged greetings, Ellie pulled Manny down and whispered furiously, "What are you doing here dressed like that?"

He grinned. "I look fabulous, don't I?"

"Manny!"

He pouted prettily. "Relax, would you? It's a joke—Joan thought it would be hilarious to crash a stuffy gig. I had no idea it was the same party you were going to." He grinned and lowered his voice. "I love fooling the straight ones, and I think this Ivan guy is loaded."

"He's Mark's partner, you idiot!"

Manny looked hurt. "But he likes me."

"He likes *Molly*," she said, using his stage name. "There's a big difference."

"Joan and I are splitting in a few minutes, anyway."

"Don't do anything foolish—Ray just caught us practically naked in the car. Mark is worried to death."

Joan and Monica slipped away. Ray Ivan stepped to Manny's side and smiled at Ellie. "Are you a friend of Molly's?"

"Ellie's my roommate," Manny purred in a low, silky voice. "She's here with Mark Blackwell."

Ellie smiled tightly. *Gee, thanks, friend.*

"Blackwell?" Ivan's eyebrows shot up. "I gather you are, er, close."

Embarrassment flooded over her and she floundered for something to say.

"They're practically married," Manny assured him, patting his arm.

MARK WANDERED OVER to a drink tray and picked up a martini, then scanned the room for Ivan. He needed to extend an apology for what had happened, and he wanted to get it over with. Not sure what he'd say when he did find him, Mark just prayed the right words would come to him. He removed the lipstick-stained handkerchief from his pocket. Between cat allergies and various mishaps, he'd have to remember to carry two hankies with him when Ellie was around. He used the soiled cloth to wipe the sweat from his forehead.

Raising his glass to take another sip, he glanced back to Ellie and choked on the liquid in his throat. Ray Ivan stood talking to her and an attractive brunette. He hurried over to the group as unobtrusively as possible.

"Blackwell!" Ivan boomed. "Glad to see you finally came—I mean, made it—er, good to see you, son." Mark felt the heat climb up his neck as he shook the senior partner's hand.

"Good to see you, sir."

Ivan gestured to the striking woman at his side. "I assume you've met Molly since she's your lovely fiancée's roommate."

So, she had another roommate. "No, I haven't had the pleasure—" His hand stopped in midair. "Did you say fiancée, sir?"

Mark and Ellie exchanged panicked glances, then spoke at the same time.

"I'm not really—"

"She's not really—"

Ivan raised his eyebrows. "What's that, Mark?"

Mark thought about the picture they'd presented earlier to his conservative partner who'd been married for forty years. Mark reached over to put an arm around Ellie's shoulders and squeezed her against him. "Yes, she is lovely, isn't she? Could I have a word with you in private, sir?"

"Certainly."

Mark loosened his grip on Ellie and steered the senior partner to a quiet doorway. "Sir, I want to apologize for what you saw—"

Ivan raised his hand and waved Mark's words away. "Perfectly natural for a man and his bride-to-be, son. When's the big day?"

Mark's mind raced. "Well, we really haven't discussed a day, sir."

"Molly told me you and Miss Sutherland met when she came to the office to paint your portrait a few days ago. Love at first sight, eh?" The older man chuckled. "You're a lucky man, Mark, with good taste. I like to see my partners settle down, become family men. It's important to the firm's image, you know." He winked at Mark, then turned to the room at large and stepped forward. "Everyone," he called, "may I have your attention?"

Dread ballooned in the pit of Mark's stomach as the room quieted.

"I'd like to propose a toast. To our new partner, Mr. Mark Blackwell, who has two reasons to celebrate tonight."

Mark's bowels twisted.

"Raise your glasses with me to honor him and his bride-to-be, Ms. Ellie Sutherland."

The room erupted into gasps and applause. Mark

swayed, but caught himself on the door frame, then swung his gaze to Ellie. He pleaded for forgiveness with his eyes. A bewildered smile froze on her face as she nodded to those around her.

Mark soon found himself engulfed by well-wishers. Patrick seemed especially surprised and elbowed him. "You sly dog, what was all that nonsense the other day about remaining single?"

"What can I say?" Mark conjured up a tight smile, his stomach cramping.

"Dinner's served," Patrick's wife announced.

Ellie watched Ray Ivan walk Manny to the door, and to her horror, plant a kiss on her roomie's smooth cheek. Manny waved to her gaily, and she raised her hand halfheartedly in response. Her mind still reeled when Mark took her arm. As they walked toward their table, she whispered, "An engagement wasn't part of the deal. What's going on?"

"I'll explain later," he muttered. "Just remember, I've got your cat."

Ellie reached for another rum and cola as they passed a drink tray and finished it before they were seated. He held out a chair for her at one of the six-person, cloth-covered tables and took the adjacent seat on the end. His leg nudging hers when he spread his napkin across his knee sent tremors through her body.

She knew the alcohol had affected her, but the events of the evening were taking their toll, as well. First, his assault on her senses in the car, then Manny showing up, and now everyone thought they were engaged. She nearly laughed out loud at the irony. She wondered what he would do if she stood on the table and announced that he'd hired her to make his mother hate her, and that a pregnant cat was the only reason she'd come with him tonight?

Well, not the only reason, she conceded, choosing a skewered scallop from a platter on the table. She studied his face as he talked to the man on his right. Mark was one great-looking man, and right now the pheromones were running in her favor. So what if his interest in her was short-lived? There were worse things than having a raging three-week affair with a gorgeous wealthy man.

Time to have some fun.

She slipped off her shoe and snaked her foot around his ankle. Mark jerked his head toward her a fraction, and seemed to stumble on his words, but continued speaking to his companion. Ellie smiled seductively, then worried his shin and calf with her traveling toes. Mark shot her a sharp glance, obviously trying to concentrate on his conversation. Popping the scallop into her mouth, she rolled it on her tongue suggestively. Mark swallowed visibly and shook his head as if in warning, then turned back to the man.

Smothering a giggle, she extended her left leg farther over her right and nudged his knee open. She ran her foot down the inside of his thigh. Suddenly, he jerked again, his hand grabbing her foot to halt its progress. She tried to pull away, but he held her steadfast, and suddenly his other hand claimed her foot, as well. His face was averted from her and he remained deep in conversation.

Teasingly, he swept his finger across the pad of her stockinged foot, sending shudders up Ellie's spine. Her toes crinkled in response, but he slowly and sensuously inserted a large finger between her big toe and its neighbor. Rhythmically, he explored the shallow valley, running the length of his finger in, then out, in, then out.

The ability, as well as the desire, to withdraw her plundered foot vanished. Ellie relaxed into her chair as much as possible without drawing attention to herself, then began squeezing her toes together, clasping his finger harder and harder. As the minutes passed, she grew moist between her thighs, imagining his strong fingers dipping elsewhere. As his finger became more forceful, she increased the pressure. Faster and faster he plunged. Ellie could feel her body pulse inside in tune with his finger's song. The tension mounted, mounted...

"OOOOooooHHHHhhhhhhh!" she screamed, bringing her hand down upon the table with a solid smack. Every eye in the room turned to her, and even Mark seemed surprised, his ministrations halting momentarily.

"Are you all right, dear?" the woman next to her asked, leaning closer.

Ellie recovered, sitting ramrod straight. "Oh!" she repeated, slapping the table again, "Oh, boy, are these scallops good!" She popped several into her mouth, smiling and nodding to everyone at her table, then waving assurance to Patrick's wife across the room. Every woman at the table lunged for a portion.

Afraid to look at Mark, Ellie kept her eyes turned away. What would he think of her now? She withdrew her ravaged foot from his relaxed hands and stretched her cramped toes. Who could have guessed learning to pick up pencils with her toes would come in handy one day?

When at last she chanced a glance at him, his eyes were still on her, slightly widened with an expression that asked, "Was that what I think it was?" She chewed on her bottom lip and nodded ever so slightly.

At her affirmation, amazement washed over Mark. He, too, had become aroused during their little game under the table, but he couldn't believe she'd really—

"As I was saying." The man to his right laid a hand on Mark's arm to resume their conversation. Mark frowned at him, and in the few seconds he broke eye contact with Ellie, she disappeared from sight. Confused, Mark craned his head to search the room, then noticed the tablecloth moving at her place setting. Then he felt her crawl over his feet. Mark stiffened in disbelief, then noticed other people at the table jump, then frown and shift in their seats. She was obviously traveling the length of the table.

He excused himself once again from the man bending his ear. With a quick glance around, Mark swallowed and, as inconspicuously as possible, bent over, then cautiously pulled up the white tablecloth.

For the second time tonight, he was treated to a mouthwatering view of Ellie's rump, but Mark didn't have time to stop and ponder his good fortune. "Ellie!" he whispered sharply. She had to back up, her rear coming very close to his face, in order to twist around and look over her shoulder.

"What?"

"What the hell are you doing?"

"Looking for my shoe," she said simply, slurring her words slightly.

"Get out from under there and I'll find it for you," he said, trying to remain patient.

Suddenly, two other heads joined them under the table, both male. "Is there a problem?" asked one fellow who had been paying rapt attention to Ellie all evening.

"No!" Mark barked.

"I can't find my shoe," Ellie said, pouting.

"Well, now," said the other man, tsk-tsking at Ellie, "that will never do."

Mark sighed in exasperation. "For God's sake, Ellie, get out from under there!"

But now nearly everyone at the table was peering beneath the cloth and asking if something was wrong.

Mark reached forward and grabbed Ellie by her upper arm, then steered her out backward. When she stood up and plopped down in her seat, her hairstyle a little worse for wear, Mark ground his teeth in frustration. Their table companions were slow in rejoining them topside, as if Ellie had found something wonderful under the table and they wanted to experience it, too.

"Is this what you're looking for?" The chatty fellow to his right held up a black pump. Sex appeal fairly dripped off the stiletto heel.

"Oh, thank you," Ellie said, grinning, then she reached across the china and crystal to retrieve it. The man looked curiously pleased, until his wife elbowed him sharply in the ribs.

Mark closed his eyes and counted to ten. When he opened them, Ellie was walking away from the table, presumably to find a bathroom, but wearing both shoes, thank goodness. He watched her hips sway, then suddenly realized nearly every man in the room feasted on the same sight. This woman packed a powerful punch.

Mark felt a ridiculous urge to follow her, lock the bathroom door, lift her onto a porcelain sink and wrap her legs around his waist. If a little foot flirting sent her into orbit, what kind of reaction could he elicit with no holds barred? And where would he find her tattoo? Shoulder? Hip? He swallowed. Bikini line?

A tap on his right shoulder startled him. A smiling waiter set a plate of exquisitely arranged salad in front of him, and he was glad to have his attention diverted for the time being. That woman was going to be the death of him, or at least his career. He would eventually need a wife who could entertain a group on this scale, but not one who could double as the entertainment.

Ellie returned a few minutes later, looking refreshed. She nodded at him when she took her seat, smiling brightly. He noticed the color in her cheeks seemed high, and he assumed it had something to do with the amount of rum she'd ingested since they'd arrived. Not that he blamed her, with everything that had happened. Engaged. How on earth was he going to get out of this mess?

She seemed a little flustered still, making small talk with the ladies at the table, one of them his secretary, Monica. He felt a sharp pang of guilt at the questions she had to answer. Yes, she was so proud of her fiancé for making partner. She patted his hand. No, they hadn't shopped for a ring yet. Yes, they planned to have several children. Mark choked on a cherry tomato, but was saved by the gabby man who pounded him hard between the shoulder blades.

Children? Mark patted his mouth with a linen napkin. Would he make a good father? Would Ellie make a good mother? He studied her profile as she spoke to someone across the table, nodding and smiling. She was a beauty, no doubt. Her features were elfin, small and chiseled. Her blond hair was cropped in short layers, a style only a woman with exquisite features could wear with panache. With her outgoing nature and easy smile, Mark suddenly knew she would be a wonderful mother—romping with her children, singing and dancing to keep them entertained, finger painting the walls if necessary. He smiled and Ellie turned to him at that instant, coming up short at something she read in his eyes. Mark blinked to clear his head and she visibly relaxed.

For the rest of the meal, Mark tried desperately to concentrate on anything but the woman beside him. He puzzled over the power she seemed to wield on his senses. This attraction—it seemed almost supernatural. Not one single aspect of Ellie Sutherland set her apart from any number of beautiful women he'd met, but in totality, she was sensational. Ellie defied science because her whole far outweighed the sum of her parts. The woman was walking synergy.

And he was completely taken by her.

Mark's hands shook slightly as alarms went off in his ears. He'd read about this in men's magazines— and it didn't bode well for his future as a bachelor. No sir, he wasn't about to don the albatross of commitment when he'd just reached a zenith in his career. Yet even as he nodded his head resolutely, Mark's chest clogged with dread when he thought about taking Ellie home and being alone with her. The answer? Stall as long as possible, of course.

"How much longer?" Ellie whispered a few hours later, trying to smile. Only a few guests lingered over coffee. She could feel her eyelids dragging, threatening to close for good. She'd had no chance to talk to Mark about their abrupt engagement, and she wanted to be somewhat awake on the ride home.

Mark squinted at his watch. "You're right," he said. "We should be going."

They said their goodbyes to their hosts, and a few minutes later they were off.

She waited until they had driven a couple of miles in silence before she cleared her throat. "Well?" she asked.

Mark glanced sideways. "Well what?"

Ellie sighed. "Well, what the heck is going on?"

He passed a hand over his face and pinched the bridge of his nose, squinting. "Believe me, I was as surprised as you were at Ivan's announcement. He's old-fashioned and, after witnessing our little, er, display, he must have arrived at his own conclusion."

Manny's offhand comment to Ivan about she and Mark being "practically married" crossed Ellie's mind, but she didn't mention it. She angled her body toward him. "Why didn't you correct him?"

In the dim interior, she saw his shoulders fall in defeat. "He started telling me how important it was to him that all his partners be settled down, you know—family men—and I couldn't tell him the truth. Next thing I knew, he was toasting our engagement."

Ellie's heart drooped. Mark Blackwell's career

meant more to him than anything else in the world. Maybe she'd caught his eye, or rather, his crotch, for a few days because of these pheromones, but she was fooling herself if she thought she'd ever be able to compete with his first love—his job. He had no room for a woman in his life, least of all a woman like her.

"I'm sorry you got dragged into this," he said, reaching over to grasp her hand. "It'll die down in a few weeks, and I'll simply say we broke it off." He squeezed her fingers. "By the way, Ivan seemed taken with your roommate Molly. Why haven't you mentioned her before?"

His hand was so warm, his touch so welcome. Ellie said nothing and just stared at his fingers. "It never came up," she mumbled distractedly. Just a few hours ago she'd told herself to seize the moment. And that was before she knew he could induce her to orgasm, fully dressed and in a crowded room. She felt heat travel up her face. Would he kiss her good-night, or had she scared him off completely? Surely he'd guessed how long she'd been celibate if toe sex sent her over the edge.

When he parked in front of her building, he hesitated slightly. "It's okay," Ellie rushed to assure him. "You don't have to walk me up." She scrambled to loosen her seat belt and find her purse.

"No," he said, turning off the ignition. "I want to."

They walked quickly and quietly into her building and up the stairs. Ellie's heart pounded furiously as she fumbled with the key. Mark took it from her, then unlocked the door easily. The door swung inward, creaking, and darkness stretched before them. Was it her imagination, or had her bed suddenly become a living, breathing entity, palpitating and calling to them from down the hall and behind a closed door?

"Coffee?" she squeaked, flipping on the kitchen light.

"Sure," Mark answered. "A shot of caffeine for the drive home won't hurt." He smiled at her, lowering himself into a kitchen chair. She rummaged nervously for a filter, and managed to get the coffeemaker going within a few tense minutes. "Well," she said brightly, turning to face Mark. "What an interesting evening." She bent to remove her shoes, nudging them under a chair as she rubbed one throbbing arch.

"Yes," Mark agreed in a choked voice. She glanced up to see his eyes riveted on her stockinged feet, and she immediately realized her mistake. She watched as Mark moved in slow motion, standing and reaching for her, pulling her into his arms. Lifting her face to his, she offered her lips to him. His mouth descended on hers, his lips moving hungrily, as if he were a starved man and she a bountiful fare.

Ellie's knees weakened and she swayed into him, twining her arms around his neck for support. He groaned and his voice vibrated inside her mouth, inciting her to respond in kind. Drawing her against him, he lifted her off the ground to settle fully against his arousal. Wild barbs of desire knifed through her as Ellie inhaled the scent of his skin, felt his need for her pushing against her stomach. Mark's hands slid over her back and waist, gripping, massaging, caressing. She felt her nipples bud and bloom against his chest, and raised one leg to hook around his thigh. Immediately, his hands sought her lace-covered rear, exposed by her movement. His breathing became more ragged, until he finally raised his head.

"Ellie," he whispered hoarsely. "I'd like to see that tattoo."

She smiled languidly, desire and...love?...expanding her heart. She might regret this tomorrow, but tomorrow lay a world away, and tonight she needed to live. "I can't walk unless you put me down," she said, referring to her dangling toes.

In response, he swung her up into his arms. "Where's your bedroom?" he asked, his eyes dark with passion. Ellie directed him, her arms still around his neck, her pulse beating out of control during their brief journey. Mark lay her on the bed, then left her long enough to close the door. The only light came from a small window. She watched him move across the room, his movements unhurried. When he returned, he was removing his tie.

"Let me," she said, reaching for him. She sat up, and with deft fingers, made short work of his shirt buttons, then stripped the garment from his back. How many times had she thought of him standing before her like this, bare-chested, the way he looked in his office when she'd taken his picture? He was breathtaking. His hands stilled her when she moved to his waistband.

"I want to see you," he breathed. "I have to see you." Blazing a trail across her skin, his hands enveloped her, moving around to find the zipper at her back. Ellie heard the slide of the enclosure giving way, and felt the fabric fall from her shoulders. Mark leaned toward her, easing her onto the soft comforter, and slipped the dress to her waist. Instantly he found her lace-covered breasts, kissing and suckling through the fabric. Ellie moaned and arched her back, thrusting the small peaks up for his onslaught. Without taking his mouth from her, he lifted her hips and eased the dress down her legs. She heard the whoosh of the fabric as it landed somewhere on the floor.

When Mark drew back long enough to take in the sight of Ellie lying before him in black bra, panties, garter belt and stockings, he had to clench his teeth in resolve. *Hold on, man, hold on.* The fact that his body had been in a near-perpetual state of arousal throughout the evening convinced him his present control bordered on tenuous, at best. Slender and smooth, she was beautifully arched to reveal endless valleys and peaks to explore. From her shapely collarbone to the divot in her flat stomach, to the valley between her thighs hidden by her raised knees. Where to begin? Hours seemed woefully inadequate to sample Ellie's gifts, yet his body told him he had scant minutes left.

A loud groan escaped him as he stretched out beside her, capturing her mouth in a kiss that threatened to be his undoing when she wriggled against him. She turned in his arms and he managed to undo her bra, sending her small, full breasts tumbling into his hands. He dipped his head to taste their richness and grew heady from the overwhelming desire flooding his body. The intoxicating scent of her skin took him near the brink.

Her small fingers splayed across his back then down to his waist, struggling briefly with his zipper, then helping him drag the pants down with her feet. He kicked them off, his breath leaving him when Ellie reached to clasp his stiff manhood. She stroked him within milliseconds of exploding. He grabbed her hand to still her movements.

"I'm not superhuman," he groaned, rolling over to lie between her legs. Mark took a few deep breaths to steady himself, then undid her garter belt. Thoughts of slowly rolling her thigh-high stockings down and off her pretty feet flickered through his mind, but he knew he'd be lucky to remove her panties in one piece. Hot need billowed in him, and he tugged her underwear down hurriedly, raising her knees to speed the process. A glimpse of dense dark blond curls registered in his mind before he returned to the cradle between her legs. His heat-seeking member rushed to her entrance.

"Mark," she whispered, "I'm not protected."

Sanity flashed and he lowered his head. "Of course," he said, then gritted his teeth. Sighing, he gently rolled off her and lay still, fighting to gain control. "I'm sorry," he said. "I lost my head."

Ellie sat up and reached to open a drawer in her nightstand. "I have regular and extra-large," she announced, rummaging through its contents.

Mark bounced upright. "Whichever you think."

She peered at him, a smile playing on her lips. "Extra-large."

It seemed to take hours for her to roll the condom into place, and Mark shook with his need to make love to her. At last, she lay back and pulled him to her, her neck arched, leaving it exposed for his kisses. He licked at the hollow beneath her chin, then found an earlobe to nuzzle as he eased himself into her warmth. Their moans mingled as he stilled, taking a few seconds to experience her. She tightened around him and Mark tensed to hold on a little longer. Just long enough for her to—

A long scream escaped her lips and she clawed his

back in the throes of her passion. Amazement registered for an instant, but quickly gave way to gratitude as he began to move within her, feeling free now to expend himself. The mewling sounds she moaned into his ear urged him on. He felt his senses soar, his body tense in preparation for release, then shuddered again and again as ecstasy delivered him from his suffering.

Not until minutes later, as he lay nuzzling a pert nipple and feeling her heart beat against his cheek, did Mark realize he still hadn't noticed a tattoo.

MARK OPENED HIS EYES, disoriented at first. Then he remembered he slept in Ellie's bed. He turned his head to see the clock. Three in the morning.

Usually he lingered with a lover until morning, but now he had an overwhelming need to go home. Or more to the point, to get out of Ellie's bed. The walls of her bedroom, covered with eclectic groupings of prints and various bric-a-brac, suddenly seemed to close in on him. As noiselessly as possible, he got up, gathered his clothing and dressed. He winced at the sight of the wadded pile he'd made of the dress in which she'd bewitched him and every man at the party. Carefully, he picked it up and folded it neatly, placing it on the dressing table.

Mark walked back to the bed, planning to kiss her, but instead stopped to watch her sleep, her breasts easing up and down with her deep, even breathing. A tingling sensation settled in his chest and made his own breathing difficult. After a last glance, he opened her bedroom door, stepped into the hall and closed it behind him.

Silently, he retraced his steps to the front door, then

stopped when he realized someone was unlocking the door from the hallway. His heart raced. A burglar? Then Mark relaxed. It was probably just one of Ellie's roommates.

Molly stepped inside, then her eyes widened in fear, a key dangling from a manicured hand raised to defend herself.

Mark rushed to explain in a loud whisper, ''I'm Mark Blackwell, Ellie's, uh, friend. We met earlier this evening.'' He smiled apologetically and pointed to the door. ''I was just leaving.'' He stepped into the hall and closed the door behind him.

The short drive north seemed interminable, not just because Mark fought falling asleep, but because his big lonely bed no longer seemed so inviting. Ellie's sleep-softened face came to him, and her plump nipples sitting atop her breasts like puffs of pink whipped cream. He moistened his lips involuntarily, and nearly ran off the shoulder of the highway. Loud music from his stereo and a full-blast air conditioner got him home safely.

The clock on his nightstand read ten minutes past four. Mark began to strip off his clothes again, then grimaced as his shirt raked across his uncomfortably tender back. One glance in the mirror showed why, and his mouth fell open. Bright red welts and a few tiny drops of dried blood marked his back where Ellie had clawed him in her passion. Too tired to register more than passing astonishment, Mark climbed into bed. He had just closed his eyes, when his nose began to itch. He rubbed a knuckle over it, annoyed. At the same time, something warm and furry touched his foot. Mark shouted and sat up in the bed, scrambling for the light.

A muffled yowl sounded under the covers. Mark jumped out of the bed and watched the lump travel beneath the covers to the pillow where his head had rested. Esmerelda poked her orange head out to peer at him angrily.

"Scat," Mark barked, buck-naked and waving his arms. The cat blinked. A fit of sneezing seized him, sending him in search of a handkerchief. "Get out of my bed," he commanded, gesturing again. Esmerelda yawned. When Mark reached for her, she flattened her ears against her head, and flung an evil hiss toward him. He jumped back, wondering if the beast had been declawed. Deciding he'd rather not find out tonight, Mark tramped noisily down the hall to a guest room, sneezing the entire way.

As he punched down a lumpy pillow, Mark cursed sourly. He'd left one unsettling she-cat only to come home to another.

7

ELLIE AWOKE with the most delicious feeling in her bones. Her hazy mind struggled to remember what event had triggered this languid, buoyant state. She'd won the lottery…no. Her paintings were being offered at an exclusive auction…no. She'd slept with Mark Blackwell…

Ellie's eyes popped open. Yes! A tentative lifting of her knee triggered soreness in several little-used muscles, and she grimaced. Sitting up and pulling the sheet around her breasts, she scanned the room for evidence of Mark's presence. Her dress had been folded neatly. The indention in the pillow next to hers felt cold.

A foreign scent assailed her nostrils. Sex. Their fragrances lingered on the morning air. Ellie pulled her pillow higher against the headboard, and reclined against it with a sigh. On impulse, she pulled the other pillow over her face and inhaled his aroma, then settled it across her stomach. Her heart raced. Now what?

A knock at her door stymied her rising panic. "Ellie, are you up?" Manny's voice was soft but insistent.

"Just a minute," she called, reaching to pull a short terry robe from its home on the bedpost. She still wore her stockings and loosened garter belt, although the garments had twisted uncomfortably. She tied the frayed robe belt around her waist and tucked the ends under her hips, then straightened the covers around her. "You can come in."

"Breakfast in bed," Manny announced grandly, entering with a laden bed tray.

Ellie grinned. "And what, may I ask, is the occasion?"

Manny smiled wide, his eyes knowing, as he set the tray on her lap. "Your introduction back into a morally bankrupt society."

"What makes you think—"

"Don't bother denying it." Manny held up his hand. "I passed Mark on his way out this morning." He smiled, triumphant. "So?" he prompted, settling in cross-legged at the foot of the bed.

"So what?" she said, taking a bite of toast.

"For heaven's sake, give me the details."

As Ellie chewed, the events of the entire evening began to resurface in florid detail. She winced.

"Come on, 'fess up," Manny urged. "You set Ray Ivan straight about your engagement, right?"

Ellie bit into her bottom lip.

Manny's eyes rolled back. "You didn't?"

"There didn't seem to be a good time to mention it."

"Unbelievable," he said, shaking his head. "Your life is better than a soap opera. So tell me, how did you go from being a fake fiancée—" he leaned over to retrieve a stray earring from the floor "—to a genuine seductress?" He dangled the bauble for emphasis.

The quick sip of juice did not lessen the heat that rushed to Ellie's face. "He brought me home, then I asked him in for coffee, and the next thing I knew, he was carrying me in here." She shrugged.

"Well, that explains the full pot of cold coffee," Manny said sarcastically, then he brightened. "Was it earth-shattering?"

Ellie tried to hold back a grin, but couldn't. "I can't remember having two really great orgasms in one night."

"Two? I'm impressed. Didn't think Mr. Republican had it in him."

"Well, one occurred at the dinner party—"

"What?"

"It's not what you think. We were fully clothed, and sitting down. After you left, I got a little tipsy and started playing footsie with his...well, anyway, he grabbed my foot and the next thing I know, I'm screaming like a banshee in the middle of the appetizer course."

"You got off on him playing with your *feet?* You were in worse shape than I thought, woman." He howled with laughter, pounding his knees with his fists. Wiping his eyes, he suddenly sobered. "Has anything like that ever happened before? I mean, do you think the pheromones had something to do with your reaction?"

Ellie took another drink. "No, it's never happened before, and yes, I think it has everything to do with the pills." She hadn't meant to sound so glum.

"Did Ray Ivan ask about me?"

"Manny, you're playing with fire."

"I think it's fun."

"He's a sweet, *straight* old widower. If you took off your skirt, he'd probably have heart failure."

He waved off her concern. "It doesn't matter, El,

I'll never see the man again. By the way—'' he wagged his eyebrows ''—when will you see Mark?''

Ellie gasped and looked at the clock. ''I have to be at his office for a sitting in forty-five minutes! What am I going to say to him after last night?''

''Hmm.'' Manny tapped his cheek in mock deep thought. ''How about 'thank you'?''

''THANK YOU,'' Ellie said as Mark held the door to the office building open wide enough to allow her to wheel in her bike. They'd arrived at the same time, Mark rounding the corner from the parking garage just in time to see Ellie ride up in front of the building.

He smiled stiffly at her, feeling awkward. She certainly looked chipper today in pink bike shorts and a glove-fitting zebra-print tank top. But then, she didn't have to apply salve to her battle wounds, then don a starched dress shirt for a sitting. Her dangling black claw earrings were a staunch reminder of the injuries she'd inflicted last night. Still, he had to admit it was the greatest sex he'd experienced. He rolled his shoulders, trying to ease his taut skin as they walked through the reception area to the elevators. Neither of them spoke on the ride up. She looked completely at ease, and he didn't have a clue what to say about last night. Finally, she broke the silence.

''How's Esmerelda?'' she asked, reaching over to extract a long orange hair from his shirtsleeve.

Mark frowned and brushed his sleeve with his hand, dislodging more hairs. He promptly sneezed. ''Your cat has taken up residence in my bedroom. In my bed, to be more precise.''

''Really? She hardly ever leaves her bed at night.

She must be under a lot of stress, being in new surroundings. Or there could be something wrong with the
room where you put her bed.''

A flash of annoyance surfaced, but he forced patience into his voice. ''Your feline already has the run
of my house. What could possibly be wrong?'' The bell
sounded and the doors slid open.

Ellie stepped off the elevator and guided her bicycle
toward his office. ''The room where you put her bed,
what color is it?''

''Blue.''

Ellie smacked her handlebars with one hand and
nodded. ''That's it—she hates blue.''

Mark took a mighty breath and rubbed one temple.
His aggravated allergies were giving him a headache.
And now the allergen didn't approve of his decor.

''Hey, you two,'' Patrick called, walking toward
them, smiling.

''Oh, damn,'' Mark muttered, then donned an appropriate smile. ''Hey, yourself,'' he said as Patrick
drew nearer. ''Nice party.''

''You two were the spotlight,'' Patrick insisted, then
turned to Ellie. ''And I can't tell you what a pleasure
it is to meet the woman who's tamed this maverick. I
never thought I'd see the day Mark Blackwell settled
down.''

Ellie shrugged and nodded, her expression one of
agreeable shock. ''Amazing, isn't it?''

''Actually, Patrick—'' Mark began.

''Good morning, all!'' Ray Ivan boomed from down
the hall. ''Well, if it isn't the happy couple.'' He
walked up and patted Ellie's arm, then clapped Mark

on his raw back, sending spasms of pain down his spine.

Mark inhaled sharply. "Good morning, sir."

Ivan pointed to the canvas and paint-stained tackle box strapped to the panniers of Ellie's bike. "Working on the portrait, today, are we?"

She smiled wide, her eyes bright. "We sure are."

Mark's partner nodded agreeably, then said. "Listen, kids, let me know as soon as you set a wedding date, because it's been my policy to start a brokerage account for my married employees as a college fund for their children. Right, Patrick?"

"Right," Beecham said.

"Children?" Mark and Ellie said in unison.

"Monica told me last night that you plan to have a big family," Ivan said.

Mark remembered Ellie's words at the dinner table and felt his underarms grow moist. They'd very nearly started a family last night. He looked at Ellie, and she looked back, eyes wide.

Ivan laughed, slapping Mark's back again, twice. "Didn't mean to put you on the spot. Just let me know, Blackwell. And congratulations again, you picked a beauty." He winked at Ellie, then engaged Patrick in a conversation as they walked away.

"I need some aspirin," Mark said, moving toward his office.

Once the door closed behind them, Ellie took a deep breath. Trying to sound casual as she lowered her kickstand, she said, "Why did you leave in the middle of the night?"

"Huh?" Mark swallowed the pills he'd shaken into his palm. "Oh, well, I knew I had to come in here this morning, and there were some papers at home I wanted to go over.'' His voice sounded vague. ''And don't forget about the cat,'' he added, his eyes darting around the room. ''I had to check on her.''

Ellie frowned slightly. He wasn't very convincing. Obviously he preferred hurrying home to handle work details to dawdling in her bed. A career man, through and through.

''By the way,'' he said, ''I ran into Molly while I was leaving your apartment. I didn't see a third bedroom. Where does she stay?''

Ellie's mind raced. ''Uh, she stays in Manny's room.''

''Ivan will be heartbroken,'' he said.

''Oh, they have an open relationship,'' she improvised. ''You never see them together.'' She swallowed, then scrambled to change the subject. ''This session shouldn't take too long. All I really need to do is a composition sketch.''

''Sure,'' he said in a distracted tone. ''Where do you want me?''

They locked gazes. Ellie's heart pounded as snatches of their lovemaking spun through her mind.

Mark cleared his throat. ''We really should talk—''

The phone rang, breaking the spell.

''I'll get set up,'' she explained, gesturing to her supplies. She kicked herself mentally. Mark Blackwell was the epitome of her father in his younger days. Hadn't she always promised herself she deserved more than her mother had put up with? So why on earth was she entertaining thoughts of a future with him? It had to be the pheromones.

She heard Mark push a button. "Mark Blackwell," he said, all business.

"Marcus!" his mother's voice screeched over the speakerphone.

Ellie watched as Mark rounded his desk to sit down, worry in his face. "Mom? Where are you calling from? Is everything all right?"

"No!" she continued more shrilly than before. "How can everything be all right when I arrive at Stella's house for bridge and she announces to me that my own son is getting married?"

"Mom—"

"And *please* don't tell me it's to that fruitcake you brought to the reunion. I lived in the bathroom for three days—"

Mark stabbed the intercom button and picked up the receiver, then spun around in the chair, his back to Ellie, murmuring low into the phone.

Oh, great, Ellie thought, the woman *does* hate me. And the only thing she needed in her life less than a workaholic boyfriend was a workaholic mama's boy.

"Mom, don't worry," she heard him say. "It's all a big mistake that got way out of hand." He paused. "Mom, if I were getting married, don't you think you'd be the first to know?"

Probably even before the bride, Ellie mused as she unpacked her supplies.

"Yeah, you can reassure Stella she doesn't have to buy an expensive wedding gift, after all. I have to go, Mom. I'll call you later." He hung up and sighed. "Sorry about that." He stood and walked toward her, shrugging sheepishly. "Mom is a little excitable, if you hadn't noticed."

"Did you set her straight about our little pretend engagement?"

He did have the good grace to blush. "I told her it was all a mistake."

"She didn't sound like the same woman who's desperate for you to get married."

He smiled wryly, shrugging again. "I guess when it comes right down to it, she doesn't want another woman in my life."

"More to the point, she doesn't want *me* in your life."

Mark pursed his lips. "That's my fault. I shouldn't have asked you to pull all those stunts at the reunion. I guess my behavior was childish." He looked into her eyes, and reached over to touch her hand. "I'm sorry, Ellie."

His voice and expression were genuine. Ellie blinked furiously to stem her welling tears. "All those stunts" were natural events.

"Where were we?" he asked. Restlessly, he shoved a hand through his light brown hair, leaving it disheveled. For a few seconds, she felt sorry for him. His life had been turned upside down inside a week of meeting her. But then, so had hers.

"You messed it up," she said, reaching up to smooth the errant strands. His hair felt silky and thick, fresh from a recent shower, she guessed. Memories of twining her hands through it last night came to her, but she brushed them aside. He stood perfectly still, his eyes locked with hers while she fussed with his hair. Desire lurked in the depths of his forest green eyes. And what else? Affection? What might her traitorous eyes be revealing to him? "There," she said, giving his hair a final pat and easing the moment.

"I think we should talk about last night," he said.

"Well, I am curious about the blood on the sheet."

Mark gestured loosely over his shoulder. "I didn't realize your nails were so long." He smiled and added, "Or so effective."

Embarrassment sent heat rushing to her face. Ellie gasped, covering her mouth. "I did that?"

"You were the only other person in the bed."

"I'm so sorry, are you okay?"

Now he laughed. "I only regret I won't be in senior gym class tomorrow to gloat in the locker room." He reached for her, and she went to him, her kiss a peace offering.

The phone rang again. They parted. Mark glanced at the display, and reached for the handset. "It's Ray," he said. "Hello, sir." He paused. "Yes, she's still here."

Ellie's eyebrows shot up.

Mark listened for a few seconds, then surprise registered on his face. "Hold on and I'll ask." Mark pushed a button to mute the sound and said, "He wants to take Molly to dinner. Can you arrange it?"

Ellie's stomach dipped. "But Manny—"

"I thought you said they had an open relationship."

"I, uh…Molly's not exactly your partner's type, Mark."

"Okay, she's younger than Ray by a couple of decades, but you have to admit she's showing a little wear herself. He's a young and wealthy sixty-two. She could do worse."

She floundered. "But she hardly knows him...I don't think she'd be comfortable."

"So we'll double."

Her heart pounded. "As in a double date?"

"Sure. It would give me a chance to get to know Ray more informally. And maybe we can find a way to explain away our pseudoengagement."

"I'm not sure—"

"Help me out, Ellie. I need to redeem myself for that little car-necking incident, which was really your fault, by the way."

"*My* fault?"

He leaned toward her and nuzzled her earlobe. "It wouldn't have happened if you weren't so damned irresistible."

Ellie's pulse jumped erratically. He was right—the episode before the party *had* been her fault. All roads led back to the pheromone pills. "Well..."

He pushed a button to retrieve his partner. "How about the four of us going to dinner? The Lexington Diner? Tonight?" Mark looked at Ellie for affirmation and she nodded resolutely. "Ellie will talk to Molly and get it all set up. I'll pick up the girls and we'll meet you there around seven."

"Thanks," he said to Ellie after he'd hung up. "Ivan hasn't dated at all since his wife passed away. This is a big step for him."

If he only knew how big. Ellie coughed. "I have to go to Underground this afternoon to stand in for an artist friend," she said apologetically. "I guess I'd better get started here."

"Explain to me again what you'll be doing today," he said distractedly.

The Puritan-white canvas she withdrew begged for paint. She loved the faintly pungent odor of newly dried gesso. "I'll be applying a base coat of thin oil paint to develop a working composition—what objects are placed where in the painting." She gestured to the canvas with a dry paintbrush for emphasis.

"I thought it was just me in the painting," he said, grinning.

That smile of his threatened to be her undoing. "It *is* just you, but the background will also have its place in the painting. And the size of your shoulders, face, etcetera, is very important."

His grin deepened. "How low are you going?"

Ellie rolled her eyes. "Just to your chest, Mark." Not that she wouldn't enjoy painting a full-length portrait of him, and nude, at that. In art school she'd drawn professional nude models who cut a less impressive figure than Mark Blackwell.

"Anyway, the important thing today is to sort out the colors and placement. Then I can begin the detailed work. By the way, the thinned-down paint I'll use now will dry quickly, but once I start layering in color, I'll be using long-drying oils. At that point, it's going to be difficult to transport the canvas," she smiled, suddenly fidgety. "Especially on a bike."

He looked confused. "So?"

Ellie sighed. She hated doing this, it would seem as if she was trying to get him back to her place. "So, since I don't have a studio to work in, I'll have to set up the easel in my apartment and ask you to come there when I need you to, uh…sit." Her face burned, but the situation couldn't be helped.

"And how often would I get to come and…sit?" he

asked, leaning close. His dark green eyes danced merrily.

"Not much at first, but then about every other d-day."

His face fell. "Is that all? I've got a better idea. Why don't you set up at my place? I've got plenty of room, and you could take care of—I mean, check in on your cat." He stopped for a moment, concern on his face. "Is it a problem getting to my house that often? I'd hate for you to have to take a taxi every time."

"No," Ellie said slowly, thoughtfully. "I could ride my bike to the train, take the train to the Dunwoody station, then ride the short distance to your house. It's only a couple of blocks." Ellie's mind spun. It did seem like the perfect solution. And she missed Esmerelda terribly.

Mark nodded. "Good, then it's settled."

"But I'd have to be there during the day," Ellie warned.

"I'll give you a key. No big deal."

Sure, Ellie thought miserably. Obviously he didn't perceive their working together in an intimate setting as a big deal. And why would he? He didn't intend for their "relationship" to go anywhere.

Of course, she had more immediate problems to deal with. Like matchmaking between Mark's partner and her transvestite roommate.

8

"THIS I'm not sure about," Manny said, drumming his painted fingernails on the kitchen table.

"Me, neither," Ellie admitted, sorting through the junk mail. "But you owe me one for leading Ray Ivan to believe Mark and I are engaged."

Manny threw his hands in the air. "I was only trying to save your reputation. He jumped to his own conclusion."

"Okay, okay. Go to dinner as Molly and you can help us explain the misunderstanding. Then you can make excuses the next time Ray Ivan calls." She lifted a finger in warning. "But no funny stuff."

Manny reached over to toy with a rose petal that had dropped onto the table's surface from the bouquet of a dozen in the delivered vase. "The man does have class," he said, fingering the card with "Molly" written on it. "I take it you haven't told Mark about the real me?"

Ellie chewed the corner of her lip. "No."

His mouth tightened. "I can't blame you. He'd die if he knew he'd come within a hundred feet of a drag queen."

"Manny, Mark's a big boy raised in a big city—he's not *that* naive. But I didn't want to divulge details about your life to a man who was a stranger little more than a week ago.'' She stood and tossed a handful of envelopes in the trash can. ''And once the painting is finished and I'm out of pills, he'll be a stranger again.''

''Why do I feel a Barry Manilow song coming on?''

''Look,'' Ellie said in exasperation. ''I need to know if you can pull this off tonight.''

''*Moi?* I've been a woman nearly as long as you have, El. Of course I can pull this off.'' He brightened at the challenge. ''It'll be fun.''

Warning bells sounded in her ears at his exuberance. Manny loved nothing better than performing—she hoped he didn't outdo himself.

Indeed, when Mark picked them up, a bewigged Manny looked a picture of cool, tall, slender femininity in a short wrap skirt and fitted jacket. Ellie, on the other hand, was sweating profusely in her red silk shift by the time they reached the restaurant. She hadn't expected Mark to recognize Manny—she sometimes had to look closely herself to believe the metamorphosis—but still she was a nervous wreck.

The Lexington Diner enjoyed the reputation of being one of the swankiest eateries in the upscale area of Phipps Plaza. Not only was the menu famous, but the establishment also boasted a celebrated orchestra that played big-band tunes behind a large dance floor. According to Mark, all the attorneys at his firm held memberships.

Ray Ivan sat waiting for the group at a secluded table. Everyone exchanged pleasantries. ''You look stunning, my dear,'' he crooned to Manny, standing to pull out her chair. The older man looked flushed and excited. Ellie noted the half-empty wine bottle on the table with a shiver of premonition.

"Thank you," Manny responded, his voice honeyed.

The waiter brought more wine posthaste, and Mark ordered appetizers. Ellie didn't take her eyes off the couple across from her, and concentrated hard to hear every word.

"Molly, what do you do for a living?" Ray asked.

Manny smiled coquettishly. "I'm a performer."

"A singer?" He seemed quite pleased.

"And a dancer," Manny confirmed.

Ray leaned in to Manny's ear. Ellie leaned forward to listen. "I should have known by those legs," she heard him say, his words slightly slurred.

"Oh, my!" Manny jumped, slapping playfully at Ray's hand beneath the table.

"Ellie," Mark whispered, "didn't your mother ever tell you not to eavesdrop? Let's dance and leave them alone for a few minutes."

"But—"

"Come on." He stood and tugged her along behind him.

Thoughts of a masquerading Manny were swept away when Mark pulled her to him in a slow, close waltz. She fused her curves to his hollows, tucking her head beneath his chin, and gave herself up to his liquid movements. He was a wonderful dancer, graceful and strong. She loved the feel of his muscles moving against her, his hips melded to hers, guiding her to the low throb of the music. His hand stroked her lower back, stirring volcanic reactions in her midsection.

"You smell wonderful," he breathed into her ear. "Can I take you home with me?"

Ellie winced. She was oozing pheromones again. *There's nothing quite so romantic as an old-fashioned synthetic chemical reaction.* She lifted her head. "What about Molly?"

"If things go well, and it looks like they will, I suspect Ray will want to see her home."

Worry pooled in her stomach. "I didn't expect Ray to be so...taken with her so quickly."

"Why not? He's lonely, and she's a striking woman. Let's just let nature take its course."

Right now at that table, nature is being stood on its ear. Ellie bit her tongue hard.

"So you'll sleep in my bed tonight?" he murmured.

Ellie lowered her chin to hide her eyes. She was falling for this man, and setting herself up for a fantastic tailspin. "Let's just let nature take its course," she said, settling into his broad chest.

When she opened her eyes a few seconds later, she saw that Manny and Ray had joined the dancers on the floor. Manny held himself rigidly, but Ray's hands were roaming freely. When he grabbed a handful of Manny's rear end, Ellie missed a beat and stepped on Mark's foot.

"Ow," he said, chuckling.

"Sorry. We'd better get back to our table—I'm starved." She tugged him back to their chairs, and, thankfully, Manny and Ray followed suit.

The waiter came around to take their entrée orders and delivered yet another bottle of wine on the house. Ellie lost count of the glasses Mark's partner downed. When the saucers of escargot arrived, everyone dug in but Ray, who appeared to be well on his way to becoming smashed.

Mark leaned over to whisper to Ellie. "I've never seen Ivan drink like this—he must be nervous."

Ellie nodded, glanced at Manny and swallowed a snail whole. His left eyelash was coming unglued and flapped precariously when he blinked. She looked over at Mark. He, too, had noticed and was studying Manny closely.

"Um, Molly," Ellie said, trying to keep alarm out of her voice.

Manny looked up and Ellie winked hard at him several times, then wagged her eyebrows.

"Is something wrong, Ellie?" Ray asked, exaggerated concern evident in his blurry eyes.

"I, uh…" Ellie's mind raced. "I need to go to the bathroom, and I need Molly to come with me." She jumped up, grabbed Manny by the forearm and dragged him away from the table.

"What is it now?" Manny demanded.

"You're losing an eyelash," she hissed, herding him toward the lounge.

He reached up to finish yanking it off. "Damn, you can't find good adhesive anymore. I've got more in my purse—it'll just take a minute."

They shuffled into the bathroom where Ellie wet a towel to hold to her perspiring face.

Manny leaned into the mirror, carefully reapplying the lash. "Gee, El, Mark's partner is as horny as the brass section of the Atlanta Symphony."

She threw him a sarcastic look. "And you're complaining?"

"Let's just say what little appeal the man *had* evaporated a vineyard ago. And I don't know how I'm going to get rid of him."

"Maybe our best strategy would be to wait for him to pass out."

"And when do we get to the part about your engagement being a farce?"

"Even if we tell him, he won't remember tomorrow."

"You're right, which is why I'm going to tell him to kiss off."

Ellie's eyes bulged. "You can't! You have to let him down easy so he won't hold it against Mark. You and I got Mark into this mess, we have to see it through."

Manny pointed a long nail at her. "Let's get this straight—I'm doing this for you, not Mark. And believe me, you can't be gentle with men like Ray Ivan. He'll have to be hit over his balding head, or he'll be calling me from now on. This has gone too far. I think we need to tell Mark the truth."

Ellie's throat constricted. "You mean, about you?" Manny's occupation and alter identity would not be within Mark Blackwell's scope of understanding. And she didn't want Manny to be offended by a confrontation.

His face fell. "Are you ashamed of me?"

"Oh, no, Manny," she rushed to assure him. "But Mark is pretty conservative. He might not be very accepting."

"Then let's get Ray away from the table and broaden Mr. Blackwell's horizons."

Ellie felt faint as they left the ladies' room. The only guaranteed outcome of this evening would be a retraction of Mark's invitation to share his bed tonight. Manny stopped at a pay phone outside the lounge and dialed the restaurant's number, asked for Ray Ivan to be paged, then left the handset lying on its side.

"We're back," Manny said brightly as they approached the table.

"Are you okay?" Mark asked Ellie when she claimed her seat. "You look a little pale."

She mumbled she was fine, and took a long drink of wine for courage.

The maître d' appeared. "Mr. Ivan, a phone call for you. Right this way."

Ray straightened his suit, and managed to walk away with only a slight stagger.

The entrées had arrived during their stint in the bathroom. Ellie let a few seconds of silence pass watching Mark eat two bites of rare steak. Her salmon sat untouched.

Manny cleared his throat violently and frowned at her, nodding toward Mark's bent head.

"Mark," Ellie said, moistening her lips. "We have something to tell you."

"What?" he asked, taking a swallow of wine, then proceeding to carve off another cube of prime rib.

She looked at Manny, and he nodded encouragement. Ellie gripped the napkin in her lap into tight fists. "Well, the truth is—"

"The truth is," said Manny in his own voice, "looks can be deceiving."

Mark stared at Manny and blinked, his lips parting slowly. He leaned forward, squinting, then his eyes bulged. "M-Manny?"

Manny lifted a manicured hand in a small wave. "How's it hanging, Mark?"

Mark dropped his silverware with a loud clatter, and felt the blood drain from his face. "Oh...my...God." He gripped the chair arms and gaped at them for interminable seconds. "You're telling me—" His voice was high and shaky. He stopped and looked around, then cleared his throat and began again, this time speaking low and deliberately. "You're telling me I set my partner up with a *man?*"

Ellie winced and Manny nodded.

Mark gripped his head with both hands. "This can't be happening." Blood pounded in his ears and he felt faint. He looked at Ellie. "Why the devil didn't you *tell* me?"

"I tried, but you said you needed to make amends for us being naked in the car—"

"*I* wasn't naked—"

"Technically, neither was I—"

"Kids," Manny snarled, "we don't have time for this. Here he comes, and he already asked me to go home with him." Their heads pivoted to see Ray striding toward the table, having eyes only for Manny.

"You have to get out of here," Mark hissed to Manny. "Right now!"

"That won't keep him from calling me and sending flowers," Manny insisted. "I'll have to hurt his feelings sooner or later. We have to nip this in the bud. I've got an idea—work with me."

Ray slid into his seat and flashed them a bleary smile. "False alarm." He moved his chair closer to his date, looping an arm around the back of Manny's chair. "Now, where were we?"

Mark's career flashed before his eyes. Sweat popped out on his forehead, and he downed the glass of wine. Manny leaned forward to whisper something to Ellie, and she nodded in response, her eyes darting to Mark. *What are they up to now?*

"Mr. Ivan," Ellie said sweetly. "Would you like to dance?"

"Well, of course, dear." Ray tore himself away from Manny and accompanied Ellie to the dance floor.

Mark narrowed his eyes at Manny. "Don't even think about asking me to dance."

Manny waved him off, exasperated. "Don't be ridiculous—you're not my type at all. But I do need for you to go to the men's room with me."

"Excuse me?"

"I need to borrow your pants."

"*What?*"

"Look, for both our sakes, I've got to shake this guy once and for all. Are you with me?"

Cornered and out of options, he gestured toward the rest room and relented stiffly. "This is against my better judgment."

"I'll go first, and you follow in a few minutes."

Manny escaped and Mark played with his empty wineglass for a few seconds, then whistled tunelessly while he watched the second hand on his watch. When exactly one minute had passed, he strolled toward the men's room.

He breathed a sigh of relief to find the room empty. Perhaps Manny had gone home. He'd make excuses to Ray and somehow convince him not to call her, uh, him again.

"Pssst!"

Mark jerked his head toward the sound. One of the stall doors was closed, but no legs or feet were visible.

"Pssst, over here, Mark!"

Mark walked over to the stall and said, "What the hell are you doing?"

"I'm getting undressed."

"Are you suspended in midair?"

"I'm standing on the toilet."

Mark put his hands on his hips. "Did Ellie teach you that trick?"

A man entered the bathroom and walked to the sink, eyeing a large red stain on his lapel. He nodded to Mark and reached for a towel.

"Would you stop clowning around and take off your pants?" Manny whispered loudly.

Mark groaned inwardly. The man's head snapped up. He made wide eye contact with Mark, then turned and bolted out the door.

"Great," Mark said, walking into the adjacent stall. "We just scared a customer to death. He's probably reporting us right now. What are you doing, anyway?"

"I'm going to get Ray off Molly's back. Hurry up— I need your shirt, pants, socks and shoes."

"And what am I supposed to wear in the meantime?"

"Oh, that's right—Ellie says you don't wear undies."

"Does she tell you everything?" Mark sputtered.

"*Every*thing—you can hang on to your jacket for security."

Mark began stripping off his clothes and handed them over the top of the stall. "This had better work."

"Trust me."

"The man wearing the WonderBra says 'trust me.'"

"Don't knock it till you've tried it."

Why hadn't he worn boxers tonight? Mark felt utterly ridiculous standing naked in his suit jacket and holding his tie in front of his crotch while Manny dressed in his clothes. He wondered briefly if he could be disbarred for public nudity. Probably.

A couple of minutes later, a wad of clothing sailed over the top of the stall. Mark dodged panty hose, girdle, a set of fake boobs, wig, high heels and other mysterious items, watching them settle onto the tiled floor around him. ''What's all this crap?'' he demanded.

''All that crap is my wardrobe,'' Manny said hotly. I can't leave it in here—someone might take it. Keep it with you until I get back.''

Mark crossed his arms and shook his head in defeat. ''I saw this once in a movie. If you leave me stranded with nothing to wear out of here but women's clothes, I'll track you down and kick your ass. You've got ten minutes.''

''I'll be back,'' was Manny's acid response. Mark heard the stall door open and close, then lots of water splashing, then finally Manny exiting the outer door.

A few seconds later, the outer door opened again, this time admitting someone with a slow lazy stride. Mark looked down at his hairy legs and bare feet and imagined how it would look from the other side. He quickly stooped to snatch Manny's clothing from the floor and out of sight. Sweat beaded on his forehead.

''Having problems in there?'' the man asked haughtily, walking over to stop in front of the stall.

Mark's heart stopped. He knew that voice.

''Hey, buddy.'' The man knocked, and raised his voice in a challenge. ''I said, are you having problems in there?''

His co-worker, Tony Specklemeyer. The little hotshot who'd come to his office for a showdown over cheating on a client's tax forms. Mark cursed silently, scalding the air. The ambitious little jackass would hang him out to dry if he saw him like this. A drop of sweat dripped off his nose.

Mark pictured the headlines: Partner of Prestigious Atlanta Law Firm Found Buck-Naked In Men's-Room Stall Amidst Pile of Women's Underthings. He could visualize himself saying, ''Honest, Officer, I was just loaning my clothes to my fake fiancée's transvestite roommate so the senior partner of my law firm wouldn't find out I'd set him up with a man.''

Specklemeyer's feet had disappeared, and Mark prayed the man would simply leave. He nearly had a stroke when he heard a gasp above him. Mark turned and looked straight up into his co-worker's astonished face hanging over the top of the stall.

''Blackwell?''

Mark reached up to grab him by the throat, dropping most of the clothing he held. ''This isn't what you think, and if you so much as breathe a word of this to anyone, I'll rip out your spleen, got it?''

But Specklemeyer wasn't shaken. ''Gee, Blackwell, you're much more intimidating when you're not wielding a pair of size eleven turquoise pumps.''

Mark looked down at the shoe in his other hand. His fury exploded, and he shook the man until his head rattled. His voice was low and deadly. ''I mean it, Specklemeyer. You did not see this.''

Tony held up his hands in surrender and rolled a smile around on his lips. ''Sure, man, sure. Whatever you say.'' He jerked loose from Mark's grip, and Mark heard him step down from the toilet seat and leave the rest room.

Mark sank to the toilet and put his face in his hands.

My career is definitely over. Next week, being partner would be a distant memory.

He clasped his hands together. "Please, God, let me get out of here alive so I can wring Ellie Sutherland's neck!"

ELLIE HELPED an unsteady Ray into his seat before she slid into hers. She glanced around frantically for Manny and Mark. They'd been gone for several minutes.

"I need to visit the men's room," Ray announced, half standing.

"No!" Ellie yelled, drawing the attention of patrons around her.

Ray looked at her, startled.

"I mean, not yet," she said, laughing nervously. "Can you wait until Mark or Molly get back so I won't be here by myself?"

Ray sat back down obligingly. "Where *are* those two?"

Good question.

"Ellie!" Manny's voice exclaimed behind her. She turned to see Manny, clad in Mark's clothing, striding toward her. Despite her panic, she had to suppress a giggle. His feet were swimming in the bigger man's shoes, and he'd rolled up the cuff of the dress pants to keep them from dragging.

"Where's Molly?" Manny asked dramatically.

"I think she's in the ladies' room, Manny."

"Is this a friend of yours, Ellie?" Ray asked cautiously.

"Ray Ivan, meet Manny Oliver."

Ray stuck out his hand, perplexed. "Pleased to meet you."

Manny didn't shake his hand, and instead cried, "Are you the man who's trying to steal my Molly?"

"What?" the older man exclaimed.

Manny swooped down on one knee and clasped Ray's hands. "Don't do it, sir. If you have a heart, don't do it."

"Don't do what?" Concern lined Ray's face.

"Don't take my Molly." Big tears filled Manny's eyes. "I love her, but she keeps a flock of men on the side. She's so beautiful, I can't compete with them all. You understand, don't you, sir?"

"I guess so," Ray said dubiously.

Ellie hid a smile behind her napkin. Manny hadn't removed his eyelashes, and his long fingernails were still blood red, but the sodden Ray didn't seem to notice.

The maître d' approached the table with a worried look on his face. He addressed Ray. "Is everything all right here, sir?"

Manny's sobs increased, his head bent over Ray's hands.

"I think so," Ray said in confusion.

Manny raised his head. "So you'll give me your word to not see her, no matter how tempting she is."

Ray looked at Ellie, then back to Manny. "I guess so."

"Oh, thank you, sir." Manny's sobs began anew. "You've made me a new man. But please, when she comes back out, let her down gently. I love her so much, I couldn't stand for her to be hurt."

Ray nodded rapidly. "Sure."

Manny kissed the man's hands, then made a tearful exit.

"I'm so sorry, Ray," Ellie said, patting his hand. "Perhaps it really is for the best."

He nodded wisely. "Better to have loved and lost..." His voice faded as he lifted his wineglass to his lips for the hundredth time.

A few minutes later, Mark came walking hurriedly back to the table, glancing around the room and tugging at his tie.

"Where've you been?" Ray slurred. "We've been worried about you, son."

Mark glared murderously at Ellie, but turned a smile on Ray. "The snails didn't agree with me, sir."

"Have you seen Molly?" Ellie asked, her eyebrows raised.

"I believe she'll be here any minute," he said through clenched teeth.

"Hello, all," Manny said in his sugary Molly voice, swinging into his seat.

He looked slightly worse for wear, his wig askew and lipstick hastily applied. He turned a smile on Ray. "Miss me?"

"Yes," Ray admitted, his voice sad. "But I'm afraid I must call it an evening."

"But why?" Manny's eyebrows furrowed dramatically.

Ray took Manny's hand in his. "Well, the truth is, Molly, you're too much of a woman for me, and I don't think this is going to work out."

"Oh, no." Manny pouted prettily.

Mark rolled his eyes, and Ellie kicked him under the table.

"Shush, my dear," Ray said gently. "It's for the best. You've been a lovely dinner companion, and I thank you very much."

"Well, if you're sure," Manny said cautiously.

Ray waved for the maître d' and asked him to hail a taxi, then signed for the meal, folded a fifty into the man's hand and bid everyone good-night.

When he was out of sight, Ellie sank into her chair in relief. "Whew!"

Manny snapped his fingers. "Told you it would work."

"Except," she added glumly, "he still thinks we're engaged."

Mark scanned the room again, obviously agitated. His scowl was black and ugly when it landed on Ellie. "Although being engaged to you is a harrowing prospect, believe me, it's the least of my problems right now."

FREDA ESCORTED ELLIE to the first available closet-room. "So," the clinical assistant said in a tired voice. "How's it going?" She sat down heavily in a creaking metal chair and flipped through Ellie's journal, stopping occasionally to scratch at her temple with the end of a pen.

"Fine," Ellie replied nervously, sitting on a stool wedged between a trash can and a Formica desk. Absolutely nothing in her life was fine.

Freda had stopped on one page to read intently. "Well, I can see things have progressed nicely with Mr. Mark."

"Keep reading," Ellie said dryly.

Freda squinted, bringing the book closer. "Try to remember to print your entries next time."

"But I printed them *this* time."

"Well, it's hard to make out what you've written. You had 'toy' sex? Is that something new?"

Ellie felt her skin redden. She coughed lightly. "Mmm, that would be 'toe' sex."

"*Toe* sex? Okay, you had, er...*toe* sex once and regular sex once?"

"That's right."

Freda studied a form on her desk, pen poised, then shook her head. "I never seem to have the right checkboxes for your answers."

"Being categorized under 'other' is the story of my life."

"Do you see this moving toward a long-term relationship?"

"Definitely not."

Freda kept writing. "How often do you see him?"

"For the next few weeks, possibly every day—I work out of his home now, but it's temporary, and partly so I can look after my cat."

"He's keeping your cat?"

"Uh-huh."

"But last week you told me he's allergic to your cat."

"He is, but we made this deal he'd look after her until she had kittens if I would go to a swanky work dinner party as his date. Except it didn't go very well because his partner caught us making out in the car and then announced to everyone that we're engaged."

Freda's eyes widened. "You're engaged?"

"No, but everyone thinks so. Except his mom—he

told her the truth because she nearly had a heart attack when she heard it through the grapevine. She hates me because I—''

"Ruined the family reunion," Freda cut in. "You told me."

"It was an accident," Ellie insisted. "Then we double-dated with his partner and my roommate, only Mark didn't know my roommate is a transvestite—"

"Wait," Freda said, holding her palm stop-sign fashion. "That's a whole different study. Let's get back to the pheromones. Have you had sex since you started working in his home?"

"He's not speaking to me."

"Because of the roommate?"

Ellie nodded. "It's a long story, but a co-worker of Mark's saw him in the bathroom naked and holding a bunch of women's clothes—"

"Wait, I thought your roommate was the cross-dresser."

"He is."

Freda looked at her questioningly. "Then why was Mark naked in the bathroom holding women's clothes?"

"He had to loan *his* clothes to my roommate to convince his partner that the woman he thought he was with had a boyfriend."

Freda looked totally confused. "And that boyfriend would be…?"

"My roommate."

Pursing her lips, Freda said, "Okay."

"Anyway, Mark hasn't spoken to me since he dropped me and my roommate off Saturday night."

"I thought you said you were working in his home."

"But I only started yesterday. He worked late, probably on purpose, and I left before he got home."

"Why don't you stick around one night until he comes home and see what happens?" She winked, surprising Ellie. "See how long he can resist you."

"The problem is, these pheromones seem to be working both ways."

"What do you mean?"

"Why else would I be so drawn to a man who is everything I would hate in a partner? It has to be these pills."

"Probably," Freda agreed, nodding. Spreading her hands, she added, "Think of it as one big science project."

"Oh, no," Ellie groaned.

"What?"

"I blew up the science lab my junior year in college."

9

WHY, oh, why had he ever thought he'd be able to resist her, and in his own home, no less? Purposely working late each night, Mark half hoped she'd be gone when he arrived, half prayed she wouldn't be. Tonight was Friday and his prayers had been answered. Classic rock thumped through his centralized stereo system when he stepped into the entryway. He inhaled, filling his lungs with her fresh-air skin scent that had permeated his home.

"Ellie," he called, and although he knew she couldn't hear him above Lynyrd Skynyrd, he added, "I'm home." For a few foolish seconds, the image of an aproned June Cleaver flashed through his mind, coming to the door to welcome Ward home from a hard day's work.

"Mark, is that you?" Ellie bawled, coming to the top of the stairs to peer over the railing.

Except June had never worn an apron like that, he mused, admiring the way the short work smock emphasized Ellie's breasts and small waist. And Mrs. Cleaver would have been holding a spatula instead of a paintbrush.

Mark waved, deciding not to yell over the music. He hated himself for being so glad to see her. She held up a finger to indicate she'd be back, then disappeared.

Mark set his briefcase by the bottom step and loosened his tie. Walking toward the kitchen, he bellowed, "How have you been?" His last two words reverberated through the house because the music abruptly ended. Then he heard the sound of Ellie's feet descending the stairs lightly and rhythmically.

"Oh, fine," she said cheerfully.

When he turned to her, he noticed immediately she'd lost the smock. Black hip-hugger shorts and a ribbed lime green turtleneck would have been unforgivable on most women, but Ellie, as usual, looked delightful. Right down to the smudge of gold paint on her chin. Then he realized her cheer had been forced. Her wide smile could not hide her bright, panicked eyes. He slowly placed the two bottles of beer he'd withdrawn from the refrigerator on the counter. "What?" he asked, alarm setting in.

"You might want to have something stronger than a beer," she warned.

Mark bit his lip and summoned patience. "What?" he repeated quietly.

Ellie's face took on a pleading look. "She's just a sweet little kitty, Mark, please don't be mad."

Mark snorted and twisted off the beer cap. "What did Sheba do today? Pee on another blue cushion?"

He lifted the bottle to his mouth, but stopped at the look of dread on Ellie's face. Obviously this was much worse than a couple of throw pillows. "What did she break?"

"She didn't break anything, exactly."

"What the hell did she do, *exactly?*" Suddenly Mark realized the buzz from his fish-tank filter was absent. His head jerked around. "Oh, no. Not my fish?"

Ellie stood wringing her hands. "I guess the fish video got her wound up—"

Anger bubbled inside his stomach. "Your cat *ate* my fish?"

She bit her bottom lip, then said, "Well, she didn't eat *all* of them, mostly just batted them around—"

Mark strode through the kitchen into the den to stare at the fifty-gallon tank of serene, still water. Artificial sea grass drifted up from the bottom. A labyrinth of elaborate ceramic sand castles sat vacant. A single black severed fish tail floated on the surface.

"I turned off the filter," she offered. "And sang 'The Circle of Life' when I flushed them down the john."

"At that point, I'm sure they were glad to be dead," Mark retorted, remembering her singing voice. "What happened to the lid?"

"The veterinarian says Esmerelda has an above average IQ—"

Mark cut her off. "If that were the case, the animal would be smart enough to know not to devour seven hundred dollars' worth of exotic fish!"

Ellie blanched. "Seven hundred dollars? Are you crazy? That's two months' rent."

Mark narrowed his eyes.

Smiling nervously, Ellie quietly stammered, "Well, you certainly can't f-fault her good taste."

Irritation triggered a finger twitch. Soon his hands were jumping at his sides. "I'm filling it up with piranhas tomorrow." He strode back to the kitchen, gulped half the beer, then added, "Big, smart piranhas that say, 'Here, kitty, kitty.'"

"I'm sorry, Mark, really I am, and I know Esmerelda

is sorry, too, if only she could tell you," she pleaded, hot on his heels.

"Oh, so *that's* what she's trying to say when she bares her fangs and runs me out of my own bed."

"Please, Mark," Ellie begged softly. When he turned, she slipped inside the circle of his arms. Desire bolted through him against his will. Wrapping her arms around his waist, she turned huge blue eyes up to him, batting her lashes shamelessly. "She's going to be a mother in a couple of weeks," she said earnestly, as if that explained everything.

"Meow," Esmerelda announced, walking regally into the room, tail held high. She glanced toward the den and licked her lips, then blinked at Mark.

"Long live the queen," Mark grumbled, but set his beer down to draw Ellie closer to him.

Ellie inhaled sharply when he tightened his hold. Her breasts, without the protection of a bra, responded immediately. Mark's voice was low as he lowered his mouth to her ear. "If you think kissing up to me is going to make up for that murdering cat of yours, well, then—"

She moved her lips to his and drew his breath into her mouth with a slow, deep kiss.

When she withdrew, he simply stared down at her. "Well, then...you're much smarter than your pussycat." He shook his head in wonder. "Between last weekend and my empty aquarium, I should be furious with you."

"But?" she asked hopefully.

"But...there's something about you that makes me forget what I was feeling or saying before you walked into the room,'' he said, hearing the wonder in his own voice.

Ellie's smile was tremulous. ''I'm sorry. I should have told you about Manny. Does his cross-dressing bother you?''

Mark thought about it for a few seconds. ''No. I mean, it takes a little getting used to, but he seems like an okay guy.'' He smiled wryly. ''I just didn't want to be the one who paired him up with the man who respected me enough to make me a partner.''

She played with a buttonhole in his jacket. ''So did you get in trouble for...you know.''

''For my stint as a naked clothes rack for your friend?''

She giggled and nodded.

He loosened his grip on her waist, took a drink of his beer and leaned against the counter. ''Specklemeyer hasn't come out and said anything, but he's flirting with disaster.''

''How so?''

''We had a meeting this morning with an old client, and Ray told him I was engaged.'' He watched her expression, curious for a reaction, perplexed by his own curiosity. Her face remained unreadable, and he continued, ''I opened my mouth to set the record straight, but Tony sat gloating across the table. He really thinks I'm covering up some kind of kinky lifestyle. I figured telling everyone we're not engaged would only add fuel to his fire. I'm sorry to keep prolonging this.''

She shrugged, a smile on her lips. ''Do you think he'll say anything?''

''If I know Specklemeyer, he'll wait until he needs

my support for something big, then he'll threaten to tell what he thinks he saw.''

''Is he that vicious?''

''He's so blinded by ambition, I wouldn't put anything past him. The man has a vanity license plate that says 'HUNGRY.'''

''Would they really fire you?''

''Of course not—even if I were a cross-dresser, it would be illegal to fire me. But it's a label I'd rather not have to defend.'' God, she smelled wonderful. He pulled her to him and kissed her neck. She felt dangerously good and his body hardened in need. No, his mind screamed, a thousand times no. ''Do you have dinner plans?'' he asked, nuzzling her ear.

She pressed her breasts against him, moaning slightly. ''Nothing I can't get out of,'' she whispered. ''What did you have in mind?''

''Getting you out of something,'' he murmured, ignoring the warning bells in his head. ''Do you think Esmerelda would let us borrow my room for the night? I still haven't seen that darn tattoo.''

ELLIE SAT UP GINGERLY so as not to disturb Mark, her heart catching at the sight of him sprawled in the tangled sheets. They'd made love, then ordered Ellie's favorite ham and pineapple pizza, washed it down with beer and made love again. He'd asked her to accompany him to a regatta today in Savannah, and she was looking forward to spending the day together. It seemed he did have time for rest and relaxation, after all. Maybe he wasn't the work machine she had imagined.

At the moment, she sincerely doubted if even Esmerelda could rouse the man. Mark's soft snores attested to his deep state of sleep, but it was his state of undress that mesmerized Ellie. She studied the proportion of his torso, the hard planes of his stomach and the length of his semihard sex with an artist's trained eye. On impulse, she began to frame a composition with her joined thumbs and extended index fingers. Some scenes were meant to be captured on paper. Mark Blackwell in the buff was an artist's dream.

Silently, Ellie rose and lifted his blue-and-white-striped pajama top from the bedpost, then pulled it over her head. She rolled up the sleeves and padded to Esmerelda's room where she had set up an easel and paints.

The corporate portrait was progressing nicely. Mark was coming alive on the canvas surface, devastatingly masculine and authoritative in his olive suit. She'd coaxed him into sitting for her last night in the few minutes between their lovemaking sessions, and had taken advantage of the time to render his eyes. This most important feature was most accurately portrayed if painted directly from the model in order to capture light and expression. They glistened back at her, serious, but with a teasing twinkle at the edges. Volumes of dark leather-bound reference books made up the background, the books' gilded accents a perfect foil for the green in his suit and eyes.

Ellie snatched her large sketch pad and flipped past the quick sketches of Esmerelda until she found a clean sheet. Then she reentered Mark's bedroom, sighing when Esmerelda dashed through the door before she could close it. Mark remained deep in slumber. She'd bet he hadn't so much as twitched since she'd left.

Sinking into an overstuffed chair in front of the bay window, Ellie propped her feet on an ottoman and spent a few seconds drinking in the sight of Mark's glorious body. The thick charcoal pencil in her hand began to move almost involuntarily. Within minutes she'd scrawled a rough sketch of him across the page. On the second pass, she worked more slowly, blocking in shadows to delineate limbs and muscles. Finally, she added more detail, like body hair and facial features. Taking particular care, she rendered his privates in precise proportion on the paper. Not hard, yet not soft, his current state of semiarousal would aptly reflect his size, yet not come across as vulgar.

The sketch turned out so well, Ellie decided a painting must be done. She grinned. It would be her unique thank-you to Mark for taking care of Esmerelda. He'd probably get a big kick out of it. What man hadn't fantasized about being immortalized in the nude at the peak of health? She'd work on the new painting at her apartment to keep it a secret.

She closed the sketchbook and put it aside to crawl back into bed. Mark grunted contentedly when she spooned up next to him. *I can't believe I'm so stupid. I fell in love with him knowing full well he's devoted to his job. I promised myself I'd never get tied to a man who thought being with his family was an option. Besides, the study ends in two weeks, along with my sex appeal.*

The phone rang, jarring Mark awake. Ellie reached for the handset on the nightstand and gave it to him. He pulled himself up, rubbing the sleep from his eyes, and spoke into the phone. "Hello? Yeah, Patrick…no, I'm fine, what's up?" Mark reached for the pen and pad beside the phone and began to jot down notes. "No, I'll be glad to take care of it." He glanced at Ellie and frowned apologetically. "Have Monica make the arrangements and clear my calendar for next week. I'll be at the airport in forty-five minutes." He was already standing when he hung up the phone.

"Sorry about today," he said simply, tearing off the sheet of paper. "Something came up—I have to go to Chicago with Beecham and Ivan for a week or so." He bent over and kissed her quickly.

Déjà vu. How many times had her father missed planned outings with the family because his boss had called at the last minute? "Oh, come on, can't you wait until this afternoon?" Ellie cajoled.

Mark shook his head. "Sorry, I have a plane to catch. Grant was supposed to go but had to cancel at the last minute. That leaves me."

"Can't we at least have breakfast?" Ellie pleaded, hating herself for sounding like her mother.

"Sorry," he repeated. "I'll make it up to you when I get home. I promise." Then he walked toward the bathroom. After he closed the door and the shower spray started, Ellie frowned.

Sorry, sorry, sorry. Her father had had an endless supply of apologies. Rising from the bed, she scooped her clothing from the floor. She cursed under her breath, and shook her head. She had no one to blame but herself. She'd seen the train coming, but had barreled past the warning signals to straddle the tracks, welcoming the light with open arms.

SATURDAY AND SUNDAY NIGHT had both been late work nights in Chicago. And since what little sleep time he'd had left he'd spent thinking about Ellie, Mark arrived at the hotel's continental breakfast Monday morning in a less-than-rested mood.

He couldn't get the woman off his mind. Of course, the irritating rash he'd developed from the foamy whipped cream she'd covered his privates with served as a constant reminder of their romps. Granted, she had removed it in a most satisfying way. *It's just a strong physical attraction.* Unfortunately, the one area in which they seemed to be most compatible was in bed.

He purposely hadn't called her since he'd left. Somehow, calling long distance to check in just seemed too…relationship-y. Still, the idea of spending a lot of time with Ellie had begun to sound appealing. The mere thought of the tiny pink mouse tattoo, apparently barely concealed by her garter belt that first night, sent the blood rushing to his groin. Ellie was beautiful, sexy, funny, and he craved her company. He could do much worse, he knew. He might give this novel idea of a committed, monogamous relationship some serious thought.

"How's Ellie?" Patrick asked, breaking into his thoughts.

Mark glanced at Ray, who also seemed interested in his answer. For an instant, Mark wondered if Specklemeyer had leaked the information, after all. Maybe they knew his engagement was a charade and were calling him on it. Shifting in his seat, he replied, "Fine, thanks for asking."

Patrick looked sympathetic. "Big step, isn't it?"

Mark nodded, swallowing a dry bite of bagel.

"Of course it's a big step," Ray declared, snapping open a newspaper. "The last woman you'll sleep with for the rest of your life, the one woman you'll wake up to every day for the next fifty years, God willing.''

Patrick nodded solemnly. ''Of course, the bedroom gets a little chilly once kids come along, but you get used to it.''

Ray grunted his agreement. ''Bone-cold.''

Mark pursed his lips and shook his head, smiling wryly. ''So why don't married men reveal this stuff to single men *before* the engagement?''

Ray chuckled. ''We're not trying to talk you out of it, son. Marriage has its good points. If the right woman came along, I'd do it again.'' He rattled the newspaper. ''Probably.'' Mark thought about Manny and winced.

''Yeah,'' Patrick said, ''Lucy is fabulous, it's her mother I can't stomach. By the way, how's your mother taking this?''

''She's not ecstatic, but—''

''Uh-oh,'' Ivan announced from behind the paper. ''Not a good sign, but it's to be expected. Don't worry, things will probably work out before one of your parents has to move in.''

''Move in?'' Mark parroted.

''Sure,'' Patrick said. ''After Lucy's father passed away, her mother was so heavily medicated, she came to stay with us for a couple of weeks. She's been living with us going on two years now.''

Mark swallowed. He doubted he could live with his *own* mother, and he didn't know the first thing about Ellie's family. Except that her dad had been a workaholic. But hadn't she said something about a nudist colony? His collar grew warmer and tighter.

''That's nothing,'' said Ray, bending down a corner of a page to peer at them. ''My mother came to live with us back in 1970. She and my poor wife argued so much, the police were at my house three times the first week because the neighbors complained.''

Mark imagined his mother and Ellie in the same house. Not in a million years. He pushed his plate away and grabbed a glass of water. He'd never experienced heartburn before, but it didn't take a medical degree to perform a quick diagnosis. His previous notion of entering a relationship with Ellie ended along with his appetite.

10

ELLIE WAVED at the messy painters as she ducked through the entryway of the clinic. She was almost sorry she wouldn't be around to see the finished product.

Freda stood behind the receptionist's counter when Ellie walked in. "Well, if it isn't the woman with the experienced toes." The woman's eyes were actually twinkling. She led Ellie back to a tiny room and asked, "So, what's the latest?"

"Nothing kinky this week," Ellie informed her as she took a seat and handed her the journal. "I consider whipped cream to be pretty standard stuff."

"Oh?"

"We were together Friday night, then he left town Saturday."

"Sounds like he came around."

Ellie grinned sheepishly. "Around and around and upside down."

Showing uncharacteristic concern, Freda asked, "Have you heard from him?"

Ellie shook her head sadly. "It's the pheromones, isn't it? He's not near me to be affected by them, so he's not interested."

"Is that what you think?" Freda asked, her pen poised.

Ellie nodded.

"Could be," Freda admitted, making notes. "But haven't you heard the saying 'Absence makes the heart grow fonder'?"

"I thought it was 'Absence make the heart wonder.' Or is it 'wander'?"

"You don't have much confidence in your relationship, do you?"

Ellie's laugh was short and dry. "Relationship? What Mark and I have is a physical attraction brought about by these…these fake love-inducers." She pointed to the bottle of pills sitting in front of Freda. "It's not fair—they mess with a person's mind—they make you think something's there that really isn't." She blinked away tears and tried to smile at Freda. "Tennyson was wrong—it's better *not* to have loved at all than to have loved and lost."

"You haven't lost him yet," Freda said.

"Yeah," Ellie said miserably, gesturing to her final supply. "This should delay the inevitable by about one week."

"Have you considered the possibility you might feel differently about *him* once you quit taking the pills?"

Elation zigged, then zagged through Ellie's heart. She lifted her chin and flashed a genuine smile in Freda's direction. "You're right!" A burden the size of Mark's cellular phone bill rolled off her back. Since it was a chemically induced fluke she'd fallen for the very type of man she'd sworn to avoid, this attraction would probably disappear as quickly as it had surfaced.

"Anyway," Freda said, "it'll be interesting to see what happens when he returns." She handed Ellie the final week's supply of pheromones.

Ellie fingered the bottle, the pills suddenly weighing heavily in her palm. The honeymoon was almost over, and she was happy to see the end in sight.

Wasn't she?

"WHERE HAVE YOU been keeping yourself?" Manny asked, dumping his bags of groceries on the counter. "As if I didn't know," he added.

Ellie angled her head at him across the room. She'd set up an easel in a corner of the breakfast nook by the window. After wiping a brush on a turpentine-soaked rag, she stretched her cramped fingers. Sometimes, a picture practically painted itself. This was one of those times when once she started painting, she couldn't bring herself to stop. She checked her watch. Three hours, nonstop.

Manny walked over to peek at the painting and gasped, his hand to his chest. "My, my." Mark Blackwell lay slumbering on the canvas, his sleek and muscled nude body accented, not covered, by the twisted sheets. "Now I know where the phrase *too big for his britches* originated."

"Manny," Ellie warned, "if you let on you've seen this painting, I swear I'll burn your gowns."

With his hand, Manny made a zipping motion across his mouth, then turned back to the painting. "It's divine, El," he said with sincerity in his voice.

"One of my best," she agreed. "A shame no one will ever see it."

"Then why on earth did you paint it?"

"It's a surprise gift to Mark for taking care of Esmerelda."

Manny looked incredulous. "He doesn't know about it?"

"Nope."

"Well, that explains a few things. I thought it was rather loose of Mr. A. Retentive. How's the other painting going?"

"Almost finished. Mark's in Chicago."

"When did he leave?"

"Saturday morning."

"This is Tuesday. You've been at his house three entire days by yourself?"

"Esmerelda was there," Ellie said defensively.

"What have you been doing?"

"Working on the other portrait, weeding his flowers—"

"Sleeping in his bed. Did you rearrange the furniture, too, Goldilocks?"

"No! Although the couch in his den *would* look better under the window."

"You're getting too comfortable at this house," Manny warned. "What's going on with the two of you?"

"That's a very good question."

"And?"

"And I intend to pursue an answer once he returns from his trip."

"Which will be?"

"Soon, I think."

By Friday, when she still hadn't heard from Mark, Ellie was decidedly depressed. Pride kept her from calling his office to see when they expected him to return. She'd put the final touches on the business portrait still drying at his home. The finished nude, drying on an easel in her bedroom, no longer seemed like such a grand idea.

Mark Blackwell was firmly entrenched in his career, and had made it crystal clear this week he didn't care enough about her to spare five minutes of his busy schedule to call. For all she knew, he could be flitting around the Windy City with a busty woman on each arm. In fact, the more she dwelled on it, the more convinced she became he was doing just that. Misery wallowed in her stomach.

Saturday afternoon, Ellie returned home with new sketches for two more Atlanta landmark paintings she intended to add to her portfolio. A quick glance at her answering machine told her there was one message. Her heart lifted. Mark? She rushed over to the machine and pushed the play button.

"Ellie, this is Monica. I wanted to let you know in case Mark hasn't called that he'll be back Wednesday morning." So, she'd been relegated to receiving messages through his secretary, and probably only because Monica had taken it upon herself to forward the information. She knew the routine—some weeks her mother had talked to her husband's secretary more than she'd spoken to her own husband.

Ellie's heart crumbled in disappointment. She deserved more than a philandering businessman who slept with his briefcase. More than a man who would fly off for weeks at a time and never check in. She refused to expose herself to it, she refused to expose her children to it. Ellie made a painful decision. If Mark Blackwell ever came home, she wouldn't be seeing him anymore. Which was just as well, she noted. The end of the study loomed in plain sight.

She went to the Dunwoody house that afternoon to check on Esmerelda, and decided from the looks of her cat's bulging tummy, she'd better start spending the nights again, at least until Mark came home. To soothe her guilty pangs, Ellie slept in a guest room and bought groceries, then puttered around the yard, weeding, watering, trimming, even transplanting. She found a tiny vacant mulch bed which would have made a perfect herb garden, but she swept the thought aside. Better to concentrate on reality, such as finding a job.

So the next morning, she and Esmerelda pored over Mark's Sunday-paper classified ads. She would receive the last check from the study on Tuesday when she turned in her final journal, which was practically blank this week, except for the occasional street admirer. She'd be able to collect the largest and final installment on Mark's portrait from the law firm in a couple of weeks. But she needed to look for something steady and, preferably, with insurance.

Ellie sighed, circling possibilities, tears filling her eyes when she remembered the last time she'd done this. It had been the day Mark Blackwell had bumbled his way into her life. Only this time, tears, not displaced soda, wet the paper. Ellie wished she'd never heard of pheromones, because if not for those darned pills, she wouldn't have lost her heart to Mark. She put her head down and cried in earnest. Esmerelda licked Ellie's hand.

IF ELLIE HAD ANY DOUBTS about whether she wore her heart on her sleeve, Freda put them to rest Tuesday morning.

"I take it he's still in Chicago?"

Ellie nodded forlornly.

"And you haven't heard from him?"

She shook her head, just as forlornly.

"When is he due back?"

"His secretary left me a message he'll be back to-morrow."

"And you'll be taking your last two pills this eve-ning, right?"

Ellie nodded again.

Freda sighed. "Don't fret about it—you'll just make yourself sick." She smiled and patted Ellie's hand. "Good luck."

"WHAT'S THE PROBLEM?" Mark grumbled to Patrick. They'd been sitting on a runway at O'Hare for over forty minutes waiting for their plane to take off.

Patrick looked up from his magazine. "Relax, man, this is typical."

"You think they could at least serve us a beer while we wait."

Patrick raised an eyebrow. "Are you cranky for a particular reason or can I look forward to this every time we fly together?"

Mark frowned. "Sorry."

His partner laughed. "Hey, I miss Lucy, too. You'll be home before you know it. And reunion sex is the best, don't you think? It's the only time I can get near Lucy anymore." He went back to his reading, leaving Mark to brood.

He'd decided earlier in the week he wouldn't be see-ing Ellie anymore. That is, he wouldn't be *dating* her anymore. She'd still be at his house occasionally during the next few weeks until that darn cat dropped her kittens and weaned them. Come to think of it, he and Ellie hadn't really dated much, when he subtracted the dates he'd bartered for and the disastrous double date with Ray and Manny.

Okay, so he wouldn't be *sleeping* with her anymore. That thought sent a pang of regret through his midsection, but he remained determined. He was too young to settle down and when he did, it would be to someone better suited for him. He hadn't figured out the hold she seemed to have over him, but if staying away from Ellie and her powerful sex appeal held the answer, he'd do it. He'd made sacrifices before. He'd be happier in the long run. So how to break the news to her? The way men had been delivering bad news for decades. In the gentlest, safest way possible.

By telephone.

ELLIE'S HEART LEAPED involuntarily at the sound of the ringing phone. Manny's eyes shot up in question as he reached for the handset. She motioned for him to answer it.

"Hello? Yes, she is. May I ask who's calling? Well, Mark, how nice of you to call. We thought you'd died. Hold on, please."

Ellie rolled her eyes.

Manny covered the mouthpiece and said unnecessarily, "It's him."

After taking several deep breaths to calm herself, Ellie picked up the handset and said, "Hello?"

"Hi, it's Mark."

She couldn't read anything into the tone of his voice. But he didn't sound especially glad to be talking to her. "Oh, hi. Are you home?"

"Yeah."

"How was your trip?" She tried to shoo Manny from the room with her hand, but he smiled and shook his head, plopping down on the couch within hearing distance.

"I had a busy week," Mark said distractedly. "And long. It'll be nice to sleep in my own bed tonight."

The silence hung heavy after his loaded offhand comment.

Ellie cleared her throat. "Well, hopefully Esmerelda won't bother you."

"I see she still hasn't had her kittens."

"No, but she should any day. I hope you don't mind—I stayed over there the last few nights in case she needed me."

"So you're the one who replenished my beer."

"Yeah, I figured it was the least I could do. I can't tell you how much I appreciate your letting her stay." She was rambling, she knew, but she wasn't sure where they stood anymore.

"A deal's a deal," he said simply. "The portrait looks finished." He seemed to be grasping at conversational straws, too.

"It is. As soon as the paint is dry enough, I'll bring it home to frame."

"Would it sound conceited if I said it looked great?"

"A little, but I know what you mean. Thanks."

"Sure." He cleared his throat. "Look, Ellie, I've been thinking now would be a good time to let everyone at work know our engagement is, well…off."

Ellie bit her bottom lip to stem her tears. Although she'd been entertaining the same thoughts, it just sounded so final coming from his mouth. Manny leaned forward on the couch, looking ready to pounce on the phone. She took a deep, steadying breath. "My thoughts exactly. I'm sure no one will be surprised. We're not really each other's type, you know."

"Right." He sounded relieved. "But, hey, don't let that keep you away. I know you'll be wanting to check on Esmerelda, so hang on to that key, okay?"

"Okay," she said, forcing brightness into her voice. "I'll see you soon, then?"

"Soon," she promised, and hung up slowly. When she turned, Manny was already by her side. He pulled her into his arms, rocking her and shushing her tears.

AFTER UNPACKING and showering, Mark went to the office for a few hours, but couldn't seem to concentrate. *I'm tired,* he rationalized. He toyed with the idea of calling Valerie, but an early evening and a long night's rest sounded more appealing. He carefully kept at bay the words and emotions of this morning's stilted phone conversation with Ellie. In a few weeks, he'd forget about her. He'd probably run into her one day with a rumpled poet on her arm. He frowned, then pushed all thoughts of Ellie Sutherland from his mind.

After pulling into the garage, Mark walked back down his short driveway to check the mailbox. While idly flipping through bills and junk mail, he scrutinized his landscaping. Something seemed different, but he couldn't put his finger on it. Not one thing, but maybe everything. He stopped. The gardens were neater, perhaps. Which was odd, since the landscaping company wasn't scheduled to come out for another month. He examined the bushes and flowers more closely. Completely weed free. And showing evidence of recent pruning. Frowning, he reentered the garage, then noticed his gardening gloves were hung in a different spot. As were some of his tools. Ellie? He shook his head, a small smile curving his lips.

All was quiet when he entered the house. For a split second, he craved Lynyrd Skynyrd, but settled on a shot of bourbon. After he poured the drink, he stopped to study the expensive crystal decanter, heavy and cool in his hands. Very elegant, like all his possessions. Given the chance, how would Ellie spend his money? Leopard-skin-upholstered furniture? Baubles for the cat?

Trudging upstairs to change, Mark registered the fact that Esmerelda hadn't made her normal snooty appearance. Probably lying in wait somewhere to pounce on him, he decided. He walked into his bedroom, flipping on the light. He reached for the remote and tuned in a sports channel, then stripped off his clothes as he walked through the bathroom and into his walk-in closet to retrieve a pair of sweats. A slow, low growl sounded beneath the spot his long coats were hanging.

"Out of here, Esmerelda," Mark said sternly, moving the coats aside to shoo her away. A pungent, sweet odor reached his nostrils an instant before his first sneeze. Never fond of seeing blood, Mark noted it seemed especially graphic against the light camel of his best cashmere coat. "Nope, can't fault your good taste," he muttered, allowing the coats to fall gently back into place as he backed out of the closet, and trotted to the phone.

Manny answered it on the second ring.

"Hello?"

"Is Ellie there?"

"She's not feeling very well. Who's this?"

Mark sighed in frustration. "It's Mark. I need to talk to Ellie about her cat. There's blood everywhere."

"SHE'LL BE FINE, you'll see," Manny assured her. He'd insisted on accompanying Ellie because she felt so ill.

The rhythm of the train threatened to lull Ellie's mind to numbness. She knew she looked like hell. Passengers averted their eyes. Between the crying jags and a head cold she'd succumbed to this evening, she felt as if she'd been trampled. Her eyes were red and puffy, her nose the size of W. C. Fields's. She sneezed savagely into a large crumpled handkerchief.

"Your immunity is down," Manny chided. "All that worrying over a straight man, for heaven's sake."

Ellie felt too miserable to respond. Her chest ached. And to cap off this rotten day, Mark would see her at her absolute worst. Then he'd be kicking his heels he'd broken it off.

"You shouldn't have come," Manny mumbled.

"Esmerelda needs me," she managed to get out between parched lips. It hurt to breathe.

"*You* need you. That cat can take care of herself."

"Manny—"

"Okay, okay, I'll hush."

Mark stood waiting for her when they stepped off the train. She tried to calm the beating of her heart, but it raced at the sight of him. A look of concern came over him when she drew nearer.

"Are you okay?" he asked.

"No," Manny snapped. "I couldn't talk her out of coming."

"It's just a cold," Ellie assured them, blowing her nose noisily. "How's Esmerelda?"

"In labor, as far as I could tell," Mark said, studying her. "Maybe you should go home."

"No, I want to see her. Manny offered to meet me here in two hours, if you don't mind bringing me back."

He touched her elbow and steered her in the direction of his car. "You'll stay at my place tonight," he said firmly. Then at the look of challenge on Manny's face, he added, "In a guest room."

"El?" Manny asked, apparently not ready to relinquish her to Mark's care.

"I'll call you later," she promised.

The short trip to Mark's home was silent, punctuated only by Ellie's occasional sneeze or cough. Her arms ached to touch him, or just plain ached, she couldn't tell which. When they arrived, Ellie asked, "Where is she?"

"In my closet."

She made her way up the stairs as quickly as her complaining joints would allow, Mark following her wordlessly. Esmerelda's deep purr could be heard at the top of the stairs. Ellie rushed to the closet and gently pushed back the coats. In the dim light from the bathroom, the proud mother lay on her side with her new kittens gathered around.

"Oh, Esmerelda," she said softly. "You're a mother, five times over." The cat raised her head weakly at Ellie's voice, then closed her eyes to rest. "Look at them," Ellie whispered in awe. The tiny wet balls of fur resembled hamsters, wriggling next to their mama.

"Tiny, aren't they?" Mark asked over her shoulder. Ellie stood and turned to him. "I'm sorry about your coat. I'll pay for it, and the fish, too, out of my commission."

Mark waved his hand. "Forget it."

"The kittens are just minutes old. She'll be nursing them soon, and grooming them. Would it be all right to move her bed in here? She'll need somewhere clean to take the kittens when she's up to it. We'll put the bed back in her room later."

"Sure."

Ellie conjured up a shaky smile in gratitude. Her head started spinning, and she leaned against the door frame for support.

"I'll take care of moving the bed," he said gently. "You need some rest."

She allowed him to guide her in the direction of the guest room. He turned the covers back, an odd expression on his face. "Do you need anything?"

Her head ached too much to keep her eyes open. "Can you spare a T-shirt?" she asked. "I hadn't planned on staying over."

Mark returned in a few minutes with the shirt over his arm, but Ellie lay sound asleep on top of the covers, fully dressed. He shook his head, reaching forward to touch her smooth cheek, flushed from fever. As gently as possible, so as not to disturb her, Mark undressed her down to her panties. Stopping only long enough to caress the mouse tattoo just above her bikini line, he then pulled his baggy T-shirt over her tousled head. She murmured his name groggily, then turned on her side and curled into a sleeping ball. When the temptation to stay and cuddle her became overwhelming,

Mark rose quickly and left, closing the door behind him.

After moving the cat's bed to the closet a few feet away from the birthing nest, Mark dialed Ellie's apartment and assured a wary Manny that both patients were resting. Then he climbed into his own bed as he'd meant to hours ago. But the sleep he craved eluded him. The vibes radiating from Ellie in the room down the hall beckoned him, and Mark couldn't remember ever having to exert so much control just to lie still.

11

"ELLIE." Mark was shaking her awake, gently calling her name from a distance. She moved forward through the fog until at last she managed to open her eyes. She blinked, trying to adjust to the daylight, and attempted to raise her head. A splitting pain shot through her ears, and she groaned, resting back against the pillow.

"Ellie," he repeated, his voice slightly muffled. "I think something's wrong with Esmerelda. Who is your vet?"

She licked her dry lips with her thick tongue. "Dr. Doolittle," she croaked.

"Here, have some ice." He held ice chips to her mouth and she took them with her tongue, the wetness pure heaven in her sandy mouth. "Ellie, I'm serious, I need the name of your veterinarian."

"Dr. Doolittle," she repeated. "Dr. Edmund Doolittle. His office is in Midtown. What's wrong?"

His green eyes were full of worry. "I'm not sure, but Esmerelda's acting funny. She's sneezing. Do you think she could be allergic to *me* all of a sudden?"

Smiling, Ellie shook her head painfully. She tried to sit up, but he pressed her back. "Wait until I call the vet, then I'll help you up." With a start, Ellie realized he'd tied a white handkerchief over his mouth and nose. No wonder he sounded so far away. She pointed, giggling weakly.

He shrugged. "Between the cold germs and cat hair, I figured I'd be safer this way. Someone has to take care of the rest of you." His statement seeped into her, drenching every dehydrated pore. Watching him dial directory assistance from the phone in her room, a myriad of feelings assaulted Ellie, ranging from euphoria that this was the way life was supposed to be, to sorrow that it wasn't reality.

Ever so slowly, so as not to trigger the bolting headache, Ellie inched her way up to a semireclining position on the pillow. After a series of transfers, Mark got through to the doctor. Still talking through the handkerchief, he explained the situation of Esmerelda being in his care, then described the cat's condition.

"The kittens are clean. Five of them. Esmerelda is sneezing and wheezing a lot, plus her nose and eyes are runny."

Ellie bit her bottom lip to keep from smiling at his concerned, serious tone. As if he were talking about a child.

"Yeah, she moved them to the clean bed. They've been trying to nurse, but I don't see any liquid coming out, and they're wearing her out, I think. Yeah, I put a bowl of water and some food next to the new bed, but she hasn't touched it."

After a minute, he covered the mouthpiece with his hand, still listening to the doctor. "He thinks she might have a respiratory infection. She won't be able to nurse for a while."

Alarm shot through Ellie. Would the kittens live?

Mark scribbled on a notepad. "Thanks, Doc. I'll let you know. Sure thing."

He hung up and turned to Ellie. "He says it's probably a virus and it'll have to run its course. Just in case, he says to refill the antibiotic she was taking for the bladder infection. And I'll need to pick up a bottle and a week's worth of formula for the kittens. I called my own doctor earlier for advice on what to do for you, so I'll go get everything we need and be back in a little while, okay?"

"I thought you went to law school, not med school," she whispered.

He leaned over as if to peck her on the cheek, then remembered the hankie and straightened abruptly, saying, "I won't be long. Try to get some rest."

But Ellie's eyelids were already floating down and Mark's voice fading away.

"OPEN WIDE, Esmerelda," Mark pleaded. The tablet had been easy enough to hide in her food before, but how could he get her to swallow it if she wasn't interested in eating? Following the vet's orders, he held her head with one hand, then tickled her chin to get her to open her mouth. Once he saw her pink tongue, he pushed the capsule into her mouth. "Ow!" he yelped when her teeth caught his skin as he pulled his finger out. Then he held the struggling cat's mouth shut until she swallowed. "Sorry about that, old girl," Mark mumbled through his mask. Then before he let her go, he wiped her eyes and nose with a clean handkerchief. "Now, let's see to your kittens."

He'd scrubbed his arms raw with antibacterial soap. Now he reached for the first tiny animal next to Esmerelda and cupped it in his large hand. He smiled. Its eyes were still tightly closed, its face and front paws snowy white, the rest of its sleek fur as orange as its mother's. "Boots," he dubbed it, not sure of the sex. "Open up, Boots." Mark moved the tiny nipple of the bottle to its lips. At first it resisted, but when he drizzled a few drops of the warm formula over the kitten's mouth, the seeking tongue licked it up, finally seeking the nipple. Astonishment struck Mark as the tiny animal nursed, its miniature paws kneading his hand. A strange paternal feeling crept over him. He held the kitten within Esmerelda's sight the entire time, but scant minutes passed before the tiny stomach filled and the suckling stopped.

He named the solid black one EightBall, the solid orange one, Juice, the black and white one, Jersey, and the white one with a splash of orange under its chin, BowTie. Each of them caught on as quickly as their first sibling, and were soon sleeping contentedly next to their mother. Mark even coaxed Esmerelda to take a few bites of her food, and to drink her fill of water. Then he removed the food as the vet suggested.

That done, he checked in on his other patient, pleased to see her rousing from her nap at the sound of the guest-room door opening. She was a mess, her hair limp and matted, her eyes still red and puffy. But she was beautiful. "Hey," he said, his voice filtering through the ever-present mask.

"How is she?" Ellie asked weakly.

"The doctor says she'll be fine. I got her to take the medicine, then fed the kittens."

Ellie smiled. "I wish I could've seen that."

"How are you feeling?"

"Like I've been run over by that 'kill fee' beer truck."

I'm starting to feel that way, too. "Are you hungry?"

She paused, as if checking with her stomach. "Yeah."

"Then let's get you up for a shower, and I'll fix you some soup."

"I kind of like being horizontal."

"But you'll feel so much better," he encouraged. "I'll get the water hot, then come back for you."

As he adjusted the spray of water, Mark had the distinct feeling he teetered on some kind of threshold: seeing an attractive woman in a near state of undress and not acting upon an urge. It struck him as very domestic, and not sexy at all. Perhaps this was what he needed to work through his lust for Ellie, to see her in an unsexy light.

"Are you ready?" he asked, walking into the room.

"I rather like it here," she insisted again, obviously not looking forward to the effort.

"Up you go," he said, placing a hand on her shoulder and easing her up slowly.

"Oh, my head," she said, grimacing.

"Sit on the edge of the bed for a moment to gather your strength," he instructed.

"You look ridiculous with that handkerchief tied over your mouth."

"You don't want to know how you look. Come on, try to stand up."

After a few false starts, Ellie made it to her feet, leaning heavily on Mark's arm for support. "I feel so weak," she moaned. "My teeth hurt."

Mark guided her into the guest bath toward the large

shower stall. He'd set a stool beneath the spray so she wouldn't have to stand. The hot water had moistened the air, steam rising and swirling toward the ceiling.

"Oh, my God," Ellie said when she caught a glimpse of herself in the mirror. "Who is that?"

Mark chuckled and walked her to the shower door. "Here's your towel and some sweats. Do you need anything else?"

"While you're here, I might as well humiliate myself completely and ask you to help me with this shirt. I don't think I can lift my arms and pull at the same time."

Taking a deep breath, Mark nodded. She raised her arms slowly, then Mark slid the flimsy cotton shirt up her body and over her head. At the sight of her tan lines and skimpy undies, his body overheated immediately. *Unsexy. Yeah, right.*

"Thanks, she mumbled. She rolled down her panties and kicked them off, then opened the shower door and collapsed onto the stool. Ellie leaned forward to let the warm water run over her head. "Come back in about an hour," she gurgled.

Mark exited gratefully.

By visualizing Mitzi Gaynor singing "I'm Gonna Wash That Man Right Outta My Hair," Ellie managed to give most of herself a once-over with the soapy sponge. Then she must have dozed off for a while, because she was jarred awake by a blast of cool water from the showerhead. "Mighty scrawny water heater for such a big house," she grumbled. Only the freezing air from the ceiling fan spurred her into putting forth enough effort to leave the shower and wrap the towel loosely around her chilling body. But within another few steps, she felt light-headed. Reaching for the wall, Ellie slid down to rest on the floor, leaning forward to put her head between her knees.

She heard the tap at the door, but her neck refused to raise her head. Taking a shallow breath, she mumbled a response into the towel cave she'd created for herself. Suddenly Mark was by her side, worry evident in his voice.

"Ellie, are you all right? I should have stayed."

"I'm fine," she said into the thick terry cloth. "Just light-headed."

"Light-headed? You're probably dehydrated." He tugged on her arm to pull her body up a few inches, then swung her gently into his arms, and carried her.

Even through the haze of sickness, Ellie remembered when he'd last carried her to bed, it was to make love to her for the first time. That had happened last year sometime. Or was it yesterday? She couldn't be sure. She only knew she felt much better lying down on the fresh, cool sheets. Mark must have changed them. She opened her eyes and smiled at him. "You were right. The shower did make me feel better."

Mark pulled the wet towel from her body and helped her tug the covers up to her neck. Then he disappeared for a few minutes, returning with a tray of soup, crackers and two glasses of water. The smell alone revived her enough to sit up. And she was able to feed herself. She felt her strength returning a little with each bite. "I'm sorry, Mark, I should have stayed home. Now you'll probably be sick, too."

He smiled behind his hankie and pointed to it. "Besides," he added, "I had a flu shot in the spring."

"Is that what I've got?"

"My doctor said it sounded like the flu." He handed her two tablets. "For body aches," he said.

Got anything for heartaches? she wondered. "I want to see the kittens. Are they adorable?"

His cheekbones rose above the handkerchief and his eyes danced. "Yeah. Finish eating and then see how you feel."

"How's Esmerelda?"

"Relieved, I think, that the kittens are fed."

"She'll love you for it," Ellie said, quickly taking another spoonful of soup. When she glanced up, he was staring at her, his eyes unreadable. Suddenly her stomach rolled. "Oh, God." She brought her hand to her mouth.

"What?" Mark asked, his voice anxious.

"I'm going to throw up."

Mark jumped to his feet, searching for a container, then thrust a small trash can in front of her, not a second too soon. Between every retch, Ellie prayed a time warp would open and swallow her into another dimension. Could she be any more humiliated in front of this man?

Yes, she decided an hour later when her menstrual cramps began. Fortified with a smaller second helping of broth, Ellie dragged herself to the edge of the bed and stared in horror at her reflection in the mirror. Her hair had dried pasted to her head in the back, then straight up on end all around. "I look like the Statue of Liberty," she moaned, trying to smooth down the spikes. She struggled into the sweats Mark had laid at the foot of the bed, then stumbled into the bathroom to splash water on her blotchy face and comb her high hair.

"You're up," Mark said, his voice cheerful. He leaned against the door of the bedroom, but could see her standing through the open door of the bathroom.

"Yeah," said Ellie, embarrassment flooding her body. "And so is my hair."

He grinned. "Feeling better?"

"Uh, well, no, as a matter of fact, things have taken a turn for the worse. Is there a convenience store close by?"

"Just down a couple of blocks." He stepped into her room, concern in his eyes. What do you need?"

"Could you drive me?"

"No way you're getting out in your condition. Look at you."

"Thanks."

"I mean, look how sick you are. You're hanging on to the vanity to stand up, for Pete's sake. I'll get whatever you need."

"Okay. I need tampons."

He blinked. "T-tampons?"

Ellie raised her hands. "Forget it, I'll go."

"No," Mark said hurriedly. "That's all right, I'll be glad to." He started to leave, then turned back. "Anything else?" he asked, swallowing.

"While you're in that section, could you grab some panty shields?"

MARK SAT IN HIS CAR, scoping out the parking lot of the convenience store. He'd run into neighbors and colleagues here on more than one occasion. He closed his eyes and tried to remember which aisle held feminine-hygiene products. He'd bought painkillers once in the middle aisle and figured those two things should be pretty close. After all, it was all kind of…medical, wasn't it?

The object was to get in, get the goods and get out. If he waited until the cashier's line dwindled to one or two people, he figured he could buy what he needed and be safely back in his car within three minutes.

He watched two people pump gas and then walk in to pay for it. They were the only two customers in the store. He pulled a ball cap low over his forehead, and entered the store. He kept his eyes focused on the medicine aisle, but came face-to-face with a rack of picnic supplies. He glanced over at the beer case and saw milk instead. They'd rearranged the entire store.

A woman in a striped smock was sweeping up a spill a few feet away. "Can I help you?"

"Yeah," Mark said. "Can you show me to the aspirin?"

"Follow me, sir."

She walked slowly to aisle two and swept her arm at the array of painkillers as Mark scanned the shelves for the items he'd really come to purchase.

"We have regular, extra strength, buffered, child-proof caps, nighttime—"

"Buffered will be fine," he said, then took the bottle she gave him.

The clerk stood with her hands on the broom, looking at him. "Anything else, sir?"

"Uh, I'll just look around."

"Go right ahead." She turned and shuffled toward the front of the store.

Mark walked up and down each of the eight aisles,

keeping his eyes peeled for anything that said Personal or Feminine. Nothing. He made a second pass, this time more slowly. Nada.

He glanced around nervously and spotted the same clerk watching him closely, this time from behind a counter. She elbowed the cashier, a sour-looking teenager, and whispered something, nodding toward him. The cashier carefully pushed a button on her console, her eyes glued on him.

Mark grunted in frustration. *They think I'm stealing something.*

Within a few seconds, a jacketed, severe-looking older woman appeared. Her badge said Store Manager. *Great.*

"Can I help you, sir?"

"Uh, yeah," he said, keeping his voice low. "My...wife sent me out to pick up some personal things."

The woman frowned in confusion. "Personal things?"

"You know," he said, making vague gestures with his hands. "Woman stuff."

"Woman stuff?"

He sighed. "You know, *pads* and stuff."

"You're looking for menstruation products?"

He smiled tightly and nodded, admitting defeat.

"Right this way." She took him to an end cap in the front of the store which held a mind-boggling array of colored packages.

"Did you need pads or tampons?" she asked, her face serious, her voice rigid.

"Uh, tampons."

"Will that be deodorant or nondeodorant?"

"The pink box will be fine," Mark mumbled, heat rushing to his face.

"Slim, regular, plus or super-duper?"

"She's snug—I mean, small...she's a small lady." He reached up to rub his hand across his mouth.

"That has no relevance in this case, sir."

"Uh...regular, I guess."

She sighed. "Twelve count or twenty-four?"

"I'm not sure." Mark looked around, then leaned forward and whispered, "And I'm supposed to get some panty things, too."

"Panty shields?" she asked loudly. The clerks giggled openly, as did a few onlookers.

"Yeah," he murmured.

"Regular or winged?"

Mark sighed, pinching the bridge of his nose with forefinger and thumb, "Just give me two of everything."

She stacked his arms full, and carried a couple of packages toward the counter, herself. Except now the cashier's line had grown to about a dozen. Mark swore under his breath and inched his way forward, careful of his cumbersome load.

He maneuvered around a beer display, but his knee accidently nudged the mountain of twelve-pack bottles. The seemingly unending sound of crashing bottles was superseded only by the security alarm triggered from the shattering glass.

By the time the cops arrived, the clerks had most of the mess cleaned up and tallied.

Mark used his credit card to pay for two hundred thirty-eight dollars and fifty-nine cents' worth of "woman stuff" and beer.

"BLACKWELL!"

Mark jarred awake, his eyes flying open, his head jerking back. The men around the table chuckled as Mark shook his head to clear it, then repositioned himself in the conference-room chair. He'd fallen asleep in the middle of a staff meeting!

Ray Ivan frowned. "Are we keeping you up, son?"

"No, sir, sorry." Mark ground his teeth in frustration. Between frequent kitten feedings and Ellie's bouts of vomiting, he wasn't getting much rest. Two sleepless nights in a row had taken their toll.

When the meeting ended, Specklemeyer said, "Keeping late nights, Blackwell? I wonder what you could possibly be doing." He flashed a knowing smile, then trotted out when Mark's hands tightened on the chair arms.

Patrick walked out with him. "Why don't you take the afternoon off, Mark? You look beat."

"Ellie's got the flu," Mark explained, rubbing his eyes. "And the kids—I mean, the kittens...never mind. That's a very good idea. I'll see you tomorrow."

On the drive home, Mark berated himself over the predicament he'd gotten himself into. In just two days, he'd had his fill of domesticity. He breathed a quick prayer of thanks he'd broken it off with Ellie before all this mess. At least she'd been feeling better this morning, so he'd be rid of her and her cats soon. No more sneezing, no more litter boxes, no more heating pads. Good riddance! He'd probably have to take a nap in his car when he got home, just to have some peace and quiet.

Mark wheeled into the driveway and pulled into the garage, already dreading the melee that awaited him inside. He sighed, pushing open the kitchen door, waiting for the scents of cat milk and chicken soup to hit him. His nose wrinkled. Disinfectant?

"Ellie?" he called, walking through the kitchen. A note on the counter stopped him. Ellie's feminine writing curled across the page.

Great news! We have a new landlord who lifted the no-pet rule. Manny and a friend came over to pick us up today and take us home. I took the painting, too. It's not much, but I did a little cleaning to help repay you for all the trouble. We can't thank you enough. Ellie and Esmerelda.

A paw print in—lipstick?—stood out by Esmerelda's name. The extra key lay nearby.

Mark stood stock-still. Not even a goodbye? Who's to know she wouldn't have a relapse once she got home? And she didn't know the kittens' feeding schedule the way he did. Or that BowTie ate better when his little ears were rubbed. The kittens' eyes weren't even open yet, for heaven's sake! What was she thinking?

Wadding the note into a ball, he stomped upstairs. Not a sign of them anywhere. Every room sparkled, smelling clean and fresh. Not a cat hair in sight.

Mark sneezed.

"Say cheese," Ellie said to the furry group squirming on the love seat. She snapped several pictures.

"What are you doing now?" Manny asked, walking into the living room.

"Just finishing up a roll of film. I thought I'd send out birth announcements for Esmerelda."

"I think your fever must have risen higher than any-one realized."

"Oh, stop. It'll be fun," Ellie insisted. "And a great way to find homes for the kittens. I'll send them to everyone we know."

Manny stooped to catch a wriggling kitten before it rolled off the cushion. "How soon can they be weaned?"

"Well, they're not quite two weeks old yet, so maybe another four weeks, possibly five since Esmer-elda only started nursing yesterday."

"Have you heard from Papa Blackwell?"

Ellie's heart stirred. "No," she said brightly. "Why?"

"I was hoping I'd underestimated him. Unfortu-nately, it seems I was right again."

"He did take good care of us," Ellie said, practically to herself. The way he'd watched over them in his home did more to tangle her heartstrings than his pre-vious wild lovemaking. While he'd held the trash can for her to empty her stomach, she'd felt herself sinking deeper in love with Mark. At that point, she'd vowed to leave as soon as she was physically able. That she'd been able to take the cats with her had been a bonus.

"I suppose you'll see him when you deliver the por-trait."

Ellie glanced over at the twin portraits leaning against the wall, waiting to be framed. "I was thinking of having it couriered over when it's ready."

"Why don't you get dolled up and deliver it in per-son?"

"Manny, do you honestly think a cute outfit is going

to erase the memory of him seeing my partially digested food?''

"Okay, I see your point. What are you going to do with the nude?" he asked, his voice wistful.

"Hmm." Ellie frowned. "I'm not sure. Harry will give me a better deal on the framing if I have them done at the same time. Afterward, maybe I can alter the face enough to sell it."

"You're welcome to use mine."

She grinned. "I might take you up on that."

When Ellie rewound the film and put away her camera, she discovered the two undeveloped rolls from the Blackwell picnic. Adding them to her backpack, she then changed into riding togs and grabbed her helmet.

"Back in a few minutes," she yelled.

It was a beautiful day for a ride, and Ellie hadn't been out much since recovering from her bout of the flu. She'd avoided it since she tended to think too much while cycling. And she hadn't been ready to face the sad thoughts until now.

She loved him. With all her heart. She'd seen glimpses of the kind of partner he would be. They could have made things work.

If only he loved her, too.

Mark Blackwell might have been fooled by the pheromones in the beginning, but now that he'd seen her at her worst and without the influence of the love chemicals, she didn't have a chance of moving his heart the way he'd shaken hers. So she'd grieve for a few months, then pick up the pieces and start looking again. Maybe she'd give Steve Willis a call.

Ellie dropped off the film at a one-hour developing center, then went in search of dried fruits and herbs for her latest perfume brainstorm. One good thing about being finished with the pheromones, she could wear her customized fragrances once again.

But, she decided as she rode by the sexy traffic cop without garnering so much as a second glance, it was the *only* good thing about not taking the pills. Her sex appeal had apparently nose-dived to its normal basement level.

She took a few moments to study the photos when she picked them up. She ordered lots of reprints of the best group picture of Esmerelda and the kittens. The photos of the picnic resurrected bittersweet memories. She'd gotten several good candid shots, especially one picture of Mark with his arm around his mother. Gloria was smiling, looking flushed and pretty.

A thought struck Ellie, and she checked her watch, gauging the distance to Gloria's house. Just far enough for a good ride, she decided, and she'd be back in time to pick up the reprints.

Ellie pumped her legs furiously, enjoying the rush of adrenaline. After several blocks, apartment buildings and commercial property gave way to small older homes, with tiny picturesque yards. She slowed her pedaling to check the street signs, then turned down the road where Gloria Blackwell lived.

Wheeling into the neat driveway, she hopped off her bike and walked it to the sidewalk. After removing her helmet and running her hand through her hair, she took a deep breath, then removed the photos from her pack.

She climbed the steps leading to the pretty white clapboard home, nervousness rattling in her chest. After ringing the bell and waiting a few minutes, Ellie was tempted to leave the package of photos against the door and go, but suddenly the door opened and Gloria stood there, her hair rolled in large lavender curlers.

"Yes?" she said cautiously, her hand going to her hair.

"Hi, Mrs. Blackwell. I'm Ellie Sutherland. We met—"

Recognition dawned on the woman's face. "At the picnic, I remember," she said tartly.

"Yes, well…I brought you the pictures I snapped that afternoon." She extended the envelope to Mark's mother. "There is one of you and Mark I think you'll be especially pleased with."

"Why, thank you," Gloria said quietly. "But why didn't you just give the pictures to Mark?"

Ellie's heart lurched. "We're not seeing each other anymore."

Gloria's eyes brightened a fraction. "Oh?" She flipped through the photos, a small smile playing across her mouth. "My, Audra looks hippy in that flowered dress."

"Well, I guess I'll be going." Ellie started to turn away.

"Would you like to come in?" Gloria asked, obviously uncomfortable but mindful of her manners.

Ellie smiled and shook her head. "Thank you, but I really must be going. I have some other photos to pick up—" She stopped as an idea struck her. "Mrs. Blackwell, do you share Mark's allergies?"

Gloria smiled. "Me? Heavens, no. His father was always the sniffly one. My son inherited it from him, I suppose." She counted on her fingers. "Marcus is allergic to grass, pollen, animals, feathers—"

"Whipped cream," Ellie added without thinking.

When Gloria frowned in confusion, Ellie said weakly, "The foamy kind." Then she cleared her throat noisily. "Well, anyway, maybe I will come in for just a moment." She flashed her most persuasive smile. "Do you have any pets?"

"Oн," Monica cooed. "Aren't they adorable?"

"Um," Mark murmured, studying the birth announcement Monica had received. The question "Do you have a home for one of my babies?" was lettered in bold print across the bottom of the card holding the photo. Written as a letter from Esmerelda, the announcement doubled as a solicitation to adopt one of her precious infants. The kittens' eyes were open, their heads and paws woefully out of proportion to their tiny bodies. He noted with relief that BowTie, the runt of the litter, seemed to be holding his own with his rowdy siblings.

"I think I'll take one," Monica said. "Would you tell Ellie the next time you see her?"

Mark cleared his throat. "We, uh, aren't seeing each other anymore." He shuffled through a handful of phone messages she'd handed him a few minutes earlier, hoping one of them would be from Ellie.

"What? But you were engaged!"

Mark frowned at her wide-eyed expression. "Well, now we're not."

"Just like that?"

Irritation shot through him. "No, not just like that. We both agreed we weren't right for each other."

Monica shook her head in disbelief. "Are you blind? You're perfect for each other."

Mark raised his hands in astonishment. "We're complete opposites!"

"Like I said, the perfect match."

Shaking his head, Mark headed toward his office. "You're not making sense."

"Well, at least I know why you've been so testy the last few days," she called after him.

"I have *not* been testy the last few days!" Mark yelled as he slammed his door.

12

MARK SPENT a restless Sunday morning doing nothing of significance. It was shaping up to be a blah, overcast day, and he had a mood to match. He sat down heavily on the couch and began flipping through channels. A lump under his hip caught his attention, and he pulled out a toy cloth mouse. One of Esmerelda's less destructive pastimes. The pink mouse resembled Ellie's tattoo, the memory of which had him shifting positions again.

Why couldn't he get the woman out of his mind? Somehow she'd wormed her way into his heart, then sprouted barbs, at once anchoring her image and promising bloodshed if he tried to dislodge it.

He reached over to pick up the cordless phone and dialed his mother's number, thinking he'd probably regret this phone call later. "Hi, Mom," he said.

"Hello, dear, it's so nice to hear from you. Where have you been keeping yourself the last few days?"

He swung Esmerelda's mouse by the tail. "Mostly at the office, you know, working late."

"You're so industrious, Marcus, I suppose you get it from my side of the family." She sighed. "Lord knows, your father never hit a lick at anything, God love him."

Mark frowned and leaned forward to place his elbows on his knees. "Mom, I've never asked you this before, but you and Dad seemed so different, why did you marry him? I'm sure you could have found a better provider."

She was silent for a long moment.

"Mom?"

"I'm here," she whispered.

"I didn't mean to upset you."

"If I'm upset with anyone, it's myself. I guess it's easy to point out a person's shortcomings. To other people, I suppose your father and I seemed somewhat the odd couple. I'm sorry I never took the time to tell you why I fell in love with Rudy."

He sat in silence, afraid to interrupt her train of thought.

"Your father was a wonderful, caring man, Marcus. His heart was ten times bigger than his bank account, and I knew that when he proposed." She laughed softly. "I was a comely woman in my day, and I had a fair amount of suitors, some of them real catches. But not one of them could make me laugh like Rudy."

His mother cleared her throat. "I followed my heart instead of my head. And you know what? I might have wished for your father to be more financially stable, but I never regretted my decision to be his wife."

Mark's eyes clouded and his insides tingled. Ellie's face floated in and out of his mind, taunting him. *Follow your heart, follow your heart...*

"Well, enough about that," Gloria said brightly. "How's the little painter?"

It took a few seconds for Mark to recover from his surprise. "You mean Ellie?"

"Yes, Ellie. She came by the house the other day, you know."

He frowned. "No, I didn't know."

"Brought me pictures she'd taken at the picnic—she got a lovely one of you and me together."

"That's nice." Was that cheeriness in his mother's voice?

"She offered me a kitten, too. She said you'd helped nurse them when the mother couldn't. And got her through a bout with the flu, I hear." Her voice rolled with innuendo. "Is there something you're not telling me, son?"

"What do you mean?"

"You like this girl, don't you?"

"Well, sure I like her—"

"Do you love her?"

Mark snorted. "What kind of question is that?"

"A legitimate one considering you bottle-fed five kittens for her."

She had a point. "I haven't made up my mind how I feel about her."

Gloria clucked. "It's none of my business, but I wouldn't dawdle if I were you."

"What did you two talk about?"

"Lots of things—she's really very nice, Marcus, even if she is a bit quirky. She found me a fourth for Sunday bridge tomorrow."

"She plays bridge?"

"No, but she knew that Ray Ivan plays and she called him right up."

"My partner is playing bridge with you tomorrow?"

"Stella is making coffee cake and we thought we might splurge on a bottle of sherry."

Mark smiled and shook his head. "Sounds like a day."

"Oh, look at the time," she exclaimed. "I have an appointment to get my hair done."

He laughed and injected suggestion into his voice. "Go, Mom."

"Oh, you." She giggled, clearly pleased at the prospect of having a beau.

"Uh, Mom, I was wondering…did Ellie have anything to say about, well, you know…me and her?"

"Hmm." He could picture her squinting at the ceiling. "I recall her saying something about…" She paused.

"Yeah?" he prompted.

"No," she said suddenly, "come to think of it, I don't think she said a word about the two of you."

"Oh." Disappointment squeezed his heart.

"I'll call you tomorrow when I get back from bridge," his mother promised. "Bye now."

Mark hung up the phone, then stood and grabbed his keys, fully planning to drive to the office for a few hours. Instead, he drove around in circles before he finally parked at the train station and caught the line speeding toward Underground Atlanta. Maybe she would be there, drawing caricatures. And what if she is? his conscience probed. I'll think of something brilliant to say, he promised himself.

Underground Atlanta, located in the center of downtown, boasted nearly a hundred shops in its restored multilevel structure. The lower level, abandoned early in the century when the entire city was elevated, now resembled a town street, with shops on either side, the ceiling stretching far above the foot traffic. The quaint atmosphere and curbside entertainers combined to make it a favorite place for locals and tourists.

Mark strolled the length of the cobbled main street, moving with the crowd, stopping to watch a humorous puppeteer, tossing a dollar into the man's hat at the conclusion of the show. The small knot of people gathered at the end of the indoor street might have gone unnoticed by him, except for the glimpse of a floppy hat. He walked closer, carefully staying out of Ellie's line of vision. His heart pounded at the sight of her smile as she invited a young woman to pose for a caricature. Stepping close enough to watch her sketch, Mark marveled once again over her talent, and her ability to banter with the audience as she drew.

She must have inquired into the woman's hobbies because the finished drawing showed the woman holding a flute. The woman thanked her and paid for her drawing, then Ellie glanced around for another customer. Suddenly her eyes landed on Mark, and she stopped in obvious surprise. He tingled in response to her expression. He'd been too rash in suggesting they stop seeing each other. Perhaps she would go to dinner with him this evening.

"Sir," she called to him, "would you like to have your picture drawn?"

The crowd turned for his response, and he nodded, happily stepping up and taking a seat in front of her.

She frowned, studying him in an exaggerated fashion before beginning the sketch. Mark remembered the queen-bee drawing of his mother and wondered how Ellie would portray him.

"Tell me about yourself," she said, obviously for the crowd's sake.

"I'm an attorney," he said simply.

She smiled, and spoke to the crowd. "Shall I draw him as a shark?" The audience tittered.

He shrugged good-naturedly. Ellie picked up a pastel crayon and began drawing on her sketch pad. Mark couldn't see the picture from where he sat. She looked beautiful in a pink denim jacket buttoned up to her chin over a long flowered skirt. She was multifaceted: Ellie the artist, Ellie the perfume maker, Ellie the wild lover. He smiled. And all of her personas made him happy, made him laugh. *"But not one of them could make me laugh like Rudy…"*

As she sketched, she asked him questions she already knew the answers to.

"Are you a visitor?"

Mark played along. "No, a native."

"Are you married?"

"Single."

"Do you like cats?"

"I'm allergic."

The audience watched, their faces splitting into grins as Mark's drawing progressed. He squirmed. Would she put him in his sports car? A briefcase in one hand and a phone in the other? A fancy suit and harried expression? He wouldn't blame her if she did. Work had always been his top priority. Could it be his values were beginning to shift toward settling down? Mark felt an odd sensation settle in his stomach. What good were all his possessions if he had no one to share them with? And not just anyone. He wanted Ellie.

"There," Ellie exclaimed, finishing with a flourish. The crowd laughed outright when she shifted the easel toward him for his reaction. Mark swallowed, then smiled. She'd drawn him standing, a white handkerchief tied around his mouth, concentrating intently, a squirming kitten in one hand, a bottle in the other. Four other kittens climbed his jeans legs.

"It's great," he said, looking into Ellie's bright eyes. "How are they?"

"The kittens? I still haven't found homes for Jersey, EightBall or BowTie, but I'm hopeful."

"Mom said you'd talked her into adopting one. By the way, thanks for taking her the pictures."

Ellie shrugged and nodded. "No problem."

"And for arranging the bridge matchup."

Another shrug. "I owed your mother one—and Ray, too."

He fished around for any scrap of conversation. "Monica said she'd take a kitten."

"Great," she said, her smile jarring his heart. "Three down and two to go."

Listen to your heart...do you love her?...don't dawdle... "Ellie—"

"Hey." A fair-haired man walked up to Ellie. "How much longer?"

"This was my last drawing, Steve," Ellie said, smiling up at the man. Her face flushed a becoming rose at his appearance—she was obviously pleased to see him.

Mark's gut twisted at the man's familiarity with Ellie. She tore his drawing off her pad and handed it to him. Instantly, Mark reached for his wallet.

Ellie stopped him, holding up a hand. "It's on the house." She stood and turned to the crowd. "Thank you, everyone, I'll be back next Sunday."

The Steve guy began to gather up her supplies, and Mark stood awkwardly. Ellie folded her easel, then glanced at him with a half smile. "See you around," she said, lifting her hand in a friendly wave, then walked off with the man's hand at her elbow.

Mark stood like a statue, his eyes riveted on the couple. At the end of the indoor street, Ellie stopped in front of a bag lady who sat sprawled on the curb, her possessions huddled around her. He saw Ellie reach into her purse and extract a couple of bills, then hand them to the woman, smiling and saying a few words before she went on her way.

Ellie, already on a tight budget, giving away her hard-earned money to a needy person. *Just like Dad...Rudy would have been crazy about Ellie.* He watched helplessly as the blond man put his arm around her shoulder and kissed her hair.

Mark wondered if he'd caught a lingering flu bug, after all. He suddenly felt very sick to his stomach.

"THE PAINTINGS turned out great," Harry said, emerging from the back of the framing shop with one in each arm.

Desire washed over Ellie as Mark's face leaped from one picture, his body from the other. An ornate cherry-wood frame lent more formality to his business portrait, a simple black wood frame set off the nude perfectly.

"I'll pay you," Ellie said through her tears. "Whatever it takes, just a few weeks' supply, just long enough to show him how really good we can be together."

"The pills are controlled, I can't distribute them outside the study."

Ellie sniffled loudly. "Then put me back in the study."

Handing her a tissue, Freda said, "You've already been through one cycle of pills, you wouldn't be a pure study subject again so soon."

"You've got to help me." Ellie sobbed. "What am I going to do?" She blew her nose noisily, beseeching Freda.

The lab-coated woman sat back in her chair and sighed, then rose and crossed to a file cabinet. Opening the drawer, she fingered through several folders, finally stopping to extract one. Ellie saw her name on it. She hiccuped.

Freda studied the file, flipping through several pages quickly, obviously looking for a particular piece of information. At last she found it, because understanding dawned on her face. "Just what I suspected," she muttered thoughtfully.

Ellie held her breath. When she could wait no longer, she asked, "Can you help me?"

Lifting her head to study Ellie, Freda's eyes narrowed. "What I'm about to tell you could cost me my job, so you have to swear to keep this quiet."

Her heart pounded. "What is it?" Ellie asked, her tears now dry from fear.

"Promise?" Freda asked.

"I promise," Ellie agreed, crossing her heart solemnly.

Her new friend took a deep breath, then exhaled it roughly. "In the pheromones study we conducted..."

"Yes?" Ellie prompted, making a rolling motion with her hand. "What?"

"You were in the placebo group."

Confusion washed over her. "The placebo group?"

"That's right—you were taking sugar tablets. Any so-called effects of the pills you took were self-induced."

Ellie's arms and shoulders grew weak. She lifted her wobbly hands in question. "How can that be? Men kept smelling something."

"Maybe the extra sugar you were ingesting, maybe your natural scent—who knows? The power of suggestion is not to be underestimated." Freda sat back in her chair and crossed her arms. "Tell a woman she has the ability to attract any man she wants and watch her throw her shoulders back and begin to exude self-confidence." She leaned forward, waving a hand at Ellie. "Look at you—you have all the tools, you're pretty and funny and nice. What makes you think you need some silly old pills to make this man fall in love with you? If he's that blind, honey, then he can't be the one for you."

Ellie walked home, fighting back tears. Despite Freda's pep talk, her heart dragged heavily in the wake of the woman's revelation. If Mark had never been under the influence of pheromones, then he *had* been physically attracted to her, at least in the beginning. But it also meant whatever feelings he'd developed had waned naturally, and not because she'd suddenly run out of pills.

. She'd been trying to make a mountain of commitment out of a molehill of lust.

The many tiny balls of fur that came running for her when she stepped into the apartment lifted her spirits somewhat. She grabbed a cold cola from the fridge and one for Manny as he came sauntering through the hall.

"Hey, girl."

"Hey."

He wrinkled his nose. "Are you going to be in a blue funk over Mark Blackwell forever?"

"Maybe," she said defiantly, cracking open the soda can and lifting it to her mouth.

He did the same. "Well, I for one get a boost every time I think about him getting caught in the bathroom at that restaurant." He laughed. "You've got to admit it's hilarious, El."

She smiled, begrudgingly lifted from her bad mood. "He could still get in worlds of trouble if Tony Specklemeyer decides to make an issue of it."

Manny stopped. "Is that the guy's name? Specklemeyer... Why does that name sound familiar?" He walked around the kitchen absently. "I can't think...wait a minute!" He snapped his fingers. "Does he drive a black Jaguar?"

Ellie shrugged. "Beats me. I do remember Mark saying he had a vanity license plate that says—"

"'HUNGRY,' in capital letters," Manny finished.

"How did you know that?"

He leaned against the counter, a cunning smile warming his face. "Because that vile man circles the club where I work every other night, trying to pick up the performers as they leave.'' Manny shuddered. ''He says the most disgusting things.''

Ellie's mouth dropped open. ''You're kidding?''

''Nope.''

''Well, that's no crime.''

''No,'' Manny agreed, ''but you'd think the pot wouldn't be so anxious to call the kettle black if he could be thrown into the same dishwater.''

She grinned. ''You're right. I'll call Mark later and let him in on the news. I'll bet if he just drops a hint to this guy, he'll back off.''

''If Mark hadn't been stupid enough to let you go, he wouldn't have to worry about any silly old rumors.''

Ellie walked over and gave him a bear hug. ''You're so good for me.''

He pulled back in sudden recollection. ''El, I forgot to tell you—you got a letter back from the perfume-making contest.'' He flipped through the mail on the counter and handed her an envelope.

Ripping it open, she scanned the letterhead, and read out loud. ''Dear Ms. Sutherland, we are pleased to announce your formula, Irresistible You, has been chosen the winner—'' Ellie screamed, then grabbed Manny and jumped up and down. ''I won, I won, I won!'' After a few moments of elation in which she kissed him and every cat within arm's reach, she continued reading. ''Please contact us as soon as possible to arrange to collect your winnings, and to discuss your ideas for an entire product line. We look forward to hearing from you.'' She threw back her head and squealed in delight, dancing around the kitchen. In her exuberance, she knocked against the painting, the resulting tear in the wrapping paper exposing a glimpse of dark cherry wood.

Cherry? A tiny seed of dread sprouted in her stomach, then mushroomed when she ripped the paper farther and stared at Mark's business portrait.

"Oh, my God," she breathed. "Harry delivered the nude to Mark's office by mistake!" Her eyes locked with Manny's. Thirty seconds later she pounded down the stairs, carrying the portrait under her arm. Running into the street, she hailed the first taxi she saw with a loud, ear-piercing whistle.

13

MONICA TAPPED on the door, then opened it a few inches. "Mark," she said, holding up a letter and a bulky package. "Two things—Habitat for Humanity sent a thank-you letter for your donation, and a work schedule for the next home being built."

He reached for it. "Thanks."

"If I may say so," she began tentatively.

"Yes?"

"Your donation was very generous, Mark. And for you to volunteer to help build a home for a needy family, well, it's a side of you I didn't know, but one I'm very impressed with." She smiled and sincerity shone in her eyes.

"Thank you," he said softly, placing the letter on his desk.

She held the large package toward him. "And your portrait just arrived."

His pulse leaped. Ellie was here! Mark craned his neck to look around Monica. "Where is she?"

"Who?" Monica asked, confused.

"Ellie."

"A courier delivered the painting."

"Oh." Mark tried to keep the dejection out of his

voice, but he knew he failed miserably. "Leave it, please."

Monica leaned it against his desk and made a hasty exit. Mark turned back to the work spread across his desk and forced himself to concentrate. After a few minutes, he gave up, tossed the pen straight up in the air, then watched it bounce off a corner of his desk, disappearing over the edge.

He turned to look at the package. Even after all that work, she didn't want to hand-deliver it. She didn't want to see him. Not that he blamed her. He'd made it coldly clear on the phone when he returned from Chicago that he didn't want to see her anymore. What an ass he'd been. Mark slammed his fist on his desk, but it only brought Monica back to the door.

"Mark? Are you okay?" she asked, concern written on her face.

"Fine," he said through clenched teeth. When she retreated, he massaged his throbbing hand, then reached for the painting. He fingered the wrapping for several seconds as sadness welled in him. He didn't want to see the portrait right now. He didn't want another painful reminder of Ellie and his foolish behavior.

He pushed a button on his phone. "Monica, please have maintenance come to pick up the painting and hang it." Within minutes, she entered his office again and retrieved the picture. Then Mark heard her give explicit directions to the man as to where it was to be hung.

Walking the length of his office, Mark rubbed his temples. He wished a headache would erupt, because then he'd at least have a reason for feeling lousy. This gnawing in his stomach and this heaviness in his chest were becoming unbearable. Damn! He never thought he'd let a woman get to him. Maybe he needed a vacation. That's it, he decided. *I'll go to some paradise for a couple of weeks and get Ellie out of my system. After all, she's just a woman.*

The Piedmont Park painting beckoned to him and he smiled. The picture never failed to lift his spirits. He walked over to it and absorbed the artist's impression of a day in the sun and wind. The colors, the movement, everything about it made him feel the way he did when his father took him to the park as a child. He could almost feel the grass between his toes and see his dad doing card tricks for a crowd of kids. They'd eat a cheese-sandwich picnic and fly kites, then roll up their pants and wade in the kiddie-pool. Back then, the days seemed to last forever, and every hour brought new and wonderful pleasures. He'd loved his father fiercely. He loved him still.

I really should contact the artist someday and tell him how much I enjoy this painting. He'd never before thought about the artist, and for the first time, his eyes searched the bottom-right corner for a name. There it was, in white, but very small and not quite clear. "E. Sutherland," he muttered slowly, then froze. Could it be? He double-checked the signature. A dim memory surfaced of the first day she'd walked into his office. Nice picture, she'd said.

"Ellie," he murmured. A wondrous feeling began in his chest and slowly radiated to his extremities. "I might have known it was yours." Then he threw back his head and laughed. She had brought joy into his life even before he'd known her. Mark laughed until he had to lean against the wall for support.

Another knock sounded, and Monica stuck her head in warily. "Mark? I'm worried about you."

But Mark just grinned and chuckled, waving away her concern. "Never better, Monica." She exited with a reluctant expression, then Mark slid down the wall to sit on the floor as he dissolved in laughter once again. When he'd finally regained control, he shook his head at his own stupidity. He loved Ellie, he had from the beginning. But would she give him another chance?

"I'm not letting her go without a fight," he said, pulling himself to his feet and crossing to his desk. He hadn't felt this good in days. Mark punched in Ellie's number and waited nervously to hear her voice.

"Hi, this is Ellie and Manny's place. You know the drill." Then a beep sounded.

He frowned, but began to speak. "Ellie, it's Mark. If you're there, please pick up, I need to talk to you right away." He hesitated a few seconds then said, "I l-l-lo—" He stuttered over the words, then tried again. "I l-l-lo—" Darnit, it was harder to say than he'd imagined. Mark took a deep breath. "I l-l-love you, Ellie. Please call me." He hung up slowly.

"I love you, too," Ellie said.

Mark spun around and his heart vaulted at the sight of her standing in his doorway with a package, a beaming Monica pushing her inside, closing the door.

Ellie swallowed tears that welled in her throat. He did love her.

He leaped to his feet and rushed toward her. Ellie leaned the wrapped painting against the wall, then met his embrace. He kissed her, lifting her off the ground and spinning her around. "Where did you come from?" he asked, grinning.

"Iowa," Ellie said, laughing through her tears.

"You were born in Iowa?"

Ellie nodded. "We have a lot of catching up to do."

Mark reached behind her to lock the door, then stepped to his desk and cleared the top with one sweep of his arm. He grinned. "We can start right here." Papers swirled to the ground at their feet.

Ellie's heart swelled as she allowed him to pull her to his desk. How she loved this man.

He lowered his head to hers and drew her into a deep kiss, his hands cupping her rear, pulling her against his arousal. They grabbed at each other's clothing, Ellie's skirt ending up around her waist, her panties on the ceiling fan. Mark's pants sagged around his ankles. Buttons from his shirt missiled against the wall as she yanked the front open.

"I don't have any protection," he whispered.

"I'd like to start a family as soon as possible," she replied throatily, positioning herself for his entry.

"Lots of kids?" he asked, sounding pleased.

"Five or so."

He plunged into her and Ellie stiffened with overwhelming desire.

"I feel like I could plant at least that many right now," he warned, moving inside her. They rocked together for a few seconds, then Ellie felt her ecstasy ballooning. "Mark," she whispered urgently. "Oh, Mark." He covered her mouth with his to absorb her scream of release. She heard, rather than felt, his shirt rip as she clawed his back. Suddenly he tensed and moaned low into her mouth, his body jerking in relief.

"I've missed you," he breathed.

After a few seconds, her pulse slowed. "I missed you, and so has Esmerelda."

Mark's eyes rolled heavenward. "I guess this means I'll have to paint my bedroom blue if we're ever going to have any privacy."

A loud commotion outside caught their attention. Mark frowned, pulled away, and started righting his clothes. "What's going on? It sounds like it's coming from down the hall."

Beads of perspiration popped out on Ellie's upper lip. "Mark," she said. "Do you really love me?"

His face softened. "I really do." Pulling a chair over to the fan, he retrieved her lace panties and handed them to her.

Ellie began to dress, biting her lower lip. "Do you really, *really* love me?"

Mark's smile widened even as he surveyed his torn shirt in the mirror. "You know I do. Remind me to buy you a pair of gloves right away."

The commotion was getting louder, the sound of many voices raised. Mark pulled on his jacket, straightened his tie and walked toward the door. "Something's going on."

"Mark!" Ellie grabbed his hand and fought to keep the desperation out of her voice. "Please tell me there's nothing I could do to make you stop loving me."

He turned toward her again, taking her face in his hands. "Sweetheart, there's nothing you could do to make me stop loving you.'' He lowered his mouth to hers for a quick kiss.

A knock sounded at the door. ''Mark?'' Monica asked from the other side, her voice urgent.

''Promise?'' Ellie asked, gripping his hands.

''Yes, I promise, Ellie.'' He turned to open the door, then noticed the wrapped portrait Ellie had brought. ''What's that?''

Ellie just shrugged her shoulders, smiling wide.

''The last time I saw that look, Esmerelda had gone fishing.''

''Mark?'' Monica's voice was insistent, her knocking louder.

He opened the door. ''What's all the noise, Monica?''

His secretary wore an unreadable expression, her eyes wide. ''You're needed in the boardroom. *Right away.*''

''Is something wrong?'' he asked, concern written on his face.

Monica glanced at Ellie, and Ellie saw raw admiration on the woman's face. ''Not everyone would think so.''

Mark walked out the door and strode down the hall toward the boardroom. Ellie hesitated, but Monica grabbed her arm and pulled her along. Ellie's mind raced. How was she going to explain this one?

She stepped into the crowded room a split second behind Mark, in time to see his eyes land on the sprawling nude. A roomful of suited men and women roared, Ray and Patrick both bent double, tears streaming down their faces.

Mark's jaw fell, and his mouth worked up and down, but no sound came out. He turned his head slowly to look at Ellie, and she winced, taking a half step back. This was going to be an interesting relationship.

His eyes were round in disbelief, his hands clenched in fists at his sides. "Ellie," he said, his voice ominously low. "What the hell is that?"

All eyes turned to Ellie and the room quieted, poised for her answer. Swallowing, Ellie tried to gather her courage. She lifted her chin and smiled nervously at her glowering husband-to-be.

"That, as everyone can see," she said brightly, sweeping her arm in a grand gesture, "is one well-hung portrait."

Little bundles of trouble…

KIDS IS A 4-LETTER WORD

1

JO MONTGOMERY jumped at the shrill ring of the telephone, but her eyes never left the ominous bank notice on the desk in front of her. PAST DUE. Frowning, she picked up the handset. "Montgomery Group Interiors. This is Jo."

"This is John Sterling," the caller identified himself. "I believe my secretary spoke to you last week about the possibility of you doing some work for me."

Jo's mind raced. Her weighty appointment with the Pattersons scheduled for this afternoon had pushed other projects from her mind. As she shook her head to clear it, the observation *nice voice* skated on the edge of her subconscious.

She nudged the bank statement aside and opened a file drawer, walking her fingers through the tabs. "Yes, Mr. Sterling, my notes are right here." Withdrawing a folder, she read, "Residence on 69 Kings Court, five thousand square feet." The conversation was starting to come back to her. John Sterling was an architect from Atlanta, recently relocated to Savannah. "Your secretary mentioned this would be a comprehensive job."

"The works," John Sterling confirmed, his voice rushed. Jo could hear papers rattling and the solid thunk and click of his briefcase being closed. "Furniture, wall coverings, window treatments—everything."

Oh, that voice. "I know the street," Jo confirmed. "When would be a good time to stop by and review samples with you...and your wife?"

The man stilled a few seconds, and Jo assumed he was consulting a calendar. "I'm a widower," he said softly.

Remorse shot through Jo. "I'm so sorry—"

"Why don't you come by the house today and take a look around?" His tone was back to business. "Then we can get together in a few days to discuss the job more fully."

Eligible, affluent, successful and a very sexy voice. Of course, she had Alan, so *she* wasn't interested. But if John Sterling's looks were passable, her friend Pamela would be ecstatic.

"Will you be there?" Jo asked, intrigued.

"No, but my kids and their nanny will be."

The stirring screeched to a grinding halt. Jo winced. She'd never been particularly fond of children, but the last residential job she'd taken had had her maneuvering around the terroristic activities of the five-year-old Tyndale triplets. Now the pitter-patter of little feet struck fear in her heart. "K-kids?" she stammered, forcing cheer into her voice.

"Yeah," John Sterling confirmed, his voice slowing and flooding with warmth. "But don't worry—my children are angels."

JO INSTINCTIVELY threw up her arms only a split second before the water balloon exploded against her chest. A shocked gasp stole her breath as she staggered back. The drenched salmon-colored silk coatdress instantly puckered against her skin. Carefully selected brochures and fabric samples fluttered around her feet, absorbing the pools of water, effectively ruined. Stupefied, Jo stared at the owlish face of the little blond girl who stood motionless in the doorway before her. The child's myopic green eyes nearly disappeared behind thick lenses. Little Einstein tilted her head up to look at Jo, then blinked.

War whoops rang out behind the girl, and Jo gaped in amazement. In the open family room, two male savages, disguised as a toddler and a school-age boy, raced around a middle-aged woman tied to a chair. Each armed with a bucketful of water balloons, they alternately pelted their victim. Water ran down the walls of the large empty den and puddled on the wooden floor. Colorful rubbery remnants littered the room, including the branches of a scraggly leftover artificial Christmas tree standing in the corner.

''Help me,'' the woman cried to Jo, straining pitifully at her bindings.

Jo smoothed her hands uselessly across the front of her sopping dress and addressed the bespectacled girl. ''What on earth is going on?''

The girl seemed primarily concerned that the book she protected in the crook of her arm remained dry amidst the battle, but she shrugged and stepped placidly to one side to allow Jo entry. ''The boys are playing with Miss Michaels.''

''Help me,'' Miss Michaels pleaded again as she twisted in the chair to dodge another balloon that splattered onto the floor. The woman straightened to turn fright-wide eyes in Jo's direction. "Save me from these monsters."

The monsters seemed oblivious to Jo's arrival. Shouting and singing, they moved their half-naked, finger-painted bodies around the room in abandon. Jo cautiously stepped into the room, ducking to escape another randomly flung minibath. Reaching into her purse, she retrieved a silver whistle, raised it to her mouth and blew with gusto.

Everyone froze, the boys startled into abrupt silence.

"Wow," the older boy said as he stared at Jo in awe. "Can I have that?"

"No," Jo snapped, then bit her lip to stem her mounting frustration. She took a deep breath and continued in a calmer tone, "What's going on?" Hands on hips, she glanced from the girl to the older boy.

The red-haired boy frowned and grumbled, "It's just a game. Miss Michaels said we could tie her up."

Jo looked to the woman in the straight-back chair, whose dark jersey dress clung to her frail body, her graying hair hanging in wet strands where it had been driven from its bun. She gave Jo a beseeching look. "I didn't know they had water balloons, and I didn't realize Jamie—"

"I'm Peter!" the older boy bellowed, glaring.

"Sorry," the woman said hastily, then added in a low voice for Jo's benefit, "Jamie thinks he's Peter Pan. Anyway," she continued more loudly, "I didn't realize *Peter* could tie knots so well."

Jamie-Peter grinned, his chin lifted in pride. "Cub Scout training."

Jo addressed Miss Michaels. "Are you Mr. Sterling's nanny?"

"Yes. Who are you?"

Jo glanced toward the materials she'd dropped at the door and ran a hand through the short damp layers of her hair. "Mr. Sterling's interior decorator. I take it these are his children?"

Miss Michaels nodded, then motioned with her bedraggled head. "Claire is nine, Jamie—"

"I'm Peter!"

"—Peter is six, and little Billy is almost three." At the sound of his name, blond-haired Billy held up three chubby fingers in confirmation, then hid behind Jamie, peering at Jo around his brother's bucket.

Jo narrowed her eyes at Jamie and jerked her head toward Miss Michaels. "Untie her."

The boy engaged her in a stare-down, challenging her questionable authority. "You're not my mother," he said, resentment burning in his green eyes.

Jo felt a pang of acknowledgment over the boy's loss, but knew first impressions were crucial when establishing authority—and she did not relish a repeat of the Tyndale-triplet disaster. Walking toward Jamie, she leveraged her not-considerable height advantage as she drew herself up and crossed her arms. "But I'm bigger than you are," she said calmly, then barked, "so move!"

To her surprise, he moved. The bucket of water balloons crashed to the floor as he bolted forward to fumble with the knots at the woman's wrists. Begrudgingly, Jo admired the boy's handiwork, and how he seemed to loosen the tangles easily enough. Within seconds, Miss Michaels was free.

Displaying astonishing agility for a woman her age, the nanny leaped up and dived into a nearby coat closet, emerging with a hat perched on her wet head, pulling on a coat and retrieving keys from her boxy purse. She spoke to Jo over her shoulder as she moved toward the still-open front door. ''They're all yours. Good luck.'' With that, the nanny disappeared outside.

A full two seconds passed before the woman's words sank in. Jo's stomach pivoted. ''What? Wait a minute.'' Jo trotted after the woman, stooping along the way to scoop up a handful of waterlogged samples. ''You're not serious,'' she called. Miss Michaels strode toward an older-model sedan sitting in the driveway. Jo laughed nervously and smoothed a stray lock of hair behind her ear. ''You can't just *leave*.''

The woman unlocked the car door, then turned a victorious smile toward Jo. ''Watch me.''

Jo's mouth opened and closed like a puppet's, but she couldn't speak. She gestured wildly, finally sputtering, ''But you have an obligation to watch these children.''

''So sue me.'' Miss Michaels swung into her car, started the engine, backed up and roared out of the driveway.

Panic swelled in Jo's heart as she watched the sedan disappear down the suburban street. She turned to find the three children huddled on the stoop in the warm January sunshine, eyeing her suspiciously. Was John Sterling's lucrative project worth all this extra baggage? Jo swallowed and tried to ignore the moisture gathering around her hairline. The only thing she knew about kids was that she knew nothing about kids. In her vocabulary, kids had always been a four-letter word.

"Miss Michaels was a wimpy nanny," Jamie declared. "Just like the other two."

"We don't know you," Claire said cautiously, extending a hand to Billy to gather him closer. "And we aren't supposed to talk to strangers."

Jo's mind raced. Regroup. The last thing she needed on her hands right now were three hysterical kids. She walked casually back to the children and donned a professional smile. "I'm Jo. Jo Montgomery. So now I'm not a stranger."

Jamie scoffed. "Jo's a dumb name for a girl."

Jo felt a flash of irritation at his rudeness. "It's short for Josephine. Besides, I know a girl named Jamie."

"My name's Peter!" he shouted.

Claire's chin came up. "We need to see some identification. You might be a kidnapper."

Jo let out a dry laugh. The only person less likely than she to steal a child would be her boyfriend, Alan. She flipped open her purse and pulled out her license, leaning toward Claire. "See?"

Claire frowned, obviously unappeased. "What are you going to do with us?"

Hoping the answer would come to her out of the blue, Jo stalled, shifting from foot to foot. When it became apparent that divine intervention was not forthcoming, she sighed and asked, "When does your dad come home?"

Claire shrugged. "Usually around seven."

Jo glanced at her watch. Two-thirty, and she had a meeting with the Pattersons at four. "Then let's go call him and ask him to come home early, shall we?" She moved her arms in an awkward shooing motion to herd the threesome into the house.

Sighing, Jo massaged a throbbing temple. A touch at her knee startled her, and she looked down into Billy's big green eyes. Under all that warpaint, he was a cute kid, she supposed. His other hand tugged at his bunchy cotton shorts, the only stitch of clothing he wore. Jo frowned. "It's warm today, but it's still wintertime. Where are your clothes?"

"Poopy diaper," he said solemnly, and lifted his arms to be picked up.

Jo rolled her eyes heavenward. This she did not need.

She stooped and carefully lifted the child, catching a stiff whiff of the offending diaper. "Oh, good Lord," Jo muttered, exhaling quickly. Walking as gracefully as possible in stiletto heels while holding a thirty-pound toddler away from her, Jo reentered the house.

"Claire, Billy needs his diaper changed," Jo said, and bent forward gingerly to set him on the floor. But the toddler resisted, maintaining his hold around her neck like a death grip.

"Noooooooo!" he screamed, and Jo, at a loss for his tantrum, stood back up.

"He's difficult," Claire offered unnecessarily, pushing her wire-rimmed glasses back up the bridge of her nose.

"Just go get a diaper," Jo said, awkwardly rummaging through her purse with one hand. When she found John Sterling's business card, Jamie pointed her to a phone in the kitchen. On the way, Jo gave the house a practiced once-over.

The two words that came to mind were *big* and *bare*. The rooms boasted interesting lines, which probably appealed to the architect in John Sterling, but Jo had never seen such a complete absence of color and style as existed in this luxurious house. The wooden floors were glorious, the base and ceiling moldings ornately beautiful, but the sparse furniture looked tired and lackluster, the walls appallingly naked.

"He wants you to make the house more homey," John Sterling's secretary had directed her over the phone. No small feat, Jo now realized as she heard the woman's voice come on the line.

"Hello, Susan, this is Jo Montgomery from Montgomery Group Interiors. I need to speak with Mr. Sterling." Jo shifted Billy's weight lower on her hip and felt a wide run zip down to the ankle of her panty hose.

"Mr. Sterling isn't available, can I take a message?" Jo took a deep breath. "I'm at his house and his nanny just quit. He needs to come home right away." A flash of pain in her left earlobe nearly blinded her. "Owww!" Jo screamed, bending with the pain, realizing Billy had found her dangling earring and seemed intent on pulling it clean through her ear.

Susan clucked her regret. "Mr. Sterling is on a plane en route from Fort Lauderdale. He won't land in Savannah until—" she paused and Jo distantly heard papers rattling "—six-fifteen."

Bent double and holding Billy's hand rigid, Jo said tightly, "I have a very important meeting in an hour and a half—what am I supposed to do?"

"I haven't the slightest idea," Susan chirped.

Biting her cheek to gather her patience, Jo took another tack. "Do you have a list of sitters Mr. Sterling uses?" Jo glanced over to see Jamie standing on a tall, rickety sofa table, holding the end of a thin curtain sheer and gauging the distance to the ground. *Surely he's not going to jump.*

He brandished a plastic sword in one hand to an imaginary enemy on the floor. "Off with your hand, Cap'n Hook!"

He's going to jump. "Jamie!" Jo shouted, half lunging toward him, but she wasn't quick enough and the phone cord brought her up short.

"I'm Peter!" he yelled as he grabbed the curtain with his free hand and leaped from the tall table.

"Watch out!" Jo yelled as the curtains fell. Jamie was buried in an avalanche of dingy sheers. She dropped the phone and rushed over to the little boy. "Are you all right?" she gasped. Billy cheered for his older brother.

After a terrific ripping sound, Jamie's head popped up. He grinned. "That was fantabulous!"

Jo exhaled noisily. "Get out from under there and sit still until I get off the phone."

Rushing back to the swinging handpiece, Jo shifted Billy to her other hip and said, "Are you still there?"

"Yes," Susan said, her voice smug.

"So, do you have a list of sitters?"

"I used to."

"Used to?"

"It became a short list very quickly after Mr. Sterling moved to town. Now there isn't a nanny in town who'll take on the boys."

"You're joking."

"No, I'm quite serious."

"Well, if you won't help me, then I'll find someone myself."

"Good luck," Susan said, and hung up.

Claire emerged, empty-handed. "We're out of diapers."

Jo closed her eyes and counted to ten. "Claire, is there a neighbor you can stay with for a few hours until your dad gets home?"

The little girl shook her head. "We're not allowed to go to the neighbors'."

"Not even in an emergency?"

Claire shook her head more emphatically. "They posted signs to keep Jamie out."

"I'm Peter!"

"Your neighbors posted signs?"

Claire nodded. "Yeah."

"I'm probably going to regret asking this, but why?"

"He set off smoke bombs in all of their garbage cans."

"Cub Scout training," Jamie injected proudly.

"Claire, do you have a list of sitters your dad uses?"

"It's in the back of the phone book."

Jo could feel a new kind of wetness seeping through her dress and eyed Billy warily. "Did you pee-pee?"

Billy grinned. "Uh-huh."

She groaned, then said sternly, "You have to get down for a few minutes until I can change your diaper." When the little boy resisted, she shushed him. "Just until I make a few phone calls." Claire took Billy's hand and tried to divert him.

Jo pulled out the phone book and turned to the back page. Fifteen names or so had been handwritten below "baby-sitters," but each had been struck off with a black marker. Jo decided to try anyway.

"Hello?"

"Hello," Jo said pleasantly. "Is this Carla?"

"Yes," the girl said cautiously.

"My name is Jo Montgomery and I need a sitter for John Sterling's kids—"

Click.

"Hello?" Jo asked. "Hello?"

After receiving the same response from the next two sitters, Jo glanced at her watch nervously. If she missed the meeting at four, she'd sacrifice the biggest deal of her career, and possibly jeopardize her entire business.

She scanned John Sterling's card for his office address. Maybe she'd just leave them with good ole Susan until Mr. Sterling arrived. But the address was across town, and Jo knew she'd never be able to make the trip and get back to her own office in time to meet with her client.

Frantically, she redialed Susan's number.

"This is Jo Montgomery again. I'm taking the children to my office for a few hours." She gave the secretary her number and address. "I'll bring them back here once my meeting is over. Could you let Mr. Sterling know so he'll be home as soon as possible?"

"Sure thing," Susan said cheerfully. "I hope you have good insurance."

Jo hung up, and muttered, "What a witch. Okay, kids," she announced with much false bravado. "Everyone's going with me."

"We can't," Claire said, her face serious. "We're not supposed to leave with people we don't know very well."

Jo nodded patiently. "And that's a very smart thing but right now, I have no choice but to take you with me. Tell you what, why don't we write a note to your daddy about where you're going, and we'll leave it for him in case he comes home before we get back, okay?''

Claire considered the situation, then relented. ''But I'll write the note,'' she said in a superior tone.

''Fine,'' Jo said, glancing at the boys' painted bodies. ''I'll get these two cleaned up. Where's the bathroom?''

Jamie led the way up curving stairs to a cyclone-tossed bedroom with two beds on the floor. ''This is our room,'' he announced. ''Me and Billy.''

Jo smiled woodenly, her nerves fraying at the sight of the unkempt quarters. Toys lay broken and strewn, bedcovers loose and knotted in disarray. The dingy off-white walls were punctuated with small holes and marks from shoes, paint, markers and crayons. Juice boxes and food wrappers dotted the floor. An aquarium bubbled in the corner on a broken-down desk, its water suspiciously purple. Goldfish darted from corner to corner, apparently unaffected. At Jo's unasked question, Jamie offered, ''If you mix red and blue food coloring, you get purple.''

Jo picked her way through the mess and at last they entered a spacious bathroom. A shower curtain hung from three rings. The mirror above the toothpaste-caked sink was cracked. Gaping holes and scars above the naked window testified to another set of curtains Jamie had bested.

''Well, now,'' Jo said cheerfully, ''out of these clothes and into the shower.''

''We don't take showers,'' Jamie said, his arms crossed. ''We take baths.''

"Showers are much quicker," Jo cajoled. "Besides, I know for a fact Peter Pan took a shower every day."

"Nuh-uh," Jamie said warily.

"Uh-huh," Jo said, nodding. "He hung a bucket with holes in it from a tree and stood under it for his shower."

Jamie's eyes lit up. "Let's try that—I've got a bucket and there's a big tree in our neighbor's backyard!"

"Whoa," Jo said, catching the boy as he started to run from the room. "We'll save that for another day. Right now, we're in a hurry." She leaned into the tub and turned on the faucet, adjusting the water temperature.

Jamie obliged by stripping off his shorts and underwear, then winding them up and zinging them past her head into the bedroom. Completely comfortable with his nakedness, he jumped into the tub and squealed with glee when Jo turned on the shower.

"Where's the soap?" Jo asked, opening the vanity drawer but coming up empty.

Jamie's face fell. "We gotta use soap?"

"Definitely."

"It's under my bed," he grumbled.

Jo sighed and returned to the bedroom. She lifted the corner of the covers falling over the edge of the first bed and reached underneath, terror bolting through her when her hand touched something warm and furry. Jo fell back, screaming as a creature lunged at her from the darkness.

"What's wrong?" Jamie yelled, running into the room, dripping wet.

"A rat!" Jo shrieked, jumping out of her heels and onto a chair, peering all around for the rabid creature.

Jamie giggled. "It's just Tinker, my hamster. She got loose." He bent over and scooped up the fuzzy brown animal. "Thanks for finding her, Jo."

Jo's shoulders went limp. "Anytime." She climbed down from the chair and reclaimed her shoes, then gingerly stuck her hand back into the darkness. She sighed in relief when her hand closed around a bar of dust-covered soap. Victorious, she ordered Jamie back to the shower. She returned to the bathroom and finally managed to undress Billy, then shrank back from the horrible odor as she peeled away the heavy diaper. Jo gagged twice, fighting for control of her rolling stomach.

"Peee-yuuuuu!" Jamie yelled from the shower.

"Pee-yu." Billy giggled, his hands immediately finding the smelly mess.

"No!" Jo yelled, grabbing his wrists. "I don't believe this," she muttered. Holding his hands high with her one hand, she stuffed toilet paper in her nostrils to ward off the fetid smell, then washed Billy's hands in the sink.

"Are you finished, Jamie?" she asked.

"I'm Peter!" he roared.

"Are you finished?"

"Yeah," he said, emerging to stand on the bath mat Jo had spread on the floor.

One glance at his still-paint-streaked body and Jo jerked her thumb toward the tub. "Back in, mister, and lather up." She stood Billy in the shower and ordered Jamie to look after him while she went in search of a scrub brush. Claire helped her find one in the utility room. "I need you to find a washcloth and take care of Billy," Jo said, rolling up her sleeves and heading back to the bathroom. "I'll handle Jamie."

"How much?" Claire asked, rooted to the spot.

Jo turned back. "How much what?"

"How much are you gonna pay me?"

Jo's jaw dropped. "Pay you? You're kidding, right?"

Claire pursed her lips and shook her head slowly.

Glancing at her watch, Jo decided to postpone the lecture that came to her lips. "One dollar."

"Two dollars," Claire said stubbornly, her expression never changing.

Jo crossed her arms. The little chiseler! "A buck fifty."

After another adjustment to her glasses, Claire said, "One dollar and seventy-five cents."

"Okay," Jo agreed tiredly, taking a step toward the bathroom.

"Cash in advance," Claire said, primly holding out her little hand.

Jo stopped, sighed and reached for her purse. "I see we have a budding lawyer in the family," she declared as she counted coins. "Now, let's get your brothers washed up."

Jamie was blasting out an ear-splitting rendition of "I'll Never Grow Up," and Billy was sitting in the front of the tub, safely out of reach of the cleansing spray, seemingly fascinated with the water swirling down the drain. He giggled and hiccuped, and Jo watched in amazement as a huge soap bubble formed in the O of his mouth, then popped out and floated away. Billy laughed and more bubbles floated out.

Jamie stopped singing long enough to join in Billy's laughter. "He took a bite out of the soap," he informed Jo, pointing to a missing chunk.

"Oh my God!" Jo yelled, reaching in the tub to grab Billy by the shoulders. She hardly noticed her hair and shoulders were being splattered. "Shouldn't we call poison control or something?"

"He'll be all right," Claire declared. "He's done it before, that's why we have to hide the soap. He'll have the poops for a couple of days, that's all."

Billy giggled again and blew bubbles into Jo's face. She leaned back on her heels and clutched her hand to her heart in an effort to slow her pulse. "Let's get to work," she instructed Claire.

"Yeooowwww!" Jamie screamed when Jo reached in and raked the brush across his back.

"Stand still," she ordered. "It's soft and it won't kill you." She ruthlessly scrubbed every stain from the boy's body in between his protests. With some aggressive cleaning, Claire managed to remove most of the paint from a protesting Billy. Jo glanced at her watch again. Forty-five minutes left, and the drive would take fifteen.

Claire had found two towels and the boys were soon rubbed dry, their skin now glowing pink.

"Get dressed," Jo commanded Jamie.

"We're out of diapers for Billy," Claire reminded Jo.

Jo expelled a noisy sigh and pinched the bridge of her nose with her thumb and forefinger, summoning patience. "Find a white hand towel."

Once Claire had provided the towel, it took Jo several minutes to persuade a wriggling Billy to lie still while she found a way to pin it around him. After several false starts and a couple of bloody stabs into her own fingers, she finally fashioned a passable diaper and fastened the sides with two lapel pins from her ruined dress. "Shouldn't you be potty-trained by now?" she mumbled to the bejeweled toddler.

"He's difficult," Claire repeated.

"I'm ready," Jamie announced.

Dressed in a green sweat suit, à la Peter, he stood proudly, arms akimbo, a black towel tied around his neck and trailing down his back.

"What's with the towel?" Jo whispered to Claire.

"It's his shadow," she whispered back. "Don't you know anything about Peter Pan?"

Jo took a cleansing breath. She instructed Claire to find clothes for Billy, then herded everyone downstairs. Hurriedly, she added a few sentences to Claire's note to John, then locked the front door with a key Claire produced on a chain around her neck.

As Jo unlocked her sports sedan, however, Claire balked. "Where's the car seat?"

Jo blinked. "Car seat?"

"For Billy, he has to sit in a car seat."

Jo chewed her bottom lip. "Really?"

Jamie frowned, disgusted. "Aren't you a mommy?"

Foolishly feeling as if she'd just received the ultimate insult, Jo cocked an eyebrow and leveled her gaze on him. "As a matter of fact, no, I'm not a mommy."

"We have an extra car seat in the house," Claire offered quietly, pushing her glasses up.

The trip back inside for the car seat was followed by another for Billy's bedraggled blankie, then one more to retrieve another book for Claire. Somehow in all the commotion, the girl had managed to finish reading the first one.

By the time she strapped everyone in, Jo had eleven minutes left to make the fifteen-minute drive. As soon as she turned over the engine, her car phone rang.

Jo picked up the handset as she pulled out of the driveway. "Hello?"

"Josephine, where the green blazes are you?"

Jo smiled at her aunt's familiar habit of misspeak. "Hattie, I'm on my way. Have the Pattersons arrived?"

"With shoes on."

"You mean, 'with bells on'?"

"No bells, dear, just shoes."

Jo shook her head and muttered a prayer for strength. "Stall them—I'll be there in a few minutes."

"Jo, how was the Sterling appointment?"

At that precise moment, Billy's blankie slid to the floor. On cue, the toddler's bottom lip jutted out, his head dropped back and he howled.

"Jo? Do I hear a baby?"

"Shh, shh," Jo breathed to Billy, and switched the phone to her left shoulder. Keeping one hand on the wheel, and one eye on the road, Jo stretched as far as she could, but couldn't reach the blanket without risking life and limb of everyone in the car.

"Jo? Are you there?"

Billy's cries had reached a crescendo when he saw even Jo couldn't get his blanket back. "Hattie," Jo gasped. "I'll be right there." She slammed down the receiver and tried to console Billy, but he thrashed his arms in fury.

Jo looked in the rearview mirror for help, but Claire

had buried her nose in the new book. Without glancing up, the little girl did offer one morsel of wisdom.

"He's difficult."

Jamie seemed quietly preoccupied with making tortuous faces at the little girl in the car next to them. Both of the older children appeared adept at tuning out their little brother—an acquired skill, Jo noted.

She welcomed the next red light, and used the opportunity to unfasten her seat belt and retrieve the blanket, but Billy was wound up and not ready to relinquish his control over his captive audience. The car to her left honked and Jo looked over to see the woman passenger had rolled down her window. Jo frowned and did the same, only to hear the woman screech, "Can't you control your own children? That boy of yours is scaring my Kathy."

Jo craned her neck in time to see Jamie cross his eyes at the little girl. "Jamie!" she admonished over Billy's cries.

"I'm Peter!"

"Stop making faces!"

Jamie glared, and sat back in a huff, then shouted, "Itsy, Bitsy Spider."

"What?" Jo asked, wincing at the decibels Billy reached.

"Sing 'Itsy, Bitsy Spider,'" Jamie yelled. "It's Billy's favorite."

Jo rolled her eyes, and declared, "I don't sing." But minutes later when Billy had turned blue from his efforts at breaking the sound barrier, she sighed and started singing low and off-key.

Billy stopped midscream and looked at Jo expectantly.

"You gotta do the hand motions," Jamie supplied in a bored voice.

Jo leaned forward and slowly banged her forehead against the steering wheel.

JOHN STERLING shifted in his first-class seat, then folded a stick of sugarless gum into his mouth and began chewing to ease the pressure in his ears. Somewhere behind him in coach an infant started crying, and he hoped the mother knew enough to give it a bottle or a pacifier to suck on. An instant later, he bit down on his bottom lip and shook his head in self-recrimination. As if he were some parenting guru to dole out advice.

The faces of his children passed through his mind— Claire and Billy so blond, Jamie as darkly redheaded as himself. His heart wheeled, as it always did when he thought of his rambunctious crew. Once the plane reached cruising altitude and the drink carts emerged, he inserted a credit card into the phone slot on the seat in front of him and released the receiver. Within a few seconds of dialing, the flat peal of his home phone sounded in his ear. After five rings, the recorder picked up and Jamie's gruff little voice came on the line.

"This is the Sterling house, home of the great Peter Pan. Leave a message at the beep and my daddy'll call you back. Oh, and talk fast."

John smiled and injected extra cheer into his voice. "Hey, kids, it's Dad. Just calling to see how things are going. I'm sure you're being very good for Miss Michaels, because we're lucky to have her and we *really* need to keep her around, right, guys? I'll be home in time to tuck you in." John swallowed. "Daddy loves you. Bye."

Surmising Miss Michaels had taken the kids to the park in the unusually warm weather, John breathed a word of thanks to have acquired a nanny of her qualifications on such short notice. Both Miss Springston *and* Miss Anderson had left him in the lurch, but at last he'd found someone whom he could trust.

He dialed again and Susan's voice came on the line.

"Just checking in," John said, opening his pocket calendar on his knee. "Anything going on this afternoon?"

"Mr. Tyler called around two-thirty about the zoning for the Standler Mall. He needs to talk to you ASAP."

Susan sounded especially nasal today, he noted with mild irritation, scratching abbreviated notes on any patch of white space he could find.

"And Stewart phoned—he wants you to speak at the builders' association luncheon next Thursday."

"Anything else?"

"No, sir."

"Did Miss Michaels call?"

"Oh," Susan said with sudden recollection in her voice. "She quit."

John's heart and pen stopped. "She what?"

"She quit," Susan repeated.

John nearly dropped the phone, but juggled it back to his ear. "Wh-who's with my kids?" he sputtered.

"Jo Montgomery."

Recognition tickled the perimeter of his brain. "The interior designer?"

"That's correct."

In the past month, John had learned it was best to speak calmly and clearly when dealing with Susan, even when she didn't. *Especially* when she didn't. He sighed. "Susan, start from the beginning."

"Miss Montgomery stopped by your home today, and apparently your nanny walked out while she was there. She couldn't find anyone to watch the children, so she took them back to her office."

"You're kidding, right?"

"No." Susan sounded very serious.

Incredulous, John yelled, "You let a woman I don't even know take my children away from my home and to her office?" An older man sitting next to him lowered his newspaper to stare. John passed his hand over his face. Too late, he realized he'd gone too far. The phone line fairly crackled with Susan's indignation.

"Sir, contrary to popular belief, a secretary is not the gatekeeper to her boss's personal life."

John sighed again, this time contrite. "You're right, I'm sorry. I can't believe Miss Michaels just up and walked out."

"Yes, sir." Susan cleared her throat. "Well, Ms. Montgomery said she'd take them back home after she met with a client, and asked that you meet her there as soon as possible."

"Thank you, Susan." John hung up, annoyed and worried. He flipped to the back of his organizer to find Jo Montgomery's card. Four times he dialed the number, only to receive a busy signal on each attempt.

Never more than a split second from his mind, the

children had crowded his brain all day, leaving less room than usual for demanding work pressures. John brought one hand up and absently stroked his chin. He missed Annie every day. Unbidden, hot tears pricked his eyelids, but he bit the end of his tongue hard and the moisture vanished just as quickly. Life goes on, he'd told himself a million times in the two years since her car accident.

Moving from Atlanta to Savannah a month ago had been a good step for him and the children. Christmas in their new, empty home had been heartbreaking, but less brutal than last year in Atlanta. Jamie and Claire would enter new schools in a few days for the last half of the school year, and he'd promised himself he'd start looking for a suitable mother for his children as soon as possible. Someone like Annie...dear, sweet Annie, who wore bright aprons and made chocolate-chip cookies and gave puppet shows for all the kids in the neighborhood.

He had met several women since Annie's death, anxious to salve his deep wounds, but he hadn't been able to conjure up an interest in most of them. The few who had warranted further consideration had soon proved themselves to be less than ideal mom material—most of them were too involved with their own career. Three months ago, his sister, Cleo, had sat him down and explained the harsh reality.

"John," she'd said, smiling sadly, "you're not going to find an exciting career woman who's willing to give up everything she's worked for to take care of someone else's kids. And you're not going to find many single women in Atlanta who *aren't* career-oriented."

Thus the move to a smaller town where he thought his chances of finding a homey wife might be better. Not that he had anything against working women. Some of the most interesting women he'd met were just as driven to succeed as their male counterparts. But he felt his children deserved a full-time mom to make up for lost time.

John nodded his head firmly in silent determination. He'd date every eligible woman in Savannah until he found another woman like Annie, someone for whom mothering was...first nature.

"HURRY UP!" Jo screeched, practically dragging the children through the door of her small office building. As she trotted down the hall, Billy perched on her hip and her briefcase bouncing against her other leg, she could hear Hattie saying, "I'm sure Jo will be here any minute. She had to...er..."

Her beloved aunt turned from the man and woman standing before her and stared at Jo coming down the wide hallway, the older woman's glassy eyes bulging in shock. The consummate professional, Hattie recovered quickly. "She had to...pick up the children, of course." She beamed at Jo. "Darling, I was getting worried about...all of you."

"Forgive me for running late," Jo said, setting down her briefcase and extending her hand to the coifed, well-preserved woman standing beside Hattie. "I'm Jo Montgomery, and you must be Melissa Patterson."

"And my husband, Monroe," the woman said, inclining her blond head slightly. "Oh, aren't they precious?" Mrs. Patterson reached over to tweak Billy's rosy cheek.

The toddler gave her a toothy grin, and said, "Me Billy."

"And who else do we have?" Mr. Patterson smiled warmly at the other two children.

Jo swallowed nervously. How would she explain this situation? "This is Claire and Ja—Peter. Claire and Peter."

The tall, thin man with heavy black glasses leaned over to shake hands with the older children, then straightened. He smiled at Jo, his eyes dancing. "Ms. Montgomery, I must admit, in our eyes you already have an edge over your competition for our day-care account."

"Well," Hattie injected brightly, her eyes warning Jo to keep quiet, "why don't I take the children and let the three of you talk business?"

"Who are you?" Jamie asked, frowning at one of Hattie's trademark feathered hats.

Jo laughed nervously and scrambled to cover Jamie's gaffe. "Today Aunt Hattie is…Mary Poppins, right, Hattie?"

Hattie nodded, reaching for Jamie's hand. "Yes, indeed. Let's go fetch my umbrella, shall we? And I've got three lollipops in my office that need licking."

"Any green ones?" Jamie asked hopefully, already won over.

Hattie smiled brightly. "Let's go see."

Claire glanced at Jo with questioning eyes, but Jo nodded encouragingly and handed Billy to his sister. A remarkable feeling of relief swept over her as she saw the children walk away with Hattie. Free at last. Had she been gone only two hours? It seemed like two lifetimes. She turned to the Pattersons and awkwardly swept her arm in the direction of the meeting room. Her muscles had grown weak lugging Billy around. "Shall we?"

"Ms. Montgomery," Melissa Patterson said as they walked, "you failed to mention you had three children when we spoke on the phone. I've very glad we decided to consider your design firm for a bid on our account."

Jo's smile froze and she nearly stumbled, but caught herself and kept moving forward, flanked by the Pattersons.

"Oh, yes," Mr. Patterson continued. "It's crucial that the interior designer we hire for our day-care chain is in tune with children. We don't think we could have built such a successful business had we not raised five of our own."

Panic spiraled through Jo. The Pattersons owned twenty-one day-care centers in and around Savannah. Her business had been mercilessly slow, and she'd taken a calculated risk by investing heavily in a new sophisticated computer system. Last week her accountant had announced he wanted his quarterly fee in advance. And this morning's past-due loan notice was still vivid in her mind.

This business was her livelihood—and her aunt Hattie's. Adding the Pattersons to her clientele would provide her with the capital she needed to recover and expand. The Pattersons were looking to overhaul and update every day-care center they owned. This project promised to be so lucrative, the couple were conducting interviews just to select firms to *bid* on the job. Jo knew she could do a top-notch design job for them. But she couldn't take steps to acquire the account under false pretenses—could she?

"Well, the children aren't really mine," Jo said, then at the startled looks on the couple's faces, added, "I didn't give birth to them, that is."

Mr. Patterson smiled. "Adopted?"

"Er, no. Their father—"

"Ah, stepchildren." He gave her an understanding nod.

Mrs. Patterson touched her arm. "Very admirable of you to take on three of them, and a toddler at that."

Jo swallowed. Ethical quicksand.

Mr. Patterson squinted at Jo and laughed. "I thought it was a bit odd that a dark-haired woman like you would have blond and redheaded children."

"Do they take after their father?" Mrs. Patterson asked.

Jo had no idea. "Um, yes."

"Is he a blonde or a redhead?" the woman pressed conversationally.

"Um, kind of…strawberry blond," Jo improvised, beginning to perspire as they entered the meeting room. She hadn't given John Sterling much thought since their telephone conversation this morning, but now pictured him as an affluent absentee father who obviously neglected his children. Jo frowned, then turned her attention to the matter at hand—saving her business.

Upon entering the conference room, Jo guided the Pattersons into comfortable stuffed chairs around a small, elegant dark cherry table. Walking toward a computer in the corner of the room, Jo was alarmed to find herself shaking. The day's events and her own little lie of omission were beginning to take their toll.

Only then did Jo realize how disheveled she must appear to her wealthy clients, and, for an instant, she panicked. In less than two hours, those kids had ruined a two-hundred-dollar outfit and had undone an image of polished self-confidence she'd worked for years to develop. An instant later, she'd made a decision: So what if she let the Pattersons believe the kids were hers? She needed this account desperately. John Sterling and his brat pack owed her that much, right?

She took two deep breaths and faced the couple, remaining on her feet to give herself authoritative leverage. "I'd like to demonstrate a computer package I've invested in which I think you'll agree gives my firm an edge over every design company in the area." Jo sat down before the computer workstation and forced her quaking hands to still as she placed them on the keyboard. Within a few keystrokes, a large overhead screen mirrored the display on Jo's monitor.

"The program allows me to build structures to any specification and populate the rooms with furniture, wallpaper, window treatments, floor coverings and accessories. All of my major suppliers provide their patterns and colors on databases which the program accesses. I can develop a room's theme with only a few movements of the computer mouse." Jo demonstrated, pulling together a child's bedroom using an outer-space motif in less than two minutes.

"If you decide you'd like to see the design in a different color," she went on, "we can view the change right here without spending an additional cent." Two mouse clicks changed the room from dark blues to deep golds. The Pattersons murmured and nodded appreciatively, exchanging glances. Jo's confidence flooded back as she launched into the real selling point of the package.

"We can stroll through the rooms I design for you online just as a person would naturally. We can turn the camera, so to speak, and view the room from any direction, any angle." Jo showed them the stunning effects of the program which bordered on virtual reality.

"Once a scheme has been decided upon," she told them, "the program also estimates materials needed and labor hours required, depending upon the complexity of the decor. I can have an updated estimate within seconds of making changes." The presentation was powerful, and after twenty minutes, the Pattersons seemed appropriately dazzled.

Watching their expressions, Jo pushed down her uneasiness about misleading the couple. Children or no, she was the best person to do the work. She'd spent hours wooing the Pattersons to her office and cataloging ideas for the project—she wasn't going to lose this crucial job to a competitor just because she wasn't maternally inclined.

For an instant, anger sparked within her. As a woman, she was expected to like and want children. Even the close friends to whom she'd confided her true feelings on the subject had patronized her. "You'll feel differently someday," they'd said.

And her mother. Oh, God, that was another story.

She forced her attention back to her clients. Standing, Jo faced the seated couple and made eye contact. "I'd like the chance to visit one of your day-care centers and then take a few days to develop a full computerized presentation. My bid will be competitive, and you'll be able to view the entire job before you spend a dime.''

Mr. and Mrs. Patterson glanced at each other again, and Jo saw the woman nod almost imperceptibly. A barb of excitement bolted through her and Jo resisted the urge to grin. But Mr. Patterson frowned slightly. ''We would need to see your presentation Monday afternoon—can you be prepared by then?''

Jo's mind spun. Today was Thursday. She'd have to work most of the weekend, but she could easily finish the presentation with time to spare. ''Yes. But I'd like to arrange a visit tomorrow morning at one of your day-care centers to make a few notes.''

Mr. Patterson turned to her and said, ''We like what we've seen so far, Ms. Montgomery. It seems you have both the personal and professional qualifications for the job. If your presentation is as impressive as your preliminary legwork, I think we'll be doing business.''

Despite the worry triggered by his comment about her ''personal qualifications,'' Jo conjured up a professional smile and extended her hand to the Pattersons in turn. On the way to the door, Jo consulted her day calendar to set up a time Friday morning to walk through one of the day cares.

''We'll meet you there tomorrow at ten,'' Mrs. Patterson said, smiling. ''Bring your children along—I like to gauge the reactions of little ones to our centers.''

Jo's smile froze and she could only manage to say, ''I'm not sure what their father has planned for them, but we'll see.''

Mrs. Patterson stopped at the door and leaned toward Jo, giving her a generous smile. Pointing to the dark wet stain on Jo's hip, she said, ''I see you're potty-training your toddler. I noticed his creative diaper sticking out of his waistband. Diapering him with a towel is a wonderful idea because he'll be uncomfortable when he wets. He should be trained in no time. You're a good mother, Ms. Montgomery.''

An uneasy smile found its way to Jo's shocked mouth. She managed to nod and mumble something nice in return. As soon as the door closed behind the Pattersons, her body went slack with relief. Then she grabbed her purse and dashed into the ladies' room. One look in the mirror elicited a groan. Her hair was a mess, her dress rumpled and wrinkled. Her makeup had vanished, except for the black smudges of mascara beneath her dark eyes. She reached into her purse for a hairbrush, but her fingers touched pink vinyl. Withdrawing her palette of birth control pills, Jo impulsively popped one into her hand and downed it without water.

Another glance in the mirror revealed a dark brown stain over her left breast. Cautiously, Jo lifted the fabric and sniffed, confirming her worst fear. Closing her eyes, she valiantly fought the urge to swallow a second pill.

''THIS IS John Sterling. I need to speak with Jo Montgomery.'' He switched his cellular phone to his left shoulder and squinted at the street sign he passed.

An older woman who'd identified herself as Hattie responded in a tone somewhat higher than when she'd first answered. ''Oh, Mr. Sterling. May I say what beautiful children you have?''

Pride outweighed his annoyance at not yet being able to get through to the woman who'd taken his children without his permission. It wasn't often people praised his children. "Thank you," he said sincerely, then glanced around frantically to get his bearings. Savannah was still new to him, and, after dark, landmarks looked different. But now the third appearance of a neon sign flashing Pinky's told John he was indeed driving in circles. Banging his fist on the steering wheel in frustration, he turned his attention back to the phone and asked, "May I speak with Ms. Montgomery?"

"She just left, sir. We fed the children and she's taking them back to your house."

John closed his eyes briefly, then thanked the woman and hung up. He'd hoped to beat them home, anxious to see his children's faces and to tuck them in. A dull worry descended when he remembered he didn't have a sitter for the following day. He glanced at the digital clock on the dashboard. Seven-thirty. Probably too late to round up someone tonight. He sighed, suddenly craving a cigarette. The desire for one hadn't been this strong in the three years since he'd quit, but he forced it back.

One hour later, John pulled into his driveway. He'd left the damned garage-door opener inside, so he parked next to an unfamiliar sport sedan. A low light burned from the den window, and various other lights glowed throughout the big house. At least the children were still awake. John drew his briefcase and suit jacket from the passenger seat, and walked the short distance to his new home, shivering in the late chill. As always, he hesitated at the door.

God help him, he didn't want to go in. Into a houseful of sad kids he couldn't console or control. Into empty, unfamiliar surroundings. Into a big lonely bed. Some nights were more overwhelming than others. Tonight, unlocking the door was pure torture. Only the thought that his kids were probably unsettled and upset at having spent the afternoon with a stranger moved him forward.

Quietly closing the door behind him, John stepped into the foyer which opened immediately into the large family den. "Father Knows Best" played on the television, the canned laughter echoing in the large room. A box of disposable diapers sat in the floor. John automatically reached up to loosen his tie, scanning the room, but his hand froze in midair.

On a small cream-colored rug in the middle of the wooden floor, a slim woman lay asleep on her side, her knees and arms bent in repose, her slender legs extending from her slightly rucked-up dress. Her pumps had slipped off her shapely feet and lay on their shiny sides, a stray silver icicle from the Christmas tree wrapped around one stiletto heel. Short dark hair swept across her face, obscuring it from his view. And piled around her were all three of his children, Billy nestled against the woman's chest, Jamie close behind him, and Claire flat on her back less than a half foot away, her small fingers touching the woman's limp hand.

John inhaled sharply, stretching his neck forward and squinting to refocus. His heart pounded, and all moisture left his mouth. He swallowed painfully, then took a silent step forward before setting down his briefcase. As he moved closer, the woman moaned and turned her head. He stopped and watched the dark hair slide from her face, revealing a beautiful profile of straight nose, high cheekbones, full mouth and sculpted chin. As she worked her mouth in sleep, a dimple appeared and disappeared beneath her right cheek.

Holding his breath, John allowed his eyes to travel down the length of Jo Montgomery, taking in her rounded breasts, the curve of her hip, the fine bones of her slim legs. John felt an unfamiliar tightening in his groin and pulled at his waistband. The two years alone had been excruciatingly long. Taking a cautious step forward, he bent at the waist and searched for the one item he sincerely hoped the slumbering beauty didn't possess: a wedding ring. Her shapely left hand curled toward the rug, her fingers hidden. Damn! The most unusual scent reached him, kind of...fruity. Apples? No. He sniffed again. Pears. The woman smelled like pears. He shifted uncomfortably.

His children were motionless, except for Billy's occasional sucking on the two fingers he'd thrust into his mouth. John sighed. Between that mangy blankie, the finger-sucking and the aversion to potties, Billy was fast becoming a therapist's dream. Jamie lay tangled in his black terry-cloth shadow, his red hair in wild disarray. Shaking his head, John wondered if he'd made a mistake by playing along with his son's fantasies, which seemed to have grown more creative in the past few months.

And Claire. John smiled, and squatted to stroke the fine white-blond strands splayed across the rug. The very image of Annie, but as introverted as her mother had been outgoing. Bookish and solemn, his daughter rarely spoke, and displayed emotion even less. His concern was greatest for Claire because she remembered Annie the most and missed her so.

Nothing to worry about, a child psychologist had told him. Love, patience, and time healed all wounds. Children are more resilient than they look, she said.

And other comforting words John prayed were true. Here they were, so starved for female affection, they lay curled up to a virtual stranger. His eyes began to sting again.

"Hello," a woman's voice whispered.

Starting badly, John blinked and caught himself with one arm to keep from falling on his behind. "Hello," he said quietly. Sleeping Beauty had the biggest, brownest eyes he'd ever seen.

Jo squinted into the light of the ornate ceiling fan, trying to focus. She sincerely hoped the man squatting near her was John Sterling and not a burglar, because she didn't have the strength to run for help. Billy stirred beside her, then quieted.

"I'm afraid to move," she said, grimacing at the blurry man. "I might wake them." A thought so harrowing she was willing to lie there until the Second Coming.

"Give me your hand and I'll help you up." She immediately recognized his deep voice. Hesitantly, Jo lifted her hand and was pulled gently to her stockinged feet. She swayed to gain her balance, and his strong arm steadied her.

Jo lifted her head to thank him and stopped. John Sterling's eyes were the palest green, framed with gold lashes and set in a tanned face sprinkled with dark freckles. Deep auburn hair as thick as an animal's pelt faded to burnished gold around his temples, the same color as his sunlightened eyebrows. His square jaw glinted with a day's growth of red-gold whiskers—he looked like the type who might have first shaved in the sixth grade, a man who could sprout a beard over a long weekend. A half smile played upon the man's mouth, revealing laugh lines that promised to become deep channels with the accompaniment of a grin.

She searched his eyes, and found...surprise, awareness, confusion. His lips parted slightly and Jo experienced a strong sensation of déjà vu. She knew this man, but had never met him. An age-old acquaintance in a stranger's body. *Where have you been?* she felt on the verge of asking.

He was a tall man, broad-shouldered and imposing. His tie was loosened and his shirtsleeves rolled up just below his elbows, revealing more golden hair on his thick forearms. He could not have looked more masculine if he'd been wearing a loincloth and carrying a shank of raw meat. Jo knew her mouth hung open because she could feel her breath moving across her teeth, but only two words came readily to mind.

''Me Jane,'' she murmured.

His forehead creased and he leaned toward her slightly. ''Excuse me?''

''Me Jo,'' she said more loudly, then recovered and stepped back, causing him to relinquish his hold on her arm. ''That is, I'm Jo. Jo Montgomery.'' She smiled awkwardly, then extended her hand. He clasped her clammy hand in his warm one, sending so much electricity through her nerve endings, Jo was sure he could see her skeleton like a flash of green X ray.

''John Sterling,'' he said, the corners of his mouth lifting higher. ''It seems I'm indebted to you, Ms. Montgomery.'' He released her hand and waved an arm toward his sleeping children.

Jo glanced at the tangle of little arms and legs, and gave him a small shrug. ''They weren't much trouble,'' she lied outrageously.

He laughed softly. "Your clothing tells a slightly different story."

Self-consciously, she ran a hand over the neckline of her ruined coatdress, coming up with a gob of stale peanut butter. With a little laugh, Jo wiped it on her smudged lapel and said, "Okay, maybe they were a little less than *angelic*."

John had the grace to blush. Splaying his hands apologetically, he said, "When I made the remark this morning about my kids being angels, I didn't realize you'd be stuck watching them most of the day. I'm sorry, and I'm also very grateful. Please send the bill for your dress and the diapers to my office."

"I'll put it on your account," Jo said cheerfully, referring to her future design job.

"It's pretty bleak around here, isn't it?" John asked, surveying the room. "How soon can you get started?"

"I didn't get a chance to look around today, so I'll come back tomorrow if someone is going to be here."

Shifting uncomfortably, John said, "I don't have a sitter lined up yet, so I might have to take the kids to the office with me in the morning, but I'll be back around lunchtime. You can wait until then or I'll give you a key."

Remembering her morning appointment with the Pattersons, Jo made a snap decision. "I can come by in the morning to make some notes and watch the kids until you get home."

Incredulity registered on John's face.

"That is," she continued nervously, "if you don't mind me taking them on a quick errand."

"No," he nearly shouted, and Jamie turned over on his stomach. They both glanced down and held their breath. "I mean, no," John said, his voice lower. "I don't mind at all. But," he hastened to add, "that's not necessary."

"I want to," Jo said, smiling tightly.

John angled his head. "Really?"

Swallowing guiltily at the delight shining in his eyes, Jo put her hand behind her back and crossed her fingers. "Really."

3

"WHERE'S JO?" Jamie murmured sleepily, his eyes only half-open. Claire and Billy were already safely tucked in and slumbering. Normally, John saved Jamie until last, since he was the most difficult to persuade to go to sleep. Which amazed John considering the energy his son expended in a day.

"She had to go home," John said gently, pulling the sheet over Peter Pan pajamas and up to his son's strong little chin.

"She's a nice lady," Jamie said, blinking heavily.

John smiled. "Liked her, huh?"

"Yeah." Jamie nodded, his hair dark and unruly against the white pillowcase. "Can we keep her, Daddy?"

The question slammed into John like a steel beam. His smile vanished and he searched his son's questioning green eyes, swallowing the lump that lodged in his throat. Slowly reaching forward to tousle Jamie's hair, he said, "She's not a puppy, son."

"But she's pretty—don't you like her?"

"Jamie—"

"And she's no one else's mommy—I already asked."

John blinked fiercely. "Is that so?"

"Uh-huh."

He couldn't fault his son's taste. "Well, there's more to it than that." John spoke carefully. "Being a mommy is tough work, and not every lady wants to have children."

Jamie's face crumpled. "She didn't like us?"

"Of course she liked you," John assured him. "And she's going to fix up our house, so she'll be around a lot."

"When will I see her again?"

"She's coming back in the morning to start working. In fact, she's going to keep an eye on you guys until I get home at lunch."

A grin appeared, revealing small white teeth. "So she *does* like us."

"I guess so," John said, his heart crashing at his son's elation. He raised his index finger and wagged it with mock fierceness. "But no more quizzing her about being a mommy, okay?" He leaned forward and whispered, "We don't want to scare her off!"

Jamie giggled, and John kissed his forehead. "Now go to sleep so you'll be wide-awake when she gets here."

In a rare moment of obedience, the little boy rolled over and squeezed his eyes shut. John patted him on the behind before he stood up. He switched on the Tinker Bell night-light, cast one more glance over his sleeping boys, then left the room with a hundred emotions, new and old, jabbing at him.

Ten o'clock. Too early for bed, but he didn't feel like opening his briefcase. John slipped off his dress clothes, tossed his rumpled shirt into a dry cleaner's bag and rehung his suit. He turned his wallet over in his hands several times, then opened it, flipping past the credit cards until he came to Annie's picture.

Just a snapshot, the picture had been taken when she was pregnant with Jamie. Radiantly round, her pale blond hair was tossed over one shoulder, her hands resting proudly on her protruding tummy. John remembered the day, he'd insisted on taking the picture because she had never seemed more beautiful.

Carefully, he removed the faded photograph, cropped to fit inside the plastic sleeve, and rubbed his finger over the image of her smiling face. Gone but not forgotten. In a split second of revelation, John suddenly realized he still compared every woman he met to Annie. But it wasn't fair to the other women, it wasn't fair to him and it wasn't fair to his children.

John slowly walked to his nightstand and slid open the drawer. Annie's family Bible rested near the bottom, under paperbacks, magazines, old newspapers and other odds and ends. He opened the cover and placed her photo inside, on the page where her ancestors' names were logged, where he'd penned her date of death the afternoon he'd returned from the funeral. "Goodbye, Annie," he whispered as he closed the cover and replaced the volume.

John dragged his hand over his face and exhaled noisily, then turned toward his cavernous bed. Alone again. He was beginning to loathe the smell of his own faded aftershave on the pillows, night after night. The scent of pears suddenly seemed especially appealing.

He stretched out on top of the comforter and reached for the remote control, again experiencing the need for nicotine. John ground his teeth and wondered if Jo Montgomery had gone home to a vacant bed, and absurdly hoped so. She hadn't been wearing a ring. Then he frowned at his wishful thinking. Fat chance. A beauty like her, married or not, undoubtedly had someone to keep her warm at night.

JO REACHED OVER and ran her fingers across Victor's furred chest, and smiled at his growl of contentment. Presenting his pink tongue to Jo with a gigantic yawn, he snuggled deeper into the covers.

"I know," Jo crooned sympathetically to her aged collie. "Twenty-three hours of sleep a day just isn't enough, is it, boy?" Too late, he was already in dreamland. Which is where Jo had thought she would be by now. Especially after a day with the Sterling stampede. She sighed. Eleven-thirty, and sleep was nowhere in sight.

Flat on her back, Jo blinked at the rotating ceiling fan. She had to concede it was John Sterling who had trampled her emotions more than his needy children. Why had he caught her by surprise?

Because she associated fatherhood with thinning hair, a spare tire. The words *virile* and *sexy* shifted her parenthood paradigm. And John Sterling turned it upside down.

As Jo's lids became heavier, she brushed away the shiver of anticipation at seeing him again, and strained to remember the last time a man had shaken her to the core. Long ago, Alan had affected her that way... hadn't he?

THE NAGGING BUZZ of the alarm gave way to a nagging buzz at the base of her brain, some leftover negativity Jo couldn't dredge up until she rolled over and swung her feet over the edge of the bed. Then she grimaced. The Pattersons. In four hours she was expected to show up with her three little darlings in tow and her best mothering face in place. Jo soothed her guilty feelings by reasoning she desperately needed the account, plus she didn't plan to charge John for baby-sitting. They'd be even.

As she made the bed, she mentally ticked off her morning route: drop by the office to open up and leave instructions with Hattie, on to John Sterling's to begin her stint as interior designer/impromptu nanny, then over to the Pattersons for a combination idea-generating and schmoozing session.

Stepping over the silky pile of ruined coatdress, Jo smiled wryly. If she'd learned anything yesterday, it was what she *shouldn't* wear around children. She opened her closet door and flipped on the light. So the imminent question was, did she have anything hanging in her closet made of paper, plastic or metal?

Settling on a washable dark gray knit ensemble, Jo slipped in and out of the shower in record time, finger-fluffing the damp layers of her hair. She quickly applied makeup, then stepped into one-inch heels to lend a dressier look to the leggings. She had one dangling silver earring on before she remembered Billy's inquisitive hands and switched to posts. Then Jo shrugged into a stadium-length jacket, yanked her shoulder bag from the bureau and trotted out the door of her duplex into the chilly winter air. The sun was already shining, though, so it looked as though another record warm day was on tap.

As she backed out of her driveway, she glanced over at Hattie's half of the house to see if her aunt was up and about. Jo wasn't a bit surprised when Hattie emerged in a chic running suit, gloves and muffler, bouncing from foot to foot, warming up. Jo rolled down her window and yelled, "You're up early!"

"The early bird gets the can of worms!" Hattie shouted before waving and jogging off in the opposite direction. Shaking her head, Jo laughed out loud. Hattie was an original, and at the age of sixty-four, had more energy than most women half her age. Indeed, at thirty-one, Jo sometimes had a hard time keeping up with her.

Always a bit outrageous, her widowed aunt seemed to grow a little more eccentric every year. Several months ago she'd confided to Jo she'd been having vivid dreams about her first love, a military man she'd fallen in love with during college, but had lost track of when he left to fight in the Korean Conflict, as Hattie called it. Eventually she'd met and married Uncle Francis, but he'd died suddenly several years ago.

Jo was astounded to hear that Hattie intended to research the whereabouts of a man she hadn't seen in more than forty years, especially since she'd thought her aunt and the older woman's longtime friend, Herbert Mann, were a couple. Hattie insisted the recurring dreams meant her soldier was still alive, and wanted to reunite with her as much as she did. Jo worried what it might do to her aunt if she discovered he was married and unavailable, or perhaps had passed away. But Hattie was determined to find him.

Shaking her head, Jo wished her mother was as adventurous as her spirited older sister. It seemed that Helen Montgomery's sole purpose in life was to see her daughter properly engaged, then married.

Weekly Sunday dinners consisted of familiar rituals where her mom cleverly pried into Jo's love life, extracting updates and offering her own remedies for inducing Alan Parish to propose. "Josephine, three years is long enough for a man to make up his mind," had become a running part of her mom's matrimony monologue.

Thank goodness for Dad, she thought, tapping her finger on the steering wheel to the distinctive beat of John Mellencamp.

City police officer Madden Montgomery had raised Jo with a stern hand and a kind heart. Although he'd never said, Jo secretly suspected he'd wanted a boy when she'd been born. He'd dubbed her Jo, a nickname that her mother refused to use to this day. Since she was an only child, he'd waved aside convention and raised Jo much as he would have raised a son.

But when Jo entered college and declared interior design her major, her mom had noisily proclaimed victory, asserting she knew all along Jo was best suited to taking care of a home and children.

Which couldn't have been further from the truth.

In fact, she'd first chosen to study architecture, but an unending semester of physics and drafting, combined with a part-time job in her aunt Hattie's design firm, convinced Jo her talents lay elsewhere. Her mother refused to understand there was more to interior design than picking out pillows to toss on a sofa. Jo specialized in commercial design and not only graduated with honors but received awards for her term work in ergonomic office layouts. She was a natural to buy and take over Hattie's business, and now her aunt worked for her.

The future of Montgomery Group Interiors rested solely in her hands.

Jo wheeled into the parking lot and pulled into the first space, feeling responsibility descend on her shoulders like a yoke. She forced herself to take a deep breath and smile, then left her car in a burst of energy, feeling her spirits lift with pride as she unlocked the office door and flooded the rooms with fluorescent light.

Within minutes she had the coffeemaker bubbling and the radio on her favorite classic-rock station. Pulling out a sheet of clean paper, Jo made a list of the sample books she'd need to pull for the day's schedule, then checked her calendar for notes from Hattie. A bright yellow adhesive note announced, "Alan arriving Friday afternoon—will pick you up for dinner at duplex around seven."

Jo waited for a wave of pleasure to wash over her. After a few seconds she decided she'd be satisfied with a simple *splash* of pleasure. When none seemed forthcoming, Jo sighed and settled for a trickle.

Okay, so it wasn't…*electric* with Alan. But he was a good man and easy to look at, and they shared common goals. And he loved her very much, of that she was certain. He'd been in Atlanta for ten days, and had wanted her to go with him for a minivacation, but she'd declined. Worry over the precarious foothold she had on her business kept her rooted, guilt eating at her for concealing her financial woes from her boyfriend of three years.

But Alan wouldn't understand. He'd be furious if he knew how deeply over her head she'd dived. Alan had never failed at anything. His computer consulting firm was fast becoming one of the largest in the state, and he was well respected in the community. He could easily bail her small business out of debt, but Jo was determined to succeed or fail on her own.

Anyway, the fact that Alan hadn't called since he'd left only proved how comfortable and solid their relationship stood. The thought he might want to spend the night skittered across her mind, but she dismissed it. After mentally tracking Alan's libido for three years, Jo thought she had his schedule pinned down: every other holiday. At this point Presidents' Day looked lucky.

Jo scolded herself and began to jot down notes for Hattie on where she could be reached and what deliveries to check on today. The phone rang, a low bleeping sound. Jo glanced at her watch and frowned. No one called this early except bill collectors and long-distance companies. "Hello?"

"I knew you'd be there."

Oh, and Pamela Kaminski.

"Hi," Jo said to her lifelong friend. Then she added more cautiously, "What's up?"

"Does something have to be up for me to call? Can't I just be calling my bestest friend in the world to say I've been thinking about how much you mean to me and I hope you have a wonderful day?"

"What's up, Pam?"

Pamela sighed dramatically. "Okay, okay. I need to borrow Alan."

"Again? I'm starting to wonder about the two of you."

"Cripes, Jo, you know he's not my type—I prefer men who have a pulse."

"If you're trying to butter me up, it's not working."

"I'm joking, okay? You know what I mean, Alan's the perfect gentleman. I tend to bring home the strays. Unfortunately, my latest stray doesn't have a tux and I need an escort to the art council's charity dinner tomorrow night. Is Alan back in town?"

"Uh-huh."

Pamela breathed a sigh of relief. "Good. So, can I have him?"

"I'm not his keeper, you know. He might have other plans."

"I'll call him, but I wanted to check with you first."

Jo smiled, shaking her head. "By all means, call."

"I owe you one."

"You owe me about a thousand."

"I'll let you sleep with Nick the All-Nighter sometime."

"Promises, promises," Jo said, then hung up.

Walking to the catalog room, her thoughts lingered on her bubbly friend. A pang of envy flashed through her when she considered Pam's lifestyle, her personality. Jo fingered the familiar spines of the sample books, searching for the ones she needed.

Her best friend was a leggy blond bombshell, unabashedly sexual, and a fabulous real-estate agent in spite of it—or because of it, Jo couldn't decide which. Her flamboyance and scatterbrained bearing opposed Jo's no-nonsense demeanor in a way that defied the laws of friendship. They agreed on little, except to accept each other, which was all that really mattered, they'd decided long ago. Besides, Jo liked having Pam around. She felt like a more exciting person just for *knowing* Pam.

For Hattie's reference, Jo logged the catalogs she'd removed, then loaded everything into the trunk of her car. She refused to acknowledge her trembling fingers as she unlocked the sedan's door. The appointment with the Pattersons loomed over her like an inquisition. Had she lost her mind? How was she going to pass off the Sterling kids as her own?

Jo inhaled deeply as she pulled into traffic. Just this once. She'd pretend to be stepmother to the kids just long enough to firmly implant her momminess in the mind of the Pattersons. From that point on, she'd make excuses for being alone on the job. Suddenly the implication of her assumed role hit her dead center: if she was going to pass herself off as the children's stepmother, she would also be passing herself off as John Sterling's wife.

JOHN STRODE into the kitchen, wrestling with his top shirt button, but alert and wary. Strange smells emanating from the room had convinced him he was needed, or would be shortly.

Billy sat in his high chair, the remnants of who-knew-what down the front of the clean shirt John had put on him only minutes ago. "Daddy funny," he squealed, pointing to John's face.

John made a comical face, feeling the tightness where a half-dozen little scraps of toilet paper blotted razor cuts. "Daddy needs a new razor. Billy, do you have to go potty?" John nodded hopefully.

"No!" Billy said earnestly, his eyebrows diving center. "Bad monster potty."

John turned to Claire, who stood on a step stool at the counter, wearing one of Annie's old aprons. He smiled. ''What smells so…strong?'' he asked, gently tweaking the little girl's ear, then checking the stove for flames. A pan of oatmeal had been cooked within an inch of its life—more of it oozed over the sides than remained in the pot. The cleaning lady, Mrs. Harris, would need safety glasses to remove the mess from the stove. At least the burner had been turned off.

''Sit down, Daddy,'' Claire said, giving him a rare smile. ''I fixed you breakfast.''

John took the long way to the table, trying to find the source of the horrific odor. He stopped at the microwave, and opened it. Something had exploded. The acrid smell wafted out and scorched his nostrils. He slammed the door shut. ''Oh my God, what was it?''

''Eggs,'' Claire said solemnly, carrying a loaded plate to the table, her concentration intent. ''Jamie tried to scramble them.''

John swallowed. ''In the shells?''

''Uh-huh.''

''Where is he? Jamie!''

''I'm Peter,'' came the loud reply from the den.

''He's watching for Jo,'' Claire said, still holding the plate, a hurt look on her face. ''Aren't you going to eat, Daddy?''

John hurried to sit down. ''Of course, sweetie.'' He smacked his lips as she set the plate before him. A ball of rock-solid oatmeal sat in the center, with a spoon standing straight up in the middle of the mass. Two pieces of smoking black toast were artfully arranged around the edge. A glass of green Kool-Aid sat nearby, filled to the brim, only a little of it spilled over the sides. His stomach pitched.

''It looks great, honey,'' he said convincingly, and

took a bite out of a charred slice of toast to prove it. "Mmm-mmm!" He was rewarded with a big grin. Claire covered her mouth with her hand, giggling.

"Jamie, come and eat your oatmeal," John yelled into the den.

"Peter Pan has to keep a lookout," came the gruff response.

"We already have a lookout, it's called a doorbell. Now, come and eat."

"Do I hafta?"

"Get in here."

The tone must have worked, because Jamie came shuffling in, dragging his feet. "I don't like oatmeal," he whined.

John sighed and frowned. "You love oatmeal."

"Not when it's as hard as a baseball," he said sourly. "I want pancakes like Granny used to make us."

A flash of self-reproach stabbed John. The children missed Annie's mother, whom they'd lived near in Atlanta. She'd taken over the mothering role after Annie died, but her health had begun slipping a few months ago. John suspected that watching the kids had taken its toll on her. Savannah was still close enough for his in-laws to visit and really enjoy their grandchildren now, instead of sharing the burden of raising them.

"I know Granny was a good cook—" The ringing doorbell cut John off.

"Jo's here," Jamie yelped, tearing from the room.

John's pulse thrummed faster, and he had a hard time swallowing the dry bit of toast stuck in his throat. He could hear his son murmuring an excited greeting, and Jo's lilting voice responding. Wiping his mouth, he stood, preparing to greet her. Jamie came rushing into the room carrying a white bag with both hands.

"Look—McDonald's!" he cried. "Jo brought pancakes!" He jumped around like a pogo stick.

Jo hung back from the kitchen entrance, holding a second bag. John's stomach jumped, but he wasn't sure if the reaction was triggered by the wonderful smells emanating from the bag, or by the sight of Jo Montgomery in her leggy little outfit.

"But I *made* breakfast." Claire's voice was clouded with hurt. John looked at his daughter and saw her lower lip trembling slightly.

Jo took one glance at Claire's wounded face and realized her mistake. "I'm sorry," she said. "I should have called first to check." Awkwardness swirled in her stomach, combined with an odd queasiness at seeing John Sterling again. He wasn't quite ready for work yet, his top shirt button open enough for a plain cotton T-shirt to show. Even standing in his sock feet with a toilet paper-spotted face, he looked out of place in the kitchen, the calm nucleus in the chaos around him. She sniffed. What was that god-awful smell?

"Between Claire and Miss Montgomery, we'll have a feast," John proclaimed cheerfully. "Right, Claire?"

Claire worked her mouth from side to side, then relented with a little nod, and busied herself mining a chunk of oatmeal from the lump on her plate.

Jo recognized the retreat and said, "Claire, I brought chocolate milk."

The little girl's wide green eyes swam with tears behind the thick glasses, and she perused Jo thoughtfully. "No, thank you," she said quietly, then lifted her glass of green Kool-Aid to her mouth for a sip.

Without meaning to, she had undermined the girl's attempts to take care of her family. Jo tried not to analyze the troubled feelings Claire's dismissal aroused.

"Thank you, Miss Montgomery," John said with a grateful incline of his head. He reached to take the bag she held. "I'll pay you for the food."

"That's not necessary," she said hurriedly. *It's the least I can do for the use of your kids.* She felt a guilty blush crawl up her neck.

Jamie tore into the bag, sending packets of condiments flying. Within seconds, he was devouring a stack of pancakes, drenched in butter and syrup. Billy drank his fill of chocolate milk, disproving the claim of the spill-proof cup he used. Even Claire relented and nibbled on a biscuit. John made a big show of finishing his ball of oatmeal and most of the toast before rounding it out with some of the fast food.

Jo took in the happy, domestic scene at the circular pickled-oak table from the safe distance of the bar that separated the kitchen from the den. She leaned her hip against the counter and munched on a muffin, smiling. Breakfast with her father remained one of her happiest memories of growing up. Dressed in his navy blue policeman's uniform, he always looked so handsome and smelled so good. He'd let Jo wear his hat while he listened to her read the comics from the morning newspaper.

"Jo," John said, startling her out of her reverie. "Why don't you join us?" Hearing her name on his lips stirred something inside her, then panic rumbled in her stomach. She felt out of place in his home—she certainly didn't belong in the middle of it. She straightened. "Thanks, but I need to go back out to the car for some supplies so I can get started right away."

"I'll help!" Jamie offered, standing and sending his chair flying back. Syrup trailed off his chin.

"You, eat," John said pointedly. "I'll help Miss Montgomery." He wiped the syrup from his own chin and stood.

Already on her way out of the kitchen, Jo tried to wave him off. Despite her protests, he followed her, slipping on dark dress shoes at the door, then walking alongside her, close enough to scatter her nerve endings. What was wrong with her? After all, he was just a client.

Just a client who made her legs so weak she had to lean against the trunk of her car for support.

"Nice day," he observed.

She nodded her agreement as she lifted the lid, then proceeded to fill his arms with bulky catalogs.

"Uh, Jo."

"Yes?" she asked, surprised at the hesitant tone of his voice.

He looked extremely uncomfortable, and lifted his free hand to finger his loose collar. "This may be a bit premature, but...oh, what the heck! Would you have dinner with me this evening?"

Jo felt her face flush from an unexpected rush of pleasure. She looked into his expectant eyes, and found herself intrigued by the interest she saw there. The scraps of white tissue dotting his face gave him a boyish air, earthy and appealing. She opened her mouth to say yes, then she remembered Alan, and her heart dipped. "I'm very flattered, J-John," she said, stammering over his first name, "but I already have plans."

He looked disappointed, and nodded his understanding. "I see. And if I were to ask again, would you have plans that night, as well?"

Never before since she'd been dating Alan had she been tempted to see another man. John Sterling affected her in a way she couldn't describe, and for a split second, she desperately wanted to explore the chemistry between them. "I—"

"Daaaaa-deeeeeeee!" Jamie yelled from the front door. "Susan the witch is on the phone. She told me to come and get you."

One glance at the way he held the phone verified Susan had heard every word.

"Where on earth did he hear that?" John muttered, then more loudly, "Tell her I'll be right there."

Jo swallowed guiltily. She'd have to watch her mouth around the three little Sterling sponges.

"About dinner—you were going to say...?" he prompted.

She took a deep breath. No doubt, John Sterling was a very tempting man, but Jamie was a timely reminder that John had little room in his life for a love interest, and she had no room in her life for a ready-made family. So why jeopardize her stable relationship with Alan over a lost cause?

"I'm sorry," she said. "I'm involved with someone."

He eyed her thoughtfully for a few seconds, then to her amazement, he juggled his load, reached forward and lifted her left hand, his thumb closing over the knuckle on her bare third finger. "Either you're being untruthful," he said slowly, "or the man's an idiot." He dropped her hand, and walked back to the house.

His words bolted through her like an electrical connection searching for a ground. Jo remained rooted to the spot for a full minute, fighting to regain her composure. The vague thought surfaced that she should be angry with him for what he'd said, but she couldn't seem to conjure up any feeling except...Jo swallowed...*lust?*

She grabbed a few loose brochures, then reentered the house. John was just hanging up the phone. "Have you seen the entire house?" he asked. The awkwardness of the previous moment had vanished.

"Not all of it," Jo said, thankful to get back on business footing.

"How about a tour before I leave?"

She nodded agreeably, and grabbed a pad of paper and a pencil. John instructed the kids to finish eating, then turned to Jo with a smile and motioned for her to follow him. She did, trying not to focus on the athletic way he carried himself. He was a big man who was clearly comfortable with the space his body occupied.

John showed her the laundry room between the garage and the kitchen, then explained he'd like to make better use of the snack bar that separated the den from the kitchen. He also expressed his displeasure at the light fixtures in the stark, empty dining room.

"Do you still have furniture in storage?" Jo asked, assuming he owned a dining-room suite and den furniture she hadn't seen.

"No," he said. "My house in Atlanta was smaller than this one, and I gave most of my furnishings to my in-laws before I moved to Savannah. Some of the pieces were heirlooms from Annie's family, and I wanted the furniture to be kept out of harm's way until the children are old enough to inherit it.''

Annie. A tiny shock wave moved through Jo at the sound of his wife's name. Annie was a lovely name…Jo knew the woman must have been lovely, as well. Probably blond, based on Claire's and Billy's coloring. A woman with everything: a loving husband, three bright children. John looked at her, and Jo saw distant pain in his eyes. He must have seen the question in hers, because he said quietly, ''My wife was killed in a car accident two years ago.''

Jo analyzed his voice for longing, for desperation, but heard only acceptance. ''I'm sorry,'' she whispered, her heart constricting. In the seconds that passed in silence, she felt as if they had taken a giant step toward…something. The sensation left her head spinning with possibilities.

He nodded wordlessly, then walked across the den, through a set of French doors and into a study. This room was almost fully furnished, and Jo nodded in approval at the clean lines of the heavy desk, chair and armoire. ''I could use a couple more pieces in here, too,'' John noted. ''Maybe a chair or two, and a table— whatever you think.''

A sliding door revealed a wet bar, with another sliding door beyond leading to the formal living room, also vacant. Another set of French doors took them back into the entryway. John placed his hand on the banister and waited for Jo to join him before he began to climb the curving stairway to the second floor.

''I'm open to whatever ideas you have,'' John explained. ''I don't have the time or the patience to coordinate the decorating myself, I just want the house to be comfortable for the kids.''

They took a familiar left at the top of the stairs. The first room on the left was a guest room, empty and expansive. This room shared the large bathroom that led into the boys' room. If possible, their room was even more of a wreck than it had been the previous day. John shrugged his apologies. ''I want new furniture in here, and as you can see, the sturdier, the better.''

Claire's room was opposite the boys' room. Jo decided changes were necessary at the first glimpse of the dark-wood twin bed and matching dresser. Everything was in its place, painfully neat. ''New furniture in here, too,'' he said, his face softening. ''Something pretty for my little girl.''

As they walked past the staircase to the other side of the house, Jo's heart began to pound. He was obviously taking her to the master-bedroom suite. He stopped at a closed door, his hand on the knob. ''This is my room,'' he said, then pushed open the door.

The room was gorgeous, flanked by a deep bay window on the short end of the room, and another one on the adjacent wall. An elaborate trey ceiling contained two skylights. The pale carpet was thick and plush. Absurdly, the first question that entered Jo's mind was whether the large copper-colored wrought-iron bed was the one he'd shared with Annie. The worn comforter had been yanked up over the sheets hurriedly, the pillows were still squashed at odd angles. ''Your bed looks new,'' she said before thinking. Then, to hide her burning cheeks, she bent her head to scribble furiously on the pad of paper she carried.

"It is new," he confirmed. "But, as you can see, I need new bed linens, curtains, everything. The only other furniture was a straight-back chair with a towel hanging over it, and a wooden dresser with wrought accents to match the bed. "A comfy chair would be great," he continued. "Along with a new mattress."

Jo chanced a glance at John's face and found him studying her. "A new mattress?" she parroted.

"Yeah," he said slowly, crossing his arms and leaning against the wall. "My back hurts when I get up. I think the mattress is too hard."

Jo swallowed and willed herself not to lick her trembling lips. "So you'd like something softer?"

He stood unmoving, his gaze locked with hers. "Something softer in my bed would be a definite improvement."

"Dad." Claire's voice startled Jo. She hadn't seen her walk into the room.

John obviously hadn't, either. He stood up straight. "What is it, honey?"

She frowned slightly, her eyes glancing back and forth from Jo to her father. "You're going to be late for work."

He turned his wrist to check his watch and nodded in agreement. "You're right, sweetheart. I'm almost through showing Jo around. Can you get my beeper from my desk drawer and put it by my briefcase?"

She nodded, casting one more wary glance toward Jo before leaving.

John cleared his throat. "Anyway, the mattress aside, I'm worried I made a mistake buying the bed."

Puzzled, Jo asked, "Why?"

He folded his hands, a sheepish look on his face.

"You don't think it's too...masculine? I mean, would a woman...uh..." He blushed furiously.

Understanding flooded through Jo. John Sterling intended to remarry someday and wanted the room to be a place where a woman could feel comfortable. "It's a beautiful bed," Jo hastened to assure him. "And I'm sure any woman would...uh...like it." Now it was her turn to blush.

He grinned. "I guess I'll have to take your word for that."

"Daddy?" Claire's voice echoed from downstairs.

"I'm coming," John called back. He hurriedly showed Jo the sitting room, huge bathroom and walk-in closet connected to his room, all equally bare, then they descended the stairs together. Jo tingled from his nearness and from their earlier banter in his bedroom. This man aroused feelings in her she didn't want to scrutinize.

The children stood by the door, queued for a good-bye kiss. Jo had the ridiculous urge to get in line. Instead, she averted her eyes during the noisy smooches. When she peeked, Claire was plucking the bits of tissue from her father's face as he stood patiently, bent at the waist.

"Jo," he asked, standing and turning toward her. "Are you sure you don't mind keeping an eye on the kids? I can take them to work with me for a few hours—I've done it before."

"No," she said, smiling brightly. "I need to get started here, anyway. And I have to dash out to a client not too far from here, but it's a day care, so the kids should be fine for a few minutes." Could he see that her heart was still jumping from their encounter? Or was it racing due to her planned act of deception with the Pattersons?

He shook his head and pulled on his suit jacket. "If you're sure."

"I'm sure."

"Okay, then I'll be back around twelve-thirty or so." He stooped to pick up his briefcase.

Jo carried a catalog to the cluttered kitchen table, anxious for this unsettling man to leave. She spied his black and mustard-colored silk tie under a wad of napkins.

"John," she said, reaching for the tie and holding it up.

He turned, eyebrows up.

"You forgot something."

He tapped his forehead lightly with the heel of his hand. "Thanks. I was having so much trouble with my button, I put the thing out of my mind."

Abandoning his briefcase, he walked toward her. He reached for the tie, then draped it over his shoulder. Jo watched while he struggled with the button at his shirt collar, stretching his neck like a rooster to gain a fraction of an inch more room to maneuver.

She smiled and crossed her arms, amused to watch an accomplished man reduced to such contortions.

He fumbled with the tiny button, the tip of his tongue protruding in his deep concentration. After several attempts, he conceded defeat. "Forget it," he said, shrugging. "My fingers are too big for these ridiculous tiny buttons."

"Let me," she offered, stepping forward with her hands raised. She stopped a half step in front of him, her hands in midair, embarrassment flooding her when she felt his proximity. Her heart thudded in her chest, her throat tightening like a vise, forcing her to swallow hard and audibly. His green eyes held hers bondage, pulling her toward him. "Th-that is, if you want me to," she stammered.

He hesitated until she began to lower her arms, then said, "I'd like that very much."

Slowly, Jo lifted her hands to his neck. John raised his chin but Jo could feel his gaze riveted on her. She focused on the troublesome button, fighting to rechannel her rampant emotions, to quiet her pounding pulse. Placing her trembling fingers on his collar, Jo was struck with the intimacy of such a simple act. She might have been his wife, helping him to dress in the last hectic seconds before they both kissed and rushed off to day care, and then to work.

Except the mood now was anything but hectic. Time seemed to slow, like cooling molasses, the intensity of the act stretching out each millisecond. As she tugged the ends of his collar together, her fingers brushed the warm, smooth skin of his neck. She was close enough to smell his woodsy after-shave and see a tiny patch of missed whiskers under his chin glistening red-gold in the light.

Jo carefully twisted the tiny button through the hole. She released a breath she hadn't realized she'd been holding, and chastised herself. Right now her brain could use all the oxygen her quivering lungs could deliver. "There," she squeaked, lightly patting the area beneath the button.

"Thanks." His voice vibrated warm and low, but he didn't move a muscle as he stared into her eyes, his lips parted ever so slightly.

Jo remained frozen, her hands glued to the front of his shirt. Suddenly, a faraway sound made its way into her brain. John must have heard it, too, because he turned his head the same time she did.

One hand hiding his mouth, Jamie shook with giggles. Claire stared, too, but Jo couldn't read her expression. Billy stared because the other two were staring.

Awestruck, Jamie asked, "Are you going to kiss her, Daddy?"

4

JOHN TOOK a half step back to escape Jo's nearness, instantly missing the weight and warmth of her hand on his chest. As if on cue, she too had retreated, leaving a safe cushion of five feet between them.

"Finish your breakfast, Jamie," John admonished in exasperation.

Jamie frowned. "I'm Peter," he grumbled, returning to the kitchen.

Looking back to Jo, John said, "I'm sorry about that." Her flaming cheeks brought a smile to his face. Not that she could be as embarrassed as he at that moment. He laughed nervously and lifted his hands. "Kids say the darnedest things."

Jo smiled, and looked around the room, finally settling her gaze on him again. "It's okay," she said, then turned to follow Jamie to the kitchen.

John slid his tie around his shirt collar and began to fashion a knot, then made the mistake of glancing up. At the sight of her receding backside, he yanked the tiny knot at his neck to a stranglehold, then fumbled several seconds for relief. *I have to get out of this house.* He stooped to pick up his briefcase. "Kids, remember," he said, using his best fatherly voice, "be good for Miss Montgomery, okay?"

His answer was a chorus of okays, Billy's coming a

half beat behind Jamie's loud one and Claire's quiet one. He met Jo's eyes, and recognized a flash of panic. Had he spooked her with his desire to kiss her? He'd warned Jamie the previous night not to scare her off, yet he himself seemed to lose his head around her.

She gave him a shaky smile and nodded encouragingly for him to go. With one last glance at his motley crew and their temporary keeper, he left the house and walked to his car. He'd forgotten to stow it in the garage the night before, because his mind had been consumed by thoughts of Jo Montgomery.

Feeling slightly dazed, John let the car warm up for a few minutes, then backed out of his driveway and headed toward the interstate. Twenty-four hours ago he would never have envisioned the scene he left this morning. Jo Montgomery was a dream come true. Stunningly beautiful, intelligent, stunningly beautiful, his kids liked her, stunningly beautiful, unmarried. And to think she'd be spending lots of time at his home over the next…well, he'd have to think of a way to drag out this decorating project.

For the first time in two years, a feeling akin to pure happiness crept into his heart. She had a boyfriend, but she wasn't married yet. He felt certain he'd seen desire in her eyes more than once this morning. And if she could evoke such a powerful response from him helping him get dressed, she'd put him in another galaxy helping him get *un*dressed.

She'd looked interested. And interesting. Life was good. He turned up the radio and sang along badly with the tune, daydreaming about Mrs. Jo Montgomery Sterling.

With a start, John realized he'd driven four miles

past his exit. He frowned and banged his hand on the steering wheel. A large sign announced the next exit lay a half mile down the interstate, so he settled back in his leather seat. Suddenly, the engine light blinked and the car slowed. He maneuvered to the shoulder, pressing on the gas but receiving no response. He glanced at the gas gauge and cursed. Completely empty, much like his befuddled brain.

The steering wheel received a harder whack this time. Then he released the trunk latch, got out and locked his door, retrieved the well-used gasoline container and began walking toward the exit.

Oh, well, the walk would give him time to think of a way to get close to Jo Montgomery. He'd be an idiot to pass up this chance—even a fool could see she was a natural with kids.

"WHAT THE HECK is 'time-out'?" Jo asked Claire, flinching at Billy's increasingly hysterical wails. He fell to the floor, his little body stiff with anger. Rolling side to side, he wallowed in the remains of a building-block high-rise which had been rendered to scattered debris with one sweep of Jamie's arm.

Claire sighed, rolling her eyes mightily as though Jo were as dense as a tree. "Time-out is when Daddy makes Jamie sit in a room by himself for a few minutes until he can control himself."

"Until who can control himself—your dad, or Jamie?"

"Jamie," Claire said, clearly trying to be patient.

"I'm Peter!" Jamie screeched, attempting to pull away from the firm hold Jo had on his shirttail.

"Anyway," Claire continued in a calm voice, "you

should put him in time-out now for wrecking Billy's house."

"It was an accident," Jamie howled, straining to gain freedom.

"Good," Jo said. She reined him in a few inches and tipped his chin up with her cupped hand to force him to look at her. God, he was a carbon copy of his father. Every feature—from the shape of his eyebrows to the set of his stubborn little mouth—mirrored John's, only smaller and softer. Her heart tripped double time. "Since it was an accident, you'll sit down and rebuild it with Billy, okay?"

While Jamie turned over this option in his mind, Jo realized she couldn't make the boy do it, so what if he refused? Kids today baffled her. She'd seen plenty of preschoolers talk back to their parents, turning adults into quivering masses, pleading with their children to behave.

She bent down to his level, still holding his chin gently but firmly. "Okay, mister?"

Jamie worked his mouth, then gave her a lopsided frown. "Okay," he grumbled.

Jo smiled and nodded. "I knew I could count on you." She gave him a pat on the shoulder as he turned toward his quaking brother. Billy quieted and sat up when Jamie began sorting the blocks in preparation for construction. Within a couple of minutes, they were playing together quietly.

Claire poked at her glasses, her mouth set in a straight line. "Daddy would have put him in time-out."

Jo eyed her carefully. This one would not be won over easily. "Come on, I'll help you clean up your kitchen.'' She was careful to give ownership of the domain to the little girl.

"Mrs. Harris will be here in a few minutes—she always cleans it up.''

"Then let's tidy it a bit,'' Jo cajoled. "I need the table to spread out my decorating books and I could use your help coming up with a color scheme for all the rooms.''

Claire squinted while she thought it over. Then she looked at Jo and asked, "How much?''

Jo blinked. "How much what?''

"How much you gonna pay me?''

She should have seen that one coming. Jo pondered the question, crossing her arms and tapping a finger on her chin. "Does your dad pay you to do everything?''

"Uh-huh.''

Just like a guilty parent, Jo decided. "Tell you what—I've got a set of Nancy Drew books I've had since I was your age. Fifty-four, I think, plus the cookbook. If you help me, they're yours.''

Claire's eyes bulged. "Really?''

Jo smiled. The books were among her most prized possessions, but she and Alan didn't plan on having a family, and she'd probably never meet another girl who enjoyed reading as much as Claire obviously did. "Really.''

The deal struck, Claire skipped to the kitchen and started gathering used napkins from the table. When the table had been cleared and the dishes loaded in the dishwasher, Jo spread her catalogs open on the smooth surface of the wooden table. "First, we decide on a color scheme for each room. Let's start with your room,'' Jo suggested, and Claire nodded eagerly. Pointing to a page covered with matching swatches of solid, striped and polka-dotted fabric, she smiled at the plain little girl and asked, "How about pink and white?"

This nod was enthusiastic enough to cause Claire's glasses to slip down to the tip of her nose. She poked them back in place, her eyes shining. Jo felt a funny little stir in her heart for this solemn little bookworm, denied the warmth and love of her mother at such an impressionable age.

For the first time, Jo scrutinized the girl's clothing, and her heart squeezed. While undoubtedly good quality, her clothes were dull and shapeless, unflattering to the child. She wore stiff little khaki pants and a button-up shirt that was too small for her. Her small feet were shod in ugly, sensible black shoes. Her father hadn't recognized that her fair coloring required bright accents. The child nearly disappeared in all that bland.

Jo looked back to the samples and carefully said, "Do you pick out your own clothes, Claire?"

Shaking her blond head, Claire replied, "No, mostly I just wear clothes I wore at our old school in Atlanta."

"Was it a private school?"

"Uh-huh."

Which explained the uniform quality of her outfit. "The spring semester starts here pretty soon, doesn't it?"

Claire nodded. "One week. We're going to a public school, though, so I don't have to dress like everyone else."

"Have you gone shopping for new clothes?"

She shook her head vigorously. "Aunt Cleo's coming over from Atlanta next Saturday to take me—she said it would be a day for just us women." She smiled timidly, and Jo nodded, satisfied the Sterling family had the situation under control. It had been foolish of her to think otherwise.

Heads together, they pored over the heavy sample books. They quickly chose shades of blue for the boys' bed and bath, then moved on to the guest room.

"Granny Watts would like the rose color," Claire asserted, pointing.

"Good choice," Jo responded, impressed. "Rose is a great color to lie down beside your pink room and the boys' blue one." She couldn't resist finding out more about John's relatives. "Tell me about your grandparents."

"There's just Granny and Grandpa Watts. They're my mom's parents and they live in Atlanta. Granny took care of us after Mom died, but then she got sick and we moved here." Her mouth drew down and she chewed on her lower lip. "We were too much trouble, I guess."

Jo wanted to hug her, but instead she swallowed and said, "I'm sure that's not true. People just get sick sometimes, that's all. I bet you miss them."

Claire nodded. "They were going to get us a dog."

"You'll be able to visit them," Jo said kindly, immensely sorry she'd raised the subject. "And thanks to your help, the house will look great when they come to see you." This coaxed a smile from Claire.

"Now for your dad's room." Jo's stomach squirmed annoyingly.

"Make it purple," Claire said, her confidence growing.

"Hmm." Jo pondered the color, then brightened in

agreement. "Purple it is—that's the color for royalty, you know."

Claire beamed, and Jo decided the little girl was quite pretty when she was happy. With a slight pang, Jo wondered how often that was. "We'll throw in cream and black for accent colors," Jo added enthusiastically. "I'm sure your dad will like it." She paused and leaned toward Claire. "You're very good with colors."

Claire's eyes dipped, then she glanced back up at Jo beneath her lashes. "I like to paint." She poked at her glasses unnecessarily.

Delighted, Jo asked, "You like to paint pictures?"

She nodded. "My mom painted pretty pictures, but Daddy has them all packed away."

Jo felt another tug for Claire's loss. Jamie's memory of his mother would be dim at best, and Billy would never know what he missed. But Claire remembered and still nursed the pain. Smiling, Jo reached forward to place her hand over the girl's small one. "Promise me you'll paint a picture someday for my office."

Claire brightened. "I promise."

They moved on to the rooms on the first floor and before long had selected taupe and white for the living room, brown and gold for John's study, and coral and gray for the den. All that remained was the kitchen, and Jo turned to a palette of beautiful clear greens. "Since the bar will allow both rooms to be seen at once, green in the kitchen will be a perfect complement to the den's coral," she said, patting her notepad in finality.

But Claire's face wrinkled into a dark frown. "Red."

"Red with coral?" Jo asked, perplexed.

"The kitchen has to be red, with strawberries," she said, crossing her arms resolutely. "It's what Mom always wanted."

Unknowingly, she'd hit an exposed nerve, but Jo knew when to back down. She glanced at her watch. "We'll have to leave a few loose ends. Right now, we need to get going." But almost another hour had passed by the time she herded up the boys, combed everyone's hair, tamed one red cowlick, washed two sticky faces and knelt on the floor to change one diaper.

Jo shook her head and clucked as she bent over the toddler sprawled patiently on the floor, naked from the waist down. "Billy, if you're old enough to get a diaper, bring it to me and ask for a change, you're plenty old enough to go to the potty."

Billy's eyes turned dark. "Bad potty."

She sat back on her heels and glanced around the room. "Where's Jamie?" she asked Claire.

Suddenly a car horn sounded in the driveway. *Her* car horn. Fear stabbed Jo's heart. "Oh my God, he can't be in my car!" She raced to the door, threw it open and tore down the steps, nearly tripping in her haste.

Jamie was not only sitting in the driver's seat, elevated by two thick catalogs, but he had the engine running, the windows down, the stereo blasting, and was sporting Jo's sunglasses. But by some miracle, the car hadn't moved from its spot in the driveway. She glanced at the busy street at the end of the driveway and shuddered at what could have happened. Some mother she would make, all right. No kid would last a month in her care.

"Can I drive, Jo?" Jamie asked excitedly, turning the steering wheel sharply left, then right.

Make that a week—she'd kill them with her own hands.

"Whoa, he really needs a time-out now," Claire breathed.

Jo was so scared and angry, she didn't trust herself to speak. Her hands were shaking and her heart thudded in her chest. Finally, her feet propelled her to the car, where she reached in and yanked the keys from the ignition.

"Hey!" Jamie said in a loud, cross voice.

"Don't you 'hey' me, young man," Jo said, her voice low and trembling. "Do you have any idea how much danger you put yourself in?"

His chin went up. "I wasn't afraid."

"Out of the car, *right now!*"

Jamie quickly obliged, his towel-cape swirling around him as he jerked to a halt before Jo, his green eyes wide.

Jo took a deep breath and knelt in front of the little boy, her hand on his shoulder. "If the car had gone out into the road, you could have been killed, Jamie." Her voice was shaking. "Do you know what that means?"

"Yeah," he said. "Like my mom was killed by a car."

Jo hesitated, then said, "That's right. And you know how sad your daddy was when that happened?"

He nodded solemnly. "Daddy cried."

Her heart was getting an aerobic workout this morning, she thought as it squeezed tighter. "I'm sure he did. But if something happened to you or Claire or

Billy, your daddy would *never* stop crying. Do you understand?''

Jamie nodded, tears welling in his eyes. ''Don't tell Daddy, okay, Jo?''

She sighed, then pulled the little boy to her for a hug. ''Okay, but if you *ever* do this again, I'm going to give you time-off for a jillion years, got it?''

He sniffed, then giggled against her neck. ''It's time-*out*, Jo.''

His small body melted into hers, his arms going around her neck like a vise. ''Whatever,'' she mumbled, her insides turning over at his touch. When he loosened his grip, Jo glanced at her watch and gasped. ''We're late!'' She dashed back into the house to rustle up light jackets for everyone and to grab her purse from the hall table. The housekeeper Mrs. Harris was pulling in when she came out carrying Billy's car seat. The kids ran to the buxom gray-haired woman and received hugs and kisses in return. Jo introduced herself and chatted for a few minutes before hurrying the kids into the car. This time she instructed Jamie to sit up front, and put Billy in the back where Claire could tend to his needs if necessary.

Jamie turned around and stuck his tongue out at Claire. ''I get to sit up front!''

''And Claire gets to on the way home,'' Jo interjected smoothly, sticking her tongue out at Jamie. In the back seat, Claire giggled.

Aside from stopping to make Jamie apologize for throwing a wad of bubblegum onto the windshield of the police car behind them, the trip to the day care was relatively uneventful.

A row of four-foot-tall red lockers lined the walls of

the entryway for the day care, colorful coat sleeves hanging out here and there. A big-boned brunette woman dressed in chinos and a sweatshirt greeted Jo. She looked to be in her mid-forties. At first, she presented a wide smile to the group, then her eyes swept the children and the smile froze beneath her bulging eyes.

Jamie lifted his hand in a wave. "Hi ya, Cap'n Hook."

Already nervous, Jo's stomach dived and her eyes darted to his impish grin. "Jamie, do you know this nice lady?"

"He should," the woman said sourly. "He did everything short of cutting off my hand the week he was here." She looked at Jo, then straightened, as if suddenly remembering her place. "I'm Carolyn Hook," she said, "the director here at KidScape. As I explained to Mr. Sterling and to his *last* nanny, the boys are too disruptive to attend our day care." She smiled tightly and angled her head in a sympathetic gesture. "I'm sure you understand, Ms...."

"Jo Montgomery." Jo extended her hand, fighting a frown. Some bedside manner for a day-care director. She didn't love kids herself, but at least she hadn't made it her career. "But I'm *not* Mr. Sterling's nanny." She paused for a few seconds to let the woman ponder her role in the Sterling household. "My design firm is going to bid on redecorating all the area KidScape day cares. Mr. and Mrs. Patterson said it would be all right if I stopped by to have a look around." She hesitated, but the woman's bearing bit into her, so she delivered the kicker. "And they asked me to bring the children along for feedback on how things are run." A smile tickled her mouth as she watched realization dawn in the woman's eyes.

"I beg your pardon, I had no idea Mr. Sterling had gotten mar—I mean…"

Say nothing that can't be explained away later, Jo reminded herself. She donned a tolerant smile and bent to set Billy on his feet, then took his hand firmly in hers. "I'm still getting used to the children myself, Ms. Hook."

Cap'n Hook straightened and for a moment Jo thought the woman might salute. "Right this way, Ms. Montgomery. Mrs. Patterson is in the storytelling room."

Melissa Patterson sat on a tiny stool, reading aloud from a bright storybook to a group of preschoolers on the floor. She winked at them, then wound up the story with a flourish, and the children clapped their hands. Rising from her stool, she smiled and addressed Jo. "I'm so glad you brought the children," she said, then bent over and patted Jamie's arm. "You'll like it here."

"No, I won't," he said simply. Jo winced.

Mrs. Patterson recoiled in surprise and said, "But you just arrived."

"Me and my brother and sister were here for a while when we first moved here," he explained in a bored voice.

"Why did you leave?" she asked, concern on her face.

Jamie jerked his thumb toward Carolyn Hook. "Ask Cap'n Hook."

"Um, Mrs. Patterson," the woman began nervously.

"Yes, Carolyn?"

"These are the Sterling children," she said politely, but distinctly.

"The Sterling children?" Melissa Patterson looked confused.

"Remember?" Cap'n Hook asked, her eyes wide with meaning. "The flood in the boys' bathroom? The *huge* insurance claim?"

Mrs. Patterson's eyebrows went up. "Ohhhhh, you mean…" She pointed to Jamie, and Cap'n Hook nodded.

Great, Jo thought. *I'm playing stepmother to impress these people and I pick the kid who nearly destroyed their day care.* Jo sighed. "Jamie, why would you do such a thing?"

"Because," he said, shrugging, "it's boring here. All they do is tell stories."

But before Jo could apologize, Mrs. Patterson raised her hand. The woman clasped Jamie's hand and asked, "Would you come with me and tell me the kinds of things you'd like to do at day care?"

Jo allowed herself a small smile at Jamie's accidental coup.

An hour later, Melissa Patterson followed Jo out to the car. Once the children were inside with seat belts fastened, she said, "I would appreciate it if you would incorporate some of your stepson's ideas into the design bid—a multimedia room, a stage, a nature room— all of them. He's a very creative boy…and that Peter Pan act is adorable."

Guilt tugged at Jo's heart as she looked in the car at the children. "They're all special," she agreed.

"I didn't realize you'd married John Sterling," the

woman said, startling Jo. "I assume you still go by your maiden name?"

Jo nodded numbly, then, very near panic, asked, "Do you know John?"

"I spoke with him once over the phone about the flood incident, and he was a wonderfully gracious man." She pursed her lips and frowned slightly in recollection. "In fact, I would have allowed the boy to come back, but poor Carolyn said she couldn't take it, and I couldn't afford to lose her." She smiled apologetically, then brightened. "I'll have a talk with her and see if we can work out something."

"That would be very helpful," Jo said, smiling gratefully. "Mr. Ster—I mean, John a-and I—" she felt heat suffusing her cheeks "—would appreciate taking the kids to a place we feel good about, at least for the next few days until school starts again. After that, it'll just be Billy."

"Consider it done," Mrs. Patterson assured her in a professional tone, then changed the subject with an inquisitive tilt of her head. "Your husband just moved here from Atlanta and took over as head architect for Wilson Brothers, didn't he?"

Jo's mind raced, then she remembered the firm name from his business card. "Yes, that's right."

"Whirlwind courtship?"

Jo laughed nervously. "You could say that."

Mrs. Patterson's eyes narrowed slightly. "He must be a very persuasive man."

"I PICKED UP LUNCH on the way home," John said, holding the basket high. "It's such a warm day, I thought we'd go to Forsythe Park and have a picnic."

GET 2

HOW TO GET YOUR
2 FREE BOOKS AND FREE GIFT!

1. Peel off the MIRA® sticker on the front cover. Place it in the space provided at right. This automatically entitles you to receive two free books and an exciting surprise gift.

2. Send back this card and you'll get 2 "The Best of the Best™" books. These books have a combined cover price of $11.98 or more in the U.S. and $13.98 or more in Canada, but they are yours to keep absolutely FREE!

3. There's <u>no</u> catch. You're under <u>no</u> obligation to buy anything. We charge nothing – ZERO – for your first shipment. And you don't have to make any minimum number of purchases – not even one!

4. We call this line "The Best of the Best" because each month you'll receive the best books by some of today's most popular authors. These authors show up time and time again on all the major bestseller lists and their books sell out as soon as they hit the stores. You'll like the convenience of getting them delivered to your home at our special discount prices . . . and you'll love your *Heart to Heart* subscriber newsletter featuring author news, horoscopes, recipes, book reviews and much more!

SPECIAL FREE GIFT

We'll send you a fabulous surprise gift absolutely FREE, simply for accepting our no-risk offer!

5. We hope that after receiving your free books you'll want to remain a subscriber. But the choice is yours – to continue or cancel, anytime at all! So why not take us up on our invitation, with no risk of any kind. You'll be glad you did!

6. And remember...we'll send you a surprise gift ABSOLUTELY FREE just for giving THE BEST OF THE BEST a try.

Visit us online at
www.mirabooks.com

® and TM are registered trademarks of Harlequin Enterprises Limited.

BOOKS FREE!

THE BEST OF THE BEST™ — Here's How it Works:

Accepting your 2 free books and gift places you under no obligation to buy anything. You may keep the books and gift and return the shipping statement marked "cancel." If you do not cancel, about a month later we will send you 4 additional books and bill you just $4.74 each in the U.S., or $5.24 each in Canada, plus 25¢ shipping & handling per book and applicable taxes if any.* That's the complete price and — compared to cover prices starting from $5.99 each in the U.S. and $6.99 each in Canada — it's quite a bargain! You may cancel at any time, but if you choose to continue, every month we'll send you 4 more books, which you may either purchase at the discount price or return to us and cancel your subscription.

*Terms and prices subject to change without notice. Sales tax applicable in N.Y. Canadian residents will be charged applicable provincial taxes and GST. Credit or Debit balances in a customer's account(s) may be offset by any other outstanding balance owed by or to the customer.

If offer card is missing write to: The Best of the Best, 3010 Walden Ave., P.O. Box 1867, Buffalo, NY 14240-1867

BUSINESS REPLY MAIL

FIRST-CLASS MAIL   PERMIT NO. 717-003   BUFFALO, NY

POSTAGE WILL BE PAID BY ADDRESSEE

THE BEST OF THE BEST
3010 WALDEN AVE
PO BOX 1867
BUFFALO NY 14240-9952

NO POSTAGE
NECESSARY
IF MAILED
IN THE
UNITED STATES

Jamie and Claire cheered, and Billy chimed in.

"Jo, too, Daddy?" Jamie asked, his eyes shining.

John turned his gaze on Jo. "I hope so."

Jo tingled under his stare. She was still reeling from her morning of pretending to be Mrs. John Sterling, mother of three. The merry slant of his eyes tempted her. She could think of worse ways to while away the afternoon than sharing a sunny picnic with John Sterling. But her anticipation scared her. Two days ago she didn't even know the Sterlings—in an alarmingly short time, she'd become tangled in their lives. "I really can't," she said. "I need to get my notes together so we can talk about the contract."

"There'll be plenty of time to talk at the park," John said.

A very persuasive man.

"Please, Jo?" Jamie hugged her waist and pulled at her hands, his eyes soft and expectant.

"Well..." She wavered and her stomach growled audibly.

John must have heard it. "Fried chicken," he prompted, angling his head and lifting one side of the basket to allow a wonderful spicy aroma to escape.

What could it hurt? she wondered, other than her cholesterol count. It would give her a chance to review her notes with him. Alan would understand—it was strictly business. It had nothing to do with the fact she found John breathtaking in jeans and a pale blue sweatshirt. And how intimate could it be with three children along?

"Maybe just for a little while," she agreed softly, but added, "I'll drive my car in case I need to leave early."

Jamie and Billy clapped their hands. Claire looked at Jo, her tiny green eyes neither friendly nor adversarial, just questioning. For an instant, Jo wondered how much the girl might have picked up on this morning at the day-care center. "Want to ride with me, Claire, and keep me company?"

The little girl nodded listlessly, and everyone piled into the cars. When they were under way, Claire remained quiet, sitting forward in her seat, engrossed in the passing landscape. At last, she seemed to relax, and settled back in her seat.

"Were you smart in school?" Claire asked, fingering a loose thread on the seam of her pants.

Surprised by this odd, lone question, Jo nodded cautiously. "I guess so."

"Did you wear glasses?"

Jo smiled. "As a matter of fact, I did. I switched to contact lenses when I started high school."

Claire pondered this bit of information for a few seconds. "Did you have a boyfriend before you...you know—" she stabbed at her glasses "—started high school?"

Another heart tug. These kids had a knack for causing tugs. Apparently, Claire had heard the old "boys don't make passes at girls who wear glasses" saying. Jo fastened her teeth on her lower lip. But nine years old was a little young to be interested in boys...wasn't it? She glanced at Claire's troubled eyes. "Well," she began, keenly aware of the girl's fragile confidence, "David Knickerbocker followed me around trying to carry my books, so I guess you could call him my boyfriend."

Claire giggled, a tinkling sound. "Was that his real name?"

Jo nodded, grinning. "He was shorter than I was and his ears were as big as dinner plates."

They both laughed, then Claire asked, "What happened to him?"

"I gave him a black eye in the sixth grade on the playground and he didn't talk to me again until we were sixteen. By that time he'd grown into his ears and was very, very cute."

Riveted, Claire murmured, "What did he say when he talked to you again?"

Jo leaned toward her conspiratorially, "He said he thought I was prettier wearing my glasses, but he asked me to the sweetheart dance anyway."

Claire looked hopeful. "Really?"

"Really," she said, and Jo looked back to the road. She poked at her glasses. "Is he still your boyfriend?"

Jo hesitated when she thought of Alan. "Uh, no, I have a different boyfriend now."

"Are you going to get married and have babies?"

Squirming, she reached to fiddle with the radio knob and tried to tamp down her irritation. It wasn't Claire's fault that her father was causing her feelings for Alan to short-circuit. And to think she was having dinner with him tonight after spending the afternoon with John. "Alan hasn't asked me to marry him yet."

Claire tipped her head back and looked up at Jo. "But what if he does?"

"Then I'll…I'll give him an answer." Relief flooded through her when she spied their turn. "Oh, look, here we are."

From the parking lot, Jo saw colorful blankets dotting the green expanse of sunny lawn of Forsythe Park. Other couples and families were already enjoying the break in the January weather. She retrieved a Frisbee from the trunk of her car, along with a jacket and ball cap for herself. Predictably, Jamie wanted to know why she had the Frisbee. ''I bring my dog, Victor, here all the time to play catch,'' she said. The children froze.

''You have a dog?'' Jamie asked, his eyes huge.

''A real dog?'' Claire asked.

''Puppy?'' Billy piped in.

''Oh, no,'' John groaned. ''They've been after me for months now to get them a dog.''

''What kind is he?''

''Is it a boy or a girl?''

''Puppy?''

Jo laughed and described her collie. ''He's kind of old,'' she said. ''I've had him since I was little, but he's still pretty spunky.''

''Can we see him?''

''Does he do tricks?''

''Puppy?''

She looked at them and burst out laughing. ''The next time we come to the park, I'll bring Victor, okay? Meanwhile, you can play with his Frisbee, if your dad says it's okay.''

John nodded. ''For a few minutes while we get the picnic out. Don't go far,'' he warned. Jo handed the orange toy to Claire and watched them scamper off to an empty strip of grass and begin flipping it back and forth.

''I give them five minutes before at least one of them

is crying," John said, spreading the blanket he'd brought on a smooth patch of grass.

"Maybe six," Jo said, biting back a smile.

It was a glorious day, a southern breeze whispering through the limbs of the nearly naked trees on the park's perimeter. In the distance, behind the fountain, a game of touch football was under way. They were only a few miles from the ocean, so the air smelled and tasted vaguely of salt.

John knelt on a corner of the blanket and opened the basket. He lifted out container after container of great-smelling food from Houchin's Deli.

Jo inhaled and groaned appreciably, sinking to her knees a few feet away from him. "I see you've found the best deli in our fair city."

He turned his face toward her and smiled faintly, rocking back on his heels and resting his big hands on his thighs. He studied her until she became fidgety, then his grin widened. "I seem to have found all the best the city has to offer in a relatively short time."

The tingle started in her ears, quickly enveloped her head, zigged through her torso, then zagged out to her extremities. Her pinkies had grown quite numb. She shouldn't be surprised, she chided herself. He'd made it clear this morning he was interested when he'd asked her to dinner. She knew she shouldn't indulge this flirtation...but she'd come along on the picnic anyway. What did that say about her?

John cleared his throat and bent forward to remove the lids from the containers. "Well," he said, his voice animated, "how were the kids this morning?"

"Not bad," Jo said uneasily, trying to put Jamie's near-driving incident out of her mind. "Claire has her heart set on a strawberry-red kitchen.'' She reached into the basket, carefully dodging his hands and forearms to withdraw a vinyl tablecloth and silverware.

John's mouth tightened. ''Annie always talked about a strawberry-red kitchen.''

''I heard,'' Jo said sympathetically. ''I can make some modifications if that's what you want.''

He shook his head and gave her a wry smile. ''I don't think that would be a good idea. I'll talk to Claire,'' he promised. ''It's really been tough on her, first losing Annie, then moving away from her grandmother.''

''I can only imagine.''

''She needs a woman around the house,'' he continued, then shrugged and smiled, glancing over at her. ''I guess we all do.''

Her pulse quickened at his forthright implication. ''I'm sure you'll remarry someday,'' she said softly.

He studied his children at play for a few seconds, and Jo turned, too. For once, they were all playing together and laughter abounded as the Frisbee bounced along the ground. ''Yes,'' he said confidently. ''I'm sure I'll remarry. I owe them that much.''

Jo swallowed audibly. How had they gotten onto such an intimate subject when all she'd mentioned was the kitchen decor? ''Well,'' she said, withdrawing her notebook, ''Claire was a big help. We did get a lot accomplished this morning. Were you busy at the office?'' Instantly, she bit her tongue at the wifely question.

''Swamped,'' he said quickly, but for some reason couldn't meet her eye. She suspected he, too, was caught by the domesticity of her simple question.

Hurriedly she reviewed the color schemes she'd chosen and talked about one or two pieces of furniture she envisioned for each room, just to get a feel for his tastes.

"I'll leave it all up to you," he said, raising his hands in acquiescence.

"That could be expensive," she told him, laughing.

"I trust you to do a good job and to give me value for my money," he said. "If it suits your taste, then I'm sure it will suit mine."

She averted her eyes from his clear green ones. "I'll work up the design on my computer this weekend. Can you come by on Wednesday to take a look at it?"

He nodded. "I'd be glad to."

Jo snapped her fingers in recollection. "Do you have a sitter lined up for next week?"

His face collapsed into a worried frown. "No."

"I talked to the director at KidScape on Morrow Road this morning—that was the errand I had to run." She swallowed her guilt, and brushed at a fluff of blanket fuzz on her sleeve. "The director said she'd be willing to take them for the week until school resumes, and Billy after that."

John's head came up and he straightened. "Really?"

Jo grinned. "You sound like your kids."

He was visibly relieved. "I can't thank you enough. That's one huge load off my mind."

"No problem," she said.

He looked at her, and she blinked under the intensity of his stare. The wind ruffled his hair, lifting it and tossing it over to one side. He studied her mouth intently. Involuntarily, her lips parted and she moistened their dryness with the tip of her tongue. John leaned forward, his face stopping scant inches from her face, inviting her. As if drawn to him by some invisible force, Jo leaned toward him, her mouth suddenly parched. She stared into his eyes, narrowed and dark with desire. The bill from her cap shadowed his nose. She could feel his breath on her lips, she could see the gilded tips of his eyelashes.

Suddenly the Frisbee bounced off John's forehead. She heard Jamie giggle and ask, "Are you gonna kiss her, Daddy?"

5

"HOW ABOUT a welcome-home kiss?" Alan asked, lowering his mouth to hers.

For a split second, Jo didn't respond while his lips moved soft and familiar upon hers. She couldn't help thinking that John's two near misses had evoked more passion in her. She recovered, though, and kissed him back hard, trying to conjure up a stab of desire.

At her intensity, Alan's eyes widened. He lifted his head and leaned back to give her an appraising look, chuckling. "I guess I was gone longer than I realized."

Jo smiled, feeling sheepish. "Ten whole days."

"I asked you to go with me to Atlanta," he reminded her, his tone faintly shaded with annoyance.

"I know," she said quickly. "But I've been working. Yesterday I picked up a big residential account, and the Pattersons agreed to let me bid on the KidScape account, as well."

He gave her arm a squeeze and angled his blond head indulgently. "Sounds like yesterday was an eventful day."

An understatement of gigantic proportions. She nodded shakily. "You might say that."

Suddenly, he squinted at her, and reached up to smooth a thumb over her cheek. "If you've been working so hard, how did you get the sunburn?'' he asked in a teasing voice.

Jo swallowed. ''I, uh…that is, I sat outside with a client to review preliminary ideas.'' It was *sort of* the truth.

''Did it happen to be a man with a white goatee?''

Jo frowned, puzzled.

''You smell like fried chicken.''

Her mind raced, then she forced herself to relax. ''We had a box lunch while we went over the prep work.'' It was *sort of* the truth.

''This would be your new residential project?'' he asked, not probing, but out of courtesy, Jo felt.

She nodded, adopting what she hoped was a convincing smile.

''Anyone I know?'' He dropped his hands to her waist, and leaned against the back of the couch.

''N-no,'' she assured him. ''The man is an architect from Atlanta. New in town.''

He nodded pleasantly. ''What's his name?''

''John. John Sterling,'' she said, nodding with him. ''K-kids,'' she stammered, lifting her hand in an awkward wave. ''He has lots of kids.''

Alan pulled a comical face. ''A repeat of the Tyndale fiasco, huh?''

''Well, they're not *that* bad, I guess,'' she said, frowning slightly. ''But it's a lively place, that's for sure.'' She was still nodding. ''It took longer than I expected—th-that's why I'm running a little late.'' She glanced at his impeccably creased slacks and collarless dress shirt, then down at her grease-stained tunic and leggings. ''Just give me a few minutes to change.''

Alan looked at his watch. "Sure, but we need to hurry."

Jo gave him a tight smile and made a hasty exit to her bedroom. She closed the door behind her and leaned heavily against it, sighing in exasperation. Normally she wouldn't mind Alan letting himself in to wait, but for some reason anger had flared through her when she'd pulled into the driveway and spotted his Mercedes. Of course, being annoyed with Alan was completely unreasonable considering she'd been late because she was having such a good time with another man.

Victor roused, lifting his head from the rug to greet her with a nose twitch.

"Oh, Vic," she whispered, stepping forward and sinking to her knees to ruffle his silky ears. "I've been a very bad girl."

His groan sounded comforting, his brown eyes moist and sympathetic.

"There's this guy who has three kids—don't look at me like that, I realize I'm nowhere near mom material, but this guy is so...I don't know how to explain what happens to me when he's around."

Victor blinked and yawned.

She laughed wryly. "Okay, I get the hint." Jo rose and walked over to the mirror and leaned in close. With a small amount of relief she noted the absence of a forehead banner reading, Alan, Your Girlfriend Has The Hots For Another Man. Yet she was terrified her body language might somehow betray her before the night ended.

Jo stepped into the bathroom and turned on the shower, then inspected her closet with a thoughtful eye.

At last, she withdrew a snug-fitting full-skirted yellow dress and navy high heels. She was in and out of the shower in two minutes, dressed in another two, dusted on powder to tone down her picnic glow, then slicked a layer of bright color on her lips. Bending forward, she brushed her hair upside down, then swung back up and fluffed the layers with her fingers.

The low whistle Alan emitted when she walked into the living room was gratifying. He drew her into his arms for a brief turn around the living-room floor to imaginary music. She fought to banish the stiffness from her body—Alan didn't deserve to have his evening ruined just because she was feeling out of sorts.

"You look wonderful," he said, wagging his light eyebrows. "If I didn't trust you so much, I'd be afraid someone might snatch you up while I'm traveling."

Jo forced a laugh to join his, then spun around to retrieve her purse. "Ready?" She maintained a tight smile while she slipped her arms into the coat he held for her.

"You know, Jo," Alan murmured as they walked to his silver roadster. "I could stay over tonight."

She shivered involuntarily.

"Chilly?" He held open the passenger door of the two-seater.

"A little," she said, lying.

He frowned. "It's still so warm, I was hoping we could leave the top down."

"By all means," she said hurriedly, smiling wide. "I'm not that cold, after all."

Alan looked perplexed, but hopeful, as he shut her door. "Are you sure?"

She gave him a big nod, still smiling. "Absolutely."

There goes my hairdo. She opened the glove compartment to pull out the scarf she kept inside and instead withdrew a long black satiny glove.

When he swung into his seat, he glanced over at the glove dangling from her raised fingers and shrugged good-naturedly. ''Lower your eyebrows—it's Pamela's. She left it in here after the Chef's Gala last month.'' He inserted the key, turned over the ignition, then waited until her seat belt was fastened and her scarf tied in place before shifting into gear.

''Did she call you?'' Jo asked as they turned out of her neighborhood.

''She called,'' he confirmed, giving her a lopsided grin. ''I'm just a tux for hire. Don't you want to do something together tomorrow night?''

''Actually, the Pattersons want to see my presentation Monday afternoon, so that'll give me a chance to work on it tomorrow evening. Go—I don't mind at all.''

''If you're sure…Pam said Daniel Gates will be there and I've been trying to wangle a meeting with him for months to talk about replacing his mainframe computers.''

''Then you should definitely go.'' For a moment, Jo studied Alan's perfect profile in pure appreciation. There was no denying he was a very handsome man, with Ken-doll good looks and an enviable wardrobe. And very charismatic. His blue eyes sparkled behind tiny wire-rimmed frames, and his blond hair was cut in a trendy, precision style. He was almost as beautiful as Pamela. They probably attracted every eye in the room when they went places together. Her mother had been incredulous when Jo mentioned that Alan often

escorted Pamela to special events. ''Are you mad?''
she'd demanded. ''The woman's a man-eater.''

Jo had laughed then and chuckled now. There were
no two people on this planet less compatible than Alan,
the uptight obsessive-compulsive, and Pamela, the
ditzy nymphomaniac. Alan had made it clear what kind
of woman he was looking for: career-minded, poised,
successful and above reproach—not to mention willing
to share a childless marriage. Jo had always felt fortunate that she fit the bill and shared many of Alan's
goals—she'd never relished the thought of trying to
juggle a career and family.

John Sterling and his half-pint gang galloped into
her mind. T-R-O-U-B-L-E. Trouble she did not want
or need. She pushed them from her thoughts, then
reached over to cover Alan's hand with hers. He lifted
her hand to his mouth for a kiss, and grinned. She
laughed and nodded to herself in affirmation. Alan was
one of the most eligible bachelors from one of the fin-
est families in the old coastal town. Thousands of
women would trade places with her in the blink of an
eye. She was a very lucky woman.

It was *sort of* the truth.

''BUT MOM WANTED a red kitchen with strawberries,''
Claire whined, her voice and chin trembling.

John sighed and nodded. He lowered himself to sit
on her narrow bed and wrapped an arm around her
shoulder to draw her close. ''I know she did, sweetheart, but Mom's not here anymore, and I don't think
it would be such a good idea.''

Claire stared at her hands. ''Would it make you
sad?''

"Probably," he admitted.

"Her furniture and paintings made you sad, didn't they?"

His chest squeezed. Either he'd been wearing his heart on his sleeve, or his nine-year-old was more perceptive than he'd imagined. "Yes, sweetie, they did make me sad."

"Do you want to forget her?" Claire whispered, her voice barely audible.

John's throat clogged with emotion, but he swallowed heavily. His and Annie's personal relationship had had its pitfalls, but she was an impeccable mother, and he'd loved her. "I could never forget her."

She placed her small hand in his. "I don't want to, either, but sometimes I can't remember her face and that scares me."

He tipped her chin up and kissed her on the nose. "All you have to do is look in the mirror, sweetie, because you look just like her."

At last, a tiny smile appeared. "Mommy was pretty, wasn't she, Daddy?"

"Very pretty."

"Do you think I'm pretty?"

He pulled her into his lap and tickled her. "I think you're Miss America."

She giggled. "You're funny, Daddy."

"Claire," he said gently, studying her fair face, "wouldn't you like to have a new mother someday?" She stiffened, her eyes wide, and John held his breath.

"Who?" she asked, a slight note of accusation in her voice.

"No one," he said quickly, keeping his tone light. "I mean, no one yet. But I need to know how you feel about having another woman in the house, just in case.''

Her green eyes narrowed almost imperceptibly. "Jo already has a boyfriend—she told me today they're gonna get married."

The air left his lungs as if he'd been kicked. Was Jo that seriously involved? "I wasn't talking about Jo," he insisted.

"Then why did you almost kiss her?" Claire asked, struggling to get up.

John let her go. "I didn't kiss her."

"You would've if Jamie hadn't butted in," she said, and pouted, arms crossed.

"Maybe," John admitted. "But I didn't know she had a serious boyfriend, and now I do." He leaned toward her, softening. "Don't you like Jo, Claire? I know she likes you."

She mulled over his question, hugging herself and working her mouth. "I guess she's okay. She said she'd give me her Nancy Drew books for helping her with decorating the house."

He felt a little relieved. "That's great. How about let's go downstairs and watch television with the boys? That is—" he grinned at her "—if they haven't killed each other by now."

She grinned, too, and took his hand as they left the room.

"Dad!" Jamie yelled from the bar as they walked into the den. "Billy drank two whole cups of cola!"

John nearly staggered with the knowledge of the effect the caffeine and sugar would have on his already active toddler. He'd be bouncing off the walls. "He's not supposed to be drinking it this late."

"I know," Jamie said in a grave tone that announced he was really gleefully waiting for John to pronounce Billy's punishment.

Billy looked up from his seat on the floor, his chin stained dark from the sweet drink. "I drink pop," he said, holding up the cup for John's inspection.

John pressed his lips together, trying to hide his frustration. "Jamie, how did he pour soda into that little cup from that great big bottle?"

Jamie didn't hesitate. "He's too little, so I had to help him."

"I see. Well, I'll let you clean up this mess while Billy and I visit the potty."

Billy's eyes widened. "Bad potty."

But John didn't give in to his toddler's resistance this time. When Billy succumbed to tears, John scooped him up, talking to him in a low voice, but heading to the downstairs bathroom off the foyer.

John set Billy on his feet just inside the closed bathroom door and squatted to talk to him. "Billy, don't you want to be a big boy?"

Billy nodded, sniffling through his tears, but calming.

"Then you have to learn to pee-pee like a big boy."

"Daddy a big boy?"

"Uh-huh."

"Jamie a big boy?"

"Uh-huh."

"Billy a big boy?"

John pointed to his son's diaper. "Big boys don't wear diapers. Big boys pee-pee in the potty."

Billy's lower lip protruded and the tears welled again. "Billy want to be big boy."

John sighed in relief. "Good. If you learn to use the potty, we'll throw away the diapers and then you'll be a big boy, okay?"

"Okay," he agreed happily.

"Okay, so here we go." John took him by the hand and led him toward the commode and the bright red and blue potty-chair sitting next to it. They'd gone less than a step when Billy froze and began to howl, yanked his hand loose and ran back to press his face against the door.

"Bad potty," he cried. "Monster get Billy."

"No," John said soothingly. "Good potty. Watch Daddy." As John unzipped his pants, he smiled over the age-old father-son lesson. "See," he said patiently. "Daddy's a big boy."

"Mean, monster potty," Billy insisted, grabbing at the doorknob to escape.

Exasperated, John zipped up, then declared, "I know you have to go after all that cola. Come over here and stand by Daddy."

Billy shook his head wildly. "Billy no be big boy."

He strode to his son and lifted him, but Billy stiffened and shrieked hysterically when they neared the commode. Finally, John relented and carried him out of the bathroom. They were both exhausted.

"Claire, why is Billy so scared of that darn potty-chair?"

She looked up at him from her cross-legged position in front of the television and shrugged her thin shoulders. "He's difficult."

John's prediction about the combination of caffeine and sugar on his youngest son proved to be hair-raisingly correct. After an hour of chasing, catching and reprimanding, John wearily dropped onto a bright green beanbag chair and watched little Styrofoam balls pop out of the splitting seams. "We need furniture," he said to the ceiling. A paper airplane sailed over, scant inches from his nose. He blinked, but remained otherwise motionless. Children were like an anesthetic, numbing a parent's normal reflexes.

"What are those, Daddy?" Claire asked, pointing to the television.

John lifted his head and glanced at the screen, then froze. A perky brunette was extolling the virtues of a new and improved tampon design. He watched as the device expanded impressively when dipped into blue water. All moisture left his mouth.

By his estimation, it would be at least two, maybe three years before Claire would begin her cycle. Isn't that what Annie had told him once? *Oh, God, help me.* He cleared his throat. "That's a…thing, yeah, a thing that…women use…in the bathroom…when they're, uh…old enough to…have a baby." Not bad.

"Oh," was her only comment. The commercial had ended, and she turned her attention back to the teenage situation comedy she'd been watching.

He lay his head back and mentally patted himself on the back for handling the matter so smoothly. But he'd call his sister, Cleo, tomorrow and ask her to talk to Claire when they went shopping next weekend, let her know what she could expect to happen over the next few years. His gut tightened at the thought of his little girl maturing, and boys buzzing around her like little bees with big stingers. He groaned and pushed the tormenting thoughts from his mind. He had enough to worry about in the present without heaping on future problems.

His thoughts skipped around, searching for a more pleasurable resting place, and settled on Jo Montgomery. Despite his insistence to Claire that he wasn't entertaining thoughts of marrying Jo, he had to admit the idea of wedding and bedding a gorgeous woman who liked his kids held more appeal with each passing millisecond. Smiling, he absorbed her image fully into his mind, remembering their close encounters of the day. If he had kissed her, would she have kissed him back? He puckered involuntarily. Those velvety dark brown eyes, that wonderful dimple, that luxurious mouth.

Which was probably kissing another man right now.

John frowned. His dream woman was most likely sharing a romantic dinner with her boyfriend, discussing plans for having their own family someday soon.

"NO KIDS," Alan told the maître d'. "Smoking is fine, but no kids."

The balding tuxedoed man nodded quickly and consulted his seating chart. He frowned in concentration, then gave the hostess a table number. "Right this way, sir."

Jo squashed a twinge of annoyance at Alan's words as they were led to a table partially hidden by miniature palms and giant ferns. She, too, had had more than one good meal disturbed by rowdy children. She just wished he wouldn't announce his disdain for kids quite so often and so publicly.

Alan looked around the table suspiciously, pulled out Jo's seat for her, then took his own.

"Don't you want to check under the tablecloth?" Jo asked, her voice slightly sarcastic.

Alan grinned, then reached to cover her hand with his. "I don't want anything or anyone to spoil our dinner."

"Tell me about Atlanta," she said, opening the menu. While he talked about his business in the city, Jo forced herself to concentrate on his words. John's face kept appearing in her mind and she couldn't seem to find anything on the pricey menu that looked as good as fried chicken from Houchin's Deli. A waiter appeared and took their wine and food order, then left them alone. Jo realized she had never felt so uncomfortable around Alan—and hoped he wouldn't notice.

"Is everything all right?" he asked, leaning forward.

"Oh, sure," she said, conjuring up a smile. "I guess I'm just preoccupied with the Patterson account."

"Baby-sitting, isn't it?"

"Day cares," she corrected. "Twenty-one day cares."

"I can't believe there's so much demand for that kind of service," Alan said, shaking his head. "Why do people have children if they're not willing to raise them?"

The waiter arrived with the wine, so Jo bit back her retort. As the pale liquid splashed into their glasses, she gathered her thoughts, but saved her reply until the man had moved out of earshot.

"Some people have to work, Alan," she said tightly, lifting her glass to take a sip. "So they have to place their children in day-care centers." The wine tasted sharp and slightly bitter.

"If it takes both parents working to make a living,

then they shouldn't have children,'' he said matter-of-factly.

"What about single parents?" she pressed.

He took a long drink, then held up his half-empty glass to inspect the wine, nodding in satisfaction. "With both people working and kids to deal with, too, no wonder the divorce rate is so high."

Jo felt her ire rising by the second. "What if one of the parents has passed away and the survivor has no choice but to work to feed his children?"

"This is starting to sound personal."

Jo shrugged and looked away.

"This new client of yours—Mr. Extra Crispy—is he by chance a widower?"

Her pulse vaulted, but she tried to sound nonchalant. "As a matter of fact, he is."

His expression softened and he nodded congenially. "And you feel sorry for him. That's understandable." He stroked the back of her hand, smiling. "I'm just glad we'll never have to worry about it."

Toying with the hem of her linen napkin, Jo spoke quietly. "Alan, just because we don't want to be parents doesn't mean you should hold it against other people who do."

He propped his elbows on the table and leaned forward in a conciliatory manner. "You're absolutely right—if other people want rug rats underfoot, it's nothing to me, right? Just as long as they don't insist on bringing their monsters to nice restaurants."

As if on cue, something flew through the wall of ferns and smacked Alan on the temple. In disbelief, he watched a buttered dinner roll bounce onto their table and stop beside the silver candlestick holder. A woman's big blond head appeared immediately through the same opening. She smiled apologetically, her eyes shining.

"I'm so sorry, sir. Preston got carried away and threw his bread." She poked an arm through the foliage and swiped a napkin at the trail of butter on Alan's head, then grabbed the roll and disappeared with a smile.

Alan clenched his jaw and narrowed his eyes dangerously in the direction of the ferns. "Of all the—"

The reappearance of the woman's head cut him off.

"Tell the man you're sorry, Preston," she said in a pleading voice. She held a small boy horizontal by his waist and thrust him into Alan's face.

"No!" the boy yelled, and stuck his tongue out, nearly licking Alan's nose.

"Say it," his mother cajoled. "Say you're sorry and Mommy will buy you a toy on the way home."

"I sorry," the little boy snarled.

"There," his mother said brightly. "He's such a good boy." And they promptly disappeared again.

Jo maintained the silence for a full minute as she watched Alan slowly wipe the remains of the greasy mess from his cheek with shaking hands. "That," he said with venom in his voice, "is a prime example of a parent who doesn't know the merits of discipline. Imagine, that child will be operating a vehicle one of these days."

She tried to keep her eyes down, but her shaking shoulders must have given her away.

"Josephine," he said in a shocked voice. "This is *not* funny."

"I'm s-sorry, Alan," she said, fighting to keep down

the giggles. "But if you could have seen the look on your face—" She erupted into laughter, holding her napkin over her mouth to muffle the sound.

"Oh, and what kind of message are we sending these pint-size terrors when we laugh at their antics?"

Dabbing at her eyes, Jo said, "Lighten up, Alan, he's just a little kid." A movement across the restaurant caught her eye and she glanced over, then froze in horror.

Melissa and Monroe Patterson were striding toward their table, all smiles.

6

JO'S STOMACH somersaulted. She jerked her head over to look at Alan, who was wiping his face so intently, he hadn't yet noticed the couple.

"Alan!" she gasped, holding the cloth napkin to her forehead. "I feel faint—please get a pitcher of ice water."

He glanced up, frowning with worry. "You've never felt faint in your life."

"Well, I do now!" she said desperately, lurching forward. "Would you just find the waiter and get me some water?"

"Okay," he said, his eyes wide. "I'll be right back."

He had just walked out of earshot when Melissa Patterson glided up to the table. "Ms. Montgomery," she exclaimed coolly, extending her hand. "What a nice surprise."

Jo shot to her feet and yanked a smile from thin air. "Hello, Mr. and Mrs. Patterson." Pumping their hands furiously, Jo angled her body to block the couple's view of Alan's receding back.

"We were just leaving," Mr. Patterson said with a smile, "when Melissa looked over and saw you sitting here."

Mrs. Patterson craned her neck to peer around Jo. "I see we just missed your husband, John."

Jo nodded emphatically, then changed directions abruptly, shaking her head just as emphatically. "No, that's just a friend—a friend of mine and John's, actually," she said cheerfully. She used the napkin to dab at the perspiration on her forehead. "John is...home with the children, of course."

Smiling tightly, Mrs. Patterson said, "I hope you enjoyed the visit this morning—your stepchildren are just so adorable."

Jo couldn't stop nodding. "John's children are adorable, aren't they?" Then she cleared her voice, and glanced over her shoulder, alarmed to see Alan returning. She swung back to the Pattersons. "Well," she said brightly, "don't let me keep you."

"Hello," Mr. Patterson said to Alan as he walked up and stood next to Jo.

"Hello," Alan said politely, extending his free hand, holding a pitcher of ice water in the other. He looked to Jo for an introduction.

"Oh," she said, straightening. "Alan, this is Melissa and Monroe Patterson. And this is Alan Parish."

"Nice to meet you," Melissa said, smiling wide. "I hear you're a friend of John Sterling's."

Alan looked confused. "Well," he said with a small laugh, "Jo knows him a little better than I do."

The Pattersons laughed uproariously, and Jo joined in belatedly, elbowing Alan into a small bewildered smile.

"Well, we'd better be going," Mr. Patterson said, and his wife nodded, waving as they walked away. "We're looking forward to the presentation Monday."

Jo slid into her seat and heaved a sigh of relief.

"I see you recovered," Alan said, setting the pitcher of water on the table.

"Not quite," she mumbled, ignoring the water and downing her glass of wine.

He sat down. "Did I miss something?"

"N-no," Jo stammered, unable to meet his gaze.

"What's the connection between the Pattersons and your other client?"

She opened her mouth and let the words fall out, hoping they would make some sort of sense. "Remember I told you the man has kids? Well, they go to the Pattersons' day care I visited this morning, that's all."

"Oh," Alan said, already losing interest.

But Jo's anxiety had reached dizzying proportions by the time their entrées arrived. Although her salmon smelled delicious, she did little more than push it around on her plate.

"Jo," Alan chided, "you've hardly eaten a bite. Are you still feeling ill?"

"Yes," she said truthfully, the full weight of her lie wallowing heavily in her stomach.

"Should we go?"

"No," she said quickly. "My appetite's gone, that's all. Enjoy your meal." It took her a few more minutes to convince Alan they should stay, then, to distract him, she asked him to tell her more about his business trip. With an air of satisfaction, he described the deal he'd arranged with a former competitor, punctuating the details of the final meeting with a flourishing twist of his fork. When he finished, she asked, "Did you get to have any fun?"

He shrugged. "A couple of dinner shows that were pretty good."

"Were you able to find the watch you were looking for?"

Alan shook his head and smiled, a beautiful picture of curvy lips and straight, white teeth. "No, but I did find something for you today."

Her heart blipped. They'd often joked about looking for a ring, but surely he hadn't bought one—not *today*. "S-something for me?"

He grinned. "I wasn't going to tell you, but you know I can't keep surprises. I left it in the car—I can't wait to give it to you."

"What is it?" she asked, smiling tremulously and raising her refilled wineglass for another deep sip.

Alan tilted his head and gave her a sly smile. "Let's just say it's something you've needed for a long time, something we've both been putting off. I bought one to match for myself."

She inhaled sharply, choking on the wine sliding down her throat. Collapsing into a seizure of coughing and sputtering, she quaked in her chair, aided in no way by the backslapping, arm-jerking actions of Alan and a nervous waiter. When she'd finally regained composure, Jo asked again, "What did you buy?"

But he only shook his head. "Let's wait until I take you home, I've already given away too much."

Jo sweated through dessert, and fretted through cappuccino. By the time they pulled into the driveway of her duplex, she was nauseous with dread.

"Go on in," Alan encouraged with an engaging grin. "I'll get the surprise."

The few steps into her living room seemed like her

last, taking her to the pit of doom. Jo's head spun. What was she going to tell him when he gave her the ring? Her mother's face popped into her head. "Tell him yes, Josephine, what else?" Then Hattie's face appeared, her finger wagging. "Is he the man who floats your goat?" Then John Sterling's face appeared. "Either you're being untruthful, or the man's an idiot."

Her heart was nearly leaping out of her chest when she heard Alan enter the room.

"Don't turn around," he warned. Paper bags rustled behind her.

"Okay," he said. "You can look."

Jo turned around ever so slowly, her throat closing in anticipation. Alan's grin was blinding as he proudly presented matching tan lizard-skin briefcases. Her knees weakened in relief.

"Do you like it?" he asked excitedly, thrusting the more streamlined version toward her. "The leather is virtually indestructible, the combination lock is solid brass and the handle is guaranteed for life."

"It's beautiful," she murmured, fingering the nubby finish and feeling somewhat foolish. How like Alan— so practical.

Alan smiled happily, stroking his own briefcase. "Now I can toss my old one and you can get rid of that worn-out black bag you've been carrying for years."

Jo bit back a frown. Hattie had given her that worn-out black bag for college graduation—it was the same leather briefcase Hattie had used for most of her own professional life, and it meant a lot to Jo.

"Don't you love it?" he pressed. "It's made out of top-quality lizard—look, hardly any seams at all."

"Mhmm," she agreed, grasping for some level of enthusiasm for his thoughtful, expensive gift. "It's just lovely, Alan," she said, walking into his arms for a hug and a quick kiss.

"I wish you were feeling better," he murmured. "I could be talked into spending the night."

She drew back from him, both surprised and annoyed he'd chosen today of all days to become so amorous. Had she last seen him naked on Halloween? "Maybe next time," she said softly. "Thank you for the briefcase, it's beautiful."

"I knew you'd like it," he breathed, making her feel a little worse. He gave her a sweet, lingering kiss, then said, "I'll call you on Sunday and let you know how Pam's banquet went."

Jo nodded, then walked him to the door. She waved as his car lights passed over her when he backed out of the driveway. Sighing, she hugged herself tight and leaned against the door frame, trying to sort out the jumbled thoughts in her head. Why had John Sterling's name been on the tip of her tongue all night? Why had she seen his face instead of Alan's every time she glanced across the table? And why had she been so terrified when she thought Alan was going to propose?

Hoping Hattie was home, Jo stepped out onto her tiny porch and pulled the door shut behind her. A slight breeze had kicked up, chasing dried, dead leaves across the small lawn. She walked down the steps and all the way around the side of her house to the other house-front nearly identical to hers. Except where her shutters and door were dark green, Hattie's were bright yellow. While Jo's fall mums were long gone, Hattie's double-bloom pink and white camelias were lovely in the winter moonlight. And where Jo's doormat read simply Welcome, Hattie's read, Don't Bother Knocking, Come On In.

Only Jo did knock, because she knew Hattie's penchant for late-night meditation—in the nude.

Within a few seconds, Hattie answered the door, predictably knotting the belt of a housecoat at her waist. She smiled wide. "Jo, my dear, come in."

"Am I interrupting something?"

Her aunt scoffed as she stepped aside to admit Jo. "I don't have a man in here, if that's what you mean." She grinned, smoothing her silver hair, and added, "Darn it."

Jo shook her head and laughed. "Hattie, you're shameless. I'm surprised Herbert can keep up with you."

"He can't," quipped Hattie, "which is why I'm waiting for my soldier to come home. Has Alan already gone home?" At Jo's nod, Hattie winked and said, "Since he's been out of town for so long, I figured the two of you would be celebrating all night."

Smiling wryly, Jo said, "I wasn't feeling well." She followed Hattie into a modest-size country kitchen decorated with a rooster motif, and sat at the table while her aunt poured greenish tea into two stoneware cups.

"You do look a little flushed," Hattie said, squinting at her and sitting down.

Jo winced sheepishly. "It's a sunburn."

"Oh?" Her aunt's eyebrows rose over the cup she lifted to her mouth. "Do tell."

She shrugged, avoiding Hattie's gaze. "Nothing to tell."

Hattie sipped loudly. "Would there happen to be a client of yours sporting the same sunburn?"

Jo sipped. "Maybe."

Hattie sipped. "And would this happen to be the same man with whom the Pattersons think you share three children?"

Jo sipped and looked up into her aunt's bright blue eyes. "Maybe."

Hattie set her cup down. "So tell me about this John Sterling."

Shifting in her seat, Jo contemplated her answer, and decided to go with the innocent version. "He's a widower—"

"Jo," her aunt chided gently, "skip the résumé and tell me why he has you so flustered."

Sighing, Jo said, "Okay, he asked me to dinner."

"And?"

"And I told him I was already involved with someone."

"So what gives with the sunburn?"

"When I brought the kids back from our visit at the day-care center, he had a picnic packed and asked me to go so we could discuss plans for his house."

"Ah." Hattie nodded, satisfied, then retrieved her cup for another sip.

"What's 'ah'?" Jo inquired defensively.

Hattie shrugged. "Go on."

"There's nothing else to tell."

"So are you interested?"

Jo nearly choked on her tea. "No!"

"Why not? Is he hard on the eyes?"

Taking a calming breath, Jo spoke carefully. "Beauty is in the eye of the beholder."

Hattie nodded agreement. "And do you behold him?"

Jo couldn't help smiling at her aunt's persistence. "I suppose he's handsome in a rugged sort of way."

"Ah."

"What's with the 'ah'?"

"Why don't you go out with the man?"

Jo pretended to ponder the question. "Let's see," she said, holding up one hand to count. "He has three children, I have a boyfriend, and he has three children."

"Well—" Hattie grinned "—at least you know he can get it up."

"Hattie!"

"Which brings us back to your second point—of having a so-called boyfriend."

"Hattie, I know you've never been crazy about Alan, but—"

"I only want what's best for you, Jo, and Alan Parish is so much like his dad, he couldn't be very good in bed."

Jo's jaw dropped. "Hattie, you mean you and Aldred Parish actually…"

Hattie clucked. "Call it two weeks of insanity before I found your uncle Francis, and while I was still mourning my soldier, Torry." She sighed dreamily. "Ahhh, Torry. Now *there* was a lover. A Frenchman had sold him this fuzzy little contraption—"

"Hattie," Jo interrupted, trying to steer the conversation back to the present. "I've never complained about Alan's…virility."

"You didn't have to," Hattie drawled. "The man's always gone by ten o'clock."

"He respects me," Jo said, frowning slightly.

"Which is a good thing," Hattie agreed, studying the dregs in the bottom of her cup. "But the real question is—" she raised her eyes, suddenly turning serious "—does Alan *move* you?"

Jo allowed the words to sink in, turning them over in her mind, dissecting and analyzing them. Alan was gorgeous, successful, intelligent—everything a woman could want, everything she'd ever wanted. So why was she suddenly feeling so...restless? Straightening her shoulders, she said, "Hattie, it takes more than great sex to make a relationship work."

"Maybe so," her aunt relented with a nod. "But you can't have a good relationship without it." She smiled at Jo. "The nighttime secrets you share are the memories that make you feel close to your lover even when you're apart. I think that's why Torry is still so strongly on my mind after all these years." Her grin deepened. "I simply can't wait to see him again."

Jo's eyes bulged. "You've heard from him?"

"No, but the detective called me this afternoon and said he had some promising leads."

While fairly sure this "detective" Hattie had hired to find her lost soldier was a bit of a swindler, Jo nonetheless tried to mirror her aunt's enthusiasm. "That's wonderful, Hattie. I'm sure you'll find him soon."

Hattie nodded happily, then said, "Life is short, Jo—don't settle. Wait for the man who warms your heart *and* heats your bed."

John Sterling's face came to Jo again, this time in alarming clarity. She stood up to shake the unsettling feelings her aunt had stirred. "It's getting late—I'd better go." She headed toward the door, then turned around at the last second. Hattie still sat at the table, cradling her teacup. "Thanks for the talk, Hattie."

Her aunt smiled and nodded wisely. "Just remember, Jo, a hard man is good to find." She raised her cup in a good-night salute. Jo smiled and shook her head, then pulled the door shut.

"I CALLED TO ASK YOU to bring your puppy the next time you come over."

Whistling under his breath, John walked into the kitchen in time to overhear his son's words. He frowned, hands on hips. "Jamie, who are you calling at this hour?"

"Jo," the little boy said matter-of-factly, not bothering to cover the mouthpiece.

John's heart vaulted. *"Jo Montgomery?"*

"Yeah."

Astounded, John gasped. "Where did you get her number?"

"If you dial zero, the lady that answers will tell you everything," Jamie said earnestly. "Do you want to know where Jo lives, too?"

"No!" John sputtered. "I mean…" He thrust out his hand. "Give me the phone, young man."

"Bye, Jo," Jamie said breathlessly into the mouthpiece. "Daddy wants to talk to you now." He tossed the handset to John and scooted out of the kitchen, just clearing his father's light swat.

John cursed under his breath as the handset slipped through his fingers and bounced twice on the hardwood floor. He scooped it up and juggled it a few seconds longer before he raised it to his ear. "Hello?"

"Hello," Jo said, the laughter clear in her voice.

"Jo, I'm so sorry. I can't believe my son called you." He laughed nervously, wondering if the man she was involved with was sitting—or worse, *lying*—beside her, rolling his eyes at the Sterling family antics. "We interrupted your evening," he asserted.

"Not really," she replied. "I'd just returned from visiting my aunt Hattie. She lives in the other side of my duplex."

"You don't have…company?" he asked lightly.

"Just Victor, my dog," she said, then laughed. "By the way, I didn't get to tell Jamie that I usually don't take Victor to work with me."

John relaxed. "I guess the Sterling men keep hoping you'll make exceptions in our case."

"The picnic was an exception," she said pointedly.

He grinned. "Then we're wearing you down?"

She laughed again. "You both get points for persistence."

"I had a good time today."

"It was fun." Her voice sounded cautious.

He took a gamble. "I can be fun without my three groupies, too."

She was silent for a few seconds during which he was sure she could hear his heart thumping across the line. Finally she said, "John, I've always made it a rule never to mix my business and personal lives." Was that the tiniest hint of regret in her voice, or was he simply wishing too hard?

"Okay," he said, not even trying to keep the disappointment from his voice. "Business it is."

After an awkward pause, Jo said, "I need to swing by your house Monday morning with my laptop, if that's okay."

"Fine," he agreed quickly. "In case we're already gone, I'll leave a key under the mat." He coughed lightly. "I want to thank you again for making the arrangements with KidScape—you must do a lot of work for them to be able to call in a favor."

She laughed, a musical sound. "Well, actually, I'm still vying for their business, but I think I'm making progress."

"I wish you luck," he said, then winced as a crashing sound reverberated from upstairs. "I have to say goodbye," he said. "Unless my ears deceive me, I'd say yet another piece of the boys' bedroom furniture has bitten the dust."

"Are they okay?" she asked, sounding alarmed.

"I don't hear any screaming, so that's a good sign," he said. "I'll talk to you soon, I hope."

"Soon," she parroted softly, then quickly added, "Goodbye."

John stared at the phone for a few seconds, then turned and bounded up the stairs.

"So what do you think?" Pamela Kaminski asked, turning sideways. Jo blinked and glanced at her mother who seemed a bit awestruck by Pam's silhouette in the shimmering minidress.

She looked back to her curvaceous friend. "It's smashing, Pam. The gold is perfect with your hair."

"Think so?" the blonde asked, squinting in the mirror.

"You look cold," Helen said, frowning.

Jo elbowed her. "Mother, please," she hissed out of the side of her mouth.

"Well, she does," Helen whispered. "That's not a dress—it's a belt."

"Try the black one," Jo urged, smiling at her friend.

When Pamela disappeared into the dressing room, Helen sighed loudly. "Josephine, I cannot believe you're actually helping this woman pick out a gown to wear on a date with *your* boyfriend."

Jo inhaled deeply. She should have her head examined for inviting her mother to join them shopping. "It's not a date, mother—it's a business obligation and I don't mind."

"You're practically *asking* him to be unfaithful," her mother mumbled.

"I trust Alan," Jo said earnestly. "And Pam, too." More than she trusted herself these days. She rubbed her eyes and stifled a yawn. John Sterling had haunted her dreams all night and she'd awakened feeling cranky. A distracting morning of shopping had sounded appealing a few hours ago. Now it stretched before her like a life sentence.

Minutes later, the demure black dress cast aside and the gold belt-dress bagged and paid for, Jo strolled toward the food court between her best friend and her mother. "How about ice cream?" she asked, trying to cut through the tension emanating from her mother.

"I'm game," Pam said cheerfully.

"Are you sure?" Helen asked, cocking one eyebrow toward Pam. "That zipper looked a bit strained to me."

Pam's eyes narrowed, and Jo angled herself between the two women. "Now, Mother—" She broke off when Helen was jostled from behind.

"Well!" her mother huffed as a child streaked by.

Jo's breath caught when she recognized the unfurled edge of a black towel.

"Jamie!" John's voice reached her ears through the crowd. "Come back here, right now!"

Jo sprinted forward and caught the edge of the towel just as the boy yelled, "I'm Peter!"

She pulled him up short, then spun him around. His frown changed to a huge grin when he saw who held him. "Hiya, Jo!" he exclaimed.

John jogged up to them, bouncing Billy on his hip, with Claire lagging behind. "Jo," he said, his voice full of surprise.

"John," she acknowledged, alarmed at the rush of pleasure she felt. He wore a dark green leather bomber jacket and loose-fitting jeans topping athletic shoes.

He swung Billy to the ground, then straightened and grinned, brushing back waves of auburn hair from his forehead. "Fancy seeing you here."

"Jo?" Helen asked, walking up with a small frown. Pamela's eyes were devouring John's bare left hand and Jo was dismayed at the twinge of jealousy that pulsed through her. Quickly, she made introductions, feeling ridiculously nervous as Pamela extended her beautifully manicured hand to John and batted her gorgeous eyes.

John nodded to Pam, then turned back to Jo and smiled, sending her pulse racing. "Shopping?"

She waved toward her friend. "Pam needed a party dress for tonight."

"A business engagement," Pam quickly assured him. "Jo was good enough to lend me her boyfriend as an escort. I'm not currently seeing anyone," she told him with a slight tilt of her head.

"Hey, Jo," Jamie said, tugging on the hem of her shirt. "When are you bringing over your puppy?"

Billy raised his arms to her. "Poopy diaper," he said. Jo winced, then bent over to pick him up.

"Jo," Claire said, stabbing her glasses back in place. "Daddy said you're coming to decorate our house while we're at day care this week. Can't I stay home with you?" she pleaded. "I want to help."

"Me, too!" Jamie yelled. "I want to stay with Jo."

"Me, too!" Billy shouted, sticking out his bottom lip.

"That's enough," John said. "Jo can't work if she's got the four of us underfoot, can she?" He reached for Billy, but the toddler only tightened his grip around Jo's neck.

"Don't worry, Claire," she said, winking. "We'll work out something." Then to John, she asked, "Shopping?"

He looked sheepish. "Not really. The VCR is broken." He frowned in Jamie's direction. "And I was hoping to find something here to entertain them while Mrs. Harris cleans the house." He lowered his voice and leaned toward her. "Any ideas?"

Jo thought for a few seconds. "There's a pet store down the west wing," she said, pointing.

He brightened. "Great idea. Come on, Billy," he said. "Let's go see the puppies."

Billy clapped his hands and allowed John to take him. The older children shouted goodbye and scampered ahead.

"The rest rooms are a few doors down," she said to John. "They probably have a changing table."

"I'm trying to potty-train him," John said, frowning at his youngest.

Billy's face screwed up. "Monster potty."

They both laughed, locking gazes for a few seconds. Jo's heart thumped against her chest. When she remembered their audience, she looked away. "Well," she said, "good luck at the pet store."

"Nice to meet both of you," John said, inclining his head to Helen and Pam.

"The pleasure was mine," Pam said smoothly, offering him a model smile.

Jo watched him walk away, laden with Billy and a diaper bag, fighting the urge to follow them. Pam walked up beside her and watched, too. "Yummy," she said, her eyes reflecting blatant admiration.

Helen pursed her lips and smirked. "I didn't know you were so fond of children, Pamela."

Pam's gaze was still glued to his retreating backside. "I didn't say I wanted to marry the guy, just—" Her eyes snapped to Helen as if she suddenly remembered who she was talking to. "Just *see* him," she finished with a smile.

Protective feelings curled low in Jo's stomach, but she remained silent. She had known it would only be a matter of time before Pam discovered the eligible John Sterling. The two of them might even hit it off.

The thought bothered her immensely.

EARLY IN THE EVENING Jo drove to her office to work on the Patterson presentation. Because hers had been the last firm granted permission to bid on the day-care account, she had less time to prepare, but her software lent her a huge advantage in the design stage. A few hours tonight, a few more tomorrow, and she'd be ready for the presentation Monday afternoon. As she turned on her computer, she chuckled at Jamie's adamant assertion that the day care was boring. Within two hours, she'd assembled a media room and a nature room just as he'd described.

Jo relaxed in her desk chair and stretched her arms overhead. She felt sure the Pattersons would be pleased. Mentally she ticked off the hours until she made her proposal. Three o'clock Monday afternoon. While reaching for her calendar, her hand touched the Sterling home file, and Jo opened it impulsively.

She itched to begin the project. Although commercial jobs were her bread and butter, the residential jobs were some of her favorites because they unleashed her creativity. And the Sterling house...well, she was looking forward to making it more comfortable and homey for the children. Guilt over her lie to the Pattersons pawed at her. Making sure John's kids had a warm, attractive environment was the least she could do.

The peal of the delivery bell broke her reverie. Jo glanced at her watch. Nine o'clock—but some of her new vendors delivered at odd hours. She glanced down at her tattered jeans and faded pink jersey. At least it wasn't a client. She picked up her ring of keys and headed to the front door, frowning at the shadow of a large man through the lightly frosted glass. She was always wary when she worked alone, especially at night. When she reached the door, she yelled, "Do you have a delivery for Montgomery Group Interiors?"

"Sort of—Jo, it's me...John Sterling."

Her pulse leaped and she immediately thought the worst. Had he discovered her little lie? Had he come by to confront her? What on earth was she going to say? Her hand shook as she tried to insert the key into the lock.

John had convinced himself on the drive over that delivering the catalog she'd left at his house was a legitimate excuse for seeing Jo. But now, standing in the semidarkness and shouting through the woman's office door, the idea seemed slim at best.

"John," she said from the other side of the door, "what are you doing here?"

He couldn't tell if she was annoyed or simply surprised. *Say something provocative, Sterling.* "I wanted to see for myself a woman who works while her boyfriend goes out with her beautiful girlfriend."

A few seconds passed. "Is that all?"

So much for provocative. "No—I brought a catalog you left at my house."

She was silent for so long John wondered if she'd walked away from the door. Well, one thing was sure—she wasn't nearly as anxious to see him tonight as he'd been to see her. He cleared his throat. "How about if I just leave it here on the doorstep?"

She swung open the door and squinted into the glare of the outdoor light. "Sorry," she said, offering him a small smile. She looked all of eighteen in her jeans and adorable ragged sneakers. She blushed, fingering the hem of her shirt. "I wasn't expecting anyone."

He looked into her big brown eyes, unnerved by the longing she evoked in him. "You look great," he said softly.

She laughed awkwardly. Peering toward his car in the darkness, she asked, "Are you alone?"

"Yeah," he said. "My in-laws came down from Atlanta to spend the night with the kids, so I'm on my own.'' He thumped the catalog. "Mrs. Harris found this under Billy's bed, and since I knew you were working late..." His voice petered out because she crossed her arms under her breasts and his throat suddenly closed. She was not wearing a bra and she obviously felt the chill.

"Would you like to come in for a few minutes?" she asked. "I was just about to make some coffee."

"Sure," he said too quickly, dragging his gaze from her chest. "The temperature has definitely dropped."

"Mmm," she murmured agreement as she shut the door. Her skin and eyes were luminous. "I knew the heat wave wouldn't last long."

Sweat popped out on his upper lip as he stared at her, completely taken with her beauty. "It's warm in here," he said softly, feeling his temperature rise with her every movement.

Jo laughed nervously and nodded toward the light streaming into the hallway from an open door. "I hope you like decaf."

John nodded agreeably, then unabashedly watched her rear end as she led the way to a brightly lit office. The room contained a desk, a computer workstation, a small couch, plus a worktable in the corner stacked high with fabric and paper samples.

"I'm obviously taking you away from something," he said.

Glancing up from the coffeemaker, she said, "Actually, I'd just finished a segment for a large account I'm bidding on, and I'd picked up the folder on your house."

Hoping to extract more information, he kept his

voice light and teasing. "I hope my project isn't keeping you from spending time with your boyfriend. I'd hate to stand in the way of true love."

She caught his gaze for a few seconds, then looked down again and said, "You're not."

He bit his lower lip, then threw caution to the wind. "Do you mean I'm not standing in the way, or it isn't true love?"

She looked up again and he saw the briefest glint of desire in her eyes. "Like I said, I don't mix my personal and professional lives." Jo reached for the catalog, her hand brushing his in the exchange.

Encouraged by her expression and bolstered by her touch, he shrugged good-naturedly. "My kids would never forgive me if I didn't give it my best shot." Grinning, he added, "They're crazy about you."

Something unreadable passed over her face, but she remained silent.

Trying to smooth over the awkward moment, he said, "I should thank you for the pet-store idea. The kids had a blast, although now they're begging me for a dog more than ever."

She seemed relieved with the change in subject and waved a hand toward the small couch, gesturing for him to sit. "Is there a reason they shouldn't have a dog?" she asked.

This time he laughed out loud. "In case you haven't noticed, my household isn't exactly orderly. A dog would take it a step beyond chaos, don't you think?"

"It might help the kids become more responsible—" She broke off and blushed. "Not that I'd know," she said softly. "About kids, I mean."

He sat down, grimacing at the distance between the

couch and where she seated herself behind her desk. "You seem pretty maternal to me," he said breezily. "Do you see children in your future?" He wondered if his question would seem as transparent to her as it sounded to him.

But she only laughed, her dimple appearing at last. "You sound like my mother."

"Uh-oh," he said, enjoying the banter. "One of *those* mothers."

Rising at the beep of the coffeemaker, she nodded. "She can be pretty relentless." He watched her move gracefully around the room, loving the way no movement was wasted. When she turned her back, he feasted on her behind in snug jeans, the faded pockets worn white around the edges, the fabric papery thin. He squinted, trying to make out the design on her underwear, then straightened when she turned toward him.

"Cream or sugar?"

Mesmerized, he shook his head dumbly.

She handed him a steaming cup, then set her own on a small table beside the couch. Walking back to her desk, she retrieved a folder. "While you're here," she said, "perhaps you can answer a few questions about your house."

John didn't care if the folder contained crossword puzzles as long as it got Jo Montgomery next to him. He inhaled sharply as she sat down, her leg brushing against his. Jo opened the folder, the motion wafting the wonderful pear scent from her skin to his nose. His groin tightened at her nearness, his hand twitching with the need to touch her face. Biting his tongue hard, he gave himself a mental shake. One would think he'd never been around a woman before.

A delectable, smart, great-smelling, mommy-material woman.

"—so I'll let you decide," she finished, smiling at him expectantly.

He had no idea what she'd been saying. The various sketches she held gave him no clues. "You're the expert," he said with a shaky laugh. "I'll defer to your judgment."

"But it's *your* bedroom," she said, glancing up.

He caught her gaze and dared her to look away. She didn't. "I'll love anything you do in *my* bedroom," he said, his voice husky.

The pupils of her eyes dilated, and he moved toward her ever so slowly, determined this time to capture her lips. Jo remained motionless, but he saw her lips part, as if she was readying herself for him. Carefully, he angled his head and closed the distance between them until their noses touched and her breath whispered against his mouth. He searched her dark eyes a split second before his lips caressed hers. Her lips softened beneath his, but she didn't respond until he offered the tip of his tongue. Then a moan erupted from her throat, and she melted into him. Nearly weak with desire, John groaned and reached to gather her against him.

Suddenly a bolt of white-hot pain exploded in his groin, a sensation so horrific, he tore his mouth from hers and howled, jumping to his feet. His empty coffee cup rolled from his lap and bounced on the carpet. With no thought other than getting the wet heat away from his privates, John unzipped his fly and pulled the heavy fabric away from his skin. A dark stain covered the crotch of his chinos.

"Oh, my," Jo gasped, her hand over her mouth.

Feeling like an idiot, John angled himself away from her as much as possible to hold the thin cotton of his boxers out and fan his scorched skin. He didn't even want to look down. The pain had subsided to a screaming throb.

"John," she said, stirring behind him. "Are you okay?"

"Yeah." He cringed. "But it's a good thing I already have a family."

"Is there anything I can do to...help?"

He turned back to see her biting her lip, clearly torn by the implied intimacy of the situation.

John gave her a lopsided grin. "Can you help me find a hole to crawl into?"

She smiled.

He laughed.

She chuckled.

John's shoulders shook with mirth and mingled pain. Jo crossed her arms and pressed her lips together, her amusement bubbling to gay laughter. After several minutes, John wiped his eyes, and said, "Well, this would be hard to explain to someone walking in, wouldn't it?"

She nodded, her dimple highlighted, her eyes shining.

Still cloaked in embarrassment, he fastened his pants and zipped them, then turned back to face her. "This isn't what I had in mind when I came over here."

Jo pursed her lips, her expression growing serious. "Good." She studied the toe of her sneaker for a few seconds.

"Jo," he said nervously. "About what happened—"

"It can't happen again," she said firmly, lifting her

gaze to his. "Alan and I have an understanding, and kissing clients isn't part of it."

He took a deep breath and swallowed his disappointment, chewing on the inside of his cheek as he nodded and turned to leave. At the door, he paused. "Next time, you should try to negotiate in that 'kissing clients' clause."

"DISCIPLINE," Helen Montgomery said, wagging her head in dismay. "Discipline is what kids need today. Have another piece of meat loaf, Josephine." Without waiting for Jo's reply, her mother plopped a second generous slice onto her plate. "Take those kids yesterday—what was the man's name? Sterling? His children are completely out of control."

"Mom," Jo murmured. "The man lost his wife—"

"Sad, I know," her mother agreed, spooning more whipped potatoes beside the unwanted meat on Jo's plate. "But he's not doing his kids a favor by not making them mind."

Jo's father glanced her way. "She's even harder to follow when she starts talking in double negatives."

"Hush, Madden," Helen warned with a fork.

"I've met them," Hattie said, holding a green bean up to the light as if to inspect it for lint. "They seemed like pretty good kids to me."

"Uh-hmm," Helen responded, clearly voiding her sister's opinion. "I know what I'm talking about—just three more kids who'll grow up with no respect for authority, no sense of right and wrong—"

"Mother," Jo broke in, supremely annoyed. "I think John Sterling is a moral person, able to teach his children the difference between right and wrong."

"Did you salt the potatoes more than usual?" her father asked her mother.

Helen dipped her fork in for a taste. "No," she said, frowning. "Does it taste like it?"

"No," Madden said, winking at Jo. "I was just trying to get you to stop talking, Helen."

Her mother frowned. "All I'm saying is the man obviously spoils his children—"

"Mother," Jo interrupted again, stabbing her meat loaf, "can't you understand why he would?"

"Well, Josephine," Helen huffed, "I certainly hope that when you and Alan have children—" she frowned at Hattie's snort "—you teach them discipline."

"Helen," Jo's father said sternly, "I've heard Jo and Alan both say at this table more than once that they don't intend to have children."

"Oh, posh." Jo's mother waved off the notion. "Josephine will change her mind once they're married and her biological clock starts ticking." She crinkled her nose at Jo and sang, "Tick, tock."

"Aren't you putting the cart before the camel?" Hattie asked. "Jo doesn't even have a ring yet."

"Well," Helen chided, "if she'd invite him over to Sunday dinner more often, he might be more eager to join the family."

"Oh, he'd be dragging her to the altar," Jo's father agreed earnestly, causing Jo to giggle.

"Although," Helen said, completely ignoring her husband and fixing Jo with a pointed look, "no doubt today he's still recuperating from a night on the town with Pamela Kaminski."

Jo sighed, her guilt mushrooming over the kiss she

shared with John. "Mother, I told you, it was a business function—"

"Josephine, Alan is never going to propose if you continue to give him freedom."

"That's right, Jo," her father said, smacking the tabletop. "Dangle that ball and chain in front of his nose and watch him fall to his knees."

"That's enough, Madden," her mother snapped. "Eat, Josephine—you're much too skinny."

"Helen," Hattie said. "What makes you think Jo's going to say yes to Alan, anyway?"

Jo glanced at her aunt, wondering how much she had given away with her body language on the drive over to her parents'.

Helen laughed. "Of course she's going to say yes, aren't you, dear?"

All eyes landed on Jo. She squirmed nervously, then said, "Let's wait until he asks before everyone gets in an uproar, shall we?" Then she lowered her gaze to her plate and pretended to eat with relish, feeling her aunt's knowing stare upon her.

When they left her parents' house, Jo expected more probing from her aunt, but Hattie simply sat with her eyes closed and her palms turned upward on her knees until Jo had parked the car and turned off the engine.

She twisted and looked at her aunt expectantly in the dark.

"I sense that you're going to have to make a decision soon, Jo," Hattie said, breaking the silence.

Jo frowned. "About what?"

"About your men," Hattie whispered gravely, her eyes still closed. "You can't burn your bridges at both ends, you know."

"Hattie—" Jo began, then stopped. "Good night," she said simply, then hopped out of the car.

She released a frustrated sigh as she flipped on a light in her living room. Reaching for the remote, she sank onto the floor and sat cross-legged, her back against the couch. For a few hours, she wanted to forget about John Sterling and Alan Parish and the Pattersons and how much trouble she'd be in if someone uncovered her pack of lies.

But the thought that throbbed like a hangnail was that perhaps one of her biggest lies was denying her attraction to John Sterling.

Lifting a hand to her lips, she closed her eyes and relived the sensation of the few seconds before and during their abbreviated kiss. Her phone rang, startling her badly. She pushed the mute button on the TV remote—Alan would be calling to tell her about the banquet.

"Hello," she said, trying to sound cheerful.

"Hey," Pam said, her voice bubbling with excitement. "Guess what I just did?"

Jo frowned, instantly wary. "I can't imagine."

"I called John Sterling and asked him out."

Her stomach pivoted, and she tightened her grip on the phone. "What did he say?"

"He said yes, on one condition."

Jo tried to ignore her pang of disappointment. "What?"

"That we go on a double date—me and him, you and Alan. Won't that be a blast?"

7

Jo stood motionless and listened to a sound she'd never heard before in John Sterling's house: complete silence.

No whining, no crying, no tattling, no pushing, no hair-pulling, no jumping, no running, no falling.

And no laughing.

Jo frowned and set her new lizard briefcase on the cluttered snack bar, her finely tuned day-care design presentation on a diskette locked safely inside. From another case, she retrieved her laptop computer, then scooted a hardened glob of orange modeling clay out of harm's way, and created a small work area. While the machine booted up, she looked around the kitchen. One glance at the stove revealed that Claire had cooked breakfast again, except this time the secret weapon appeared to be scrambled eggs instead of oatmeal.

She ran her fingers through her hair and sighed, feeling nervous and restless. She hoped a morning of ''drawing numbers,'' as Hattie often called the tedious preliminary work, would both relax and distract her from the afternoon's presentation. But on top of worrying about filing for bankruptcy if she didn't pull off this charade, she now had another tiny problem: she was dangerously close to falling in love with John Sterling.

Jo leaned against the counter and smacked her palm repeatedly against her forehead, hoping if she cracked her head open, a bit of good sense might fall inside. She had every reason to avoid the man, so why couldn't she?

A hysterical laugh escaped her lips. Alan assumed she would marry him someday, the Pattersons thought she was married to John, and John thought she was "maternal"—the biggest joke of all.

With a sigh, Jo withdrew her rolling measuring stick and began to record dimensions of every flat surface in the kitchen: walls, floor, countertops, windows. She then entered the figures into a program on the laptop and the structure of the room emerged on the screen, plane by plane. Stepping around toys, she moved through the house and repeated the process, saving each room in a separate file which would serve as input to the sophisticated design software at her office. Nearly two hours had passed when she nervously made her way toward John's bedroom suite, the rooms she'd saved for last.

The door creaked loudly when she swung it open. Slowly she stepped inside, allowing John's essence to envelop her. He was in every corner of the room: stray clothing, loose papers, his earthy scent. Desire stabbed Jo, warming her midsection, shocking her with its intensity. The rumpled bed beckoned her, and she imagined John's body stretched out on top of the covers, smiling at her, inviting her to join him. Her fantasy continued to unfold, then took a left turn as she visualized Claire, Jamie and Billy running past her and leaping onto their father's bed. John wrestled and tickled them until they were all laughing, then they settled around him to watch TV. She imagined John suddenly remembering her, and patting a tiny spot beyond the children where she could sit.

Her desire disintegrated. John Sterling was looking for a mother for his children, and who could blame him? Jo mentally shook herself. She had no business lusting after him. The children aside—a *huge* aside— she had a loving boyfriend.

She willed herself to get back to work. The measurements were more tricky in the master bedroom because of the bay windows and trey ceiling. Jo extended the handle of the ruler as far as possible, then stood on a solitary straight-back chair to reach every nook and cranny. She nearly fell when the ring of the telephone on the nightstand broke the silence. Jo hesitated, then decided to answer in case John or Hattie was calling for her.

''Sterling residence.''

''Mrs. Sterling?'' a worried female voice asked.

Jo's tongue felt thick. ''Um, this is Jo Montgomery.''

''Oh, good. This is Carolyn Hook at KidScape, and we have a little problem.''

Alarm bolted through her. ''Are the children okay?''

''Uh, yes. But Jamie started a little fire—''

Jo gripped the phone. *''What?''*

''No one was hurt.'' The woman's voice sounded soothing, with only a little panic around the edges. ''Actually, there wasn't a flame, only a little smoke, but the sprinklers went off and we need to close early to clean up.''

Jo's heart pounded. ''Does Mr. Sterling know?''

''I called his office first since it's the number listed

for emergencies, but when I reached his voice mail, I said I'd try his wife at home.''

"*What?*"

"That was all right, wasn't it?'' Ms. Hook sounded confused.

Jo forced herself to remain calm. "Y-yes, that's fine. I'll be there to pick up the children immediately.''

After banging down the phone, Jo squeezed her hands into tight fists. *Relax, breathe.* She retrieved the spare car seat and jogged to her car, then dialed John's office from her mobile phone as she pulled out of the driveway. Susan answered on the second ring.

"Wilson Brothers, this is John Sterling's office.''

"Susan, this is Jo Montgomery.''

"Oh, hello. Mr. Sterling's not in.''

"When will he be back?''

"I'm not sure.''

Jo sighed in exasperation. "I need you to page him.''

"Is this an emergency?''

"Haven't you checked his voice mail?''

"No, he checks it. You see, if I'm on the phone when someone calls—''

"Never mind,'' Jo cut in impatiently. "Just page him and tell him I'm picking up the kids from the day care, but I've got a very important appointment this afternoon, so he needs to come home as soon as possible.''

"Haven't we had this conversation before?'' Susan asked dryly.

"Thanks, Susan,'' Jo said, then hung up. Her next call was to the Pattersons' office, where she was immediately connected to Melissa.

"Jo,'' the woman said warmly. "How are you?''

Jo frowned at the phone. She'd expected her reception to be a little frosty, considering the boy Mrs. Patterson thought was her stepson had nearly set fire to one of her day-care centers. "I'm fine, Mrs. Patterson. Have you talked to Carolyn Hook?"

"Yes, she called me immediately." The woman's voice sounded almost singsongy. "My husband and I both apologize for the workers leaving your stepson alone for even a minute—I mean..." She laughed. "Well, you know what I mean. They're so...rambunctious at that age. I'm sure you and your husband both understand that accidents can happen."

Realization dawned on Jo that Mrs. Patterson feared a lawsuit. Being a business owner herself, she understood the apprehension of liability. But she felt sure John wouldn't hold the Pattersons responsible for Jamie's behavior.

"John and I are reasonable people," Jo said slowly. "I'm on my way to pick up the children now. What happened exactly?"

"According to Carolyn, Jamie was showing the other children how to start a campfire from scratch."

"Oh my." Jo swallowed, suddenly grateful he wasn't her child to deal with. "Mrs. Patterson, I may need to reschedule my demonstration this afternoon. I haven't been able to reach John yet and I don't want to leave the children alone."

"I understand," Mrs. Patterson said soothingly. "But can we make it later this evening? Monroe is leaving the country tomorrow for several weeks and we wanted to make a decision soon. Yours is the only proposal we haven't seen, so we'll be able to make a decision rather quickly."

With a jolt, Jo wondered what effect today's events would have on the Pattersons' choice—would they favor her in an attempt to lessen the possibility of a lawsuit over today's accident? Guilt barbed through her, but the ominous letter from the bank flashed before her eyes.

"Later this evening would be better—can I call you?"

"Of course," the woman said sweetly, and Jo once again felt a flash of remorse. "I hope your children aren't too upset by what happened today."

Jo hung up, her foot pressing harder on the gas pedal. She shook her head when she thought of Jamie trying to start a fire with a rapt audience of preschoolers. Her heart shivered when she thought of all the horrible things that could have happened.

A moment later, she slid into the parking lot at KidScape, squealing tires, then jumped out of the car and hit the ground at a full run. Carolyn Hook, drenched and completely unraveled, opened the door and ushered her in. The Sterling children, apparently the last ones to be collected, were huddled together in a damp playroom. "Here's your mommy," Carolyn announced to them.

Jo started to react to the woman's remark, but tears sprang to her eyes when she saw Jamie's clothes were dingy from smoke. A sooty streak zigzagged his cheek.

"Jo!" he yelled, jumping to his feet. "I knew you'd come!"

She knelt to pull him into a fierce hug, then held him at arm's length, her arms shaking. "Jamie Sterling—" her voice was louder than she intended "—what on earth were you thinking, trying to start a fire?"

"I'm Peter," he mumbled, his eyes welling up with tears.

"No," she said sternly. "You are not Peter Pan. You're Jamie Sterling and you did a very, very dangerous thing. You could have been hurt, or someone else could have been hurt—do you understand?"

He bit his lower lip and nodded, the tears spilling down his cheeks as he dived into her arms. "Don't tell Daddy, Jo," he pleaded. "Don't tell Daddy."

Jamie clung to her, and Jo's heart nearly exploded at the feel of his little body against hers. The sound of more crying reached her ears and she looked over her shoulder to see Claire and Billy holding on to each other. She waved them to her and they ran to join her group hug. "Jo-mommy," Billy whimpered over and over. With three wet, sticky bodies clinging to hers, Jo said a resigned goodbye to the cream-colored crepe pantsuit she wore. And she now fully understood why she'd never wanted to have children—because the responsibility and commitment were more than she could bear. What if these were her children? And what if something had happened to one of them? Worse, what if something happened to one of them while they were in her care?

When she could no longer endure the feeling crowding her chest, Jo cleared her throat and pulled back from the children, looking at each one of them in turn, then smiling sadly at Jamie. "Your daddy has to know about this," she said softly. "But we'll tell him together, okay?"

"Okay," he said, sniffling.

"Okay," Jo said as she straightened. "Let's go home." The words slipped out, sending shock waves through her already sensitized nerves. Her legs felt quite shaky as she swung Billy into her arms.

"Jo-mommy," he declared.

"Not Jo-mommy," she said, glancing around for Carolyn Hook. "Just plain Jo."

"Just Plain Jo," he whispered loudly in her ear, then added, "Poopy diaper."

Jamie claimed Jo's free hand, then Claire chained on to his, and the four of them traipsed outside together.

"JO MONTGOMERY to the rescue," John whispered as he read Susan's message on his text pager, already moving toward his car. At the last minute, he turned and yelled an explanation to the inspector he was abandoning at the site of the new strip mall, then sprang into his car and peeled away.

He tapped the steering wheel impatiently as he dialed KidScape on his car phone.

Carolyn Hook answered. "Oh, yes, Mr. Sterling, the children are fine. Your wife just left."

"My wife?" he asked, puzzled.

"Yes, I was able to reach Jo at your home and she came right over to get the kids."

John started to correct the woman, then it occurred to him that even though the day-care director had incorrectly assumed Jo was his wife—a thought that pleased him immensely—she might be nervous if she knew she'd turned over the children to a nonrelative. He thanked her, then hung up and continued toward his house.

Concern for his children assuaged, John's thoughts turned to the woman who had so quickly become an important person to him and to his children. Jo had

wanted him to kiss her the other night at her office—
he would have bet his house on it. And she had responded to him enthusiastically before the humiliating
coffee incident had given her time to reconsider. He
frowned. If he could just get this boyfriend of hers out
of the picture, he might stand a better chance of winning her over. Which, he acknowledged with only a
slight jab of guilt, was the reason he'd accepted Pamela
Kaminski's dinner invitation on the conditional double
date. He was looking forward to meeting the man of
Jo's dreams on Friday night.

When he pulled into his driveway beside Jo's familiar car, he decided he could get used to this routine—coming home to her and his children, to a peaceful, orderly, happy home.

He stepped into the foyer, closing the door behind
him quietly. Claire and Jamie stood in the den, staring
at each other belligerently, arms crossed. "I'm not
cleaning up your messy building blocks," Claire declared, raising her chin.

"Then I'm not picking up your books," Jamie retorted, dropping the armload he'd collected.

"Hey!" Claire shouted, giving him a shove. "Those
are my books!"

He shoved her back. "Then pick them up yourself!"

John started to speak, when Jo appeared from the
direction of the bathroom. Her light-colored pantsuit
looked a little worse for wear. She carried a diapered
Billy almost horizontally under one arm and held a
whistle between her teeth which she blew heartily to
get the attention of the older two. "Time-out," she
said. "Claire, you pick up the books, and Jamie, you

pick up the building blocks. No more arguing and no more pushing, understand?''

Claire's lower lip protruded, but she nodded. Jamie gave Jo an adoring glance, then jumped to finish the task she'd given him. John laughed out loud, giving away his presence.

''Daddy!'' the children chorused, and ran to meet him.

He hugged each of them in turn, then looked at Jamie with a grave face. ''What's this I hear about almost setting a fire, young man?''

Jamie bit his bottom lip. ''It worked just like it was s'posed to,'' he said, a shadow of pride in his voice. ''But Jo told me I could have hurt somebody. I'm sorry,'' he finished bravely.

Frowning sternly, John said, ''Don't ever try that again, and don't ever play with matches, okay?''

Jamie nodded solemnly, then leaned forward and whispered, ''Daddy, Jo came and got us, just like a real mommy would!''

John felt his heart stir, then raised his eyes to Jo standing in the background, out of earshot. A tiny smile curved her lips, and he stood to greet her. ''Hi,'' he said lamely as he walked toward her, he and his children moving forward as a unit.

''Hi.''

''Nice whistle.''

She laughed and shrugged. ''My dad's a police officer, he makes me carry it for protection.''

He looked into her eyes until she dropped her gaze and cleared her throat. She was remembering their kiss, he knew it.

''Kids,'' he said, still watching her carefully, ''why

don't you finish picking up your toys and let me talk
to Jo alone for a few minutes, okay?''

Jamie tugged on his pants leg. ''Are you gonna kiss
her, Daddy?''

John sighed, exasperated. ''I'll yell for you if I do,
okay, son?''

The kids scampered away, giggling. He smiled at Jo
apologetically. ''I must thank you again—I know you
have better things to do than to deal with the Sterling
family crises.''

She shrugged, then nodded slowly. ''I did have to
postpone an appointment with the Pattersons this afternoon, but since they were aware of the extenuating
circumstances, they agreed to meet with me later.''

''Do you think they'll give you the account?'' he
asked.

''I'm not sure—there's a lot of stiff competition.''

''I hope your association with my notorious children
doesn't hurt your chances.''

''I d-doubt that,'' she said unconvincingly.

He suddenly recalled his conversation with the day-
care director. ''Oh, and by the way—'' he smiled
sheepishly ''—Carolyn Hook has the notion that you
and I are married.''

Jo's eyes widened. ''Did you correct her?''

''No, I'm sorry, I should have, but I figured it was
an honest mistake and that she might be alarmed at
having signed out the children to a nonrelative.''

''Th-that's okay—no harm done.''

''Were you able to get anything done around here
this morning?''

She nodded. ''I'll be ready for our meeting Wednesday." She seemed nervous as she retrieved her briefcase and grabbed her purse, then reached for her laptop.

"Let me," John offered, covering her hand with his.

She stared at their hands for a few seconds, then lifted her gaze. "Okay," she relented, pulling her hand from beneath his.

John followed her outside to her car. "I hear we have a date Friday night."

Jo's shoulders straightened. "Yes," she said with a smile. "My friend Pam seems quite taken with you."

"Seems like a nice woman," he said smoothly.

"Pam's a lot of fun," Jo said, offering a glimpse of her dimple.

"I'm anxious to meet...uh, Adam, is it?"

"Alan," she corrected him, and blushed furiously. She lifted her chin slightly. "I think you'll like each other."

"We should," John agreed. "We have a lot in common."

Jo didn't respond, only swung into her seat. "Bye." She started to shut the door, but John caught the edge and held it open.

"Good luck with the Pattersons," he said. "I'll see you Wednesday."

She nodded, then closed the door and backed out of the driveway.

John stood watching her car until it disappeared.

THE PATTERSONS had not yet arrived when Jo pulled into the parking lot of her office building. She stepped from the car and frowned at her wrinkled, stained pantsuit, then retrieved her laptop and briefcase. Her heart thumped with anticipation as she walked through the front door.

"Hi," Jo said, sticking her head in her aunt's office.

"Hi, yourself," Hattie said, her smile beaming beneath the brim of her fruit-bearing straw hat. "Another emergency with the Sterling family, I presume?" she sang.

"Don't start, Hattie."

"What was it this time?"

"Jamie almost set fire to the Pattersons' model daycare center."

"Oh my," Hattie said, wincing. "Was anyone hurt?"

"No, but I think it might influence the Pattersons' decision today."

"You're afraid they'll drop you because your presumed stepson has caused them so much trouble?"

"No," Jo said, sighing. "I'm afraid they'll sign me because they're afraid of a lawsuit."

"Oh my," Hattie repeated.

Jo frowned. "How do I get myself into these messes?"

"No one need be the wiser," her aunt offered.

"But I know the truth," Jo insisted, exasperated.

"Well, if it bothers you that much, just tell the Pattersons it was all a misunderstanding."

Right, Jo thought, and risk losing all we've both worked for. Of course, she could call Alan, and he'd have her delinquent loan payment—or the entire loan—taken care of with a simple transfer of funds.

The doorbell chimed, announcing the arrival of the Pattersons. Jo's stomach twisted.

"Hello," Mrs. Patterson said as she entered, her hair

and clothing impeccably neat and stiff. As Jo shook her hand, she noted that Melissa Patterson could be a very daunting woman if she deemed it necessary. Mr. Patterson was his cordial self.

"I trust you found your children in good hands at the day care?" Mrs. Patterson asked, her eyebrows raised hopefully.

"Oh, yes," Jo said, her stomach queasy.

"I hope Mr. Sterling wasn't too upset," she continued, her tone probing.

"Just relieved the children were okay," Jo said quickly. She nodded toward the meeting room. "Shall we begin?"

Avoiding Hattie's eyes, Jo followed the couple into the room and switched on the powerful workstation in which the design software resided. She chitchatted while tweaking the presentation screen and preparing the machine for the data she'd developed. Hattie slipped in with mugs of flavored coffee, then left again.

Jo reached for her briefcase to withdraw the computer diskette containing her work for the Patterson account. She frowned when the brass latches refused to budge, then smiled nervously at the attentive couple. "New briefcase," she explained, then pressed the buttons again with all her might, to no avail. Double-checking the line of shiny digits that made up the combination, she smiled in relief, seeing the numbers were no longer aligned. She remembered finding Jamie playing with it—he must have turned the brass wheels to different numbers. She adjusted them back to her combination, then tried once again to open the latches. Nothing.

She lifted her head and smiled again at the Pattersons. "I'll be right back," she said, exiting the room with her briefcase in hand.

"What's wrong?" Hattie said when she saw Jo's face.

Closing the door to Hattie's office, Jo fought her panic. "My presentation is in this briefcase—the diskette, the written proposal, graphs, contracts, everything—and I can't get it open."

"I noticed you'd finally traded in my old bag," Hattie said.

"I didn't," Jo said in exasperation. "Alan bought this for me while he was in Atlanta."

"Hmmph, figures—it's pretentious as hell."

"I can't get it open. I think Jamie must have jammed it somehow."

Hattie grunted in her effort to move the latches, then gave up. "Did you make a backup of the files on the machine's hard drive?"

Jo shook her head miserably. "Dumb, huh?"

"Yep."

Groaning, Jo said. "This is an omen. What am I going to do?"

Hattie sighed. "We'll just have to break inside."

"How? Alan said it's virtually indestructible."

"Except in the hands of a six-year-old."

"Good point."

"Let's gather our tools and see what we've got."

Five minutes later they surveyed their options. A metal ruler, a pair of pliers, a hammer, a flathead screwdriver and a nail file.

"Okay," Hattie said, "so we're not Bob Vila. Let's try the nail file."

Jo slid the pointed tip under one of the latches and

tried to pry it loose. Nothing. One by one, they exhausted the tools. After ten minutes, the briefcase remained intact, but Jo had one smashed thumb, three broken nails and a gash across her palm.

"That blood will never come out," Hattie said mournfully, fingering Jo's crimson-spotted crepe jacket.

"Hattie!" Jo exclaimed, wiping the sweat from her forehead. "Help me think of something."

"Do you care about ruining the briefcase?"

"No," Jo admitted. "I'll think of something to tell Alan."

"Well, it's a risk," Hattie said.

"What?"

A few minutes later, Jo sat behind the wheel of her car, shaking her head. "I can't believe this."

"Okay, Jo," Hattie yelled. "Back up!"

Jo put the car in reverse, then cringed when she bumped up and over the briefcase. She stopped and waited while Hattie bent to inspect it. "No, try again."

Swallowing hard, she pulled up, then backed over it again.

After the seventh time, Hattie squinted and nodded. "I think it's giving a little. Do you have a crowbar in the trunk?"

Jo nodded, sick to her stomach. When Hattie lifted the briefcase, she nearly choked. The beautiful, nearly seamless lizard hide was tire-crossed and scarred. Numb, she pulled herself from the car and opened the trunk.

"Ms. Montgomery?" Monroe Patterson yelled from the door of the building. "Is everything all right?"

Jo hid the briefcase behind the trunk lid and smiled. "I'll be right there, Mr. Patterson."

He nodded and disappeared inside.

Hattie jammed the crowbar into the tiny opening between the two halves of the battered briefcase and twisted hard. The latches groaned, then popped under the strain, the lid bouncing up with a sickening tear. A familiar hardened ball of orange modeling clay rolled out and onto the pavement.

"Wha-lah!" Hattie exclaimed, gasping for breath.

"Wha-lah," Jo mumbled, grabbing the diskette and the papers she needed, then dashing back inside. "Here we are," she said cheerily, dimming the lights before the Pattersons noticed her dirty, streaked and spotted suit.

At least the presentation went smoothly—a little too smoothly, Jo thought. Halfway through, Mrs. Patterson announced they had seen enough and asked to see the contract. Five minutes later, they shook on the deal, the Pattersons signed a hefty check for the advance, then walked toward the door.

"Once again," Mr. Patterson said solemnly, "please tell your husband how much we regret today's accident, and how pleased we are to be doing business with you."

After they left, Jo sat slumped in her desk chair staring at the check, riddled with guilt. The advance was more than enough to cover her late loan payment.

She sighed, leaning her head back. Facts were facts—she'd won the coveted account based on a series of lies. She'd saved her business but, in the process, had flushed her integrity down the toilet. How could she face John on Wednesday?

8

"DID YOU GET the Patterson account?" John asked.

Jo stood in the doorway of her office. "Y-yes," she stammered, her pulse racing. *Thanks to you and your kids.*

"Good," he said, flashing her a white smile. "Then we'll have something to celebrate Friday night."

Her stomach dived at the thought of the double date, then she waved him toward the meeting room to show him the results of her design ideas for his home. He walked so close to her, she could hear the crisp swish of his jeans as he moved. He looked earthy and handsome in a snug ribbed white henley shirt tucked into his loose waistband, no belt. Jo stumbled on a carpet fiber and he grabbed her arm, unnerving her further when he maintained his hold on her until they entered the meeting room.

"Nice," he murmured, scoping the room. He pulled a seat close to where she'd be sitting in front of the computer.

"Um, the view is better in the back," she murmured, pointing to the wall screen only a few feet in front of them. "This is a little close."

"This is fine." He inched his seat even closer.

She dimmed the lights with a handheld switch, and with a deep breath launched the presentation.

He emitted a low "Wow" as the rooms in his home came alive on the big screen, the walls painted and papered, the furniture functional and smart. He nodded, impressed with each room on the first floor, then smiled his approval when they viewed the kids' rooms.

She tensed when his bedroom suite appeared on-screen. Through the magic of animation, she'd designed the room around one theme: inviting. She'd elevated the bed with a platform so the piece dominated the room. A black and grape-colored comforter was turned down to reveal matching sheets, piled high with large, deep pillows. She'd arranged a dark-wood entertainment center along the opposite wall to house a television and stereo equipment. With the press of a few keys, jazz sounded low and sexy from her computer, giving the illusion that the sound came from the stereo speakers featured in his bedroom. Deep upholstered chairs punctuated the open spaces, along with low tables and tall lamps.

"I knew I'd like it," he said, giving her a warm smile in the dim light.

The sitting room had been converted into a pseudo library, with glass-fronted bookshelves and a chess table. A fire glowed in the fireplace between matching reading chairs, flanked by an overstuffed couch. He nodded, obviously pleased. Jo progressed through the bathroom, then opened the doors to the large walk-in closet. She'd inserted an organized system of racks, drawers and shelves. A man's wardrobe hung on one side, a woman's on the other. John looked at her, eyebrows raised, an amused expression on his face.

Jo blushed at the implication of the redesigned bedroom suite—rooms that could be comfortably shared.

"You seemed to be worried about, um, the rooms not being *too* masculine," she reminded him.

"Oh, I'm more than pleased," he assured her, then leaned near her ear. "And do you think a woman would be cozy in these surroundings?"

She scanned the planes of his handsome face and decided that even Pamela Kaminski might forgo her flamboyant taste and aversion to kids for a chance to conjugate with this man. "I don't think you have anything to worry about," she croaked, staring straight ahead, then turned up the light. "That's it."

John squinted and nodded. "When can you start?"

"Don't you want to see how much all of this is going to cost you?"

He shrugged. "Sure."

Jo walked her fingers through several papers on her desk, then withdrew one and handed it to John.

He frowned. "Are you sure this is right?"

Jo bit her bottom lip. "If it's more than you had in mind—"

"No," he cut in and lifted his gaze to hers. "I've been in this business long enough to know what a job like this should cost, Jo. This figure looks suspiciously like wholesale—you can't be making any money."

She shuffled the remaining papers nervously. She already felt guilty about the wealth she'd be gaining from the Pattersons' account—she wasn't about to capitalize on his project, as well. "I—I'm giving you a preferred-customer discount."

He laughed. "I'm flattered, but I wouldn't accept this kind of cut unless you were my wife."

Her gaze bounced to his and held there.

His smile was slow and sweet, and oh so tempting.

With a slow movement, he turned her swivel chair so that she faced him. "Of course, if this price comes with a marriage proposal, I'll consider it," he said.

Warmth flooded her limbs, melting her muscles and loosening her tongue. "The price or the proposal?" she whispered.

His hands stumbled along the table, then came up with the dimmer control. Jo inhaled sharply because he leaned closer as the lights lowered.

"Are you sure your aunt won't be back for a while?" he whispered.

"Yes," she breathed. Dusk descended around them.

"No flying Frisbees around?"

"No." She could barely make out his face.

"No spillable hot drinks within reaching distance?"

"No." Blackness enveloped them.

"You mean it's just us?"

"Just us." She couldn't see him, but the breath left her lungs when his lips descended on hers hungrily. Jo lifted her hands to both sides of his face, to meet him, to guide him in his exploration of her mouth. With a groan, he shifted and lifted her to his lap, surrounding her with his warm arms, kneading her skin with his big hands. His fingers grazed her neck, then skimmed down her back to span her waist. Jo arched into him, biting at his tongue, clicking her teeth against his.

She realized they'd been careening toward this moment since the second their eyes had met. Her hands clawed at his shoulders, his back, drawing him closer to her. His hand slipped up the front of her untucked blouse, and she moaned at the feel of his fingers burning through the flimsy fabric of her bra. He captured a hardened nipple between forefinger and thumb, and Jo shivered in response.

His mouth traveled up her cheek and over her eyelids, punctuated by his hushed whisper of her name. ''Jo...Jo...Jo.'' At the sound of his desire for her, physical need billowed hot within her, stealing her body's ability to support her weight. She melted into him, driving her fingers into his thick hair, and urging his mouth lower.

He clasped her hips and twisted her around so that she was straddling him. His mouth moved with greater intensity, nipping at her collarbone and nuzzling the top of her cleavage as low as her buttons would allow. Jo strained into him, desire for him crowding out any rational thought. All she wanted was for his hands, his mouth, to be on her skin. She tore at the buttons of her blouse, freeing them, inviting him to explore further. Within seconds, he found the front closure of her bra. Beneath her loosened blouse, she felt the silky straps of her bra fall down her shoulders.

With another groan, he sought her mouth again for a hard kiss. A rush of cool air whipped across her bare nipples an instant before he claimed both breasts with his warm hands. Desire stabbed her low and moisture gathered between her thighs. She moaned into his mouth, he breathed hot air into hers.

Jo had never felt such exquisite pleasure. She felt alive, on fire, desirable, wanton. He dragged his mouth from hers, breathing her name against her skin as he moved lower to capture the peak of her breast between his lips.

Jo's groan of approval coincided with a loud knock at the door.

She jerked her head up, her back ramrod-straight. Panic bolted through her as reality came crashing down. The enormity of their indiscretion settled around her even as she struggled to her feet and fumbled with the buttons on her blouse. "Oh my God, oh my God, oh my God." She snapped on the lights to speed her frenzied dressing.

John blinked against the bright light and sighed heavily in exasperation. "Is this a conspiracy?"

"Jo," Alan's voice sounded low and polite through the door.

"Oh my God." Dread washed over her, and her knees nearly buckled. "If it is, now my boyfriend's in on it," she whispered frantically.

"Oh, great," he murmured, slowly raking a hand through his disheveled hair.

She straightened her clothing, the blood pounding through her ears. Sweat popped out along her hairline. John's lazy perusal of her from his seated position unnerved her. After smoothing one hand over her blouse, she stepped forward, raised the hem of her shirt and wiped her lipstick from John's mouth with a hard swipe.

"Ouch," he complained, holding a hand to his lip.

Jo ignored him and walked toward the door.

"Wait!" he whispered hoarsely.

She turned back, her eyebrows raised. "What?"

He sighed, then pointed to his crotch. The long, hard ridge of his erection was painfully evident.

She waved her arms. "Make it go away."

His face was incredulous. "I can't just say abracadabra and, presto, it's gone!"

''Jo?'' Alan asked through the door, knocking lightly.

''Just a minute, Alan,'' she said carefully. ''We're just winding down in here.'' She turned back to John. ''Do something!'' she hissed.

''I have to stop thinking about you for it to go away,'' he said calmly.

''Well?''

''Well, I can't stop thinking about you while you're still standing there.'' He rose to his feet, the bulge still as imposing. He lifted his hands palms up, and smiled. ''In fact, I can't stop thinking about you no matter what.''

Her heart flipped over. ''John—'' She stopped. ''Stay right here.''

Trembling, she slipped from the room and closed the door behind her. Alan stood across the hall, hands in the pockets of his designer suit, critiquing a sculpture sitting on an antique sofa table. Guilt and sadness bolted through her as he turned around and smiled. Dependable, predictable Alan.

''Hi,'' he said, walking toward her.

''Hi,'' she said, lifting her cheek for his quick kiss. He sniffed. ''New cologne?''

She stiffened, then waved her hand in front of her nose and lowered her voice. ''My client is wearing so much cologne, I've been choking through the presentation.''

''Sorry to bother you,'' he said. ''Hattie wasn't around, and I didn't realize you were busy. Is it the Pattersons?''

''No,'' she said, then turned when Alan's eyes focused beyond her. She swallowed. John was walking toward them and, thankfully, it appeared that he'd managed to stop thinking about her.

"Hello," John said, extending his hand to Alan. "I'm John Sterling."

"Alan Parish." The men stood toe to toe. Their handclasp stretched on and on as their gazes locked. Jo felt age-old territorial hormones emanating from both of them. She cleared her throat loudly.

At last Alan released John's grip, lightly shaking off his hand. "I understand you're interested in Jo's friend Pam."

"Well," John drawled, "I'm discovering Savannah is full of interesting women."

Alan's eyes darted from John to Jo, then back to John. "Jo says you have three small children."

John nodded. "Ages three, six and nine."

Alan whistled low, his smile smug. "Sounds like a handful."

John's grin was slow and wide. "I have big hands."

Jo bit her tongue at the unmistakable implication. "Alan," she said brightly, "did you need something?"

After a few seconds, Alan's eyes finally cut back to her. "I wanted to see if you were free for lunch."

She smiled. "That's nice, but John and I still have a few papers to sign before we finish."

Alan looked at John and rocked back on his heels in quiet confidence. "I'll wait."

"Hattie should be back in a few minutes," Jo said quickly, "then I can leave. You can wait in my office, Alan."

The men stared each other down for a few long seconds, then Alan inclined his head in parting. "Sterling."

"Parish."

Jo turned and walked back to the meeting room, all too aware of the still-unfastened bra beneath her blouse. As she stepped into the room, she closed her eyes in trepidation. What was she doing playing post office with another man? And enjoying it, for heaven's sake.

"Nice boy," John observed, closing the door behind him.

Jo frowned. "Alan doesn't deserve that, and he doesn't deserve what I've done to him, either."

"Jo," he said, "you don't owe him your undying devotion if you don't love him."

She raised her chin. "Who said I don't love Alan?"

He angled his head. "Unless I'm mistaken, you did—with your mouth and your hands and your body."

Jo's mind spun, and she inhaled deeply. "Just because I'm physically attracted to you doesn't mean I'm not in love with Alan." Oh, God, she was starting to sound like her mother.

John frowned as he sorted her words. "You don't have to beat around the bush with vague double negatives, Jo. Are you in love with the man or aren't you?"

Her bottom lip trembled as loyalty toward Alan ballooned inside her. "I love him, yes."

"Ah," he said, walking up to stand a few inches from her. "But are you *in* love with him?"

Jo's chest heaved as she fought the sexual gravity pulling her toward John's body. "That's between me and Alan, don't you think?"

John lowered his mouth toward hers, then just as her lips parted, raised his head again. "Not if I'm what's standing between you,'' he whispered, his eyes dancing with his proven point.

She watched as he whipped out the contract she'd shown him earlier. He scribbled a note at the bottom, then signed his name. ''I'll see you Friday,'' he said calmly, then left the room.

Jo stood quietly, breathing deeply, desperate to regain some sense of normalcy. She walked over to gather up the papers, palmed the door key he'd left and scanned the contract he'd modified.

With the unfortunate absence of a marriage proposal, amount due will be exactly double the price quoted. Signed, John Sterling.

THURSDAY MORNING found Jo at her desk, feeling skittish and out of sorts, as if she were coming down with something. After nearly twenty-four hours of reliving John's mouth and hands on her body, she was finding it hard to concentrate.

''Jo?'' Hattie stood in Jo's office door, her forehead creased. ''Are you feeling okay, dear?''

''Fine,'' Jo said, forcing a bright smile. She reached for her coffee cup and nudged it, sending the liquid splashing across the top of her desk. Biting back a curse, Jo snatched up the papers she'd been working on, and turned a cheerful face toward her aunt. ''Why do you ask?''

''No reason,'' Hattie said, her tone wary. She glanced at her watch. ''Didn't you have an appointment with the seamstress this morning at the Sterling house?''

Jo gasped, picked up the clock on her desk, then banged it back down. ''Thirty minutes ago!'' She grabbed her purse and swung her coat around her shoulders as she dashed out. ''If she calls, I'm on my way!''

Between getting stuck behind a mail truck and hitting every possible red light, the trip to the Sterling house crawled. As she pulled into the empty driveway, the woman she'd missed called on the car phone to reschedule in two hours. Jo sighed and thanked her, then hung up and sat staring at John's beautiful house.

White brick made the large structure seem even more imposing. Double columns flanking the steps added a touch of southern-plantation charm, and dark green shutters contributed warmth to the expanse of white. The landscaping provided by the builder was attractive, but on the lean side, which was typical these days. She squinted and imagined a towering trellis of pink roses on the left side of the house, and a row of red azaleas under the limbs of the massive oak tree squatting near the road.

Jo opened her eyes and shook her head to clear it. This wasn't her homestead to be planning—John Sterling would decide what kind of landscaping he wanted. She'd do well to take care of the job he hired her to do. Pressing her lips together, she drove the memory of his kisses from her mind and straightened her shoulders. She might as well get a jump on the window measurements.

When Jo opened the front door, she thought a television or stereo had been left on, but as she entered the den, she recognized John's voice coming from the open door of his office. She froze, debating whether to turn and run for her life before he heard her. But John appeared suddenly in the doorway, a telephone between his ear and shoulder, his hands full of blueprints. He wore burgundy pajama bottoms…and nothing else. He grinned when he saw her, and Jo's mouth went dry. Gold hair sprinkled his muscled chest, then grew more dense over his flat abdomen before disappearing into his waistband. She tried to swallow. It was too soon after their close encounter yesterday to face him while he was so…bare.

He juggled the papers and held up a finger indicating he was winding down the conversation. Jo nodded and wheeled back toward the den, trying desperately to stem the flood of adrenaline in her blood. She shrugged out of her coat and busied herself with measuring tools, suddenly wishing she'd worn something more utilitarian than the stretchy skirt and short jacket. Although she'd have to strip down to her turtleneck later, for now, every stitch of her clothing, no matter how restrictive, was going to stay put. For emphasis, she reached up and fastened the top button on her hunter green jacket.

"Well," his voice sounded behind her. "This is a nice surprise."

Jo turned and met his gaze, conjuring up a casual smile while she fought to keep her eyes above shoulder level. His jaw was darkened by morning beard, his auburn hair sticking up slightly in the back. He was knee-weakeningly handsome. She suddenly remembered her voice.

"I—I was supposed to meet the seamstress here to measure for curtains, but I missed her, so I thought I'd get a jump on the legwork." She gestured awkwardly toward her supplies, then crossed her arms, trying to gather her defenses against his blatant appeal. "I didn't realize you were here, I should have knocked first."

"I parked in the garage," he explained. "But don't worry, I left the key yesterday so you could come by whenever you need to—or want to." His eyes teased her, and his voice softened. "But be forewarned, you might occasionally find me in a state of undress."

The turtleneck was growing uncomfortably tight around her vocal cords. "Wh-why are you home?" she asked, ignoring his remark.

"Small emergency." He waved toward his office. "I got a call this morning at five, and I've been working ever since." John laughed, his eyes sparkling. "And I thought the mornings couldn't get more chaotic around here."

"How did the kids get to day care?" She glanced at his skimpy outfit, then quickly back to his face.

"Mrs. Harris came by to straighten up and offered to take them for me."

Jo nodded, trying to ignore the fact that he was standing only a few feet from her looking so decadent. He scratched his shoulder, the muscles in his arm dancing with the movement. Jo felt her body blush in awareness and uncrossed her arms self-consciously. "So," she squeaked, "did you get the problem worked out?"

"Yeah," he said, hands on hips, nodding.

Jo pressed her lips together and nodded. "Good."

"Yeah," John agreed, still nodding.

Jo couldn't stop nodding.

They spoke at the same time.

"About yesterday—" he said.

"We need to talk—" she said.

Jo stopped and laughed along with John until he stepped closer. Then her humor vanished and she stiffened at the proximity of his naked torso. He stood within arm's reach, the waistband of the pajama bottoms sagging slightly, revealing a vague tan line and a glimpse of his white briefs. The hair stood up on the nape of her neck. He reached forward to clasp her hands in his, and his touch jolted her into motion. "J-John," she protested, stepping backward.

But he kept pace with her, holding her hands loosely and giving her a knowing, serious smile. "Jo, you have to admit there's something between us."

"I—I don't know what you mean," she said, still moving steadily backward. Her pulse raced and she nearly groaned at the desire welling inside her chest.

He walked with her, squeezing her hands, and shook his head slowly, obviously unconvinced. She felt the wall at her back and inhaled sharply as he closed in on her. "Liar, liar, pants on fire," he whispered, his mouth inches from hers. He held her arms down at her sides, but she could have pulled away at any second...if only she hadn't been exactly where she wanted to be. His mouth descended on hers with authority, and Jo resisted the heady kiss for a heartbeat before opening her lips for his searching tongue.

Then all was lost.

John moaned and pressed his body against hers. Jo could feel his swelling need for her and strained into him, her nerve endings screaming. *No, no, no,* her head warned, but her body would have none of it. "Yes," she murmured. "Yes, yes."

He gasped, driving her mouth wider to accept his foraging tongue. Releasing her hands, he reached around to cup her rear and lifted her against the wall. She opened her knees, allowing him to wedge into the cradle between. He was a vocal partner, and his guttural sounds excited Jo in a way she would never have imagined. Delicious chills ran across her shoulders as he slid his hands under her skirt and pulled the stretchy fabric up to her waist. She inhaled deeply, drawing his sleep scent into her lungs. Her clothes were choking her. She pushed him away gently, her gaze remaining locked with his as she slowly unbuttoned the jacket and let it drop to the floor. He held her suspended, his breathing ragged as she drew the turtleneck over her head, the choppy layers of her hair swishing against her cheeks as it fell back into place.

John's gaze dropped to her cream-colored satin bra, then he closed his eyes and smiled, as if to savor the sight. Jo felt a welling of pride, thrilled he was pleased with her body. With a savage moan, he pulled her away from the wall and lowered her to a rug on the wooden floor. The nubby yarn felt coarse and stimulating against her back, arousing her further. John stopped long enough to roll her panty hose and skirt down to her knees, then Jo kicked them off and lay before him in bra and panties. He fumbled with his own clothes, never taking his eyes off her. Jo smiled languidly at his haste, then bit her bottom lip when he stood nude before her. Doubts nipped at her, but John was beside her, on top of her in an instant, and the touch of his skin against hers crowded all other thoughts from her mind.

He breathed her name before kissing her again, then moved lower. He quickly unfastened the front closure of her bra, then moaned his appreciation as he freed her breasts. Cool air and warm breath swirled over her nipples, bringing them to bud. He teased first one peak, then another with his tongue, then his teeth, causing Jo to writhe beneath him. He frantically tugged at her panties, and she raised her hips to allow him to whisk them off. Jo tore at his shoulders and arms, drawing him up and closer to her, until his hard shaft branded her thigh. He reclaimed her mouth and moved between her raised knees. Jo's breathing was beyond erratic as she reached down to clasp him and guide him inside. John eased in, gritting his teeth in obvious restraint, filling her inch by slow inch.

Surely heaven was no sweeter, Jo thought. Even as he began to stroke her inner depths, an urgent rhythm was beginning to surface. She threw her head back and rocked beneath him, stiffening in preparation for an intense release. She ran her fingernails over his back, down his waist, across his clenched buttocks as they moved together with increasing urgency. John's murmurings were sweet and encouraging as he trailed hard kisses over her neck and fingered a sensitive, rigid nipple. "I want to hear you, Jo," he whispered fiercely. "Let me hear you."

"Yes," she moaned. "Yes, John, I'm almost there."

"I'm waiting for you," he gasped.

His husky whisper sent her over the edge. Jo opened her mouth and released a long, low cry of climax, which John chorused seconds later. They moved in unison, their hips connecting in unbelievable intensity as they rode out their mutual pleasure. At last, they lay quiet, melded together, their heartbeats mirrored.

Slowly, very slowly, reality drizzled, then flooded

into her brain, and Jo tried to move. The enormity of what just transpired washed over her.

"Mmmph," John said in her ear.

"John," she said softly. Panic stirred deep in her belly.

"Uh-huh?"

"We...I have to get up."

He sighed heavily, then kissed her ear. "Not yet, love."

His words spurred her into motion. She pushed hard against his shoulders. "Yes, now. I have to get up."

John raised his head and frowned slightly, looking confused, but gently extracted his body from hers and sat up. "What's wrong, Jo?"

Jo scrambled to her feet and began to gather her clothes. "We just had sex, that's what's wrong." Her hands were trembling as she tried to cover herself with her clothes. Suddenly his arms came around her from behind to still her movements.

"Call me old-fashioned," he murmured into her hair, "but I'd say it was lovemaking."

Jo closed her eyes and wrenched out of his arms to spin and face him. "What we just did had nothing to do with love. It should never have happened, and it will never happen again."

John pursed his lips and crossed his arms. "What about Parish?"

Jo inhaled deeply and lifted her chin, trying to regain her equilibrium. "I hope you'll be a gentleman, and keep this...indiscretion between us. There's no need to hurt Alan. And I hope this doesn't affect our working agreement."

His lips tightened and he was silent for a full moment, studying her. Jo clutched her wad of clothes to her chest trying to quell the embarrassment and panic mushrooming inside her. John took a deep breath and bent to scoop up his own clothes. Unable to bear his silence, Jo said, "John, I need to know you won't say anything to Alan about what happened here."

He stepped into his clothes and pulled up the loose pants, snapping the waistband. "What do you mean?" He shrugged, his voice casual. Leveling his gaze at her, he spoke softly, resolutely. "Absolutely nothing happened here." He turned and headed toward the stairs, adding over his shoulder. "I have to shower and get to the office."

Jo watched him climb the stairs, a sense of loss overwhelming her.

"JOHN, you're even more handsome than I remembered," Pam said, smiling widely. Casting aside convention, she kissed him on the cheek, brushing an imaginary crumb from his collarless bottle-green shirt, her fingers trailing down to the waistband of his chocolate-colored pleated slacks.

"I hadn't forgotten how lovely you are," he said easily. Pamela Kaminski was a gorgeous woman who filled out the long-sleeved white stretchy dress to alarming proportions. Her legs were deeply tanned for January, curvy and long, lengthened further by three-inch heels. Her hair swished across her golden shoulders, curly and full. Her lips were bee-stung and her pale eyebrows perfectly arched. But John didn't find her as intimidating as most men probably did—his mind and heart were full of Jo Montgomery. He felt comfortable flirting with Pam because he had nothing at stake.

The short ride to the riverfront restaurant was pleasurable. Pamela was a bright conversationalist who knew most of Savannah's upper crust and had lots of juicy tidbits to share. His stomach was rolling at the prospect of watching Alan Parish make a fuss over Jo all evening, but he'd determined the only way he was going to get their lovemaking off his mind was to see her with her boyfriend. Pamela chattered comfortably, demanding little response. He forced himself to relax, lulled by her silky, sexy voice.

Cruising slowly along the cobblestone alleys and streets, John seized an empty parking spot within easy walking distance from the restaurant. When they entered the establishment, his eyes instantly settled on Jo. She stood in the crowded waiting area, smiling up at Alan—dammit—looking like an entrée herself in a long fitted red dress. Now he knew what treasures lay beneath the snug garment. She turned and caught his gaze, her smile slipping a little before she raised her hand in a wave. John's breath caught in his chest as he steered Pamela in their direction.

The women embraced, and Alan's handshake seemed a little more cordial, but not much. Jo's expression was unreadable, but she appeared at ease with Alan's arm wrapped around her waist. Alan was a good-looking man, John acknowledged, with model-perfect hair and teeth. And he'd done some checking of his own—the man was loaded and on his way to the top. Young, rich, with no children, versus older, poorer, with three children. John's heart suddenly dipped. Who was he fooling? He didn't stand a chance.

But when his eyes flicked back to Jo, he was surprised to find her gaze upon him. Pamela and Alan were eyeing someone across the room and talking in low tones.

"Hi," he ventured. "Staying busy?"

She nodded, her gaze dropping to the mixed drink in her hand. "Working on the Patterson project. How are the kids?"

Nice, safe conversation. "Fine. My sister, Cleo, is coming down from Atlanta tomorrow to take Claire shopping."

Jo nodded. "I remember Claire talking about it."

"I need to pick up a few things for the boys, too."

"That's nice," she said, lifting her drink for another sip.

She looking completely at ease, he noted. Did she often indulge in brief affairs? He didn't think so, but obviously she hadn't been quite as shaken by their encounter as he'd been.

Their name was called and a young hostess showed them to a preferred table by the window. John strategically positioned himself opposite Alan, with Jo to his left and Pamela to his right.

"So, John," Alan said once they'd ordered appetizers, "who's baby-sitting tonight?" The blond man's smile was deceptively pleasant.

John bit the inside of his cheek. "A baby-sitter."

Pamela laughed gaily, touching John's arm. "I'll bet your children are adorable," she crooned.

"Well, I'm a little biased," John said, smiling.

Alan gave John a watery smile. "Jo and I don't plan to have children."

"Oh?" John asked. "I didn't realize you were engaged."

Alan's face remained impassive as he studied John. "We're not, but someday we'll be married." He reached over and patted Jo's hand possessively.

"Well, some people are not cut out for the responsibility of parenthood," John said agreeably.

Alan frowned. "It's not that we can't handle it, we don't *want* to handle it—there's a big difference."

"It's not for everyone," John repeated, smiling. "Me? I wouldn't trade it for the world. A lover can pass through your life," he paused, hoping his point landed home, "but children—they're forever."

"Yeah, forever," Alan said, chuckling and trying to gain Jo and Pamela's support with his sideways glances. "That's exactly what I mean."

John shook his head sadly. "You're right, Alan— some people just can't commit."

Alan blanched, but the arrival of their appetizers prevented his response.

Everyone placed their order except Jo, who frowned at the menu while the waiter hovered. "I can't decide," she said, shaking her head.

Alan and John spoke at once.

"Try the chilled pasta."

"Try the grilled chicken."

Jo looked from man to man, shifting uncomfortably.

Alan's eyes narrowed slightly as he spoke to John across the table. "You obviously don't know Jo very well, because she doesn't eat a lot of meat."

"No, I don't know Jo very well," John agreed slowly, "but I happen to know she does like chicken." He smiled at the man, knowing from Alan's quick, accusatory glance at Jo that he'd heard some version of their picnic in Forsythe Park.

Jo cleared her throat and handed her menu to the waiter. "I'll have the grilled chicken pasta," she said, lifting her drink for another sip.

Alan frowned, then his gaze bounced around the restaurant. "Pamela," he asked suddenly. "Is that Charles Browden in the next room?"

Pamela turned discreetly in her seat to look in the direction Alan indicated, then nodded. "He's with his wife, Evelyn. I found a house for their oldest daughter a couple of months ago—a gift from Daddy, of course."

"Do you know them well enough to introduce me?" Alan pressed.

"Sure," Pamela agreed, curls bouncing. The California couple excused themselves and left John and Jo alone, much to John's delight.

"Well," he said, lifting his glass in the air, "here's to chicken."

She hesitated, unsmiling, then chinked her glass to his. "You're determined to get me into trouble, aren't you?"

"If you didn't tell him everything about our little picnic, I don't suppose you got around to mentioning—"

"John—"

"Ms. Montgomery, I don't believe it!" a female voice said behind him.

From the look on Jo's face, she didn't believe it either. "M-Mrs. Patterson," she said weakly.

John turned around to see a well-preserved blond woman smiling at both of them.

"Savannah is small, but I seem to be running into you everywhere!"

Jo smiled woodenly, her complexion ashen.

"This *must* be John, he looks so much like Jamie."

John rose and shook the woman's hand. "John Sterling."

"Mr. Sterling, I'm Melissa Patterson."

He smiled. "It's a pleasure to finally meet you."

"You must be so proud of your new wife."

John blinked. "My new wife?" He glanced at Jo and found her staring at him with pleading eyes. Pleading for what?

"My husband and I both are so impressed with her operation, and by the fact that she has taken on three stepchildren, as well."

John looked back to Mrs. Patterson and nodded non-committally. What the heck was this woman talking about?

The woman laughed merrily. "In fact, when we first saw Jo herding those kids through the door of her office, we knew we'd found the right person to handle our account."

He was completely baffled. "Is that right?"

"Oh, yes." Her smile was blinding. "We told her up front the fact that she had children gave her a definite edge in vying for our account."

John's fingertips tingled as realization began to dawn on him. "Really?" He gave the woman a tight smile, then glanced back to Jo. She held her fingers to her lips and her cheeks ballooned as if she might heave any second.

"Oh, yes, it's important that our designer be in tune with the needs of small children."

He pressed his lips together and nodded as anger began to well within him. *Jo had pretended his children were hers in order to get the Patterson account.*

"And I'm sure Jo expressed how concerned my husband and I were about your son's little mishap earlier this week."

"Yes," he said through clenched teeth. "My new wife is good about telling me everything."

"She assured me the two of you understood it was simply an unfortunate accident—our workers are typically very diligent."

Fury boiled through his veins, but he remained calm. "No, I don't hold the day-care center or the workers responsible for the, um, mishap. I know my son's tendencies."

"Well," she said brightly, tilting her head, "it was so nice to meet you. And might I say you make a very handsome couple."

"Thank you," John said tightly. She waved goodbye, then walked away. John turned his head ever so slowly to look down at Jo. Her eyes were closed, her napkin covering her mouth.

He sat down heavily, his eyes flicking over her gray complexion. Hurt, anger and betrayal washed over him with such force he, too, felt physically ill. "The least you can do," he said in a low, deadly voice, "is look at me."

Jo's shoulders rose as she inhaled deeply, then she opened her eyes. They swam with unshed tears.

Incidents flashed in his mind with a new perspective—Jo watching his children and taking them on "errands," her picking them up from day care, the voice message from Carolyn Hook referring to his "wife,"

Billy's confusing reference to her the last couple of days as "Jo-mommy." His heart shivered in disappointment.

"You've been using me and my children to position yourself with the Pattersons." Was that his voice? He sounded like a wounded animal.

Jo lowered the napkin slowly. Her mouth opened and closed, but no sound came out.

John laughed harshly. "Well, I guess you can nominate me for fool of the decade. I had actually convinced myself that you had grown fond of us. Although I can't imagine why," he added sarcastically, picturing them grappling naked on the rug.

"John," she said, her voice scratchy. "I'm sorry. I—I'll understand if you want to cancel our contract."

Business...she was all business. There wasn't a maternal cell, muscle or bone in her great body. He stared at her. "Well, at least now I understand why I qualified for such a deep discount."

She blinked rapidly. "John—"

Alan and Pamela chose that precise moment to return to the table. Alan was so pleased with the outcome of the conversation with Charles Browden, he failed to notice the change in Jo's demeanor. But John saw Pamela glance between them suspiciously before asking, "Jo, are you feeling all right?"

Jo coughed into her napkin, then straightened and said, "A bit of an upset stomach, that's all."

Pamela squinted at John. "You don't look so swell, either."

John shifted miserably in his seat. "Unfortunately, Jo and I shared a bitter morsel while you two were gone." Jo suddenly jumped up from her seat and sprinted toward the ladies' room.

9

SIXTY-EIGHT and a half. According to her digital clock, the blades of the ceiling fan in her bedroom turned exactly sixty-eight and a half times every minute. Jo lay staring at the movement, wishing the monotony would lull her to sleep. From the floor, Victor snored happily, his conscience obviously less burdened than Jo's.

She had hoped the staggering feeling of deceit might ease as the evening wore on, but every time she looked at John's face, shame washed over her anew. He had been coolly cordial, turning his attention to Pamela, leaving Jo to converse with Alan, who was already plotting his strategy to obtain Charles Browden's account. And all she had to do was look across the table to be reminded of her betrayal to Alan.

A tiny voice rationalized that Melissa Patterson's revelation was for the best. Her feelings for John Sterling were ridiculous, considering where they might logically lead. Marriage and motherhood? She laughed out loud, the sound startling her in the dark emptiness of her bedroom. She was no Carol Brady, and John's children deserved a mother who…well, a mother who knew how the heck to be a mother. Not a clueless, shoot-from-the-hip, career-minded woman with an aversion to grubby fingerprints on her silk suits.

Toward dawn she dozed fitfully, her dreams a mishmash of chasing hellion kids and growing old alone. Her eyes snapped open when her telephone broke the silence of the late morning. She sat up and glanced at her clock as she reached for the handset. Ten-thirty.

"Hello?"

"Jo?" Claire sounded breathless.

Immediately, Jo tensed. "Claire? Is something wrong?"

The little girl started to cry. "Aunt Cleo can't come to take me shopping and I need c-clothes for school Monday. Can you take me? Daddy doesn't know how to buy g-girl things." She sniffled, waiting for Jo's answer.

Jo bit her bottom lip. "Claire, does your daddy know you called me?"

"No," Claire said miserably. "I didn't want to hurt his feelings."

Jo smiled. "That's nice, but maybe you'd better put him on the phone."

Sniffing mightily, Claire relented. "Okay, hang on."

Steeling herself, Jo ran her fingers through her hair and encountered a nest of tangles from her night of tossing and turning.

"Hello," John said abruptly.

"John, it's Jo," she said quickly.

"I'm sorry Claire bothered you." His tone was clipped. "I'll let you get back to…whatever you were doing."

"It's okay," Jo said hurriedly. "She said your sister couldn't make the trip from Atlanta."

"Emergency at work."

"Claire was so looking forward to shopping for school clothes."

"I'll take care of it," he said evenly.

Jo gripped the handset so tight her fingernails hurt. "John, I'm glad Claire called—I needed to talk to you anyway."

"If it's about the house, just use your key—"

"It's not about the house," she cut in nervously. "It's about the situation with the Pattersons." She sighed. "Please believe that I didn't fabricate an elaborate lie to convince them I was your w-wife and the children's m-mother." The words were extremely hard to get out. "They simply assumed the children were mine. At the time, I thought I had a good reason not to correct them—I really needed their account—but now..." She inhaled a shaky breath. "But now, I realize it was thoughtless and hurtful and embarrassing for you. I'm very sorry."

After a few seconds of silence, John asked, "Is this where I'm supposed to say all is forgiven?"

"No," she said softly. "I wouldn't ask that of you— I just wanted you to know how I feel about what I've done." When he didn't respond, she hurried on. "And I'd be happy to take Claire shopping—you know, just us girls."

John sighed heavily into the phone. "Jo, I don't think you realize how attached to you my children have become. I don't want them hurt any more than they already will be."

Jo swallowed the lump in her throat. "I understand how you feel, but it means so much to Claire that she have the right clothes for her new school—you know how girls are at that age."

His laugh was hollow. "Actually, Jo, no, I don't, but I'm muddling through."

"Well, I know," she said, "because I was just like Claire. Let me do this for her."

"I don't think—"

"It's the least I can do under the circumstances," she offered. He hesitated, so she pressed on. "I'll shower and meet you at the front entrance of the mall in…thirty minutes?"

He sighed. "Better make it forty-five. Billy and I are tackling the potty again this morning."

She laughed and agreed, relief flooding her. When she replaced the handset, Jo's heart lifted a little. Perhaps she could repair a fraction of the damage she'd wrought.

The phone was ringing again when she stepped out of the shower. "Hello," she said, wrapping a towel around her hair.

"Hey, beautiful." Alan's voice rumbled low.

"Hi," she said, swallowing guiltily.

"I was hoping I'd catch you before you left for the day. Are you feeling better?"

"Much," she said truthfully.

"Good. How about dinner on Tybee Island tonight?"

"Uh, sure," she said breathlessly.

"Pick you up at six?"

"Six is fine," she said, then hung up slowly. Victor stared at her sorrowfully as she jumped up to finish dressing.

NOT SURPRISINGLY, the Sterlings were late, their noisy entry to the mall causing Jo to smile. Jamie ran up to her, looking naked without his black cape.

"Taking a break from flying today?" she asked.

His lower lip protruded. "Daddy wouldn't let me wear it—it's too new."

"Nui*sance*," John clarifed, walking up. "Too much of a nuisance."

Jo smiled tentatively, her heart tripping at the sight of him. "Hi."

He nodded, his expression neither friendly nor adversarial. "Hi."

"Jo-mommy!" Billy exclaimed happily, sharing a toothy grin.

She avoided John's gaze and smiled at the toddler. "Just plain Jo, okay, Billy?"

"Just Plain Jo," he mimicked.

"Hi, Jo," Claire said, slipping her small hand into Jo's. She pushed up her glasses and smiled shyly.

Jo felt a tug at her heart. Maybe this wasn't such a good idea, after all. "Are you ready to spend some money?"

Claire nodded, her white-blond hair swinging around her face. "Daddy gave me his credit card."

Jo grinned. "Terrific." She looked at John. "Is there anything special we should look for?"

"I'm leaving it up to you," he said, his voice and expression showing his reluctance.

She nodded, and dealt with the flash of pain in her chest. She couldn't blame him for being angry with her.

He looked at his watch. "It's eleven-thirty now, let's meet back in the food court for lunch around two, okay?"

She and Claire went in one direction, John and the boys went in another. As they passed other shoppers, Jo studied the clothing girls Claire's age were wearing. They walked into the girls' section of Jo's favorite department store and Claire became more shy than ever. She chewed on her lip and poked at her glasses every few seconds, and only nodded or shrugged when Jo held up outfits. After thirty minutes, they'd gotten nowhere. "Tell you what," Jo said. "You tell me your three favorite colors and go into the dressing room. Then I'll round up several outfits and you can try everything on at once." Claire nodded happily and Jo left her in the hands of a dressing-room clerk. She returned a few minutes later with an armload of bright-colored clothing, thrilled to watch the transformation as Claire pulled on the pretty clothes.

The little girl grinned and laughed easily, her cheeks glowing. After buttoning a particularly becoming pink polka-dotted blouse, Claire looked at herself in the mirror, enchanted with the way she looked. "I'm almost pretty," she breathed. "Do you like it, Mommy?" Her eyes cut to Jo in the mirror, then she realized her slip. Her eyebrows crumpled and she pressed her lips together, trying her best to still her quivering chin while unbuttoning the blouse as fast as she could.

"Hey," Jo said softly, leaning down to squeeze Claire's shoulder. "It's okay."

"I forgot," Claire whispered, her eyes full of tears.

"Shh," Jo said, holding her tight. "It's okay, really." She pulled back and smiled sadly at Claire. "Did your mommy take you shopping?"

The little girl nodded.

"I wish she could see how smart and how pretty you are, Claire. I know she'd be so proud of you."

"Daddy says I look like her."

"I'm sure she was a very beautiful woman."

"Daddy wants to find us a new mommy."

Jo's stomach flipped over. "Did he tell you that?" she asked softly.

Claire nodded. "I think he wants you to be our new mommy."

Jo blanched, then she touched the little girl's silky cheek. "I think you misunderstood, Claire. He'll find you a new mommy someday, but it won't be me."

Claire frowned and studied her sock feet. "I don't blame you for not wanting to be our mommy—we're a lot of trouble."

Swallowing to dispel the lump in her throat, Jo pulled Claire down beside her on a tiny bench. "Claire, this is hard to explain. It's not that I don't want to be your mommy, but I don't think I'd do a very good job of being *anyone's* mommy. Do you understand?"

Claire sighed and nodded sadly. "I guess so."

"Good." Jo smiled. "And you three are not so much trouble. I'm sure there are lots of women out there who would love to be your mommy."

"I hope so," Claire whispered. "I'm not a very good cook."

Jo laughed out loud, then glanced at her watch. "We'd better hurry if we're going to meet the boys!"

Claire quickly tried on jeans, skirts, shirts, and vests. For the briefest moment, Jo visualized watching a little girl of her own try on school clothes, and for the first time, a distant longing echoed deep in her heart. Seconds later, the feeling had vanished and Jo decided she'd imagined the faint stirring.

After they'd settled on several mix-and-match outfits, they bought hair ribbons, socks and shoes. Laden with packages, they were only ten minutes late meeting John and the boys, who had already claimed a table and were somewhat less burdened by purchases.

"Wow!" Jamie exclaimed. "I'm going with Jo the next time."

John surveyed the bags with amusement and tweaked his daughter's nose. "Am I going to have to sell the house to pay for all these?"

"No," Claire said, giggling. "But I might need a bigger closet."

"Just Plain Jo bring puppy?" Billy asked, tugging on Jo's shirt.

"No," she said sadly. "He's at home sleeping."

He held up his arms. "Poopy diaper."

"Again?" John sighed as Jo swung him into her lap. "I just changed you, Billy."

The little boy shrugged his little shoulders, unable to offer an explanation.

Jo laughed, then for a moment, all was quiet at their table. Jamie looked at Jo, then at John. Claire looked at John, then at Jo and Billy. Billy looked at John, then at Jo. Jo looked at the kids, then at John. And John simply looked at her. Her heart pounded at the intimacy of the situation—an all-American family. All around them, mall shoppers talked, laughed, walked and bustled by, insulating them in a quiet pocket. A trickle of sweat slid between her breasts, but Jo couldn't bring herself to end the peaceful moment.

A flash exploded in their faces. Jo blinked, then focused on a round man who lowered a camera and grinned at John. "Nice-looking family, sir. Five dollars for the memory." The man winked at Jo and waved the instant photograph in the air.

"WHAT A NIGHT," Alan said, spreading his arms to the night stars and inhaling deeply.

Jo smiled wide, glad Alan was in such a congenial mood. Her own thoughts had remained with the Sterlings long after she'd escaped the photo opportunist. After their unforgivable lapse at his home and the dinner disaster last night, her relationship with John—whatever its label—would never be the same, but she was glad they could at least be cordial.

"The water is gorgeous, hmm?" Alan asked, slipping an arm around her shoulder.

"Mmm," she agreed. The night air was chilly, so they had the beach to themselves.

She looked up at Alan's profile, boyish and handsome, his golden hair glowing in the moonlight. Admiration, fondness and genuine love washed over her. Alan had been her rock when she was getting her business off the ground. He'd introduced her to all the right people around town and treated her with respect and kindness throughout the three years they'd dated. Alan might not inspire the same depth of emotions she experienced with John Sterling, but he shared her goals. She sighed and leaned into him, grateful for the good times they'd shared and for the good times still ahead.

"Do you remember the first time we walked this beach, Jo?"

She smiled and nodded. "Our first solo date."

He stopped and looked into her eyes. "That's the night I knew, Jo. I knew I wanted to marry you."

As he withdrew a small square jeweler's box, tiny hairs raised on the nape of her neck, triggering a full-body shiver.

"I thought it only fitting to bring you back here for the proposal." He lifted the hinged lid, revealing a huge solitaire diamond twinkling and flashing in the moonlight.

Jo felt her jaw loosen and drop.

"Jo Montgomery," he whispered, removing the ring and sliding it onto her finger. "Will you marry me?"

She stared at the winking stone for several long seconds, alarmed when John Sterling's face appeared in her mind. Then she heard Claire saying, "Daddy wants to find us a new mommy." She didn't want a package deal—she wanted a man to love her for herself, not because he was a struggling single dad. And even if John ever could love her, she wasn't ready for an instant family.

Jo lifted her gaze to meet Alan's. His love for her shone in his eyes, and Jo said the words she'd imagined saying hundreds of times since they'd first started dating. "Yes, Alan Parish, I will marry you."

He swept her in his arms for a long, sweet kiss.

When he pulled back, he was beaming. He lifted her off the ground and swung her around, whooping. They continued walking down the beach, their hands clasped tightly together.

Squashing her anxiety, Jo laughed nervously and said, ''Well, you certainly surprised me.''

Alan smiled. ''To be honest, I should call your friend John Sterling and thank him.''

Jo's head snapped up. ''John? What does he have to do with this?''

''I'm not blind, Jo, I can see the guy has eyes for you. Besides, he said something last night about commitment that hit home.'' Alan shrugged, palms up. ''I called a jeweler first thing this morning.''

Jo conjured up a watery smile.

''Do you have any feelings about a wedding date?''

''Soon,'' she whispered. ''As soon as possible.''

''Great,'' he said. ''That will keep both of our mothers from making a big production out of the whole thing.''

Jo nodded. ''Yeah.''

''So,'' he shouted into the night air, ''thank you, John Sterling, wherever you are!''

''WELL, it's about time!'' Helen shouted, pulling Jo close for a suffocating hug. ''Let me see the ring.'' She pursed her lips as she inspected the diamond, nodding her satisfaction. ''Looks like a carat and a half, what do you think, Madden?''

Jo's father squeezed her hand, smiling. ''I think it's none of our business how much the stone weighs, Helen.''

From her perch by the sink, Hattie held up a glass of iced tea. "Here, here."

Helen frowned at her sister, then turned back to Jo. "A spring wedding would be nice, don't you think, dear? I'll call first thing tomorrow to book the string quartet that played at Margaret Fitch's wedding. Remember the little crab quiches they served?"

"Whoa, Mom," Jo said, holding up her hands. "I hate to disappoint you, but Alan and I have decided on a small church wedding in the very near future."

"How near?"

"Three weeks."

"What?" Helen screeched, clutching her chest. "It's impossible to organize a wedding in three weeks, Josephine."

"No, it isn't. Alan and I compared our work schedules and it's the best time for both of us. It'll give me time to finish a residential job I'm working on." She felt a pang in her side. "When I come back, I'll start a big commercial job that will probably take at least a year to finish." Another pang, this one worse.

"Where are you going your honeymoon?"

"Fort Myers Beach."

Her mother's face crumpled. "But that's so common! With Alan's money you could go to Hawaii, or Europe!"

Jo felt for her mother, she really did. Her only daughter was marrying a wealthy man and she was being robbed of the social recognition that accompanied a glamorous wedding. "Mom, we discussed it, and neither one of us wants to be too far away from our business in case there's an emergency."

"What does it matter?" Hattie asked. "All a couple needs is a bed and a remote control."

Jo's mother shot her sister an annoyed glance while Jo flushed and pressed her lips together to conceal a smile. Hattie swept over to Jo to scrutinize the ring, then whispered, "Or in Alan's case, just a remote control will suffice."

Jo pinched her aunt on the back of her hand. "Behave," she said.

Sunday dinner was even more stressful than usual, with Helen making suggestions and Jo gently shooting them down. Exasperated, her mother finally said, "Josephine, will I be invited?"

"Of course," Hattie said quickly. "With that hair, Helen, you're the something old *and* the something blue."

"Mother," Jo said softly, "why don't you meet me for lunch tomorrow and we'll pick out invitations?"

Somewhat assuaged, Helen nodded morosely.

Later, Jo's father followed her outside to wait for Hattie.

"This is a big step, sweetheart," he said. "Are you sure you're ready for it?"

Jo looked up into her father's warm eyes and nodded. If nothing else, her experience with the Sterling family had proved to her that her personal life had reached an impasse. She needed to move on. "Dad, did you always want children?"

He crossed his arms. "I think so, yes."

She bit her bottom lip. "Did you ever regret it?"

"Not for one second," he said, drawing her into a

hug. "Besides," he added, pulling away to smile at her, "that would have left me with just your mother."

Jo laughed, poking her dad in the ribs.

On the drive home, Hattie was quiet—not meditating as usual, just studying her hands in silence.

After the first mile, Jo sighed. "What, Hattie?"

Her aunt's eyes widened in innocence.

"Out with it," Jo said. "You haven't said twenty words since I broke the news."

"I was wondering what your Mr. Sterling thinks about you getting married."

"He's not *my* Mr. Sterling, and it doesn't matter what he thinks."

"You haven't told him, have you?"

"Alan only asked me last night, Hattie. Anyway, after the way I used John and his kids, I'm sure his reaction would be 'good riddance.'" And that wasn't the worst of it, she thought as scenes of their lovemaking flashed in her mind.

"Did you tell John you played along with the Pattersons because you were close to defaulting on your loan?"

Jo nearly swerved off the road. "How did you know that?"

"I know how much it takes to keep the office running, much less make that hefty loan payment every month."

Jo winced. "Do you think I made a bad decision?"

Hattie sighed. "Jo, my dear, some of your decisions are questionable, but the software was a good investment—it helped you land the Patterson account."

"No," Jo said painfully. "The Sterlings helped me land the Patterson account."

"Which brings me back to your questionable decisions."

"You're right. If I had it to do over, I'd never have let the Pattersons believe I was a supermom."

"Jo," Hattie said, and sighed impatiently, "not *that* decision. I'm talking about your decision to marry Alan."

"Hattie, we've been over this ground before—"

"And I would keep my mouth shut if I thought you were completely happy."

Frowning, Jo asked, "Don't I look happy?"

"No," Hattie murmured softly. "You don't. I think you're more attached to those children than you care to admit."

Alarm ballooned in Jo's stomach. "Y-you must be imagining things, Hattie. I've never wanted children."

"Have you ever thought that could be because you've never met a man you wanted to have children *with?*"

Jo swallowed, wanting her jumbled feelings to go away, to be replaced by confidence that she was doing the right thing. "John doesn't love me, Hattie," she said. "He's attracted to me, but he's looking for a woman who can be a full-time mom to those kids. At least I know Alan loves me and I can be my own person with him."

After a few seconds of silence, Hattie said, "If you're sure."

Inhaling deeply with resolve, Jo said, "I'm sure."

"Well, I was hoping Torry would be here for your

wedding, but three weeks might be a little optimistic, even for me.''

Her tone cautious, Jo asked, ''Have you heard from him?''

''Yes.''

''Really?''

''He spoke to me in a dream last night—he said we'd be together soon.''

''Oh. That's nice.''

Hattie clasped her hands together. ''Jo, that's the kind of love I want for you—the kind you don't have to question—a love for all time.''

''I've made my decision, Hattie.''

Her aunt clucked. ''You've made your bed, but you still have time to decide who's going to lie in it with you.''

10

FRIDAY AFTERNOONS were normally low-key around the office. As with every day this week, she'd spent the morning with the painters at John's house, careful to arrive after she was sure he was gone, and leave well before everyone came home. The workers had accomplished a lot in five days, but there was still plenty to do in the two weeks that remained. Jo was determined to cut all ties with the Sterlings before she walked down the aisle with Alan.

She had just put down her purse and switched on her computer when the phone rang. "Montgomery Group Interiors, this is Jo."

"Miss Montgomery, this is Mary Avondale, the school nurse from Brookwood Elementary."

Her mind spun as to why she should know the woman. "Yes?"

"I'm with a student, Claire Sterling, who insists she needs to talk to you."

Sitting up straight, Jo said, "Put her on."

"Jo?" Claire sounded tearful and frightened.

"Claire, what's wrong?"

"Can you come and get me? I'm very sick."

"What's wrong, sweetheart?"

"I can't tell you over the phone—it's real bad. I need for you to come right away."

"Did you call your daddy?"

"No!" Claire exclaimed. "He can't know. Promise me you'll come instead of Daddy."

Jo's heart wrenched at the fear in the little girl's voice. "I'll be there as soon as I can. Put Miss Avondale back on the phone."

"Hello?"

"Miss Avondale, do you know what's wrong with Claire?"

"No, ma'am. She said she wouldn't talk to anyone but you."

Phone crooked under her chin, Jo scribbled directions to the school, then hung up, yelled to Hattie, and ran out the door.

Biting her nails on the way over, Jo chastised herself for not informing John that Claire looked flushed last Saturday. For all she knew, she could have spinal meningitis by now. Some mother she'd make—she couldn't even tell when a child was sick. She depressed the gas pedal harder, sliding into a parking space in the school lot at an odd angle.

Running from office to office, she finally found the nurse's station, relieved to see Claire hugging her knees, sitting on a low padded bench in the small reception area.

"Jo!" She jumped up and threw her arms around Jo's waist. "I knew you'd come."

Kneeling, Jo felt the girl's forehead. "What's wrong, sweetheart?"

"I'm pregnant!"

Jo nearly swallowed her tongue. Thankfully, her closed throat kept her from screeching her surprise. Taking a deep breath, Jo wiped the alarm from her face. ''Claire, has anyone ever touched you anywhere you didn't want them to?''

Claire frowned, looking completely puzzled. ''No.''

Breathing a sigh of relief, Jo bit back the smile that threatened to break through. ''What makes you think you're pregnant?''

The little girl shifted uncomfortably, then leaned forward, tears in her eyes. ''My boobies hurt. Stacy Whetter told me that's how her older sister knew she was pregnant.'' Her bottom lip trembled, and she fell against Jo, sobbing. ''Oh, Jo, I don't want to have a baby!''

Jo hugged her close, patting her back, trying to help her regain her composure. She wouldn't subject Claire to further indignities by laughing at her misguided concerns. ''Shh, sweetheart, don't cry—you're not pregnant.''

Claire pulled back and hiccuped. ''I'm not?''

Smiling, Jo shook her head. ''No, you're not. I suspect, however, that you are beginning to develop, um, boobies, and that's why they're hurting. Do you have any training bras?''

Eyes wide, Claire shook her head gravely.

Tilting her head, Jo wiped Claire's tears and said, ''Then we'll fix that.''

Claire sniffed, then grinned and poked at her glasses.

Consulting her watch, Jo said, ''It's only another hour before you leave. I'll see if I can sign you out.''

Predictably, the school secretary wouldn't allow

Claire to leave with a nonfamily member, so Jo dialed John's office from a pay phone in the corner. Susan put her through to John with minimal drilling.

"Jo?"

His voice was so deep and so...welcome. Jo squashed the flash of lust she felt, spinning her engagement ring round and round. "John, I'm at Claire's school. She called and asked me to come pick her up."

"What's wrong?" he asked, his voice escalating.

"Well, nothing medical exactly," Jo said, looking over her shoulder to make sure Claire was out of earshot. "But your little girl is developing breasts and it scared her so much she thought she was pregnant."

"*What?*"

"You heard me."

"I don't think so, because I heard you say the words 'your little girl,' 'breasts' and 'pregnant' all in the same sentence."

"John, I don't suppose you've talked to Claire about the birds and the bees?"

"She's only nine years old!"

"And she'll be able to conceive a child in about three years."

"Aaagggh! Don't *say* that."

"Sorry to be the bearer of unwanted news," she said wryly. "Since I'm here, I thought I'd take her out to get a few underthings she'll be needing—or would you rather do it?"

"No!" He cleared his throat noisily. "I mean, no, I'm sure she'd rather you pick out her...underthingies."

"Fine. Just call the school back and give them permission to let her go with me, and I'll drop her by the house in a couple of hours.''

''Sure,'' he said. ''Oh, and Jo…''

''Yes?''

''Um…thanks.''

AFTER HE CALLED the school, John sat back in his desk chair and scrubbed his hand over his face. It was a sad, sad day…his little girl had breasts.

John sighed, then slowly reached over to open a desk drawer, and pulled out a cigarette. Then, shaking his head, he put it back in the package and relaxed into his chair. From the same drawer he pulled a photograph—the five of them collapsed in the stiff chairs at the mall food court. He and Jo were looking at each other, and the children were all looking at them. Such a neat little fit of scattered puzzle pieces. Gritting his teeth in frustration, he forced himself to remember that Jo Montgomery had used him and the children to gain a lucrative decorating account. She wasn't attached to him and his family; she'd been pretending all along.

Or had she? He might be a little rusty, but he'd bedded enough women to know an enthusiastic response when he felt one. And she'd seemed happy to take Claire shopping last weekend, plus take time out of her work schedule today. But then again, she could be doing it to make up for her little game of deception.

Leaning back in his chair, he banked miniature paper wads into his wastebasket until it overflowed. Sighing, he stood and stretched, unwilling to dive into the paperwork for the new airport hotel. He was restless now, and he ruefully acknowledged it probably had something to do with the fact that Jo Montgomery would be coming to his house this evening, if only to drop off Claire.

He couldn't wait to see her.

"You're pathetic, Sterling," he mumbled.

Susan walked into his office and knocked at the same time. She held a newspaper in her hand. "I've been meaning to show this to you all day, but I'd forgotten until Jo Montgomery just called." She carefully unfolded the paper, then turned a couple of pages. "There," she said, pointing. "Nice picture, eh?"

John's breath froze in his chest. Jo Montgomery smiled back at him, and the caption beneath her photo heralded Montgomery and Parish Announce Forthcoming Vows.

Jo's PULSE beat more erratically the closer her car got to John's home. Claire sat in the passenger seat, clutching the bag containing six new Comfort-eeze stretch training bras, identical to the one the little girl wore under her Mickey Mouse shirt.

Suddenly Claire leaned across the car seat, staring in awe. "Is that an engagement ring?"

Laughing nervously, Jo nodded and held it out for Claire to see.

"Wow! Does that mean you're getting married?"

"Uh-huh. My boyfriend asked me last weekend."

Claire bit her bottom lip. "So I guess my daddy won't be trying to kiss you anymore?"

Jo pressed her lips together and nodded. "That's right."

"Jo, don't you think my daddy is nice?"

"Of course I do."

"Why don't you marry *him* instead?"

Jo sighed. "Because I'm marrying Alan."

"What if something happens and you don't marry Alan, *then* would you marry my daddy?"

John was right—his children had grown attached to Jo and now they were in for a letdown. Her heart ached. "But nothing's going to happen."

Claire frowned. "Will you still come and see us sometime?"

Looking over at her dejected face, Jo felt like the lowest life-form. "Sure, sweetheart."

She pulled into the driveway, then hesitated. Perhaps she shouldn't go in.

Then Jamie bounded out the door. "Jo! My room's painted all blue—it's nice! Want to see?"

She hesitated, then nodded. "Okay." After she emerged from her car, the children each grabbed a hand and pulled her toward the front door.

"Just Plain Jo!" Billy yelled a greeting from the den where he sat among a stack of building blocks.

"Hi, Billy." Jo waved. Where was John?

"Look, Jo, your picture's in the newspaper," Jamie said, reaching up to the snack bar and carrying the paper to her.

Frowning, Jo took the paper, then her eyes widened. She sighed in annoyance, then muttered, "Well, Mom, I hope you're happy."

"What does it say?" Jamie asked, tugging on her sleeve.

"It says Jo's getting married," John said, walking

into the room. He leaned over to hug Claire. "Hi, sweetheart."

Jo's stomach vaulted at the sight of him. And the fact that he knew about her engagement affected her breathing in strange ways. His hair was slightly mussed, as if after he'd pulled the holey jersey over his head, he hadn't bothered to comb it again. He wore white gym shorts that revealed his disturbingly familiar muscular legs, and stood barefoot.

"Look at Jo's ring, Daddy. Isn't it pretty?" Claire asked.

He looked at Jo and pursed his lips, then reached forward and lifted her hand, fingering the knuckle of her third finger much as he had only days ago. "Hmm, nice," he said. "I guess the man's not as big an idiot as I thought."

Jo smiled and shrugged lightly. "He said all your talk about commitment the other night hit home."

John stared at her, then crossed his arms. "Well," he said, his voice deceptively soft above the ears of the children, "the least you could have done was let me in on it—remember me, your *husband?*"

Straightening her shoulders, Jo changed the subject. "Claire has the things she needs for now, but if I were you, I wouldn't postpone the talk I mentioned for very long."

"Oh?" John asked, his eyes flat. "And you're the parenting expert now?"

The remark hit her like a slap in the face. She wasn't mommy material—not now, not ever. "N-no," she stammered. "I...I have to go."

She turned toward the door and Jamie yelled, "But Jo, don't you want to see my room?"

Blinking furiously, Jo tried her best to smile. "I'll see it tomorrow, Jamie, okay?" She walked across the foyer as fast as she could. As she closed the door behind her, she heard Jamie mumble, "I'm Peter. Daddy, why is Jo crying?"

On the way home, Jo rolled down the window and drove slowly, welcoming the bracing breeze, wishing it would blow away all her problems, all her fuzzy feelings. She owed it to Alan to stay away from John Sterling, but their paths kept crossing. It was impossible to disappoint the children, especially Claire, but she'd have to steel herself the next time one of them called. She simply could not keep riding this emotional roller coaster—front car, no hands.

She dialed her office voice mail to check messages. The third caller was Melissa Patterson. "*Miss* Montgomery," she said in a cool tone, "I was looking through the paper today and spotted something rather interesting. I think we should talk."

"MRS. PATTERSON will see you now," the young woman said gravely, sweeping her arm toward the door. She gave Jo an apologetic half smile.

Jo halted before the closed door, her heart thudding against her chest. She took a deep breath and turned the knob. Mrs. Patterson turned in her tall swivel chair and offered her a chilly smile. "Come in, Miss Montgomery."

Nodding and smiling, Jo took the seat she was offered, trying desperately to calm her rolling stomach.

Her palms were wet with perspiration. Inside her purse was a check for most of the advance the Pattersons had given her. If they insisted on full repayment immediately, she'd have to swallow her pride and go to Alan.

"Mrs. Patterson," Jo began, laughing nervously, "I suppose you would like an explanation for the announcement in the newspaper."

The woman pursed her thin lips. "I've narrowed the explanations down to two—either you're a bigamist, or you're a liar."

Clearing her throat, Jo said, "Um, yes, well—"

"I don't have all day, Miss Montgomery, which is it?"

She took a deep breath, then said, "Well, I guess if I would have to pick one—liar."

"That's fortunate since it's the only legal option. And may I ask why you felt it necessary to weave such a fantastic lie?"

Jo cleared her throat again, then spoke softly, carefully. "The day I first met you and Mr. Patterson, you assumed the children were mine. After you mentioned it would help my chances for getting your account, I simply let you go on believing it."

"You mean you played us for fools."

"I certainly didn't mean—"

"And were the children and Mr. Sterling in on it— I suppose to wangle their way back into the day care?"

"No, they're completely innocent."

"The children seemed very attached to you."

Jo took a deep breath and nodded, her lips pressed together. "I'm redecorating the Sterling house. I suppose they latched on to me as a mother figure."

"But the other night in the restaurant, I distinctly heard Mr. Sterling refer to you as his wife."

"We weren't together," Jo said, feeling like a dolt. "Our dates had excused themselves from the table when you appeared. John didn't know what was going on—he covered for me."

"I see," Mrs. Patterson said slowly, studying Jo's face as if trying to determine how a person could do such a thing.

Rising to her feet, Jo said, "I'm sorry for deceiving you, Mrs. Patterson. I feel terrible about this whole situation, and I'll understand completely if you want to cancel the contract."

Her hands steepled, Mrs. Patterson remained silent for a full minute, then shifted forward in her seat. "I'm still of the opinion that we need a designer who is able to connect with children."

Jo swallowed resolutely, then she opened her purse to remove the check.

"And," the woman continued, "I still think we have the right person in you…Jo."

Incredulous, Jo stammered. "Y-you do?"

"You're a natural with kids—you might not see it, but other people do. Those children respond to you. And we were very impressed with your software demonstration—I don't think my husband and I have ever reached a decision so quickly."

"You mean it had nothing to do with worrying about being sued for Jamie's accident?"

Mrs. Patterson shook her head. "We carry millions of dollars' worth of insurance to cover situations like that, Jo. It had no impact on our decision to give you our account.'' She smiled at last. ''You underestimate your sales capabilities.''

''Thank you. I'm flattered.''

Mrs. Patterson sighed. ''But I'm genuinely disappointed to discover those children aren't yours...it somehow seemed so right. Apparently, you underestimate your capabilities in other areas, as well.''

Jo left the Pattersons' office feeling stunned. The fact that she still had the account wasn't nearly as amazing as Mrs. Patterson's other revelation.

She actually thought Jo was good with children.

JO DROVE BY John's house seven times Monday morning, waiting for his car to leave. Finally, when the furniture van arrived, she sighed and pulled into the driveway, bracing herself for the physical onslaught of his presence.

Billy's screams of ''Bad potty, bad potty'' filled the air when she opened the front door.

''John?'' she called.

A few seconds later, he walked in carrying a tearful Billy. ''I can't figure it out. What is it about that damned potty?''

''Just Plain Jo!'' Billy exclaimed, reaching for her.

Reluctantly, Jo took him, reveling in the feel of his chubby arms around her neck, his chubby legs around her waist. ''Poopy diaper,'' he whispered.

Jo and John exchanged glances. ''He's difficult,'' they said in unison, then smiled.

''Some of the furniture is here,'' Jo said, nodding toward the front door. ''This place will be starting to take shape when you get home this evening.''

"I took the day off to potty-train Billy, even if it kills us both," John said, raising his hands palm up. "So you're stuck with me."

"Oh," Jo said, squirming. "Well, I won't be here that long—just until everything's in place. There'll be more furniture delivered every morning this week." She hesitated, then plunged ahead, "John, Claire mentioned once you had paintings packed away that your wife painted."

He stiffened. "Yes."

"Well," she said softly, "I think it would be a very nice thing if your kids could grow up surrounded by her artwork, don't you?" She held her breath.

He stared at her for a long time, then bit his lip and nodded. "Okay, I'll bring them out of storage."

She walked to the door and instructed the men to start unloading the furniture, then walked into the downstairs bathroom to retrieve a diaper. Immediately, he stiffened and whined, "Bad potty, monster potty get Billy."

Sighing, she set him down in the hall, then went into the bathroom and rummaged through the vanity cabinet. When she looked back, Billy had poked his head around the corner. "Monster potty," he whispered ominously.

Jo followed his stare and frowned at the commode and the colorful potty-chair sitting next to it. She stood and walked over to the toilet and touched the back of it. "Good potty," she said.

"Good potty," Billy parroted.

She touched the small potty-chair. "Good potty."

"Good potty." He grinned, but still hung back.

"Come and sit on the good potty, Billy," she said, smiling and nodding.

He shook his head firmly. "Monster get Billy."

"I give up," Jo mumbled, stooping to right a black plastic-dragon toilet-brush holder.

"Monster get Billy!" the toddler shrieked, cowering at the door.

Jo frowned, then looked at the cartoonish animal shape in her hand. "Is this what you're afraid of?" She held it up, and Billy fled, wailing at the top of his lungs.

Straightening, Jo covered her mouth with her hand, laughing quietly.

"What's going on?" John asked from the doorway. "Where's Billy?"

Jo turned and held up the plastic dragon. "He's afraid of the toilet-brush holder."

"You're kidding."

"Nope. There's one in the upstairs bathroom, too, isn't there?"

He nodded. "You mean, all this time…?"

"Yup."

He brought the heel of his hand to his forehead. "I *have* seen Jamie use them in his Peter Pan escapades—he probably terrorized Billy more than once." Hands on hips, he shook his head and laughed with her. "I owe you big for this one, Jo."

After a few seconds, their laughter faded, and their gazes met. Finally, Jo smiled nervously and said, "Maybe we can call it even, then."

He studied her face for a few seconds, then nodded. "Sure." To her surprise, he extended his hand.

She stared at his big fingers, then slowly lifted her

hand and slipped it inside his. Their skin touching was electric, at least for Jo. The nerve endings in her fingers throbbed. Instead of a handshake, the clasp was intimate and warm, palm nestled against palm. At last, Jo retrieved her limp hand, and tried to smile. "I'll get rid of Billy's monster and leave you two alone with the potty." Completely shaken, she left the bathroom, determined to stay out of sight the rest of the morning.

OUT OF SIGHT was not out of mind, John decided as he sat on the bathroom floor, watching his toddler read while sitting contentedly on the potty. He sighed, wishing he could stop wanting her, could stop…loving her. He blinked at his own admission, then watched as his son craned his neck.

"Just Plain Jo?" Billy asked, pointing to the door.

John nodded. "Jo's still here, Billy." Pain expanded his chest. "Just don't get used to it," he whispered sadly.

11

BETWEEN tying up loose ends at the Sterling house and taking care of last-minute arrangements for the wedding, the week flew by. Thursday afternoon Jo did a preliminary walk-through by herself in preparation for John's final walk-through scheduled that evening. On the way back to her office, she stopped at her duplex and boxed her collection of Nancy Drew books, then walked to her car to stow them in the trunk for Claire. She was startled when a handsome older gentleman came around the side of her house and approached her.

"Good day," he called, his breath white in the crisp air.

"Hello," she said, smiling. "Can I help you?"

"I certainly hope so," he said. "My name is Torry Rodgers and I'm looking for Hattie Stevens."

Jo stared at him, stupefied. "*You're* Torry?"

"Yes, I am," he said, smiling. "Do you know Hattie?"

"I'm her niece, Jo Montgomery." She couldn't stop smiling.

"Well, that's marvelous! Can you tell me where I might find her?"

"I'll do better than that," Jo said, grinning. "I'll take you to her."

He followed her back to the office. Jo didn't go inside—she simply let him in, turned the Closed sign on the door and climbed back into her car. She could work from the duplex today. After all these years, the couple deserved a private reunion. "Good for you, Aunt Hattie," she whispered.

Alan called three times that afternoon to check on minor things, and each time Jo found her patience wearing more thin. "I really don't care what kind of champagne we toast with, Alan, just make sure there's plenty of it."

To her surprise and delight, Pamela had been her saving grace the past few days, doing anything and everything Jo asked her to do, plus anticipating dozens of things Jo had forgotten.

On the way to the Sterling house, her mother called on the car phone and chatted about nothing for ten minutes, then cleared her throat and said, "Josephine, I hope you remembered to see your doctor and arrange for birth control."

Stunned, Jo realized her mother thought she was still a virgin. It took her a few seconds to recover. "Yes, Mother."

"Good, because the wedding night can be very scary if you're not prepared."

Pamela would not believe this conversation. "Okay."

"So, are you—" Helen cleared her throat again "—prepared, dear?"

Jo bit her tongue to keep from laughing out loud. "I think I know what to expect, Mother, yes."

"Good, because if you have any questions, I'll be

glad to answer them, or if I don't know, I'll ask your father.''

Jo held up the handset and looked at it, incredulous. She put the phone back to her mouth and said, ''Thanks, Mom.''

By the time she pulled into John's driveway, she was a walking bundle of nerves. The entire house was lit up, and Jo sat looking at it, realizing how accustomed she'd grown to its rooms, its lines, its ambience. She stepped out of the car, zipping her coat, then pulled the carton of books from the trunk and headed toward the door.

She'd barely reached the top step when the door flew open and the kids came running out.

''Jo!'' Jamie cried. ''My room is neato!''

''Where's your cape?'' she asked.

''I'm just Jamie again,'' he said bluntly, then smiled shyly, a first. ''You can call me that—Jamie, I mean— if you want to.''

Claire pulled her down for a whisper. ''My boobies don't hurt anymore, Jo. And guess what?''

''What?'' Jo whispered back.

''Jeremy Winder carried my books to math class!''

''Really?'' Jo's eyes widened.

''Don't tell Daddy,'' Claire begged.

''It's our secret,'' Jo promised.

''Just Plain Jo!'' Billy said, pulling on her pants leg. ''Billy is big boy now.''

She noted the lack of a diaper under his jeans with an exaggerated gasp. ''Yes, you are a big boy, aren't you?''

''Need a hand?'' John asked from the doorway.

She looked up and drank in the length of him, head to toe, leaning against the frame, his arms crossed casually. Her mouth went dry, and she could only hand him the carton. "There are two more in my car," she said, turning back to get them.

He told the kids to come in from the cold, then caught up with her and withdrew the larger box, leaving the smaller one for her. "So, Saturday's the big day."

She smiled, avoiding his gaze. "Uh-huh."

"My invitation must have gotten lost in the mail."

Glancing up, she said, "I didn't think you'd be interested."

"Who knows?" His voice was soft and teasing. "I might just crash the party."

He walked ahead of her, then said over his shoulder. "What's in these boxes, anyway?"

"Books!" Claire squealed from inside the house, lifting volumes from the first carton. They set down the other boxes and Jo watched as Claire arranged the books chronologically, fingering the spines lovingly. Once she'd finished, she rose and hugged Jo around the waist. "Thanks, Jo. I'll take good care of them."

"I know you will," Jo said, stroking her hair.

John cleared his throat loudly, then asked abruptly, "Aren't we supposed to be doing a walk-through?"

"Right," Jo said, releasing Claire. He obviously wanted her to leave as soon as possible.

To force herself to keep her mind on business, Jo grabbed a clipboard and pen, then backtracked with John to the entryway. He coolly approved each selection from wallpaper to sculpture. In his office, Jo noticed that several wide file cabinets had been added, along with a drafting table.

"I decided to move my office home," he explained. "To be with the kids as much as possible."

Jo nodded, her admiration for John growing even as her chest tightened with pain. He was a good father and deserved a partner who would be an equally good parent. She brushed aside the disturbing thoughts and forged ahead with the walk-through.

They moved throughout the downstairs, Jo's spirits alternately lifting and falling when she recognized how well the rooms had turned out and how much she was going to miss being in them. She especially liked the green kitchen, and had instructed a still life of Annie's be hung by the breakfast table. The overall effect of the first floor was homey and livable. She could tell John liked it very much because his children moved through the rooms so comfortably.

They all climbed the stairs, the boys showing off their room first, then Claire. Jo pretended she had never seen any of it before tonight, exclaiming over every piece of furniture, and every picture. After reviewing the guest room, they left the kids in their rooms and she followed John to the master suite, conscious of her physical reaction to his proximity in the intimate setting.

He opened the door, and Jo caught her breath. The room was still decorated as beautifully as she'd left it, but John had changed it to reflect the way she'd presented it to him with the software: the bed was turned down, jazz music played softly, even a fire in the sitting-room fireplace. It was stunning and titillating.

"H-how's the new mattress?" she asked, her eyes riveted to the bed.

"Heavenly—didn't you try it?"

She raised her gaze to find him staring at her. "No."

His smile was slow and provocative. "Want to?"

Unsaid words hung in the air between them. Jo blinked first. "I'll have to take your word for it," she said quickly, moving away from him. "You're happy with the rooms, then?"

"As happy as I can be under the circumstances."

She looked at him and frowned. "What do you mean?"

He shrugged. "Look around—these rooms are for lovers, not for one man to rattle around in."

She felt her cheeks grow even warmer.

He laughed ruefully. "You know, when I asked you to decorate this home to your taste, I thought it was a brilliant strategy."

"You don't like it?" she asked, alarmed.

"Oh, I like it tremendously," John assured her, then added softly, "but my strategy backfired, because you're in every room."

Jo stared at him, and her mouth opened. Her brain short-circuited and transmitted words of love to her tongue, but they stalled there. She longed to share this room with him, to lie beneath him in his bed—but a frightening thought crossed her mind. What if she sacrificed everything for this man only to discover a few months from now that the lust had diminished and she was left with a husband who didn't love her and three children she couldn't bear to leave?

"I have to go," she said suddenly, backing out of

the room. She trotted down the stairs and gathered up odds and ends she'd left lying around in far corners of the house—a ruler, a level, color strips.

When she turned toward the front door, she was surprised to see the four of them standing together. Claire stepped up and handed her a gift wrapped in ratty Christmas paper. "It's from all of us," she said. "So you don't forget."

Jo's hands shook as she removed the paper to reveal a framed picture, painted by Claire. It was the front of their house, impressively detailed and colored. In the yard stood a tall man with red hair, and three children, all appropriately sized and hair-colored. The picture blurred as Jo's eyes watered, her throat clogged with emotion.

"We signed our own names," Jamie said, his voice full of pride. "Except for Billy—he used his handprint."

"And Dad picked out the frame," Claire piped in.

"It's beautiful," Jo said tearfully, kneeling to gather them in a hug. "Thank you. I'll miss all of you."

She released them abruptly, then stood and faced John.

He looked at her, through her, not really focusing. "Good luck, Jo."

She nodded. "Goodbye, John." Then she turned and walked out the door, clasping the picture to her chest.

"Jo!" Pamela admonished. "Everyone's waiting!"

Jo looked up from her handkerchief into her best friend's concerned face. "I can't stop crying."

"It's your wedding day—you're supposed to cry."

"Not this much, Pamela. I don't think I can do it."

"Of course you can do it. Alan's waiting up there with a huge grin on his face, and I'm wearing this horrid peach taffeta dress—all for you."

Jo smiled through her tears and took a deep breath. "Okay," she said. "I can do this, I can do this." She kept repeating it to herself as she exited the dressing room and her father offered her his arm.

"You look beautiful, sweetheart," he said, beaming. "Are you ready?"

Jo nodded and kept repeating, "I can do this, I can do this." But as soon as the doors to the small chapel were opened, she began to sob and nearly buckled. Her poor father half pushed, half dragged her down the aisle past a jam-packed crowd of family and friends and deposited her beside Alan, whose forehead was slightly creased with concern.

"Jo," he whispered, "are you all right?"

She nodded, then yanked the silk hankie from his breast pocket and blew her nose mightily.

The music ended, and the preacher began, "Dearly beloved—"

"Wait," Jo said, holding up her hand. The audience gasped.

"Jo," Alan snapped, "what is wrong with you?"

"I need a minute with my aunt."

Alan looked incredulous. "What?"

Jo turned around and held her gloved hand over her eyes against the bright lights. "Hattie, where are you?"

Her aunt stood in the second row and made her way to the aisle. "Right here, dear."

Jo waved her over behind the organist, then turned to the singers and said, "Sing something."

They broke into a hesitant version of 'O Promise Me,' then Jo asked Hattie, "So, how's Torry?"

Hattie's smile was joyous. "He's simply wonderful."

"Do you think you two will get married?"

"Oh, yes." Hattie nodded convincingly, dislodging a bright orange straw hat with a white plume. "He proposed last night."

"You're kidding!"

"Like I said, Jo, you know when it's right."

"What are you going to tell Herbert?"

"That I hope he finds someone who loves him the way I love Torry."

A cold hand wrapped around Jo's arm from behind, and she turned to face her mother. "Josephine Helena Montgomery, are you trying to send me to the grave from a heart attack?"

"Mother, I just want to be sure I'm marrying the right man."

"The right man?" Helen said tightly. "Look at your groom, darling! He's gorgeous, he's smart, he's successful—"

Jo looked at Hattie. "She's right."

"But does he curl your toes?" Hattie asked.

Helen frowned. "What on earth are you talking about?"

"Oh, come on, Helen, I'm talking about the bedroom—"

"Stop right there, Hattie!" Helen held up her hand.

"I'll not have you talking about perverted things in front of my daughter."

At the sound of a deep voice being cleared, Jo looked over her shoulder.

"Jo," Alan said, motioning to the crowd. "Everyone's getting a little restless. What's going on over here?"

Jo shooed her mother and aunt back to the pews, then turned to Alan. She looked into his eyes and all the powerful feelings of admiration, respect and companionship were resurrected. Alan loved her, and would make her happy.

"I'm ready," she announced.

They took their places and the singers stopped mid-lyric. The minister began again, and so did Jo's tears. She leaned on Alan and sobbed throughout the introduction. John didn't love her. He'd move on to find a mommy for his kids—someone who could cook and sew and swap coupons with other mothers. When the minister asked if anyone objected to the joining of this couple, the only sound that could be heard were her sobs echoing off the walls.

The minister paused for so long even she looked up at him. Then the peal of a bell sounded, jarring everyone to their feet. "Fire alarm!" the minister shouted. "Everyone stay calm—"

But his words fell on deaf ears. The guests stampeded to the back of the church, out into the hall and down the front steps. Worry and relief flooded Jo when she realized the ceremony would be delayed a little longer. She and Alan were among the last to emerge into the cold, blustery wind. Rain was threatening to spill from the gray sky any moment. Remembering what John had said about crashing the party, she shivered and scanned the milling crowd for his face, wondering if he might have slipped in to sit in a back pew.

"Jo!"

She knew that voice: Jamie. Jo turned to see all three children standing together under a tree, waving. Claire's words came back to her: *"What if something happens and you don't marry Alan,* then *would you marry my daddy?"* One look at Jamie's face and she began to suspect who had pulled the fire alarm. She walked over to them as fast as her long dress would allow. "What are you kids doing here?"

Claire raised her chin and poked her glasses. "Jo, we want you to be our mommy."

"Yeah!" Jamie said.

"Jo-mommy!" Billy chimed in.

The minister called for everyone to return to the church. "False alarm!" he shouted.

Jo looked at them and sighed. "Come with me," she said, extending both hands. Linking on to her, the children followed her into the church and down the hall into the dressing room. She sat down and motioned for them to sit at her feet.

"How did you get here?"

"We took a taxi," Jamie said proudly.

"We showed the driver the wedding announcement in the paper and told him to bring us," Claire said. "Then we left a note for Daddy."

"Jo-mommy!"

"Can't you be our mommy, Jo?" Claire pleaded.

Jo's eyes watered, but she was nearly cried out.

"Claire, you'll understand this better than the boys, so please listen very carefully, okay?"

The little girl nodded.

"To make a marriage last, two people have to really love each other. Your daddy can't marry me just because the three of you want him to, do you understand?"

Claire nodded. "I think so. You're saying that daddy doesn't love you."

Jo nodded. "That's right."

"Does Alan love you?"

"Yes, he does."

"And you love Alan?"

Jo hesitated, then said, "There are different kinds of love, and yes, I love Alan on one of those levels." She heard a sound behind them, and froze. Slowly, she turned to see not only Alan, but John standing in the doorway. Alan's face was a mask of disappointment, and John's...his was unreadable.

"Kids," she said softly, "I need to talk to Alan alone for a few minutes. Would you wait outside?"

John collected them at the door and herded them into the hall, closing the door behind them.

Jo walked up to Alan and touched his hand. When he opened it, she placed her engagement ring in his palm. "I can't marry you, Alan. I'm sorry. You've been good to me, and I'll always admire, respect and care for you, but you deserve someone who loves you more than I do."

Alan pursed his lips, his blue eyes welling with unshed tears. "It's Sterling, isn't it?"

Jo swallowed, her chest aching for what she and

Alan had once meant to each other. "I didn't mean for it to happen, Alan, but yes, I'm in love with him."

"How does he feel about you?" he asked, his voice choked.

She smiled. "I honestly don't know."

"Well," he said, attempting to laugh, "I feel like a marathoner who just lost a race to a spectator."

"Alan," she said softly, "I hope we can—"

"Still be friends," he finished for her, then gave her a pained smile. He inhaled deeply and expelled the breath noisily. "If he's not good to you, Jo, he'll have to answer to me."

She reached up and kissed him on the cheek. "Thank you, Alan."

Tears gathered in her eyes as she watched him leave, then she walked toward the door to tell the children goodbye. Suddenly John appeared in the doorway and Jo stopped, unable to move.

"Am I correct in assuming that since your fiancé just left looking like a wounded animal, you are now unengaged and available?"

Jo's heart skipped a beat. "Yes."

John walked into the room and dropped to one knee in front of her. His green eyes shone soft and warm. "And if I professed my undying love, would you give your hand in marriage to me?"

She tilted her head and narrowed her eyes at him. "Start professing."

"Jo," he said, taking her hand, "I've thought of nothing but you since the first second I saw you." He bit his lip, then smiled. "I'm crazy in love with you, and I can't bear it if you don't love me, too."

Inhaling sharply, she mirrored his smile. "In that case, I have good news."

He grinned and rose to his feet, holding her by her arms. "Say it," he murmured, lowering his mouth to within an inch of hers.

"I love you," she whispered. "With all my strength."

"Say you'll marry me," he breathed.

"I'll marry you."

The sound of giggling reached their ears and they turned to see all three children crowded in the doorway.

Jamie grinned. "Are you gonna kiss her, Daddy?"

John looked back to Jo and laughed, shaking his head. "I sure am, son." He tilted his head and captured her lips in their first truly uninhibited kiss, straining toward each other, but somehow managing to keep it G-rated for their cheering audience.

Amidst the background of clapping, Jo said, "Seems a shame to waste a perfectly good dress and a perfectly good church and perfectly good food, doesn't it?"

John's smile was wry as he glanced down at his khaki pants and V-neck sweater. "I'm not exactly dressed for a wedding, but if it doesn't bother you—"

Jo didn't stay to hear any more. She herded the children in front of her to find her parents and Hattie standing in the hall.

"Josephine, I'm going to have a stroke if you don't tell me what's going on!" Helen demanded.

"Mother, you remember John Sterling, don't you? And his children, Claire, Jamie and Billy?"

"Hello," her mother said suspiciously.

"John, this is my father."

The men shook hands and exchanged greetings.

"Mother, John and I are getting married."

Helen swayed and grabbed her husband's arm. "What did you say?"

"Hattie, would you please round up the organist and the singers and tell them to start from the top? I need to find the minister and give him John's name."

Smiling, Hattie turned to go, then whirled back and patted Helen's arm. "Congratulations, sis—you're a grandmother!"

Helen went limp, but Jo's father waved them on their way. Jo found Pam nibbling her acrylic nails in the hallway and pulled her aside. "Pam, I'm not marrying Alan."

Her friend smiled wryly. "I noticed."

"But I'm worried about him…would you mind going after Alan and…well, keeping an eye on him?"

Pamela frowned and bit her bottom lip, then relented with a nod. "Sure, Jo. Call me tomorrow."

The ceremony was short and sweet. The minister raced through the vows, keeping one eye on Jo. The congregation had dwindled somewhat, but there were still plenty of well-wishers to cut the cake, once the slab with Alan's name had been removed. Jo was overjoyed when Hattie caught the bouquet, laughed when Jamie caught the garter and cried when Claire shyly asked permission to call her Mommy.

After the food had vanished, Jo danced until her feet throbbed, then kicked off her shoes and danced again. When John spun her into a slow waltz, she kissed his ear and nibbled on his lobe. "I didn't know you could dance," she said, fuzzy from the champagne.

"I didn't know you could nibble," he said, moaning.

"What other things should I know about you?" she asked, still nipping and licking.

"I have a horrible sense of direction."

"You seem to have mastered up and down," she whispered.

"Kids!" he yelled, lifting his head. "Get your things. It's time to go home."

"Home," Jo murmured dreamily. "That sounds so nice, doesn't it?"

They prodded their family through the reception hall as quickly as possible. Jo tried to tame her thoughts, relatively sure she shouldn't be thinking about sex just a few steps away from a church. They piled into the car and made one stop on the way home—to collect Victor. They were home within minutes, but it took quite a while to get everyone settled down, bathed and in bed, then up again for drinks of water and trips to the bathroom. Jo decided to take a few minutes when she tucked in Jamie and Claire to point out the dangers of pulling a fire alarm, but afterward she smothered them with good-night kisses.

Backing out of their rooms, John warned, "And no one yells or gets back up unless you're bleeding, got it?" He looked at her and smiled ruefully. "I figure we've got thirty minutes, tops."

But at last they were alone. John swung her into his arms and carried her across the threshold to his bed, where he lay her down and began to peel off the layers of her wedding ensemble, now wet with bubble bath and speckled with food.

Stripped down to wispy lingerie, she arched against

the soft mattress, offering her husband an unabashed display of peaks and valleys.

John groaned and began to tug at his own clothing. But Jo sat up to help him undress, freeing his erection into her hands, stroking him until he warned her to stop. He was beautiful, all hard planes and firm muscle, smooth skin and red-gold body hair. He knelt to uncover her breasts, and Jo tensed in preparation for his mouth. He moaned, his voice rumbling over the pebbled tip before he captured it in his mouth, sending her body into convulsions. When she thought she couldn't bear another second of the onslaught, he moved to the other breast and began anew, settling his body over hers.

She pulled at his back, straining into him. His fingers slid under the nearly invisible panties and whisked them away, opening her to his strong, probing fingers. She gasped, and he joined her in a deep kiss, moving his body against her, while readying her with his hands. A low hum of liquid pleasure began circulating deep within her, coaxed closer and closer to the surface with his deft movements. He murmured loving things into her ear, inviting her to enjoy her release, telling her how much he wanted to see her trembling in his arms. She surrendered to the ecstasy, exclaiming as loudly as she dared, bucking beneath him as orgasmic waves engulfed her. "John," she moaned. "John."

He quieted with her, although she could feel his shaft against her thigh, hard and straining. "Jo," he whispered.

"MmHmm," she said, barely able to open her eyes.

He grinned sheepishly, his breath ragged. "I feel like

an idiot, but I guess I should ask this time—are you protected?''

She laughed out loud, then nodded. He kissed her mouth, moving to settle himself at her moist entrance, then carefully, carefully, entering her until she took him completely. His guttural moans were pure, raw pleasure, sending shivers up her spine.

''Jo,'' he whispered again, his voice raspy.

''Mmm?'' she gasped, moving under him, keeping pace.

''I won't be...able to...last very long.''

''Then can we...do this...again sometime?''

He laughed and moaned and shuddered at the same time, calling her name with each spasm. She rocked beneath him, then descended with him to stillness.

They lay unmoving for the longest time, Jo reveling in the intimate weight of her husband's body on her, in her. Just when she thought he had fallen asleep, he spoke, his breath warm against her throat.

''I'll tell you a secret if you'll tell me one.''

''Okay,'' she agreed.

''You first,'' he urged.

Jo pondered his request, then murmured, ''When I was fourteen, I wrote a letter to Shaun Cassidy and asked him to marry me.''

''Really?''

''Uh-huh. Now you.''

He was silent for a few seconds, then said, ''I was the one who pulled the fire alarm at the church.''

*Who needs a wedding
when you can skip right to the honeymoon?*

WIFE IS A 4-LETTER WORD

1

ALAN PARISH DREW BACK and kicked the aluminum can high in the air, mindless of damage to his shiny formal shoe. Hands deep in his pockets, he watched the can bounce and tumble on the deserted rain-soaked sidewalk in front of him, gleefully imagining it to be John Sterling's head each time the metal collided with the pavement.

His mouth twisted with the ballooning urge to curse, but he couldn't think of an appropriate expletive to describe the basically nice guy who'd just happened to steal his fiancée—at the altar. Right now the only adjective for the man that came to mind was…smart.

Glancing around, Alan looked for something else to kick, suddenly wishing it were physically possible to make contact with his own backside. He should have asked Josephine to marry him months ago—no, years ago. Instead he'd taken their relationship for granted and she'd fallen in love with one of her clients, then canceled her marriage to him before his mother, perched on the front pew, had time to work up a good cry.

At this very moment, his friends and business associates were no doubt toasting the happy impromptu couple, at Alan's expense—literally. He winced, remembering that he'd made sure a case of his favorite champagne would be sitting behind the bar in the reception hall.

The sound of a speeding car approaching behind him, along with a telltale beeping horn, made him turn just as the vehicle zoomed through a curbside puddle and showered him from head to toe. Alan raised his arms in a helpless, deep shrug as the cold, muddy water seeped under his white shirt collar and dripped down his back. An aged white Volvo sedan jumped the curb a few feet in front of him and lurched to a lopsided halt, with one wheel up on the sidewalk.

Oh, well, he'd actually seen *worse* parking out of Pamela Kaminski.

"Sorry," she yelled, fighting and tugging her way out of the death trap she drove. "The hem of this damned lampshade dress got tangled in the pedals." She slammed the door and limped toward him. "Broke a heel, too," she reported.

Alan rubbed a finger over the lenses of his glasses to remove the water blurring his vision. Pamela should have looked ridiculous in the peach organza bridesmaid dress with the armful of stiff chiffon around her bare shoulders, but she didn't. With her typical irreverent air, and her remarkable good looks, she carried off the eighties prom-dress knockoff with panache.

From her alarmingly low-cut neckline, she dragged out a handful of white handkerchiefs. She then shoved back a strand of dark blond hair that had escaped her topknot, and began to swipe at the water streaming from his chin. "Sorry 'bout that," she murmured.

"No problem," he said tartly. "I needed to cool off."

She grimaced. "I was talking about the wedding."

"Oh." Trying to keep his eyes averted from the bosom of his ex-fiancée's best friend, Alan decided he'd never been more miserable in his life than at this moment. He stood completely still and allowed Pam to continue a woefully inadequate job of soaking up the water. "I can't believe Jo actually selected that dress for you to wear," he said sourly.

"She didn't," Pam said, painfully sticking the end of a hankie into his ear before moving on to swab his forehead none too gently. "Someone mixed up the order, but when it arrived, Jo seemed so stressed-out, I didn't want to bother her with it."

Alan scowled. "Since she only had eyes for John Sterling today, I'm sure she didn't even notice."

"It appears she did have a lot on her mind," Pam agreed.

Inhaling, then expelling his breath noisily, Alan said, "I suppose they got married."

Pam kept her eyes averted and nodded. "I heard Jo breaking the news to her mother just before I left."

"And you didn't stay?"

She pressed her full, brightly painted lips together and shook her head. "Between Jo, the groom and his three kids, I figured there were already enough people at the altar."

Grunting in frustration, Alan sputtered, "I can't believe after all these years of saying she didn't want children, Jo just up and marries a man with so much baggage!"

"Mmmnn," Pam said sympathetically. "*Three* carry-ons." She tossed the ruined handkerchiefs into a nearby trash can and pulled out her neckline, presumably to look for more.

Alan swallowed hard. He'd never thought about Pamela Kaminski romantically, but he was in the same pool as the rest of Savannah's male population when it came to admiring her generous physical gifts. The glimpse of a wildly inappropriate black strapless bra beneath the innocuous dress was enough to dry his tux from the inside out. When she plucked out two more hankies, he pulled a finger around his suddenly too-tight shirt collar. "Were you planning to shed a few tears, Pam?" he asked wryly.

She frowned and waved a hankie. "They were for Jo. The poor girl was crying like Niagara all morning."

"Thanks."

Pam glanced up and smiled sadly, her hands stilling. "I'm sorry, Alan. I didn't mean to hurt your feelings. I know how much you love Jo."

Anger, hurt and frustration welled up anew, so he cleared his throat and changed the subject. "Why did you follow me?"

She tossed the last two soiled handkerchiefs. "Thought you might need a friend. Where's your best man?"

"My guess is he's two choruses deep into the Electric Slide."

"Where were you headed?"

"To the airport."

She angled her head at him and laughed. "That's quite a walk."

"My flight to Fort Myers doesn't leave for four hours." He smiled tightly. "I allowed us plenty of time to celebrate at the reception."

"You're not serious," Pam said cautiously, as if she

wasn't sure she was dealing with a sane person. "You're still going on your honeymoon?"

"Sure." He shrugged, then lifted his chin. "Why not? It's paid for. I'll drown my sorrows in buckets of margaritas on the beach. I plan to eat enough limes to stave off scurvy for a lifetime."

Pam stared at him, the blue of her eyes startling against the wide whites. Then she blinked and looked up as a large raindrop dripped down her cheek. Within a few seconds, the rain was pelting down.

Which Alan didn't mind since his day couldn't possibly get any worse.

Suddenly a bolt of lightning streaked through the sky and struck a stand of trees several hundred yards away. On the other hand, perhaps he shouldn't tempt fate.

Pam was already tugging him toward her car. "I'll give you a ride. Where's your luggage?"

"In the back of the limousine at the church. I'll buy everything I need when I get to Fort Myers." He opened the passenger-side door, lifting it out and up at its awkward angle, then gingerly lowered himself onto the dingy sheepskin-covered seat. Once inside, he turned to look at Pam, who barked, "Buckle up," as she started the engine.

With a teeth-jarring jolt, they descended from the curb in reverse. Then Pam peeled rubber on the wet pavement, and made an illegal U-turn. As they sped toward the highway, Alan winced at the sound of her stripping gears, then braced an arm against the cracked vinyl dashboard. A dislocated shoulder was the most minor injury he could hope for when the rescue team extracted them with the jaws of life.

"Uh, Pam."

She glanced over at him, turning the steering wheel in the same direction. He gasped as the car ran off the shoulder, then sighed in relief when she jerked it back to the pavement. "What?" she asked, oblivious to his alarm.

"Never mind," he said hurriedly. "We'll talk when we get to the terminal. Do you know where you're going?"

She scoffed and made a heart-stopping weave across the yellow line, then yanked the hem of her dress above her knees. She was barefoot. "Alan, you know I practically live in my car. It's my *job* to know where I'm going."

Alan now realized why Pamela was the most successful real estate agent in Savannah—after a ride with her, prospective home buyers were probably too rattled to refuse.

To his horror, she reached over to tune the radio, and after enduring a full fifteen seconds of her not once looking at the road, Alan lurched forward and offered to find a station. He tuned in to some light rock and eased back in his seat, trying to relax.

Pam made a disapproving sound. "Is that all you can find? My *dentist* plays that stuff, as if the sound of a drill isn't torturous enough."

Alan sighed and found a more trendy station, assuming Pam was satisfied since she began singing along— badly. Suddenly he focused on the windshield wiper on his side and pursed his lips. "Is that a man's sock?" he asked.

"Yeah," she sang, weaving and shrugging. "The wiper blade fell off and the sound of that metal arm scraping against the windshield wore on my nerves."

Alan shivered.

She turned a dazzling smile his way. "The black sock is hardly noticeable and it works great."

He begged to differ, but he didn't dare. He briefly wondered which of Pam's admirers had left the handy souvenir, then pushed the thought aside. Instead, he closed his eyes and conjured up visions of sandy beaches and unlimited quantities of alcohol. He'd buy and finish the entire set of a new science-fiction series he'd been yearning to read. And Mrs. Josephine Montgomery Sterling, mother of three, would be far, far away...wiping runny noses.

Pamela respected his silence, humming and singing along with the radio, but not pressing him into conversation. After several minutes, he opened his eyes and glanced at her. Her profile was almost classically beautiful—the tilt of her nose, the curve of her pronounced cheekbones. Except Pam's upper lip protruded slightly over her lower lip, giving her the appearance of having an upside-down mouth. Combined with large blue eyes and a mane of dark gold hair, she was stunning to the point of being intimidating. She had the braver half of Savannah's bachelors running to her bed, and the smarter half just plain running.

He'd heard the stories in the locker room at the club—Pam's exploits in bed were legendary. But he'd often wondered how many of the rumors were rooted in fact and how many were pure conjecture based on Pamela's background. She'd grown up in the Grasswood projects, the black eye of Savannah's otherwise beautiful downtown face. Grasswood was notoriously populated with several generations of dopeheads, prostitutes and petty thieves.

The first time he met Pamela, he'd peeled her off another girl's back in the hallway of his private high school and she'd rewarded him with a sharp kick to his shin. In response to public pressure, Saint London's Academy had extended scholarships to a handful of families from the projects, and Pamela's was one of the lucky ones. He remembered her two brothers being hoodlums and she herself being garish and unkempt, mouthy and irreverent, courting fights with girls, boys and teachers alike. One by one, the Kaminskis had all been expelled.

When he'd started dating Jo several years later, he'd been amazed to learn the girls were best friends, and more stunned still when he discovered that dirty-faced, sparring Pamela had become a top-producing agent for Savannah's largest realty company. Jo took Pam's flamboyance and reputation in stride, and soon Alan had grown more relaxed with Pam's company, despite her unpredictable and scandalous behavior.

The first time Jo had asked him to accompany Pam to a charity benefit as a favor, he'd been slightly uncomfortable, hoping desperately his high-bred mother didn't get wind of it because he didn't want to listen to her reproof. But he'd watched with fascination as Pamela the sexy siren had morphed into a sleek and charming conversationalist as she worked a roomful of potential clients. As a bonus, she'd even procured him a few introductions that had proved beneficial in advancing his computer-consulting business.

She was as different from his reserved, proper ex-fiancée as night and day. Jo was a quiet reading bench, Pam was a tousled bed. Jo was a contented house cat, Pam was a prowling lioness.

Alan frowned. The woman *was* a little scary.

"I'll wait with you," she announced as she veered into long-term parking.

"That's not necessary," he said, hanging on while she took him on a harrowing ride through the parking garage.

They lurched to a crooked halt one-eighth of an inch from a four-foot round concrete pillar. "I'll buy you a drink," she said, and lifted herself out of her seat with the force of putting on the emergency brake. "Let me get some decent shoes."

Hiking up her skirt, she walked around to the trunk in stocking feet. Alan got out of the car and followed her. She unlocked and lifted the lid to reveal an unbelievable array of footwear—pumps, sandals, boots, tennis shoes—he guessed there were fifty or more pairs scattered to the far corners of the trunk, no doubt from her perpetual careening.

"Do you moonlight as a traveling shoe salesman?" he asked.

She laughed. "I never know what kind of terrain I'll be showing a house in—I try to be prepared."

Alan reached in and withdrew a thigh-high red-patent leather boot. He lifted an eyebrow and asked, "Where's the matching leash?"

She smirked and yanked the boot away from him. Pam hastily rummaged through the pile and came up with one light-colored high-heel pump and slid her foot into it, then stood on one leg while she searched for its long-lost mate. "Aha!" she said, finally retrieving it, then tossed in the pair with the broken heel and slammed the trunk with vigor. It bounced back up and she slammed it twice more before it held. "The catch is tricky," she informed him, slinging her purse over her shoulder. "Let's go."

They garnered more than a little attention as they made their way through the airport and settled into a booth at a tacky lounge. To send him off right, Pam ordered two shots of tequila and a pitcher of margaritas on the rocks. She licked the back of her hand and sprinkled salt on it. He did the same and lifted his shot glass to hers.

"You make the toast," she said, her eyes bright.

Her beauty struck him at that moment, and his tongue stumbled slightly. "Uh, to being single," he said, clinking her glass heartily.

"I'll drink to that," she seconded, then tossed back the tequila, licked the salt from her hand and sucked on a lime wedge.

He followed her lead, squinting when the sour juice drenched his tongue. "I really didn't want to get married anyway," he mumbled.

"So why did you propose?" she asked, then poured them each a glass of margarita from the pitcher.

Alan shrugged. "It sounds silly now, but at the time it seemed like the thing to do."

Her look was dubious, but she didn't question him further. Instead, she laughed. "You're a mess."

Alan glanced down at his wet, disheveled tuxedo and chuckled, then scanned her rumpled appearance and grinned. "So are you."

They both laughed and he loosened his bow tie, letting the ends hang down the front of his stained, pleated shirt. "What a hell of a day," he said, shaking his head and cradling the frosty glass of pale green liquid.

"Yeah," she agreed. She took a deep drink from her glass, then one more drink to finish it off. "Did you have any idea she was hung up on John Sterling?"

He frowned. "I knew he was hung up on *her,* but I never suspected she'd even consider a man with so many kids." He finished his own drink in a long throat-numbing swallow. "Did you know?"

She shook her head and refilled their glasses. "I knew something was bothering her, but I assumed it was just prewedding jitters."

"I feel like a fool," he announced, swallowing more of the tangy drink. "I know everyone is laughing at me."

She shook her head again, dislodging another strand from her stiff hairdo. "They probably feel sorry for you."

"Oh, thanks, that makes me feel *tons* better."

"Everyone will forget about it by the time you return," she said in a soothing tone as she topped off their glasses again.

The alcohol was beginning to take effect on his empty, nervous stomach. His tongue and the tips of his fingers were growing increasingly numb. He pushed his water-spotted glasses back up on his nose. "I hope so, but I doubt it. Maybe I should move."

She scowled, an expression which did not diminish the prettiness of flushed cheeks and flashing eyes. "That's ridiculous—you've lived in Savannah all your life. Your parents would be hurt. And your consulting business—" she lifted her glass again and squinted at him "—you can't leave before you get old Mr. Gordon's computer account. I went to a lot of trouble linking up the two of you at the children's benefit."

"I know," he said mournfully, swirling the liquid in his glass before taking another deep drink. "You're right, of course. But let me wallow a little—my ego is pretty tender at the moment."

"You'll bounce back," she said with confidence. "There'll be debutantes lined up at your door by the time you return from your trip."

Her words were slightly slurred—or was his hearing becoming somewhat warped? "Nope." He sat up straight and jerked his thumb to his chest awkwardly. "I'm never getting married. As of today, *wife* is a four-letter word."

"Alan," Pamela said, leaning forward, "*wife* has always been a four-letter word."

He frowned. "You know what I mean."

Feeling a little tipsy herself, Pamela looked across the sticky table at her drinking companion and a feeling akin to envy crept over her. She wondered what it would feel like to have a man so in love with you that he'd swear off marriage completely if he couldn't have you. Pam bit her bottom lip. She'd known Jo Montgomery for years, and her best friend had always demonstrated remarkable good sense—until today.

What could have possessed her to abandon her faithful boyfriend of three years at the altar to marry a widower with three kids? Granted, Jo had confided that her and Alan's sexual relationship left a little to be desired—and personally, Pam found Alan quite bookish and dull, but even a boring man didn't deserve to be jilted. But she knew Jo felt bad because she'd asked Pam to go after him. Even though she didn't say it, Pam knew Jo feared Alan might do something impulsive and self-destructive.

She watched as Alan tilted his head back and emptied his glass. In high school, Pam had triumphantly dubbed him "the Ken doll," a nickname she still used in conversations with Jo, much to Jo's consternation. His fair hair was cut in a trendy, precision style, and his round wire glasses were like everything else in his wardrobe: designer quality.

The man was painfully clean-cut, his skin typically scrubbed within an inch of its life, his preppie clothes stiff enough to stand in a corner. She perused his slim, chiseled nose and squared-off chin, complete with an aristocratic cleft. He was handsome in an Osmond kind of way, she supposed, but everything about him screamed predictable.

Alan Parish came from thick money, as her mother would say. She doubted if he'd ever experienced belly-hurting hunger, missed school because his shoes had finally fallen completely apart, or scraped together money to post bail for three family members in one week. The worlds they came from were so far apart, they were in separate dimensions.

Then she bit back a smile. Right now, with his hair mussed, his glasses askew and a narrow streak of mud on his jaw, he looked more like one of her stray lovers—disorderly and disobedient. Only she knew better. Alan was an uptight computer geek—she'd bet the man had a flowchart on the headboard of his bed.

"What's so funny?" he asked, his expression hurt.

"Nothing," she said as fast as her thick tongue would allow while waving for the waiter to bring them more drinks. Then they spent the next half hour extolling the virtues of being footloose and commitment-free while they drained the second pitcher.

At last, Alan looked at his watch, moving it up and back as if he was trying to focus. "Time to go," he said, standing a little unsteadily.

Pam stuck out her hand. "I think I'll stick around and sober up for the drive home."

"With your driving, who could tell?"

She scowled. "Have a great time, Alan."

"Yeah," he said dryly. "I'm off on my honeymoon all by myself." He bowed dramatically.

"Maybe you'll meet someone," she said.

Alan straightened, then frowned and pursed his lips.

"What?" she asked, intrigued by the expression on his face.

"Go with me," he said.

Pam nearly choked on her last swallow of margarita. *"What?"*

"Go with me," he repeated, giving her a lopsided smile.

"You're drunk," she accused.

He hiccuped. "Am not."

"Alan, I'm *not* going on your honeymoon with you."

"Why not?" he pressed. "My secretary booked a suite at a first-rate hotel, and it's all paid for—room, meals, everything." He pulled the plane tickets from inside his jacket and shook them for emphasis. "Come on, I could use the company and you could probably use a vacation."

A week away from Savannah was tempting, she mused.

His smile was cajoling. "Long days on the beach, drinking margaritas, steak and lobster in the evening." He wagged his eyebrows. "Skimpily dressed men."

At last he had her attention. "Yeah?"

He nodded drunkenly. "Yeah, you might get lucky."

But she couldn't fathom spending a week with Alan, and she'd *never* share a bed with the man, no matter how roomy. She shook her head. "I can't."

"I'll sleep on the pullout bed," he assured her.

She set down her drink. "But what will people think? What will *Jo* think?"

"What do you mean?" he asked.

Pam squirmed on the uncomfortable bench seat. "Well, you know—us being together for a week."

His shocked expression didn't do much for her ego. "You mean that someone might think that we're...that we're...*involved?*" His howl of laughter made her feel like a fool.

Of course no one would jump to that conclusion—a high-bred southern gentleman and a trashy white girl from the projects—it was ludicrous.

"And as far as Jo is concerned," Alan continued, "if she ever thought there was a remote possibility we'd be attracted to each other, she'd never have trusted me to escort you to your business functions."

Pam's fuzzy brain told her an insult was imbedded in his rambling. "I suppose you're right, but a few people might jump to conclusions."

Alan shrugged. "It's not like the whole town of Savannah is going to know, Pam."

She glanced down at the horrid peach-colored dress. "But I don't have any clothes."

"We'll go shopping when we get there," he said simply. "Come on, will you go or won't you?"

She had accrued vacation time. And only one deal

in progress that she could probably handle over the phone. And Jo *had* asked her to keep an eye on Alan. She pressed a finger to her aching temple. It hurt to think too deeply.

Pamela emptied her glass and wiped the back of her hand across her mouth, then looked up at him and smiled. "Well, I could use some new sandals...why the heck not?"

2

ALAN SALUTED the head flight attendant, then dropped into his seat, wincing when the jolt threatened to scramble his furry brain. He felt as if he was forgetting something, but the answer hovered on the fringe of his memory, eluding him. His neck suddenly felt rubbery. Laying his head back, he closed his eyes and slowly reached up to pat the wallet in his breast pocket. That wasn't it. Hmm, what then?

"Ex-schuse me," came a loud female voice. He opened his eyes a millimeter and Pamela Kaminski slowly came into focus, just as her purse whacked some poor businessman upside the head. "Sorry, sweetie." She leaned over to place an apologetic kiss on the man's receding hairline.

Alan smiled and tried to snap his fingers, but missed. Pamela! He'd forgotten Pamela.

"There you are!" Pamela said, her eyes glassy. "When I came out of the ladies' room, you'd disappeared. Thank God, my middle name is Jo. Then all I had to do was convince a woman at the gate that the last name on my license and the name on the ticket were different because I'd just gotten married." She giggled. "Whew!" She swung into the seat next to Alan, then leaned against him and squealed. "I've never flown first-class before."

"Unlimited drinks," he informed her, rolling his head.

Her grin was lopsided. "No fooling? I'm up for another pitcher."

"You'll have to settle for one drink at a time—and they don't serve margaritas."

She pouted, sighing at the inconvenience, then noisily fumbled with her seat belt until Alan lifted his head and offered to help. "It's twisted," he announced, reaching across her lap to straighten the strap. The chiffon ruffles at her plunging neckline tickled his jaw. He valiantly tried to concentrate on the silver buckle, but his eyes kept straying to her cleavage. The tiny embroidered rose front and center on her black bra made an appearance every time she inhaled. After three clumsy attempts, he finally clicked the belt together, then settled back into his seat heavily.

The flight attendant eyed them warily when they ordered bourbon and water, but served them promptly enough. They finished the weak drinks before takeoff, and Alan found himself beginning to doze as they taxied down the runway. An iron grip on his arm startled him fully awake.

Pamela's left hand encircled his right wrist so tightly her knuckles were white. Her long peach-colored nails were biting into his flesh. And her face was turning as green as the limes they'd sucked dry.

"What's wrong?"

"Remember when I said I'd never flown first-class?"

"Yeah."

"Well, I've never flown before, period."

"No kidding? Why not?"

"I just remembered—it's a phobia of mine." She put her fingers to her mouth. "Oh, dear."

He leaned forward and twisted in his seat. "What?"

"I'm going to throw up."

Alan panicked. "Oh, don't do that."

Still holding her mouth, she nodded in warning, her eyes wide. Alan fumbled for the airsick bag, and jerked it under her mouth just as the plane banked. She unloaded, missing the bag more than hitting it, although Alan accepted some of the blame for holding the paper bag somewhat less than stone still. He heard a groan go up from surrounding passengers.

When her retching gave way to dry heaves, Pamela slumped back into her seat, frightfully pale. A flight attendant was at their side as soon as the plane leveled off, extending a warm, wet towel to Pamela. "I'm going to need more than one," Pam muttered, eyeing the mess she'd made.

Organza was more absorbent than it looked, Alan decided, fighting the urge to vomit, himself, as he handed the bag to the attendant. Insisting she was too weak to make a trip to the lavatory, Pam cleaned up as well as she could sitting in her seat. The attendant, obviously at a loss, murmured the two-hour trip would pass by quickly.

"Oh, God," Pam breathed, laying her head back. "It's an omen—I should have never gotten on this plane."

"Relax," Alan said, reaching forward to pat her arm, then decided it would be more sanitary to pat her head. Her hair was stiff and had pulled free from the clasp that hung benignly above one ear. "It'll be a smooth flight—I travel all the time and I've never had any problems.''

Suddenly the plane dipped, then corrected, then dipped and banked again. The Fasten Seat Belt sign dinged on, and the pilot's voice came over the intercom. ''Ladies and gentlemen, we have encountered some turbulence.'' The attendant was thrown out of her fold-down wall seat, but she recovered and continued smiling as she fastened her own belt. ''Please bear with us while the captain climbs to a higher altitude.''

It was the worst flight Alan had ever experienced. The plane continued to pitch and roll, eliciting gasps and moans from the passengers. A cabinet door in the small galley gave way, sending trays of food into the aisles.

Alan felt terrible, willing his stomach to stay calm, and pressing his throbbing head back into the seat to keep it as immobile as possible. He felt terrible, too, for inviting Pam to come along. She'd probably be traumatized for life. He heard others seated around them getting sick, and he glanced anxiously at Pam to see if she would lose it again.

Her eyes were squeezed shut, and her lips were moving. ''Hail Mary, full of...full of gr-grace...'' She opened one eye and whispered to Alan, ''I've never said my prayers while I was loaded—do you think it cancels out?''

Alan pursed his lips and considered the question, then shook his head and she continued to stumble through the prayer, finishing with ''Pray for us s-sinners now and...and at the hour of our death. Amen.'' Then she crossed herself.

"Hey," he whispered soothingly. "We're going to be fine. It'll level out here in a few minutes."

On cue, the plane made a sickening dip. Pam swallowed and jerked her head toward him. "Are you crazy, Alan? We're all going to die and I'm going to be buried in this horrid dress—*if* they find our bodies."

He sighed. "Of course they'll find our bod—" He stopped and shook his head to clear it. "Wait a minute—we're not going to die, okay? I refuse to die in a plane crash on my wedding day."

Her eyes widened and she gestured wildly with her hands. "Oh, Mr. Moneybags, I suppose you're going to buy your way out of this?"

Alan frowned. He'd spent his entire life trying to make his own way, only to be frequently reminded he was a Parish, and therefore was forced to share the credit for his accomplishments with his family name. He crossed his arms, closed his eyes and refused to be provoked. "I'm not going to argue with you because I'm drunk and tomorrow this conversation won't matter."

"Does anything affect you, Alan?" Pam asked, her voice escalating. "You got jilted today and you still came on this honeymoon like nothing happened. Now we're getting ready to crash and you sit there like a dump on a log."

"That's lump," he corrected, his eyes still closed. "A lump on a log. Or is it bump?"

"I meant what I said," she retorted. "I'm drunk, but I'm not incoherent...I'm...I'm...oh, God, I'm going to be sick again."

His eyes snapped open. He reached for the airsick bag on his side and thrust it under her chin.

"Arrgghhh!" he cried when she missed the bag again. He looked away and tried to reach the attendant bell with his elbow. Once the remaining contents of her stomach appeared to have been transferred to the bag, the floor and all surfaces in between, she fell back into her seat, completely exhausted. At last the pilot located a more comfortable altitude, and the turbulence ceased. The passengers cheered, and within seconds, Pam fell into a deep sleep.

Alan surveyed his traveling companion and winced. If his head didn't hurt so much, he'd probably be laughing. Pam Kaminski, the perpetual playmate, looked like a rag doll in her stained, smelly, ugly gown. Her hair was lank and damp, her mouth slack in slumber. He flagged the busy attendant and quietly asked for more towels, then carefully leaned toward Pam, trying not to wake her.

With fierce concentration, he delicately wiped her face, admiring the fine texture and translucence of her creamy complexion, and the long fringe of lashes on her sleep-flushed cheeks. She never once stirred, not even when he dabbed at the corners of her upside-down mouth. But for the first time ever in the presence of Pamela Kaminski, Alan felt *himself* stir.

He shifted in his seat, trying to stem the rush of inappropriate feelings for his ex-fiancée's best friend. But sitting there in her mussed gown with her mussed hair, she looked like the grubby little tigress she'd been in high school, all piss and vinegar, and she made his blood simmer.

Passing a hand over his face, Alan blamed the lapse on his own lingering drunkenness. He hadn't made a big enough fool out of himself already today—why not make a pass at Pam and watch her laugh until she vomited again.

PAM WAS A BIRD flying over a landfill, dipping and diving, the stink of rotting trash permeating the air. She started awake and blinked, disoriented at first, then realized with a jolt that she was on a plane hurtling toward a shared honeymoon with Alan Parish, and that the stink was *her*.

"Ugh." She wrinkled her nose in disgust, and pulled herself straighter in the seat, flinching at the explosion of pain in her temples. She turned her head oh-so-slowly to see Alan zonked out, snoring softly and leaning against the wall. His expensive black tux was probably beyond cleaning, but his mottled jacket still lay folded neatly across his lap. Embarrassment flooded her when she remembered how he'd held the airsick bags as she filled them. She smiled wryly. Alan had surprised her.

A ball of white fuzz dangled in his hair, and she reached forward impulsively to remove it. Awareness leaped through her when she touched the silky blond strands, which was almost as alarming as the feeling of warmth that flooded her as she watched his chest rise and fall. Awake, he was Alan the Automaton. But relaxed in sleep, he looked downright sexy. A memory surfaced…she'd had an absurd crush on him for the short time she had attended the private school his family practically owned.

Before she had time to explore the amazing revelations, the attendant who had earlier emptied the linen closet on Pam's behalf, touched her arm and murmured, "Are you feeling better, ma'am?"

Pam nodded gingerly.

The woman smiled gently. "I'm sorry, Mrs. Parish—this flight wasn't a very promising start to a honeymoon."

Confusion clouded her brain. "But I'm not—" She glanced up at the woman and smiled tightly. The situation was too convoluted to explain. "It'll be fine once we get to Fort Myers."

"Congratulations—was it a long engagement?" the woman pressed.

"N-no," Pam stammered, suddenly nervous. "This was all quite sudden. Could you direct me to the bathroom, please?"

The blue-suited attendant pointed and smiled, then walked back down the aisle.

Pam slowly pulled herself to a standing position, but the movement stirred up a fetid smell from her dress. Swallowing her urge to gag, she gathered her skirt in her hands, hiked her dress up to her knees and sidled her way to the lavatory.

Not sure what she expected, she was nonetheless disappointed by the cramped booth. "People actually have sex in here?" she mumbled. A glance in the mirror evoked a shocked groan. Her makeup had disappeared, except for mascara that rimmed her eyes. Her hair was a sky-high rat's nest of tangles. Miserable, she looked down at her dress and shuddered—nothing much she could do there.

After washing her face with cool water, she opened her makeup bag to repair as much damage as possible. At the last minute, she held up a perfume bottle and gave her dress a couple of squirts. Too late, she realized she'd only intensified the stench. Cursing under her breath, she exited the cubicle and made her way self-consciously back to her seat, aware of passengers recoiling in her wake.

Alan was still dozing when she lowered herself into the seat. The pounding in her head had lessened, making room for reality to ooze into the crevices of her brain. In her occupation, vacations were hard to come by because time off meant missed commissions on home deals that were possibly months in the making. She'd passed up a week in Jamaica with Nick the All-Nighter, and a long weekend in San Francisco with Delectable Dale.

Only to squander seven days in close, romantic quarters with Annoying Alan.

The captain's voice came over the intercom and announced they were beginning their final descent to Fort Myers. Beside her, Alan roused and started to smile, then his nostrils flared. "Oh my," he said, his eyes watering.

Pamela frowned sourly. "You're no fresh breeze yourself."

"A shower would feel pretty good right now," Alan agreed, then touched his forehead. "Not to mention a couple of aspirin. We really tied one on."

Pam nodded. "Tequila will make you say and do strange things." She caught his gaze and studied his eyes, wondering if he was having as many misgivings about his hasty invitation as she was about her impulsive acceptance.

But his ice-blue eyes gave away nothing. "Better buckle up," he said, pointing, then smiled shyly. "Need a hand?"

Inhaling sharply, she shook her head. She could handle the guys who thought they were macho, the self-assured lady-killers—they were safely shallow. What she couldn't handle was Alan's Mr. Nice Guy persona...it threw her off balance.

It was six-thirty when they emerged from the airport, and dusk appeared to be converging. With only a few wrong turns, they found the car rental where Alan's reservations had been made.

"I'm sorry, sir," the clerk said, smiling sympathetically. "We're all out of full-size luxury cars. We'll have to step you down—with a sizable discount, of course."

Alan sighed and pinched the bridge of his nose. "Okay, I'll take a midsize."

The man tapped on the keyboard, then made a clicking noise with his cheek. "No, sorry."

"Utility vehicle?"

More clicking. "Nada."

Alan pursed his lips. "What *do* you have available?"

The man smiled and pointed out the window to a row of tiny white compacts.

Alan shook his head firmly. "No way."

Pam frowned. He was exhibiting typical Parish behavior. "Alan," she whispered loudly. "What do you mean 'no way'? It's a lousy rental car—what do you expect?"

He looked at her and mirrored her frown. "The best."

She crossed her arms impatiently and tapped her foot. "I'm tired, sick and cranky—get the stupid car and let's go."

His mouth tightened in displeasure, but he nodded curtly to the clerk.

"*I'll* drive," Alan announced firmly a few minutes later as they approached the little car.

"Fine," Pamela said, not missing the dig. "I hope this resort is close by—I'm beat."

With a lot of cursing from Alan, and frustrated mutterings from Pam, they finally managed to wedge themselves into the car. Alan unfolded the map he'd purchased, taking up the entire interior of the car. "Looks like about a twenty-minute drive." Then he spent fourteen minutes rattling the map, trying to refold it.

Pam leaned her head back, forcing thoughts of the coming week from her mind. She'd just roll with the punches, as always. Why was she letting a few days with Alan rattle her? She was safe—the man wasn't the least bit attracted to her. But it was his uptight idiosyncrasies that were going to drive her crazy. He was still rattling that damned map. She reached over and tore it from his hands, wadded it into a ball and tossed it in the back seat. "Let's go."

ALAN SQUINTED at a sign as they drove by. "Did that sign say Penwrote or Pinron?"

"We're lost, aren't we?"

He scoffed and pushed up his glasses. "Of course not."

She sighed dramatically. "Oh, yeah, we're lost, all right."

"'Lost' is a relative term."

"And I guess you're one of those guys who'd rather run out of gas than stop and ask for directions."

"Well, if you hadn't destroyed the map—"

"Forget the map—pull off at the next exit."

Suddenly the car wobbled. At a thumping sound on the back right side of the car, he slowed. "Darn it," he mumbled as he steered the lame car to the shoulder of the road. "We've got a flat."

"Beautiful," Pam said, throwing her hands up in the air. "We're lost *and* we have a flat."

"Well, it's not my fault." He shoved the gearshift into park. "You're the one who insisted we take this, this…matchbox car to begin with!"

"So call them to bring us another car."

"My cell phone is in my suitcase in Savannah."

She reached into her purse and pulled out her own mobile phone, but frowned. "The battery's dead."

"Great. This is just great!"

She pointed down the highway. "There's probably a phone off that exit."

Exasperated, Alan said, "I'm sure there is, but by the time I've walked that far, I could have the tire changed."

She sighed mightily once more, then opened the passenger-side door and stepped out. Alan did the same and walked back to the tiny trunk, swaying as vehicles passed them at terrific speeds.

"Are you sure you know how to do this?" Pam asked suspiciously.

"Sure," he said with false confidence. He'd once read a roadside manual, and he was sure the information would come back to him. Men just knew these things, didn't they?

Thirty minutes later, he was on his back, still trying to position the jack, when he looked over to see Pamela standing with her skirt hiked up to her thighs, and her thumb jerked to the side.

"What the heck are you doing?" he shouted.

"Getting us a ride," she yelled matter-of-factly.

"Would you please cover yourself? You'll attract every serial killer in the vicinity."

"I don't care, as long as he'll give us a ride to the resort."

"I've almost got it," he lied.

"Sure," she said, unconvinced, then smiled wide into oncoming traffic.

He heard the sound of a large vehicle slowing down and glanced over to see a big rig edging onto the shoulder in front of their cracker-box car.

"It worked!" she squealed, trotting toward the truck.

Alan heaved himself to his feet and took off after her, grabbed her by the elbow and pulled her to a halt. "Are you crazy? Didn't your mother ever tell you not to accept rides from strangers?"

Pam angled her head at him. "Alan, there's no one stranger than you." Then she yanked her arm out of his grasp.

He frowned at the tire iron in his hand, then tested its weight and hurried after her. At least he could break the serial killer's knees if he tried anything funny.

The burly, bearded murderer was already climbing down from his rig, doffing his cap to his vivacious victim. The man hadn't yet noticed him, Alan observed.

"Howdy, little lady, having car trouble?"

He couldn't hear Pam's response, but from the tilt of her head, he assumed it was something pathetically feminine and appropriate. She did at least gesture back to Alan, and the man looked up at him, frowning at the tire iron in his hand. Alan swung it casually as he stepped up beside Pam, slapping the metal bar against his left palm as if he wielded the weapon often—and well.

"Name's Jack," the man said cautiously as he extended his grubby hand to Alan.

Alan sized him up. *Jack the Ripper, Jack the Jackal, Jugular Jack.*

Shifting the bar to his left hand, Alan firmly shook the paw the man offered, then spit on the ground in what he hoped was a universal he-man gesture.

"I'm Pamela and this is Alan," Pam said cloyingly, her eyes shining.

Jack looked them over. "You two just get married?"

"No," Alan said.

"Yes," Pam declared.

The trucker looked between them, and took a tentative step backward.

Pam shot Alan a desperate look. "I mean, yes," Alan said, conjuring up a laugh. He shrugged and winked at the man. "Still can't get used to the idea."

"We just need a ride," Pam said quickly. "To the…" She looked to Alan for help.

"The Pleasure Palisades," Alan said, somewhat self-consciously. Pam raised an eyebrow and he felt his neck grow warm.

Turning back to the man, she asked, "Do you know where it is?"

"Yeah," Jack said, tugging at his chin. "Y'all ever been there?"

"No," Alan said. "My secretary moonlights as a

travel agent—she made all the arrangements. I hear it's a very nice place."

The trucker pursed his lips, then nodded slowly. "Yep."

"Can we get a ride?" Pam pressed. "We'll be glad to pay you for your trouble." She dug her elbow deep into Alan's rib. He gasped, then nodded.

"No bother," Jack said, turning to walk toward his truck. He swept his arm ahead of him. "Climb on in."

"What're you hauling?" Pam's new drawl and buoyant step were evidence she'd already bought into the little adventure.

"Hogs," the man said proudly as he climbed up to open the passenger-side door.

"Hogs?" Alan parroted as Pamela clambered inside. She was barefoot again, carrying her shoes in one hand.

"Yep." The man grinned as he waited for Alan to get in beside her. Still gripping the tire iron solidly, Alan glanced over his shoulder uneasily.

"You'll need to put down that tire iron, son," the man said bluntly.

Alan straightened and puffed out his chest. "And why is that?"

Another grin. "So you can hold Barbecue," the man said, pointing inside.

"Oh, it's a baby!" Pam cooed.

Letting down his guard slightly, Alan slid one eye toward the cab. Pamela was sprawled in the seat, leaning over to fondle a tiny pig on the floorboard.

"That's Barbecue," the man said, laughing. "Born a few days ago. The rest of the litter died, so I figured I'd keep him up here till the end of the run."

"He's adorable," Pam said, squealing as loudly as the nervous, quivering pig.

"Get in, son," Jack said, giving him a slight shove.

Alan spilled into the deep seat. The door banged closed behind him. "We're goners," he said to Pam.

Her forehead creased. "What?"

"The man's probably got all kinds of butcher tools on him, and a meat hook for each one of us."

"You're paranoid," she scoffed. "We're lucky he stopped."

Jack opened his door and climbed up behind the huge steering wheel, effectively halting their conversation. He pulled down the bill of his cap, then started the truck. It rumbled and coughed, then lurched into gear. "To the Pleasure Palisades," he crowed, slapping his knee. "You folks will have a dandy wedding night there."

Alan's heart pounded and he didn't dare look at Pam. He glanced at his watch and almost laughed out loud. Less than eight hours ago, he was ready to walk down the aisle to marry Jo Montgomery, hoping the act of commitment would put a new spin on their lackluster sex life. Instead he was sitting in the cab of a big pig rig with a woman who smelled almost as bad as the cargo, with only the promise of a lumpy sofa bed to sleep on—*if* they ever made it to the resort.

Pamela chatted with Jack, while Alan sank deeper into the seat. He felt moisture on his foot and looked down in time to see Barbecue squatting over his shoe. Alan didn't have the energy to pull away, so he simply lay his head back on the cracked vinyl. He'd officially sunk to the level of piglet pee post. What a poetic way to sum up the day.

3

"ARE YOU SURE this is it?" Pamela peered out the window at the four-story structure. Half of the sign's neon letters were unlit.

"Yep," Jack said.

"Linda said it was an older resort, but with a lot of atmosphere." Alan said, frowning slightly. "It's beachfront, though—I think I can see the water from here."

"Well, it's hard to tell much in the dark," Pam said agreeably, allowing Alan to help her down from the truck. His hands were strong around her waist, and he set her only a few inches in front of him. Surprised at her body's reaction, she quickly stepped back.

They looked up and waved to thank the trucker. Jack leaned out of his window and yelled, "Wish I were you tonight, son. She's a looker!"

Pleased, Pam grinned, then glanced at Alan. He'd turned beet red and his smile was tight as he nodded at the man, speechless. Pam felt sorry for Alan being put on the spot, so she scrambled for something to smooth over the moment. "Well, let's get checked in. I can't wait to get out of these clothes."

Too late, she realized she'd only added fuel to the fire. Alan cleared his throat, then turned toward the entrance. Without the lights of the truck, the parking lot was plunged into darkness. She took a step, then stumbled and grabbed the back of his jacket on the way down, very nearly taking him with her. He straightened and reached for her, his hands moving over her in search of a handhold. She felt him latch on to her shoulder and heard the rip of fabric as he came up with a handful of chiffon ruffles. He cursed and pulled her to her feet with an impatient sigh. "Do you think we can manage the last hundred yards without another catastrophe?"

She nodded, shocked at the sensations his hands were causing. It was the alcohol, the hunger, the exhaustion, the darkness—all of it combined to play games with her mind. What she needed was rest and daylight to remind her he was only uptight, dweeby Alan.

He grasped her elbow and steered her in the direction of the hotel. Pam suddenly had a premonition about the place and the week to come, but she kept her mouth shut and tucked her torn ruffles inside her bodice.

Flanked on either side by two gigantic plastic palm trees, the front entrance was less than spectacular. A dank, musty smell rose to greet them when they stepped onto the faded orange carpet of the gloomy reception area. To their right, stiff vinyl furniture so old it was back in style and more plastic plants encircled a portable TV set with an impressive rabbit-ear antenna. A home shopping channel was on, and two polyester-clad, middle-aged couples sat riveted to the screen. To their left, the gift shop was having a clearance on all Elvis items. Pam pursed her lips—maybe she could expand her collection.

She glanced at Alan to gauge his reaction. He was

frowning behind his glasses, clearly ready to bolt. "This isn't exactly what I expected," he mumbled. She bit down on her tongue, suddenly annoyed. She doubted if he'd ever spent a night in less than four-star accommodations.

The reception desk stood high and long in front of them, dwarfing the skinny frizzy-haired clerk behind the half glass. She was snapping a mouthful of chewing gum. "Can I help you?" she asked disinterestedly, not looking up. She was surrounded by cheap paneling and sickly colors. In a word, the decor was garish. Alan's ex-fiancée, an interior designer, would have fainted on the spot. Yet for Pam, the place had a certain...retro charm.

"Hello," Alan said tightly. "I'm not sure this is the right place. Are there any other hotels named Pleasure Palisades in the area?"

Twiggy glanced up, her eyes widening in appreciation as she scanned Alan. She completely ignored Pam. "Nope," she said, sounding infinitely more interested. "This is it."

Alan gave Pam a worried glance, then looked back to the clerk. "Do you have a reservation for Mr. and Mrs.—" He coughed, then continued. "For Parish?"

"Parish?" She flicked a permed hank of dark hair over her shoulder, turned to a dusty computer terminal and clicked her fingers over the keyboard. "Parish...Parish...yep, Mr. and Mrs. Alan P. Parish, the deluxe honeymoon suite through next Friday night." She glanced up and added, "With complimentary VCR and movie library since it's almost Valentine's Day."

Alan's eyes widened in alarm. "We're in the right place?" Twiggy didn't answer, only blew a huge pink bubble with the gum, sucked the whole wad back into her mouth, then smiled.

"I'm sure the room is nice," Pam whispered, trying to sound optimistic. As long as it had running water, she couldn't care less.

He held up his finger to the girl. "Just one moment." He curled his hand around Pam's upper arm and pulled her aside. "There must be some mistake. I'll call Linda and get this straightened out *immediately*. I saw a Hilton a couple miles down the road—we'll get a room there tonight."

Pam was shaking her head before he finished. "I don't have 'a couple miles' left in me or in these shoes." She stamped her foot for emphasis.

"We'll call a cab," he said, frowning.

She stabbed him in the chest with her index finger. "*You* call a cab, and *you* go down the road to the Hilton. I'm tired and I'm hungover. As long as this place is clean, I'm staying!"

He took a step back and poked at his glasses. "You don't have to get nasty about it."

She swept an arm down the front of her dress. "That's the point, Alan. I *am* nasty."

Holding up his hands, he relented. "Okay, okay—we'll stay one night."

Two minutes later, the clerk swiped his credit card, then handed them two large tarnished keys. "Room 410 in the corner, great view, cool balcony. But the elevator is out of order, so you'll need to take the stairs." She smiled tightly at Pam this time, and snapped her gum. "Have a pleasant stay."

Alan moved in the direction she indicated, but Pam grabbed his arm. "I'll need to purchase a few things to change into," she reminded him, nodding toward the gift shop.

"You need something in the gift shop?" the girl asked. She didn't wait for an answer, just reached under the counter and pulled out a piece of cardboard that read, "Back in a few," and propped it against a can of cola. "I'm the cashier, too." She snapped her gum and emerged from behind the wooden monstrosity.

Pam followed the girl into the gift cubbyhole, rubbing her tired eyes. "Alan, what does the 'P' stand for?" She quickly surveyed the dusty merchandise on the cramped shelves, searching for items to help her get through the week.

Alan moved to the other side of the store, intent on his own shopping. "What 'P'?"

She stacked toiletries in her arms, then moved to a wall rack of miscellaneous clothing. "Your middle initial, what does it stand for?"

He was silent for several seconds, then said, "Never mind."

She turned around and grinned, her curiosity piqued. "Come on, what's your middle name?"

The frown on his face deepened. "Forget it, okay?"

"Well, it has to be something odd or you wouldn't be so touchy."

He looked away.

"Parnell?"

"No."

"Purcell?"

"No."

"Prudell?"

"Pam." His gaze swung back to her, his voice low and menacing. "Don't."

She made a face at him, then turned her attention back to the shelves. She'd need shorts and a T-shirt, not to mention underwear. Pam spied a single package of men's cotton boxer shorts and picked it up, then stopped when she realized Alan also had a hand on them. They played a game of mini-tug-of-war, with each tug a little stronger than the last.

She yanked the package. "I didn't figure you for a boxer man, Alan."

He pulled harder. "And I didn't figure you for a boxer woman, Pam."

She jerked the package. "You don't know me very well."

"I *have* to have underwear," he protested, then nearly stumbled back when she abruptly released the package.

Pam acquiesced, palms up. "Since underwear has always been optional for me, they're all yours."

His Adam's apple bobbed and he looked contrite. "M-maybe we can share."

Perhaps it was the timbre of his voice, or his boyish, disheveled appearance, or Elvis's "Blue Christmas" playing softly in the background, but Pamela suddenly felt a pull toward Alan, and it scared her. "I don't think so," she said more haughtily than she meant to.

Alan shrugged. "Suit yourself. Do you have everything you need?"

Nodding, Pam yanked an Elvis T-shirt and a pair of pink cotton shorts off the rack, then heaved her bounty onto the counter.

Alan piled his items on top. "I'll get these things," he said, opening his wallet. She started to protest, but he held up his hand. "It's the least I can do," he said, then raised an eyebrow when the clerk lifted a package of rub-on tattoos from Pam's things.

Pam grinned. "I always wanted a tattoo."

Five minutes later she lifted her skirt, shifted her packages and tilted her head back to look up the stairwell that seemed to go on and on. She was exhausted and again her decision to share a room with Alan for a week seemed ludicrous. On the way up they had to stop several times to rest, then walked down a dimly lit outdoor walkway, past several doors to reach the last room, 410.

Pam could hear the ocean breaking on the beach below them, and she leaned over the railing to get a better look. Suddenly Alan's arm snaked around her waist and dragged her back against his chest. The length of his body molded to hers, and Pam gasped as her senses leaped. After a few seconds, he released her gently, then admonished in a low voice, "I don't trust that railing, and I don't want to make a trip to the hospital tonight."

Her heart still pounding in her chest, Pam laughed nervously and listened while he fidgeted with the key in the dark. "You'd think they could put up a few lights," Alan muttered. He pushed open the door, reached around the corner and flipped on a switch.

They stood and stared inside the room in astonishment.

"They obviously saved all the lights for the *interior*," he added flatly.

Pam nodded, speechless. The room's chandelier was a dazzling display of multicolored lights, multiplied dozens of times by the room's remarkable collection of mirrors.

"It's a disco," he mumbled.

And the bed was center stage. Huge and circular, it was raised two levels. A large spotlight over the padded headboard shone onto the satiny gold-colored comforter, and Pam doubted the light was meant for reading.

"At least the carpet is new," she said, stepping inside.

"Yeah," he said. "And I'm sure they paid top dollar—brown shag is really hard to find."

She glanced around the room, at the avocado-green kitchenette, the makeshift living room consisting of a battered sofa—presumably the pullout bed—and two chaise-size beanbag chairs. The sitting area was "separated" from the sleeping area by two short Oriental floor screens. The wide-screen TV was situated to be visible from the bed or from the sofa.

"It's spacious," she observed. "And functional."

"Yeah—for orgies."

She scoffed and set down her bags, crossing the room to inspect the bed. She poked at the comforter and watched the bed ripple. "It's a water bed," she said, grinning. "And look." She held up a small bottle lying on the pillow. "Complimentary body liqueur—cinnamon." She twisted off the lid, then dipped her index finger in and tasted it. "Mmm, I'm starved."

Alan rolled his eyes, then looked around the room as if plotting how to get through the night without touching anything. "It's a dump," he pronounced.

Pam replaced the liqueur. It was a repeat of the car rental—nothing but the best was good enough for Alan Parish. "Lighten up, Alan, this is fun."

"Speak for yourself," he muttered, shaking his head.

Straightening, she put her hands on her hips and threw back her shoulders. "Why don't you come down from your high horse and see how the other half lives?"

"What the hell is that supposed to mean?"

"It means life isn't always first-class, and you have to learn to roll with the punches."

He squared his jaw. "I can roll with the best of them."

"Hah! You can't even *bend,* Alan, much less roll. You're just a spoiled little rich boy."

"I resent that," he said, his eyes narrowing.

"Go ahead—it's still the truth." She jerked up the bag that contained her new toiletries and headed in the direction of what appeared to be the bathroom. She opened the door, then breathed, "Wow."

A large red sunken tub dominated the room, appropriately set off by pale pink tile. It appeared that the sink, shower and commode had been miniaturized to make room for the tub, which could easily accommodate three adults.

"Hmm," Alan said behind her. "Another novelty." His voice was still laced with sarcasm.

"But not the last," Pam said, pointing out the picture window over the tub.

Their room was the last one set in a U formation, giving them a perfect view over an open plaza of the brightly lit room on the opposite side. Though not as spectacular as theirs, the room was furnished in the same style and occupied by an elderly couple who clearly had a disdain for clothing. Pam stared, fascinated, as the couple moved around in the kitchen, completely nude—with no tan lines. "It's like watching a car crash," she murmured. "You don't want to look, but you can't help yourself."

The woman turned her gaze directly toward them, then nudged her husband. Pam and Alan stood frozen, like two animals caught in headlights. Then the couple smiled and waved.

Alan reached forward and yanked the curtain closed over the tub. "Unbelievable," he muttered. "Those people are old enough to be my parents."

Pam leaned over and turned on the hot-water faucet. The first few trickles of water looked a little rusty, but it ran clear within a few seconds, so she stopped up the tub and poured in a handful of scented salts from a gold plastic container.

"Not everyone loses interest in sex when they get older, Alan." Then her best friend's comments about her drab intimate relationship with Alan rattled around in her head. "Assuming a person was ever interested in sex in the first place," she added dryly.

She reached around the back of her dress to capture the zipper in her fingers, and began to ease it downward. Suddenly, she remembered Alan was still in the room, and stopped. Holding up her neckline, she sighed. "Alan, I don't have the energy to throw you out, but I'm warning you—these clothes are coming off in the next few seconds, so if you don't want to be embarrassed twice in one evening, you better vamoose."

He paled, then groped for the doorknob and bolted out of the room. Pam giggled, then slid the zipper down and escaped from the hideous, rancid dress. After ripping off her shredded panty hose, she unhooked her bra and stepped into the heavenly, hot bubbles.

"Ahhhh," she breathed, sinking in up to her neck. Leaning her head back, she closed her eyes, her hands moving over her body to dislodge the day's grime. She automatically lapsed into a series of isometric exercises she always performed in the tub or shower for toning and relaxing. After a few minutes, her limbs grew languid, but her skin tingled.

Gingerly, she lifted her head and looked toward the closed door. Scooping up a handful of bubbles, she trickled them across her raised leg. Alan Parish was the most conservative, stuffy man she'd ever met under the age of sixty. Of course, he did have a lot to live up to, being the oldest son of such a prominent Savannah family. A subdivision had even been named for them— Parish Corners. He was a regular pillar of the community, unlike herself, who had nowhere to go in the world but up.

And here they were, two opposing forces, thrown together in a tacky hotel room. Paper and matches. Roses and switches. Uptown and downtown.

She smiled wryly. Inviting her to come on the trip was no doubt the most spontaneous thing Alan had ever done in his life. How ironic that he was probably the only man in Savannah who would invite her to spend a week with him, without having anything sexual in mind. Pam eased her head back. She could relax— Alan Parish's relationship with her was even less than platonic.

ALAN PASSED A HAND over his face and paced the length of the room. He wouldn't have believed it possible to be so tired and yet so awake at the same time. His hungover head was screaming for sleep, but the rest of his body was rigidly aware that Pamela Kaminski, a woman who had a sexual position named for her—the Kaminski Curl—was in the next room, naked...and lathered.

He swore and ripped off his bow tie, then tossed it across the room. When he caught a glimpse of himself in one of the many mirrors, he came up short, surprised at the anger he saw in his face. He prided himself on always remaining calm, regardless of the situation, but today—he sighed and shoved his fingers through his hair—today he'd been put through the wringer by two different women. His laugh was short and bitter. If he didn't know better, he'd suspect it was a conspiracy.

His empty stomach rolled, prompting him to call the front desk. Twiggy's bored drawl was instantly recognizable. "Yeah?"

Alan bit back a tart comment, and instead mustered a pleasant tone. "My—uh, *our* package includes meals, and I was wondering if the hotel restaurant is still open."

"Just closed," she said cheerfully.

He groaned. "We're starved—can we get room service?"

Twiggy sighed dramatically. "What do you want?"

"A couple of steaks and a bottle of wine."

"I'll see what I can do."

"Thanks." He hung up and frowned sourly at the phone. How had his secretary found this place? Remembering he still needed to find accommodations for the rest of the week, he called Linda's voice mail and left her a message to call him. Then he contacted the car rental agency who promised to have another car delivered to their hotel first thing in the morning.

Trying mightily to forget the events of the last few hours, Alan removed the black studs from his buttons, shrugged out of his wrinkled shirt and folded it neatly over the back of a stiff kitchen chair. He slipped off his shoes and socks, then lowered himself to the dreadful carpet and performed fifty push-ups. Breathing heavily, he pulled himself to his feet, wincing at the odor of his own sweat. A shower before dinner would feel terrific. Glancing at his watch, he frowned and hesitated, then went to the bathroom door and rapped lightly. Steam curled out from under the door, warming his bare toes. Alan swallowed. "Pam?"

He heard her moving in the water, splashing lightly.

"I ordered room service and it should be here soon."

She didn't answer. Alan shifted from foot to foot, wondering if she'd fallen asleep in the water. Suddenly, the door swung open and Pam stood before him, holding the ends of a dingy white towel above her breasts, her hair dripping wet. His breath caught in his throat, and the room seemed to close in around them.

Pamela smiled benignly. "I left my new clothes out here," she said, pointing to a bag on the floor. She brushed by him, her clean, soapy scent rising to fill his nostrils. He watched with blatant admiration as she walked over to retrieve the articles. Her long, slender legs were glowing with bath oil and speckled with water. His heart skipped a beat when the towel sagged low enough in the back to expose her narrow waist and the top of her—

"Astringent," she mumbled, rummaging in the bag.

"Wh-what?" he croaked.

"Remind me to buy astringent tomorrow when we

go shopping,'' she said, bending over, the towel inching up to reveal the backs of her thighs.

Alan felt his knees weaken, and averted his glance to the ceiling as he cleared his throat. "Okay." The plastic bag rattled.

"And a hair dryer."

"Sure." He sneaked another peek. Her back was still turned, and she was still standing butt up, the towel barely covering her. Squeezing his eyes shut, he suppressed a groan.

"Are you okay?"

His eyes snapped open. Pam was staring at him, squinting.

"Uh, tired and hungry, same as you, I suppose."

She nodded toward the bathroom. "You'll feel better once you shower."

Gratefully, he escaped to the bathroom, where he leaned heavily against the closed door for a few seconds to compose himself. But he was still muttering to himself a few minutes later when he stepped under the cold spray of the cramped shower. Any other man would have ripped off that towel and carried Pam to the bed...so why hadn't he? Sighing, he massaged his tired neck muscles. Because Pam would have welcomed it from any other man. But he'd been around Pam enough to realize she saw him as little more than a big brother—completely asexual. Why else would she have sashayed into the room practically naked, as if he wasn't there? She hadn't acknowledged his masculinity enough even to be modest around him. It was downright insulting. Just because he wasn't like the Neanderthals she typically dated didn't mean he wasn't alive.

A tapping sound on the shower glass startled him. "Alan?"

He froze, then whirled, instinctively crossing his hands over his privates.

4

PAM BLINKED. She'd seen so-so bodies and she'd seen good bodies. But who would have thought this magnificent specimen had been walking around Savannah all this time disguised as Alan Parish? Wide, muscled shoulders, smooth chest, washboard stomach…now if only he'd move his damn hands out of the way.

Through the steamed glass of the shower door, his face was screwed up in anger. "Pam!" he yelled. "Do you just walk in on a person no matter what they're doing?"

Pam gave him a wry smile. "Don't get your bowels all twisted, Alan. Unless yours is green, you don't have anything I haven't seen before. Your secretary is on the phone."

"Linda?" he asked, talking above the noise of the water.

"How many secretaries do you have?"

"Has she found another place for me—us—to stay?"

Pam sighed impatiently. "I didn't ask, Alan. I think she's still recovering from the fact that a woman answered the phone."

His eyes widened. "Did you think to disguise your voice?"

She planted her hands on her hips in annoyance.

"Sorry, I was fresh out of helium, but I think we're safe."

Alan nodded, the water streaming down his face. "You're probably right—she'd never suspect you were here with me."

"No one would," Pamela agreed dryly. "Not in a million years."

He stared at her, nodding and dripping, then sputtered, "Well?"

"Well, what?"

"Well, hand me a towel!"

Pam grinned, enjoying his self-consciousness, then reached for the remaining bath towel folded not so neatly on the toilet tank. She dangled the flimsy cloth in front of the shower door and watched as he considered uncovering himself to retrieve it. Thirty seconds passed.

Alan shifted and blushed deep pink. "Just drape it over the top of the stall, will you?"

Pressing her lips together to control her smirk, Pam tossed the towel over the top of the shower door and Alan grabbed it just as it passed his waist. She laughed and exited the room shaking her head.

Imagine, she thought as she collapsed on a yellow beanbag chair and began to untangle her wet hair, Alan was *modest*. It was actually kind of...refreshing in an attractive man, quite the opposite from the chest-pounding antics of her transient lovers. Then she frowned. Maybe Alan was more than just a "lights off" kind of guy—maybe he harbored a host of hang-ups that kept him from enjoying sex. Her friend Jo had never gone into specifics, and even though Pam had been dying to know details, she'd respected her friend's privacy.

The sound of the bathroom door opening broke into her thoughts. Alan emerged in a pair of navy sweatpants and strode over to the phone. He was polishing his glasses with the bath towel and didn't look at her, but the set of his shoulders told her he was still ruffled by her invasion. He shoved aside the wet hair hanging in his eyes, yanked up the handset and turned his back to Pam.

"Hello, Linda?"

Unabashed, Pam used the opportunity to more closely scrutinize his startling physique. His skin was damp and glowing, golden and sleek, like a swimmer's.

"You just got back from the wedding? They must have had a blowout reception."

His shoulders were wide and covered with knotty muscle that rolled under his skin as he paced around the nightstand, gripping the phone.

"No, Linda, don't feel bad—I'm glad you enjoyed the champagne…well, thanks for the condolences, but it's probably for the best."

She could smell the clean, soapy scent of him even at this distance, stirred up every time he pivoted on his bare feet.

"Yeah, I decided to take the trip anyway."

Pam squinted at the length and width of his feet, made a few mental calculations, then pursed her lips in admiration.

"Let's just say this place is not exactly what I expected."

The baggy sweatpants dipped low to reveal the top of his hard-won boxers and a narrow waist. Being a computer nerd must be more physically demanding than she thought.

"Actually, Linda, it's a dump."

Now that she thought of it, she *had* passed him going in and out of the workout club a couple of times.

"What do you mean, this is the only room available?"

His butt was narrow and hard, like a greyhound's...aerodynamic...built for speed. Desire struck low in her abdomen, shocking her.

"The woman who answered?" Alan glanced at her over his shoulder, then quickly back to the phone. "Uh, nobody...that is...nobody you'd know." He laughed nervously. "A m-maid."

Pam frowned, but a knock at their door and thoughts of food distracted her. She scrambled up and swung open the door, then practically snatched the covered food tray from Twiggy's hands. When the girl stuck out her skinny foot to prevent Pam from shutting the door, Pam smirked, set down the tray and shoved a five-dollar bill into her bony hand.

She slammed the door with a bang and motioned for Alan to get off the phone. He nodded, his face a mask of frustration. "Just keep checking, Linda, and let me know when you find something."

By the time he hung up, Pam was already sitting cross-legged on the water bed and lifting the lid from their meal.

"Bad news." He sat on the edge of the mattress and triggered a small tidal wave.

"I know—no pickles," Pam said, staring down at a platter of grilled-cheese sandwiches.

"Linda says it's the height of the season, and with

Valentine's Day only a few days away, everything is booked.''

''Damn,'' she mumbled, sinking her teeth resignedly into the surprisingly good sandwich. ''I really wanted pickles.''

''She's going to call if something opens up.''

''Mmmphh,'' Pam said, licking gooey orange cheese from her finger.

Alan stared at the food tray. ''I ordered steak. That is not steak.''

''But it's good,'' she mumbled, cracking open a can of cold soda.

''And that is definitely not wine.''

She glanced up at him. ''You ordered wine?''

He blushed, then stammered. ''W-well, you know, the meals are already paid for.''

''I thought I was too tired to eat, but I was wrong.'' She stuffed in the last bite of her sandwich.

Alan picked up a sandwich by the corner and sniffed it. ''Cholesterol city.''

''My hometown,'' Pam said with a smile, then she tore off a huge chunk of a second greasy sandwich. ''Live a little, Alan.''

He wrinkled his nose and took a tentative bite, then chewed slowly. ''Linda said the wedding was a big hit.''

At the serious tone of his voice, Pam stopped munching and searched for something comforting to say, but nothing came to mind.

''I thought Jo really loved me,'' Alan said without self-pity. He seemed genuinely perplexed.

''She did,'' Pam quickly assured him. ''She told me so many times.''

"Then she fooled us both."

Pam shook her head, then finger-combed her wet bangs. "That's not true—Jo doesn't have a deceitful bone in her body. Look how close she came to marrying you because she thought it was the right thing to do."

Alan gave her a wry smile. "Pam, don't ever go into motivational speaking."

"Okay, that didn't come out just right, but you get the gist—she really does care about hurting you."

His blue eyes darkened. "I knew John Sterling was trouble the minute I laid eyes on him."

Pam chose her words carefully. "It takes two to tango, Alan." Then she muttered to herself, "Three in France."

He sighed heavily. "You're right. She certainly fell hard for him."

Sympathy barbed through Pam—the man *had* been robbed of the future he'd planned. She felt compelled to say something. "Well, if you ask me, Jo missed out." Pam leaned sideways to give Alan's shoulders a friendly squeeze, but she was unprepared for the electricity beneath her fingers when she made contact with his smooth skin. Alan jerked his head around and their faces were mere inches apart.

For a few seconds, neither one spoke. Pam swallowed audibly.

"Do you really think she missed out?" Alan asked, his voice barely above a whisper, his gaze locked with hers.

Sirens went off in Pam's head. She fought the waves of awareness that flooded her—his scent, his warmth, his incredible physique. Her body softened and hardened in response. Sexual energy flamed to the surface and singed the fringes of her mind. Incredibly, a message was delivered to her brain amidst the smoke and fire. *It's Alan. Alan—who's still in love with your best friend.*

Pam inhaled sharply and pulled back carefully, not wanting to make the moment even more awkward. The fluid mattress bumped them up and down. She laughed nervously. "Yeah, I do," she said brightly, then swept her arm out toward the room. "She missed all of this on her wedding night."

To her relief, Alan smiled and looked around. "Something tells me she wouldn't have appreciated all this, um, atmosphere as much as you do. Jo would never have climbed into that ridiculous tub."

"It was fun."

"And she would never have sat on a beanbag chair."

"The most underrated furniture on the market, in my opinion."

"And this bed..." He laughed, smacking the shiny comforter, then bobbing up and down with the waves. "She would *never*—" He stopped midlaugh and glanced up, then blushed.

Pam grinned and shrugged. "She might have surprised you. Water beds aren't so bad."

With one eyebrow raised, Alan reached for another sandwich. "You speak from experience, I take it."

She nodded amiably. "My first experience, as a matter of fact. Which was so unremarkable, it's a wonder I don't have a bad association with water beds."

He laughed again. "My first time was less than

memorable, too. To this day I have an aversion to spiral stairs.''

Surprise shot through her, and she couldn't keep it out of her voice. "Spiral stairs? *You,* Alan?''

His smile was sheepish. "I seem to remember that was also my first introduction to Kentucky bourbon.''

"Ah," she said knowingly. "Been there, done that.'' She dropped her half-eaten cheese sandwich onto the platter and stifled a huge yawn. "I think the day is catching up with me, but it's scarcely ten-thirty.''

He glanced toward the television cabinet. "How about a movie before we, um, turn in?''

"Sure," she said, shifting on the bed, flashing forward to their sleeping arrangements. She felt restless and uncomfortable with her newfound attraction to Alan, and grateful he didn't share her momentary indiscriminate horniness. But the thought of sleeping with Alan and then returning to Savannah to face her friend Jo was enough to have her begging her guardian angel for strength.

She watched out of the corner of her eye as Alan removed the food tray and slid it onto the dresser. He moved with casual elegance, running a hand through his drying hair, separating the glossy strands. Pam groaned and crossed her arms over her saluting breasts, squeezed her eyes shut and whispered, "Oh Holy Angel, forsake me not...''

At the sound of his moan, she peeked. Alan leaned over and arched his back, cracking and popping the stretched vertebrae, flexing his well-toned upper body. Sweat broke out on her upper lip. "...give no place to the evil demon to subdue me...''

"I hope this free video library has something decent

to offer." He straightened, then walked over to the cabinet and swung open the door. When he knelt down to finger the row of black video cases, his baggy sweatpants inched even lower, revealing more of the new pale blue boxers.

"…take me by my wretched and outstretched hand…"

"Oh, great," he scoffed, his back to her. "*Denise Does Denver, Long, Dark, and Lonesome,* and the soon-to-be-classic *Tripod Man.*"

"…and keep me from the front—I mean, every affront of the enemy…"

"Did you say something, Pam?"

Her eyes widened. Alan was squinting back at her over his shoulder. She straightened and smiled, her mind racing. "N-no, just reciting my to-do list for tomorrow."

He frowned. "To go shopping?"

"No, I, uh…I have a big home deal in the works that I have to check on." Which was the absolute truth, although she hadn't given it any thought until now.

"Anyplace I'd know?"

"The Sheridan house."

He whistled low. "That should be quite a commission."

"That's why I need to check on it."

After reshelving the tapes, he retrieved the remote control and pushed himself up from the floor to sit at the foot of the bed. With his back to her still, he asked, "Isn't the Sheridan house haunted?"

Pam felt the wave he'd started ripple beneath her rear end. "*Please* don't add fuel to that rumor—the house has been on the market for nearly two years and

I finally have an interested buyer.'' *And please don't come any closer.*

''Hey—'X-Files' reruns.'' He turned and clambered up to join her on the bed, a happy grin on his face. After stacking the slippery, bumpy pillows behind his back, he scratched his bare, flat stomach and crossed his long legs at the ankles.

Pam held her breath, rattled by his nearness. Her head bobbed from the rolling mattress. ''I've seen this episode,'' she said, exhaling.

He turned his head toward her and pushed his glasses higher on his nose. ''Really? You like this show?''

''Never miss it—I'm a big science-fiction fan.''

His eyebrows rose. ''Me, too.''

Pam sat perfectly still, her thigh a mere eight inches from Alan's elbow. ''So, do you think Mulder and Scully will ever get together?''

Alan made a clicking sound with his cheek and shook his head, his fair hair splaying against the shiny gold pillows. ''I hope not.''

''Why?''

''Because they're great just the way they are. Sex would...would—'' He waved vaguely into the air. ''Well, you know—''

''Complicate things,'' Pam offered, trying to relax.

He nodded. ''Cloud the picture.''

''Muddy the waters.''

''Yeah, I'd hate to see them backslide to the 'X-*rated* Files.''' Alan smiled and forced himself to take his eyes off Pam and concentrate on the television show. His skin tingled from her proximity and he had to keep his leg bent in order to hide the other physical reaction she provoked. "Of course it's obvious that Mulder thinks Scully is really hot."

"You think?"

"Sure," he said, sneaking another peek up at her from his reclined position. He was eye level with her chest...and she wasn't wearing a bra. She glanced down at him, twisting a lock of dark blond hair around her finger. His bent leg began to tremble. "Can't you tell by the way he, um, looks at her all the time?"

She squinted at the screen. "Does he?"

"Yeah, and haven't you noticed that they're always invading each other's personal space?"

"How can you tell?"

"Eighteen inches. Americans like to keep a private space of eighteen inches around them." He started to draw an imaginary arc around him, but stopped when he realized the line would encompass Pam. His leg was practically jerking now. "Th-that space is reserved for, uh—"

"Intimacy?" she prompted, looking completely innocent.

His pulse leaped. "Or k-keyboards," he croaked.

Her finely arched eyebrows drew together. "What?"

He shrugged, suddenly feeling foolish. "Computer humor—most of us spend more time with our PC's than with any one person."

"Agreed—more than with any *one* person," she said, smiling wryly, then breaking out in a huge yawn.

Great, Parish. Not only is your conversation putting her to sleep, but you come off looking like some kind of freak who's turned on by his mainframe. And he hadn't missed her unnecessary reminder that when it came to sex, she liked to experiment. Which was an even bigger slap in the face considering they were in bed together and she was fighting to keep her eyes open.

He turned his attention back to the television, trying to lose himself in the fantasy on the screen. His wedding night was turning out to be somewhat less exciting than he'd hoped for. Not that he'd invited Pam along as a substitute for Jo—sleeping with her hadn't entered his mind.

Well, okay, so it *had* entered his mind, but not seriously. Not any more than when he saw a gorgeous model or movie star on TV. To him, Pamela had always seemed just as distant, just as untouchable. And even though the long expanse of her bare leg beckoned to him just a few inches away, she might as well have been still in Savannah for all the good it would do him.

He bit the inside of his cheek, his frustration mounting. One half roll of his body would put him face-to-breast with the most beautiful, sexual woman he knew. Maybe all he needed to do was make the first move. Maybe she'd rip off her clothes and he'd get to see what half of Savannah was raving about. Maybe they'd be great together and he'd give her a blinding orgasm.

His confidence surged, and he made a split-second decision. For once in his life, he would seize the moment and let the chips fall where they might. Before he could change his mind, he drew a quick breath and rolled onto his side, realizing the instant his chin met soft, pliant skin that he'd underestimated the distance *and* the size of her breasts. Her light floral scent filled his lungs, and his mind spun. His eyes darted to her face as he scrambled to think of something witty to say. Panic exploded in his chest...until he saw that she was sleeping.

He pulled himself up and expelled a small, disappointed sigh as he studied her lash-shadowed cheeks and the eternal pout of her fuller upper lip. He allowed his gaze to rove over her slender neck, then down to her breasts. The dark crescents of her nipples were barely visible beneath the thin fabric of her T-shirt. Elvis smiled at him, obviously happy to be stretched over Pam's ample bosom.

Alan's body hardened and he fought back a groan. He lifted his free hand and let it hover over an area where her shirt had risen high on her thigh. Was she wearing panties? Did he dare peek? After all, she'd seen him all but buck naked.

No, he decided. He wasn't a voyeur—he wanted anything that transpired between them to be consensual. "Pam," he whispered, his voice scratchy.

She moaned and moved down on the pillows and slightly toward him, but didn't rouse.

"Pam," he repeated a little louder.

He held his breath as her eyelashes fluttered for a second and her mouth opened as if she was going to speak. His desire for her swelled even more and his heart thumped in anticipation.

"Alan?" she murmured, her eyes still closed.

"Y-yes?" he whispered hopefully.

She wet her lips, and he thought he might go mad with wanting her. He moved toward her open mouth, intending to kiss her awake, but the sound emerging from her throat stopped him cold.

She was snoring...loud enough to shake the mirror on the ceiling above them.

5

PAM'S LEG itched. Trying to ignore it, she floated deeper into the pillow, enjoying the last fuzzy minutes of sleep. But the itch persisted until at last she reached down and scratched her knee vigorously. The thought that she needed to shave skittered across her mind, but was obliterated when she realized she hadn't even felt her fingernails against her skin.

Her eyes flew open, and she froze at the image in the mirror ceiling. Alan, stripped down to his boxers, lay wrapped around her like a koala bear in a eucalyptus tree, his arm resting comfortably across her chest, his bent leg heavy upon her abdomen. She could feel his warm breath upon the side of her neck. Her mind spun and panic welled within her. The last thing she remembered was watching television—had she…did they…oh, God, what was that stabbing into her side?

She pushed at his arm, dragging him with her as she attempted to roll away from his body. The fluid mattress surged, grabbed her, then slammed their bodies back together, abruptly rousing Alan from his slumber.

"Huh?" he muttered, lifting his head.

His glasses sat askew on the top of his head and his hair had finished drying in every direction but down. "Get off of me," Pam said, enunciating clearly.

Squinting, he appeared not to have heard her.

"Alan," she repeated more loudly. "I'm not Jo—get off of me."

She knew the precise second her words registered because he stiffened and his nearsighted eyes rounded. "Pam?"

Throwing him a smile as dry as her mouth, she said, "Afraid so."

He wasted no time disentangling himself from her, but floundered a few seconds before propelling himself off the bed. Pam followed him with her eyes, averting her glance from the bulge straining at the front of his underwear. To avoid aggravating her mushrooming headache, she lay still until the waves stopped.

Patting furniture surfaces, presumably searching for his glasses, Alan walked into the half-unfolded sofa bed. Flesh collided with metal in a sickening thunk. "Son of a—" He broke off and bit his lower lip, wincing.

"They're on the top of your head, Einstein."

Alan fumbled for his glasses, jammed them on and looked back to the bed as if he still hadn't seized the situation.

She lifted her hand and fluttered her fingers at him. "I trust you slept well," she said in a sarcastic tone.

Patting down his hair, he scowled and bent over to scoop up his sweatpants. "How could I, with you snoring loud enough to rattle my teeth?"

Annoyance bolted through her, and she shot up, grimacing at the pain exploding in her temples. "Do you always curl into a fetal position when you're in agony? Our deal was *you* would sleep on the sofa bed!"

He reached down to massage his shin. "I tried to pry open the damn thing, but it wouldn't budge."

She rubbed her forehead, glancing around the sunlit room. "What time is it?"

He held the sweatpants in front of his waist with one hand and picked up his watch with the other. "Almost ten o'clock."

She sighed, pushing tangled hair out of her eyes. "At least the stores should open soon."

"Forget the stores, give me a restaurant."

"Fine. We'll have a bite to eat, then I can go shopping." Thankfully, the awkwardness was dissolving. "Wonder what the weather will be like this week?"

Alan picked up the remote and found the weather channel, then tossed the control on the bed. Without another word, he turned and limped into the bathroom.

Pam frowned after him. He didn't have to be so snotty—after all, *he* had invited *her*. He wasn't being a very gracious host.

Oh, well, at least Mother Nature was smiling on them. According to the chipper weatherwoman, they had arrived smack in the middle of a February heat wave: temperatures in the low nineties, and sun, sun, sun.

Pam gingerly pulled herself out of bed and walked to the far end of the room, away from the bathroom. In the light of day, the kaleidoscope room really was horrid. Groaning, she reached overhead in a full-body stretch, wriggling her toes in the chocolate shag carpet, then drew aside the yellow brocade curtain covering a sliding glass door. The balcony Twiggy promised was a tiny wooden structure about the size of a refrigerator enclosed by worn railings. Despite the slight pain caused by the morning sunlight, she unlatched the door and stepped out into the cool air, feeling her spirits rise along with the gooseflesh on her arms.

A set of questionable-looking narrow stairs descended to a pebbly path that disappeared into palm trees and sea grass. She took a step forward, then stopped, rubbed one bare foot over the other, and decided not to chance it. If she fell and broke a leg, Alan might shoot her to put her out of his misery.

Without the wide sign from the neighboring Grand Sands Hotel, they might have had a very good view. Despite the obstruction, a slice of the white beach was visible, dotted with morning walkers and shell-seekers. The air, full of sand and salt dust, blew sharp against her bare arms and legs. Inhaling deeply, she drew in the tangy ocean breeze and was suddenly very glad she had come. Maybe the circumstances weren't ideal, but she loved the ocean and Savannah's beaches were a bit too cold to enjoy this time of year.

Humming to herself, she turned and reentered the room, closing the sliding door behind her. Then her gaze landed on the bathroom door and her smile evaporated. Obviously, Alan already regretted the invitation to share his honeymoon. She was a poor replacement for the woman he loved. But she was here, and she'd promised Jo she'd keep an eye on him. She blushed guiltily—the amount of time she'd spent eyeing him since their arrival probably wasn't what her friend had had in mind. Lifting her chin, she gathered her willpower. She could keep her lust at bay for a lousy week, but darn it, she wasn't going to let him mope and ruin the only vacation she'd had in over a year!

She took in her appearance in one of the many mirrors at her disposal and groaned out loud. As if he'd be interested, anyway. Her friend Jo rolled out of bed looking great. She, on the other hand, looked as if she'd been dragged backward through a hedgerow.

Dropping onto the unmade bed, she grabbed the phone. She needed to check her messages and see if old Mrs. Wingate had made up her mind about buying the Sheridan house, haunts and all. She retrieved her answering service with a few punched buttons. The message from Nick the All-Nighter was wicked enough to fry the phone lines. And Jo had called, concern in her voice—had Pam seen Alan and was he all right?

She shot a look toward the bathroom door just as it opened. *Speak of the devil.* Swallowing, she scanned the tempting length of Alan in black running shorts and a tight touristy sweatshirt. He offered her a small smile, apparently in a much better mood. She lifted her finger, then turned away from him and tried to concentrate on Jo's rambling, heartfelt message. With a sigh, Jo thanked Pam for going after Alan and asked Pam to call her at John's house—Jo laughed—make that *her* house. Pam smirked into the phone, happy for her friend, but disturbed by the sticky mess she'd left behind.

She felt contrite as she replaced the handset. It wasn't Jo's fault that she was having these inappropriate feelings for Alan. "Jo left me a message."

Alan's handsome face remained impassive—perhaps a little *too* nonchalant. "What did she say?"

Pam hesitated, then said, "She was wondering if I'd seen you and how you're doing."

He exhaled loudly and cracked his knuckles in one quick movement. "What business is it of hers?"

"She's just worried about you—"

"Well, I'm not suicidal," he snapped.

Pam stood, jamming her hands on her hips. "You don't have to shoot the messenger."

"Sorry—I'm not feeling very well."

"Join the crowd," Pam yelled back, then touched a hand to her resurrected headache.

His expression softened a bit. "You don't look too bad—I mean, uh, you look…fine."

She smiled wryly, then turned toward the bathroom. "Nice try. I'll be out in two shakes."

Alan watched her retreat into the bathroom, the curves of her hips tugging at the hem of her T-shirt. A little more than *two* shakes, he amended silently, making fists of frustration at his side.

"This is insane," he said to the frantic-looking man in the mirror.

"Why are you worried about it?" his image asked. "Just *bed* the woman, for heaven's sake."

"I can't—she's my ex-fiancée's best friend."

"Even better."

Alan squeezed his eyes shut and cursed, then slowly opened them to address his argumentative reflection. "This is a fine mess you've gotten us into." Oh, well, maybe his secretary would come through with less evocative accommodations.

True to her word, Pam showered quickly, emerging like a ray of sunshine, her skin glowing, her golden hair caught up in a high, swishy ponytail. He groaned inwardly. She was even gorgeous in running shorts and a baggy white jersey sporting a multicolored parrot. "Ready?" she asked.

"And willing," he mumbled, picking up his wallet.

At the last minute, they both shoved their feet into

hard, ill-fitting plastic thongs, then stumbled downstairs to find the reservation desk deserted. A fiftyish woman sprawled in one of the lobby chairs, smoking a long cigarette and watching a church program on television. She was happy to nod in the direction of the restaurant, and as soon as they smelled food their clumsy steps quickened.

Alan's stomach rumbled when he saw how packed the restaurant was. Grasping Pam's elbow, he pointed to the buffet line. ''If you'll get us something to eat, I'll try to find a table.'' She nodded and he cased the area, his eyes lighting on a family of four wiping their chins over emptied plates. He scrambled toward the table, arriving at the same time as a busboy and an older couple holding laden plates.

The silver-haired man smiled. ''Share?''

''Sure,'' Alan agreed.

''We're the Kessingers,'' the man supplied. ''I'm Cheek and this is Lila.''

Alan introduced himself as he pulled out the older woman's chair. ''Another person will be joining me.''

''We're from Michigan,'' Lila offered.

''Savannah,'' Alan told her, as he took a seat opposite her. The Kessingers seemed nice enough, divulging they were devoted snowbirds who migrated south every January until spring.

''There you are,'' Pam said, precariously balancing two plates piled high with food. Alan relieved her of half her burden, then introduced the senior couple.

''Hi,'' Pam said cordially as she swung into her seat.

Alan frowned down at the plate in front of him. Every single item was fried. ''I see you got plenty of the *brown* food group.''

"Eat," Pam said pointedly, stabbing a sausage patty with her fork.

With visions of whole-wheat bagels and fresh fruit dancing in his head, Alan ate, stopping frequently to sop the grease from his food with paper napkins. Lila Kessinger proved to be quite chatty, which gave Cheek plenty of time to ogle Pam, he noticed, surprised at the needle of jealousy that poked him.

"Are you newlyweds?" Lila asked.

Pam glanced at him. "No, we're just…uh…"

Alan's stomach fluttered. "Buddies," he offered.

"Pals," Pam affirmed.

"Oh," the woman responded. "I assumed you were married since you're in the honeymoon suite."

Alan stopped. "How did you know we're in the honeymoon suite?"

Lila grinned. "We're right across the plaza from you, in room 400. Remember—we waved."

He frowned, trying to recall, then grunted as Pam kicked him under the table. One look at her raised eyebrows and his memory flooded back. The naked couple! He dropped his fork with a clatter and a burning flush crept up his neck. "Oh, I didn't recognize you—"

"Because we're both nearsighted," Pam cut in. "We couldn't see much." She looked at him for reinforcement. "Isn't that right, Alan?"

"Y-yes," he said, a picture of the wrinkled nude couple emblazoned on his mind. "In fact, we didn't see anything at all. You waved, did you say?" He brought a glass of room-temperature water to his mouth for a drink.

Lila beamed and nodded. Cheek leaned forward, his eyes devouring Pam.

Lifting his wrist, Alan pretended to be shocked. "*Look* at the time. We have to go," he said, eyeing Pam.

"But I'm not finished," she protested.

"We'll get a stick of butter for the road," he said through clenched teeth, casting his eyes toward the door.

"Okay," she relented sullenly, wiping her mouth and standing. "It was nice to meet—"

Alan pulled on her arm, and nearly dragged her back through the restaurant.

"Let go of me," she said angrily, then jerked away from him. "What the devil is wrong with you?"

He stared at her and exclaimed, his frustration high, "That's the thanks I get?"

"Thanks? For what?"

"That dirty old man looked like he was getting ready to have *you* for breakfast!"

Pam tilted her head and laughed. "You're jealous!"

"What?" Alan scoffed, embarrassment thickening his tongue. "That'z we—ridiculous!"

"Weally?" Pam teased.

Grunting, Alan sputtered, "I thought you wanted to go shopping."

She grinned, looking triumphant. "I do."

"Then let's go see what the car rental agency delivered." He pivoted as quickly as the stupid sandals would allow, then flapped back toward the lobby, fuming. Damn, he hated her teasing, filing him in the same category as her bevy of besotted suitors.

Twiggy had returned to her post, and looked as

bored as usual when he asked about the car. Without a word, she held up a key and pointed to the parking lot.

"Finally," he breathed, taking the key. "*Something is going right.*"

He walked stiffly across the lobby and out into the parking lot, unable to look at Pam, still smarting from her taunt. He knew she was behind him, but he didn't know how close until he spotted their car, stopped dead in his tracks and felt her body slam into his.

"What's wrong?" she asked, stepping up beside him. Then she gasped. "A limo?" She whooped, then laughed until her knees buckled.

Alan, however, did not share her mirth. "This is unbelievable." He removed the letter tucked under the windshield wiper and read aloud. "Dear Mr. Parish, please accept this upgrade vehicle as our apology for your unfortunate breakdown—" He broke off and glanced at the powder blue stretch limousine. "They sent me a damn pimpmobile!"

Pam laughed even louder, clapping her hands. "What a blast!"

He stood paralyzed in shock as she swung open the back door. "Ooooh," she breathed, her eyes shining. "A television and everything!"

I'm in the twilight zone. "We're taking it back."

Her head jerked around. "What? We can't!"

"Oh, but we can."

Pam's eyebrows crumpled, and she pulled out her secret weapon: the pout. Damn! Surely she knew what that mouth did to him. He wavered. "Maybe we'll keep it just for the day."

She brightened and tumbled inside, then stuck her

head back out. "I'll ride in the back." He felt the vac-
uum of air as she slammed the door.

Feeling like a colossal fool, he glanced around,
opened the front door and slid behind the wheel. Pam
had already found the button that operated the divider
between them and was zooming the panel up and
down.

"This is amazing," she squealed.

He glanced in the rearview mirror at her smiling
face, watched her pressing buttons and exploring, and
felt a strange tug at his heart. As exasperating as she
could be, Pam's unflagging enthusiasm was undeniably
charming. Somewhere between childhood and yuppie-
hood, he'd lost his zest for simple things...now he
wondered how many wonderfully pure pleasures he'd
overlooked the last several years.

"There's a refrigerator!" she exclaimed. "And olives!"

He pulled onto the highway, keeping one eye on
Pam. She reclined in the back seat, propping her long
legs on the bench seat running up the side. Then she
unscrewed the lid from a slender jar and popped green
olives into her mouth like a squirrel eating nuts. For
some reason, he found the whole scene provocative.

"Hey, Alan, have you ever gotten naked in a limo?"

He weaved across the centerline so far he might have
hit the oncoming car if the guy hadn't blared his horn
and punctuated it with a hand gesture.

Breathing deeply to stem the charge of adrenaline
through his body, he said, "I, uh, no, I can't say I
have."

"Me neither."

Although her admission surprised him, he didn't say

so. For a fraction of an instant, he entertained the idea of sharing Pamela's first sexual *something*. The way he figured it, the only new variable he could possibly add to her experience equation was location. Shaking the thought from his mind, he kept his dry mouth shut and his eyes peeled for signs indicating a mall.

Once he found a shopping center, it took several minutes to find a place to park. At last they were inside the mall and Alan felt some sort of normalcy returning at the sight of regular people in smart, upscale surroundings. He made a beeline for a well-known department store. "We can split up," Pam suggested.

Alan shook his head. "I'll go with you, I'm paying."

"Wait a minute—"

"Don't argue. I talked you into coming, and it's my responsibility—"

"I can take care of myself!"

He drew back at the change in her mood, the vehemence in her voice. He'd obviously hit a nerve, so he gentled his tone. "I know you can take care of yourself, Pam, but I'd feel bad if you spent money on top of taking time from your job. Let me do this—make me feel good." Immediately, he felt his skin warm at the implication of his own words.

She chewed on her lower lip, considering his words, then smiled slyly. "I think this may be the first time a guy has offered to do something for *me* to make himself feel good."

Glad her mood had lightened, he crossed his arms and mirrored her smile. "Maybe you've been hanging around with the wrong guys."

Her smile dissolved and her gaze locked with his.

"Maybe you're right," she said, her voice barely above a whisper.

Alan studied her face and inhaled slowly, sure his chest was going to explode. This woman was driving him crazy. One minute she made him feel like an inept teenager, the next minute she made him feel as if he wanted to take care of her. Which was nuts because she'd made it perfectly clear she intended to take care of herself.

His fingers curled tighter around his biceps, itching to smooth the stray lock of hair back from her soft cheek. To hold her pointed chin and tilt her porcelain-like face up to the sun. To kiss that lopsided, upside-down, top-heavy pink mouth.

"Okay, go ahead," she said, shrugging.

He actually took a half step toward her before he realized she was talking about the clothing tab. "Where to first?"

"Men's shoes."

"What?"

She pointed to his red, thong-pinched feet and grinned. "You're going to need comfortable shoes to keep up with me."

Good idea, he decided three hours later as he shared a bench with an older gentleman outside the women's dressing room.

"Birthday?" the guy asked, obviously bored.

"No."

"Anniversary?" The man tapped out a cigarette and put it in his mouth, unlit.

"Uh-uh."

"Ah—you're in the doghouse."

"Well, not really."

"Oh, God," the man said, rolling his eyes. "Don't tell me you love her."

"Pam," he said loud enough to carry into the dressing room, "I need to eat something nourishing for a change. Can you hurry up? I'm getting light-headed."

"I think I found a swimsuit," she sang, then burst through the swinging doors. "What do you think?"

"Good Lord," the man muttered, his unlit cigarette bobbing.

Alan swayed, then gripped the side of the bench to steady himself. Pam's curves were stunning. Metallic gold, the top of the string bikini barely covered the tips of her generous breasts, the veed bottoms arrowed low to her bikini line and high on the sides, emphasizing the opposing curves of her waist and hips. His throat closed and perspiration popped out on his upper lip despite the chilling air conditioner.

Her pale eyebrows furrowed. "You don't like it."

"He loves it!" the man next to him shouted, his cigarette bouncing off the carpet. Then he punched Alan's arm so hard, Alan fell off the side of the bench.

Flat on his back, Alan wet his lips carefully, then croaked, "It will do."

6

"ARENT YOU COLD?" Alan asked for the eleventh time.

Pamela jerked her head toward him, then lowered her ninety-nine-cent white sunglasses. "No."

"You look cold."

"Then stop looking." She leaned her head back against the plastic chaise lounge that suspended her several inches above the wet, white sand of the beach. "And stop talking."

After spending the day shopping with him yesterday and sharing an awkward dinner last night, she was ready to scream. They'd been at each other's throats all evening, culminating in an argument over finding someplace else to stay because he refused to sleep on the broken foldout bed. In the end, she had won separate sleeping arrangements, but he had complained about his back all morning.

Although quiet at the moment, he was driving her bananas, hiding behind those mirrored designer-prescription shades, reminding her every few seconds that she lay nearly naked within touching distance, yet he had no intention of doing so. Which was a good thing, she fumed, because she'd cuff his chiseled jaw if he laid a hand on her.

She harrumphed to herself. As if she would stoop to

fooling around with her best friend's ex. Pam winced and concentrated, desperately trying to dissolve the sexual pull radiating from him.

After all, once they returned to Savannah, Alan might run into Jo at an odd party or two, but Pam saw her at least a couple of times a week. Jo had been a true-blue friend, and Pam wasn't about to risk their relationship for a beach fling—no matter how pulse-poundingly gorgeous Alan looked lying glistening in the sun.

It was a glorious day, the sun as high as it could climb in a February Florida sky. As promised, the air temperature hovered in the mid-nineties, although she suspected the water temperature would be a bit more sobering. Still, it hadn't stopped several families from romping in the foamy waves, some with floats, some with masks to protect their eyes from the brine.

The beach was much more crowded than she'd expected. Portable stereos blared and the nutty smell of suntan lotion mingled with the salty air, barely masking the underlying scent of fish. Striped umbrellas populated the sloping stretch of pale sand and waitresses threaded their way through bodies to deliver drinks and hot dogs from the oceanside grill. The whole spring-break atmosphere was just another in a long series of surprises this trip had brought, she thought wryly, sneaking a sideways glance at Alan.

Bent over a book he'd bought at the mall, he looked relaxed and untroubled. Pam frowned sourly. *She* was wrestling with lewd and inappropriate thoughts, and *he* was reading a book.

"What is it now?" he asked, raising his head. "Is my breathing bothering you?"

Her gaze flicked across his oiled chest, watching defined bone and muscle expand and contract every few seconds, the sun dancing over every ripple. She could see her twin reflection in his gray lenses and wondered if he had any idea what he was doing to her. Unable to withstand the strain and confusion any longer, she swung her feet down, then stood, wrapping a short black sarong around her hips. "I'm going to stretch my legs."

Alan closed his book, keeping his place with one finger. "Want me to go along?"

Noting his uninterested tone, she shook her head. "I'll be back in an hour or so."

The strip of beach where fingers of water rolled in offered the clearest path for walking. She picked her way down to the front, ignoring a couple of low catcalls, then dug her toes in the cool, silky sand. Water hissed over her feet and frothed around her ankles, sending chills up her legs.

The beach snaked ahead of her, the people growing increasingly tiny in the distance, the shoreline curving left, then right again and disappearing about a mile away. Pam inhaled deeply, then set off at a brisk pace. Nothing cleared a person's head like the wind, water and sky.

As she made her way down to the water's edge, more than one good-looking man passed her, jogging or walking the other way, and more than one looked interested. A small smile curved her lips. One way to fight her ridiculous distraction with Alan was to find another man to distract her. A Robert Redford look-alike ran by her and grinned. Pam turned to watch him run away from her. A little on the short side, but he was definitely a looker. He had turned around and was running backward, scanning her figure up and down. After plowing into a group of teenagers, he saluted and went on his way.

"Don't tell me you're alone," a deep, accented voice said behind her.

Startled, Pam turned and looked up into the glinting eyes of a dark-eyed, dark-haired stranger. He looked to be of Latin American descent, his deep brown skin set off by gleaming gold jewelry at his throat, wrist and left earlobe. He grinned, exposing amazingly white teeth. Pam shivered. Dark, dangerous, good-looking…just her type.

"Uh, yes," she said, then added, "at the moment." A girl had to be careful in strange surroundings.

The man extended his long-fingered hand. He wore a diamond-studded horseshoe ring on his middle finger. "Enrico." The "r" rolled off his tongue seductively.

Pam smiled and put her hand in his. "Pamela."

"Ah, Pamela. Do you live here or are you on vacation?"

"Vacation."

"Then surely you have just arrived—I could not have overlooked such a beauty."

Enrico massaged her fingers between his. "I flew in from Savannah yesterday."

"A southern belle. I thought I detected a slight, how do you say—*drawl?*"

"Yes," she said, then gently extracted her hand. "Where are you from?"

"Puerto Rico, originally, but I have lived in the United States for several years."

Pam nodded congenially. "In Fort Myers?"

"No, I am vacationing, same as you." He leaned toward her and lowered his voice to a husky whisper. "And I was becoming *very* bored."

Odd, she felt nothing but indifference as he looked into her eyes. Not a sizzle or a zing. Not even a stir. "Well, I'd like to finish my walk," she said pleasantly, stepping around him. "It was nice to meet you, Enrico."

His eyes devoured her. "Until next time, Pamela."

She gave him a shaky smile, then trotted away. Pumping her arms to elevate her heart rate, she kept her eyes averted from passersby and walked two miles, past rows of resorts that ranged in appearance from posh to worse-than-the-Pleasure-Palisades. Finally, the crowds thinned and the sand became coarse and strewn with sea debris.

Pam waded into the waves up to her knees to cool off, watching a group of wet-suited windsurfers in the distance. It looked like fun—maybe she'd try it before they left. Sighing, she wondered if she'd be able to find enough entertainment to fill the hours between now and Saturday. Anything to keep her mind off Alan.

Anything but Enrico, that is—the guy gave her the willies. Turning to retrace her steps, she felt a surge of anticipation at seeing Alan again, then instant remorse. So much for clearing her head. She spotted him while she was still several hundred yards away—he was hard to miss since he stood at attention smiling down at a willowy brunette.

Absurd barbs of jealousy struck her low, but she squashed them. The woman was striking, thin and elegant in a simple black one-piece, wearing a large hat that shaded her face. The thought struck Pam that the woman might have been Jo's sister, she resembled her friend so closely. Regal, demure, classy...definitely Alan's type. Pam bit her lower lip, wondering if he wanted privacy, but knowing she needed sunscreen. Oh, well, she'd just swing by to pick up the lotion, then perhaps she could find the Robert Redford runner again.

Alan smiled and nodded to the lady, his book abandoned, Pam noted wryly. Above the music and the general din of the crowd, his voice floated to her in snatches as she approached the couple. "Show companies...become more productive...automation...accessibility."

The woman looked very impressed, nodding thoughtfully and lifting her expressive eyebrows. Her voice was lilting and definitely *interested*. "Client-servers...centralization...remote stored procedures."

Aha—a she-nerd. Out of all the people on this beach, how had they found one another? Pam sighed. Just like Enrico, the tongue-rolling Romeo, had found her—birds of a feather, yada, yada, yada. Oh, well, if Alan was occupied, the temptation to jump his bones would definitely be removed...or at least reduced. "Hi," Pam said cheerfully as she approached the computer couple.

"Oh, hi," Alan said, smiling awkwardly.

"Don't mind me," Pam said, waving a hand. "I just came back to get sunscreen."

"Um, this is Robin," he said, gesturing to the woman, who pursed her lips at the sight of Pam.

"Hiya, Robin," Pam said, nodding to the woman. "Nice hat."

"Thanks," Robin replied slowly, then turned to Alan. "I guess I'll be going."

"Don't leave on my account," Pam assured her, holding up her lotion triumphantly.

"No, that's all right," the woman continued. "My friends will be wondering where I've gone." She smiled at Alan and swept his figure, head to toe. "I certainly hope we run into each other again."

Alan's tongue appeared to be tied, so Pam stepped in. "I'm sure you will—he'll be here until Saturday." She leaned toward the woman and lowered her voice conspiratorially. "He's available, you know."

The woman smiled awkwardly, then glanced from Pam to Alan.

"Pam—" Alan protested, but she waved her hand frantically to shut him up.

"And you are...?" the woman asked with a small laugh.

"Alan's sister," Pam said without missing a beat. "I'm Pamela." Alan made a small choking noise, but she ignored him.

"Oh." The woman nodded agreeably. "Well, it's nice to meet you...Pamela." She winked. "And I'll see *you* later, Alan."

"Don't be a stranger," Pam sang as the woman walked away.

"What was that all about?" Alan demanded when she turned around. His arms were crossed over his broad chest, his pale eyebrows high over his shades.

Pam shrugged, her movements mirrored twice in his dark lenses. "It's plausible—we have the same coloring. Besides, who's going to believe the real story?"

Alan threw his hands up in the air. "I give up trying to follow your logic."

Falling into the chaise, Pam smeared sunscreen all

over, down to the crevices between her peach-lacquered toes. Alan reclaimed his chair and his place in the book he was reading. She glanced at the cover and smiled. "Hey, *Dr. Moonshadow.* I thought it was the best book in the entire series."

He glanced over. "You've read the Light Years series?"

She nodded enthusiastically. "Have you gotten to the part where the Light Knights return with the king's head in a box?"

He dropped his head back on the chair, looking mortified. "That would be, I take it, *the ending?*"

Pam bit her lip. "Oh...yeah, I guess it would be."

Tossing the book in the sand a few feet away, Alan cursed and pushed himself to his feet. "Now *I'm* going for a walk."

Pam watched him stride off, admiring his defined hamstrings and calves. And she didn't miss the head-turning that spread through the women on the beach like "the wave" as he walked by. Oh, well, she decided as she fished in her purse for her cellular phone and a pad of paper, maybe he'd run into Robin the RAM/ROM woman.

Pam pulled out the phone's antenna, then stabbed in a number with the end of a pencil. Then maybe *she* could stop thinking about how much she enjoyed teasing Alan, how many interests they shared, how sexy— "Hello?" she responded to the voice on the end of the line, then realized her client, Marsha Wingate, had updated the message on her service.

"Hello, this is Madame Marsha, psychic in training, Monday, February twelfth. If this is Ronald, son, wear your guardian pendant today. I communed with the weatherman this morning through the television and the winds today in Syracuse are *definitely* unfriendly. If this is Sara, dear, don't talk to any Aries men today, and don't drink the tap water. If this is Lew, give me a trifecta twenty-dollar bet on the number three, four and seven greyhounds in the fifth race. And if this is Pamela, I drove by the Sheridan house last night precisely at midnight, and the bad vibes coming from that place—jeez, Louise! I want an expert's opinion, though, so I arranged to have a crystal reader from Atlanta drive down tomorrow. If this is anyone else, I have nothing to say, so don't bother to leave a message.''

After the tone, which sounded vaguely like the theme from ''The Twilight Zone,'' Pam left an upbeat message telling Mrs. Wingate she was out of town for a few days, but could be reached through her cellular phone if she decided to scoop up the Sheridan house before someone else got wise to what a steal it was. Smiling wryly at her own transparent sales tactic, Pam then checked into the office to let them know she didn't have her pager.

When she had exhausted every nit-picking phone call she could think of, she winced at the still-strong recharged battery light on her phone, then sighed and dug out the scrap of paper on which she'd written her friend Jo's new phone number. With her heart pounding guiltily, Pam punched in the numbers and prayed no one would answer.

''Heh-wo?'' said a young voice.

''May I speak to Jo, please?''

''Jo-mommy?''

Pam blinked. Boy, did that sound weird—her friend

Jo, a mommy. The littlest one must have picked up the phone, she decided. And although she was no expert on kids, he seemed way too young to be answering the phone. "Yes, Jo-mommy," she said carefully. "Go get Jo-mommy."

"Hello?" another voice said, this one slightly older. "Who is this?"

Pam frowned. "Who is this?"

"This is Peter Pa—I mean, this is Jamie Sterling. Who do you want?"

The middle one, she decided. "I need to speak with Jo."

"What for?"

Taking a deep breath, Pam forced a soothing lilt into her voice. "Just to talk—I'm a friend of hers." Then she heard the sound of the phone being ripped from his hand, followed by a scuffle and at least two raised kid voices as they tried to claim ownership of the phone, which was being bounced around the room.

"Hello?" A girl's voice came over the line. Jamie was still yelling something in the background.

The oldest one, Pam remembered. An owlish-looking little thing. "May I speak with Jo, please?"

"May I ask who's calling?"

At least she was polite. "This is her friend Pamela."

"She's indisposed at the moment."

Pam pulled back and looked at the phone. Indisposed? Quite a vocabulary for a tyke. "I'm calling long distance—are you sure she can't come to the phone?"

"She and my daddy are upstairs jumping on the bed."

With pursed lips, Pam nodded to herself. Of course. Where else would they be? Before she could think of an appropriate reply, Jo's voice came on the line. "Hello?" she asked breathlessly.

"Gee, Jo, can't you guys control yourselves at least until the kids go to bed?"

"Pam!" Jo laughed. "It's not what you think—John is testing the springs on the new mattress."

"Oh, is *that* what married folk call it?"

Jo laughed again, this time harder. She sounded almost giddy, Pam thought irritably, despite the clatter in the background. "Oh, never mind, Pam. I called your office this morning and they said you were out of town. Let me guess—Nick the All-Nighter?"

Pam squirmed on the lounge chair. "No."

"Delectable Dale?"

Sweat beaded on her upper lip. "Uh, no."

"Someone new?"

After mustering her courage, Pam muttered, "I'm with Alan in Fort Myers."

"Excuse me? Hang on a minute." Jo put down the phone, then Pam heard the sound of a police whistle peal shrilly, followed by, "QUI-I-I-I-I-ET!" The clatter ceased, then Jo picked up the phone. "Sorry. Now, what did you say?"

Pam tried again. "I'm with Alan in Fort Myers."

"You're with Alan in Fort Myers?" Jo asked, her voice richly colored with surprise.

"Yes, I'm with Alan in Fort Myers." It was getting easier to say, but she still felt as if she was going to have a stroke. She took another deep breath. "He decided to take the trip anyway. I gave him a ride to the airport, and he talked me into coming along. I haven't had a vacation in over a year, and he was acting a little desperate—"

"Pam," Jo cut off her rambling. "You are the best friend a woman could ask for."

Swallowing guiltily, Pam ventured, "I—I am?"

"I've been so worried about Alan. Now I can relax because I know you're looking out for him. How is he?"

Pam paused, thinking of all the just plain looking *at him* she'd been doing since they arrived. "He's a little depressed, which is normal, I guess."

"I'm sure his ego is bruised," Jo said mournfully. "I feel terrible. Can you try to cheer him up?" she pleaded. "Maybe take him dancing or do something fun?"

Pam's hands were so sweaty she nearly dropped the phone. Manufacturing a little laugh, she said, "Well, I'm not so sure the words *Alan* and *fun* can coexist, Jo, but I'll give it a shot."

"Make him extend himself a little," Jo urged. "Maybe he'll meet his soul mate while he's there—or at least have a little beach fling."

"He's certainly getting a lot of female attention," Pam agreed, failing to mention how much of it had derived from her.

"Good. Eventually Alan will realize we weren't right for each other, and that our marriage would never have worked. But for now, he could probably use a diversion."

"Right," Pam said as if she were receiving an assignment. "So, how's married life?"

"Wonderful," Jo said. On cue, a hellacious howl erupted in the background. "Oops, gotta run. Thanks again, Pam—you're a savior. Bye!"

Pam frowned at the silent phone. Savior? Sinner,

perhaps, with all the wicked thoughts about Alan spinning in her head. She bit her lower lip—she should have gone to mass yesterday morning.

"What's wrong?" Alan asked as he dropped into his lounge chair, his body gleaming with perspiration. He picked up a towel and wiped his face. "Did the FDA issue a moratorium on fried foods?"

She smirked. "No. I talked to Jo."

He stilled, then pressed his lips into a straight line. "You mean, Jo *Sterling?*"

"Um, yeah."

Alan lay his head back and Pam's heart twisted at the hurt on his face. "And how are the newlyweds?"

"Busy, from the noise in the background."

"Did you tell her where we are?"

Pam studied her nails. "Yeah. She seemed relieved."

He made an indignant sound. "You mean that I haven't self-destructed?"

"Well, she didn't use those words."

"She wouldn't have."

"I think she really does feel bad about what happened, Alan."

A deep sigh escaped him. "I'd rather not talk about it."

"Fine," Pam said, also eager to drop the subject. She glanced toward the water, then noticed a young man had set up shop on the beach, guarding a half-dozen Wave Runners bobbing in shallow water.

He picked up a megaphone and yelled, "Rent a Wave Runner, by the hour, by the half hour."

"Let's do it," Pam said, clambering out of her chair.

"Do what?"

"Rent a Wave Runner," she said, tugging on his hand.

"They look dangerous," Alan said with a frown.

"Can you swim?"

"Yes," he answered indignantly.

"Then come on, take a risk for once in your life."

He pushed himself up slowly, then followed her at a leisurely pace. "I'm a risk-taker," he defended himself tartly.

"Oh, sure, Alan," she said over her shoulder. "You're a regular daredevil."

Alan bit his tongue. She was the most infuriating woman! He wanted to shake her, but he suspected that putting his hands on her and giving her breasts an excuse to jiggle would probably undo him in his current state. She strutted away from him, giving movement to the rub-on flower tattoo he'd watched her apply to her hip this morning in the room—a performance he'd been able to endure only by virtue of much teeth-grinding. His jaws still ached.

The young rental man was so bedazzled by Pam and her little bikini, he could scarcely speak. Amidst the boy's nods and a dancing Adam's apple, Alan half-heartedly negotiated a price for a Wave Runner and two wet suits, still unconvinced he would relish the ride.

Pam poured herself into a full-length neon pink wet suit with a built-in life jacket whose front zipper simply could not accommodate her chest. But leaving the zipper down a few inches only lifted her breasts higher and further emphasized her deep cleavage. Alan pulled on his own rubber suit, which was about six inches too short in the arms and legs. He performed a deep knee bend to loosen the material.

"I'll drive," Pamela announced, grabbing the handlebars and floating the Wave Runner out a few feet into the shallows.

"Oh my God," Alan gasped when he waded into the bracing cold water. "Are you sure this is going to be enjoyable?"

She scrambled up on the bobbing machine, straddling the bright yellow vinyl seat and plugging in the ignition starter. After slipping the stretchy key ring over her wrist, she turned around and held out her hand. "Would you stop complaining and get on?"

"What's that for?" he asked, pointing to the wristband that connected her to the machine.

"It's like a kill switch," she said with a grin. "If I throw us off, the engine dies."

"Oh, that's comforting," he said as he gingerly climbed up on the back and settled behind her on the long padded seat.

She pushed a button and the engine purred to life. "Better hang on," she warned over her shoulder as she turned the handlebars quickly and revved the engine, sending them into a sideways spin.

Alan grabbed the strap across the seat and managed to hang on, barely. "Have you ever done this before?" he shouted into the wind.

"Too many times to count," she yelled, leaning low and feeding the gas until they were hurtling across the waves at a breathtaking speed. They caught a wave, rode off the edge into the air, then landed with a teeth-jarring—and frigid—splash. Pam squealed in delight, then shouted, ''You're throwing us off balance. Hang on to me!''

Too shaken and waterlogged to refuse, he wrapped his arms around her waist, twining his fingers into the buckles of her wet suit. She was going to kill him. Was drowning a painful way to die? In this case, he'd probably have a heart attack first. The air whooshed from his lungs as they landed hard and a wave of freezing water swelled over the back and drenched him. At this rate, he might suffer both tragedies in the space of the next few seconds.

Several hundred feet offshore, they zigzagged the water many times, and Alan could feel her confidence growing with each pass. He could have simply let go to escape the frenzied ride, but he had to admit the experience was rather thrilling. He jammed his body up behind hers, holding fast to her waist and pressing his face into her wet hair, giving in to the sexual zing that pierced his abdomen at holding her so close and bumping against her with every jump and spin.

She drove faster and faster, jumping higher and higher, landing with belly-flipping spinouts. When they caught the underside of a particularly deep wave, Alan sensed impending doom. Pam screamed in delight, and they were airborne for what seemed like a minute, when Alan decided they would be safer to land separate from the Wave Runner. He lifted his arms to clasp her, harness-style, then twisted off to the side, taking her with him, but releasing her before they hit the water.

He plunged in, bubbles fizzing around his ears, his senses temporarily clogged with the glug, glug of enveloping water. With two powerful kicks, he reached the surface, then slung water from his eyes and immediately looked for Pam.

Alan spun all around, treading water, frantically searching for a flash of neon pink, but he saw nothing except the silent wave runner several yards away and endless foamy green-gray waves.

7

ALAN'S HEART SLAMMED against the wall of his chest and panic coursed through his veins. "Pam!" he shouted, "Pam, where are you?" He swam toward the Wave Runner using long strokes, swallowing great gulps of cold, salty water as waves pushed and pulled at him, elevating his terror. She could have hit her head on the machine when he pulled her off...she could have hit the water at an odd angle and broken her silly neck...she could have been dragged down by an undertow...she could have—

"Of all the...stupid...things...to do!"

Alan stopped, then went weak with relief as he realized her voice came from the other side of the Wave Runner. She coughed fitfully until she gagged, then coughed more, wheezing, cursing him with every breath. He swam around to find her clinging to the side of the water bike, her golden hair molded to her head and neck, her mouth open to take in as much air as possible. She confronted him with wide, blazing blue eyes.

"Were you trying to kill me?" she croaked, then another coughing spasm overtook her.

"*Me?*" Alan yelled. "I was trying to keep you from killing us *both!* We would have been thrown off for sure on that last kamikaze maneuver!"

"Would not!"

"Would too!"

"Would *not!*"

"Would *too!*"

Pam stuck her tongue out at him, then reached up to climb back on the Wave Runner. "Next time I'll leave you on the beach with your book."

Alan shook with fury. First she'd given him the scare of his life when he thought she'd drowned, then she yelled at him for spoiling her fun! "Wait just a minute," he said, grasping her arm and pulling her back into the water.

"Let go of me!"

"I'm driving back."

"Oh no you're not!"

He squeezed her upper arm and pulled her face near his. "Oh yes," he said with finality, "I am."

Her eyes widened slightly in surprise, then her mouth tightened, but she didn't argue. A drop of water slid off the end of her nose and Alan once again marveled at the smoothness of her skin. The thought crossed his mind that she was close enough to kiss, but he was pretty sure she'd drown him if he tried. Her chest heaved with her still-labored breathing, straining the already taxed wet-suit zipper to near bursting. His body leaped in painful response because there was nowhere in his wet suit to expand. But the flash of pain brought him back to reality and he released her slowly, then moved away to a safer distance.

His brain had been scrambled from Pamela's joyride, Alan reasoned as he pulled himself out of the water to straddle the Wave Runner. He took a deep, head-clearing breath before turning around to offer his hand to help Pamela climb up. Her mouth quirked left, then right, but finally she let him help her up. She slipped a couple of times, which made him laugh, then she went limp with giggles and sank back into the water.

"You," he said, shaking his head, "are wearing me out."

"Then you," she said, heaving herself up far enough for him to pull her onto the seat, "don't have much endurance." She handed him the wristband.

"I never needed it with Jo," he said as she slid behind him. He bit the inside of his cheek and turned over the engine, immediately regretting mentioning his ex.

But Pamela simply reached around his waist and laced her hands together, then said close to his ear, "But I'm not Jo, am I, Alan?"

Her breath felt warm against his cold, wet ear, and her words swirled round in his head, taunting him. *I'm not Jo, am I, Alan?* An understatement of gigantic proportions. *I'm not Jo, am I, Alan?* As if he weren't electrically aware of the fact. *I'm not Jo, am I, Alan?* And he realized with a jolt that he was having fun, more fun than he'd had in a long time—and he was very glad that Pam was, well...just Pam.

His heart strangely buoyed, he tossed a mischievous smile over his shoulder and said, "Hang on." Then he leaned low over the handlebars and mashed the gas with his thumb, sending them lunging forward. Pam squealed in surprise and delight, ramming herself up against him, which tempted Alan to squeal with delight. He mimicked her earlier technique, driving fast, catching waves and landing with a spin, drenching them with walls of water that surged over the back.

Adrenaline pumped through him and, combined with the sheer physical thrill of being close to Pamela, for the first time in his life he felt blatantly cocky.

Alan threw back his head and whooped, reveling in the pressure of Pam's thighs squeezing his. For several minutes, he sent them skimming and jumping over the sun-drenched water, slowing at last as their time remaining slipped to less than ten minutes.

Hating to see the ride end, he adjusted the speed to idle and guided them toward the rental stand several hundred yards away. All sorts of strange and inappropriate emotions were running rampant through his body, and they were all directed toward Pam, who hadn't relaxed her hold around his waist. Waves slapped against the sides of the Wave Runner, and the sounds of beach music rolled out to meet them. Although sunset was still hours away, the beach was emptying rapidly as the locals packed up their families to go home for the evening meal.

"Did you have fun?" she asked, resting her chin on his left shoulder.

For a split second, Alan considered lying—he had an uneasy feeling that admitting he enjoyed Pam's company was not in his immediate best interests. But for the past hour, he had laughed more than he would have thought possible only a few hours ago, and for that, he owed her the truth. "Yeah, I did have fun. Thanks for taking my mind off...you know."

"What are friends for?" Pam asked lightly, closing her eyes and swallowing her guilt. She'd promised Jo she'd make sure he had fun. But at some point during their outing, she had forgotten she was supposed to be entertaining Alan because she was having such a good time herself. And now, putting back toward shore, she felt deflated and angry with herself for even thinking there wouldn't be too many excuses this week to hold Alan so close.

"Maybe we can take it out again tomorrow," Alan suggested, turning his head and inadvertently bringing his smooth cheek next to her mouth.

"Sure," she said casually, already looking forward to the ride. "Unless you'd rather take Robin."

"Who?" he asked, his tone innocent.

"My, what a short memory we have," she noted dryly. "You know, the smart woman in the hat."

"What makes you say she's smart?"

"Well, she works with computers, doesn't she?"

"The computer industry has its share of incompetents."

Pam brightened. "So she isn't smart?"

"Oh no, she's smart," he corrected, evoking a little stab of jealousy in her. "But don't assume anything just because someone talks in acronyms."

"You're getting sunburned," she said irritably.

He laughed and they pulled up next to the rental stand. "Are you sure it isn't the reflection from your suit?"

The young rental man had walked out into the shallows to meet them. Pam reluctantly relinquished her hold on Alan and dropped into the water up to her knees, already tugging at the confining zipper. By the time she reached the warm sand, she'd only managed to peel the rubber suit from one shoulder and she was already exhausted. She fell to the sand, knowing the grit would only make things worse, but she didn't care. Lying on her back, she squinted against the sun and watched Alan extricate his magnificent body from his too-small suit with great sucking sounds as the rubber relented. Her breasts tightened in awareness and desire struck her low as he dragged the suit down, yanking his conservative navy trunks low on his hips. Standing in the sun with gleaming wet skin, his fair hair dry and tousled, he looked healthy and sexy, and Pam acknowledged for the first time that she was very attracted to him. And in more than just a physical sense, although simply looking at him had become a favorite pastime.

Today when he'd driven the Wave Runner, she had seen a side of him she'd never glimpsed before: carefree and spontaneous. He was actually fun to be with.

"Need a hand with your suit?" he asked, standing over her and grinning.

Pam nodded and took the hand he offered her, allowing herself to be pulled to her feet. She tugged at the opposite shoulder of the suit and succeeded in budging it an inch or so. Alan reached for the collar. "It's harder now that your skin is wet and the suit is heavy."

His fingers felt like branding irons against the cold flesh of her collarbone. He gripped the thick material and peeled the suit down her arm, turning the sleeve inside out. With both arms free, Pam was able to work the suit past her hips with some self-conscious wriggling, but had to admit defeat at her thighs. Then she lost her balance and sat down hard in the sand. Alan howled with laughter, but before she could get her breath to chew him out, she was thrown to her back because he had yanked her legs in the air to finish stripping off the stubborn suit. Sprawled in the awkward position and at his mercy, Pam felt like a too-big toddler being changed, and bristled at the hoots and laughter of the sparse but rapt audience staked out under umbrellas in the sand around them.

Alan also appeared to be enjoying her discomfort. At last he held up the pink garment as if it were a trophy and said, "I don't think this suit will ever be the same," then gestured to the deformed top of the fatigued-looking rubber suit. The comment brought him cheers from the members of the male gallery within earshot.

Pam scrambled to her feet, not sure if she liked this new, cocky side of Alan. "Well, while you strut for the other roosters," she said with a deceptively sweet smile as she brushed the sand from her bottom, "I'm going to find a beer."

Then she turned to march back to their blanket and chaise lounges they had rented for the day.

"Better go after her," some guy yelled to Alan behind her back.

"I'll go," another male voice piped up, triggering more laugher. But Pam had to acknowledge a little thrill that everyone assumed she and Alan were together.

"Hey," Alan said, jogging up beside her with a sheepish grin. "I'm thirsty, too."

Pam glanced at him, increasingly alarmed at the pull she felt toward him. "You need sunscreen."

He scrunched up his face and rubbed his cheek. "My skin does feel a little tight."

"Uh-oh," she warned. "Wait until after sundown."

He stepped in front of her, stopping her in her tracks. With eyebrows raised, he asked, "What will happen after sundown?"

Pam's pulse skipped and, not without a certain amount of panic, realized Alan was also feeling the sexual pull between them. His eyes searched her face, and she sensed that, ever the gentleman, he was waiting for a signal. They had reached the sticky point where everything they said to each other could be stretched, warped and misshapen to mean something else, an unstable area that might lead them to ruin unless one of them took control. And since Alan was freshly wounded from Jo's rejection, he was vulnerable to sexual revenge, even if he wasn't conscious of his motivation. And it was Pam's job to make sure that she wasn't a physical party to his retaliation for being dumped at the altar.

She forced lightness into her tone, ignoring his invitation to prolong the flirtation. "Sunburns are always worse after sundown," she said quietly, glad they had reached their chairs. She tossed him a bottle of sunscreen and pulled a short mesh cover-up over her head. Pointing up the sandy incline, she said, "I'm going to get a beer."

"Sounds great," he said, grabbing a T-shirt, but Pam held up her hand.

"Stay here and I'll bring them back," she said, desperate to escape his proximity. She practically ran up the stone path to the grill, but told herself she'd have to find a way to steel herself against the magnetism that had materialized between them—they would be here another four days!

The grill turned out to be a charming little outside eatery comprising a long bar and three weathered multilevel decks covered with latticed-wood "ceilings" that allowed the sun and wind to filter through. Pam glanced over the crowded tables, then walked to the bar and ordered two draft beers.

"Ah, Pamela, we meet again," came a deep, rolling voice behind her. Pam turned to see the handsome Enrico standing with an umbrellaed drink in his bejeweled hand.

"Er, yes," Pam said, offering him a small smile. As dangerous as the man appeared, at the moment he seemed the safer of two choices.

"Have you been enjoying the afternoon?" he asked conversationally, straddling a stool next to where she stood. His chest was well-developed and covered with dense, black hair. Pam made a split-second comparison to Alan's sleek physique, then bit the inside of her cheek when she acknowledged her preference.

"Sure," she answered casually, as the bartender slid two beers toward her.

"A two-fisted drinker?" he asked, his dark eyes dancing.

"For a friend," she explained, lifting one of the cups to her mouth with a shaky hand. Her revelations about Alan had her completely rattled.

"A male friend?"

Pam nodded.

Enrico formed a pout with his curvy mouth. "Is he jealous?"

Pam pressed her lips together, stalling. "I don't know," she said, licking the bittersweet liquid from her lips.

He made a clicking sound with his cheek. "Silly man." Then he leaned forward and wrapped a long blond lock around his forefinger. "I would never let you out of my si—iiiiIIIIEEE!" Enrico jerked back as a large arm descended between them on the bar with a resounding smack.

Pam swung her head up and gasped to see Alan standing between them, nursing a smirk. "I was getting thirsty," he said.

Anger flashed through her. How dare he show up while she was trying to forget about him! "Alan, what are you doing?"

He nodded at the dark man he towered over. "Is this guy bothering you?"

"No!"

"Excuse me," Enrico said, pushing away from the bar slowly. "Perhaps I'll see you later," he said, lifting his bronzed hand in a wave. Then he walked away, sipping his drink.

Alan watched him, then muttered, "Someone should tell him his back needs a trim."

"What the heck was that all about?" Pam demanded.

"I was defending your honor," Alan declared hotly. "*Again*. And a lot of thanks I get—again."

"Well, I guess I'm finally getting a glimpse of the real you, Alan P. Parish," she said through clenched teeth. "Tell me, does the 'P' stand for 'prehistoric'?"

He glared.

"Or 'paternal'?"

He glared.

"Or just plain 'putz'?"

He straightened and picked up his beer. "I can take a hint—if you want that…that gorilla with all his gold chains, then who am I to stand in your way. But if you start choking on a hairball, don't come crying to me."

A shrill ringing stopped him. Pamela reached inside

her purse and pulled out her cell phone, then flipped down the mouthpiece. "Hello?"

"Pam?" Jo asked.

"Oh, hi, Jo," she said for Alan's benefit.

He frowned and took a huge gulp of beer.

"I was hoping I could talk to Alan," Jo said. "You know, explain what happened."

"Alan?" Pam asked, raising her eyebrows.

He shook his head no and waved his arms frantically, mouthing the words "No way."

"Uh, you just missed him," Pam said. "He went to get a beer."

"Are you both having fun?"

"Oh, yeah," Pam said, laughing merrily. "Fun, fun, fun."

"Oh, good. Would you tell Alan I called and that I hope we can talk when he gets back?" She hesitated. "And that I'm really sorry for how things turned out?"

"Sure thing," Pam said, giving Alan a tight smile.

"And Pam," Jo said. "Thanks again for being such a good friend to me and to Alan."

"Don't mention it," Pam answered, then folded up the phone. "Jo said she hopes the two of you can talk when you get back, and that she's really sorry for how things turned out."

Alan downed the rest of his beer, then slid the plastic cup across the bar for a refill. "On second thought, I think I'll stay right here and get drunk," Alan said, settling on the stool Enrico had vacated.

Pam rested one hip on the corner of the neighboring stool. "I don't know if that's such a good idea," she warned with a half smile. "The last time you got drunk, you invited me to go on your honeymoon."

One corner of his mouth lifted. ''This is one for the record books,'' he said, shaking his head. ''Do you suppose I'm the only man in history who won't get laid on his honeymoon?''

''Well,'' Pam said slowly, ''it doesn't have to be that way.'' When his eyes widened, she stammered, ''I m-mean, there are lots of women on the b-beach...'' Flustered, she swept her hand in the air. ''Take what's-her-name in the hat.''

''Robin,'' he said, then began draining his second beer.

''Robin!'' she seconded, nodding. ''Nice teeth.''

''Cute figure,'' he said.

''If you go for the boyish look,'' Pam agreed, still nodding.

''Nice legs,'' he said.

''Thick ankles,'' she murmured.

''Pretty hair.''

''Sloppy dye job.''

''Are we talking about the same woman?'' Alan asked, angling his head. ''I talked to her for twenty minutes and you saw her for what—twenty seconds? How did you notice all those things?''

Pam shrugged. ''A woman knows.''

''I thought she was nice.''

''She was nice,'' Pam agreed. ''*If* you're going to settle for nice.''

''What's wrong with nice?'' Alan asked.

''It's boring.''

''One person's boredom is another person's reliability.''

She sighed, exasperated. ''We're talking about a beach fling, Alan. Reliability doesn't even make the list." She turned and gestured to the crowd around them, deciding she'd have to get the ball rolling for him. "Look—women everywhere—just pick one."

Alan turned slowly on the stool. "You make it sound so, so..."

"Spontaneous?"

"I was going to say cheap."

"What about the redhead in the corner?" she asked, pointing her pinkie.

"She's cute," Alan agreed with a halfhearted shrug.

"Well, don't get too excited," she warned sarcastically. "I suppose you prefer brunettes."

"Not really," he said, draining his beer and smiling. "It's been a while since I went looking for a woman, but I don't think I discriminate."

Pam finished her beer and accepted a refill. She was already getting a buzz since she hadn't eaten much all day. "How about the one in the green bikini?"

He looked and squinted. "She's kind of skinny, don't you think?"

"I thought men liked skinny women."

"Slender, great. Curvy, even better. But skinny, no way," he said, shaking his head.

"The yellow shorts and piled-up hair?"

"A definite possibility," he conceded slowly.

Pam frowned and gulped her beer. "She laughs like a seal, though. I can hear her barking from here."

"Wow, look at the one in the red suit," he said, leaning forward slightly.

Pam squinted, then dismissed her with a wave. "They're fake," she said with confidence.

"How do you know?"

"Can't you tell? They don't move."

"Well, she isn't on a trampoline. Besides—" he turned a wolfish grin her way "—I hate to break it to you, Pam, but most men don't care if they're real or not."

"You don't have to tell *me* about men," she said.

He adopted an expression of mock remorse. "Sorry—I forgot I was talking to the source." He frowned. "I'm curious—is there a straight man in Savannah who isn't after you?"

She grinned. "Two Baptist reverends, and you."

Alan saluted her with his drink. "Gee, thanks—you do wonders for my ego. Ever been married?"

"Nope."

"How have you managed that?"

Pam ran a finger around the rim of the plastic cup and pursed her lips. Then she gave a little shrug and said, "I've never fallen in love."

He scoffed. "I think falling in love is a vicious rumor that was started thousands of years ago by the world's first wedding director."

She giggled, then sighed as memories washed over her. "I came close once—I was seventeen and looking for a way out of the projects. He was nineteen and had the world by the tail."

"What happened?"

"He also had two other girls by the tail."

"Oh."

"That's when I decided it was much safer to play the field rather than risking it all on one horse. And I've been hedging my bets ever since."

"Hey," he said, holding up his hand. "Forget the horses—I don't want to hear about the kinky stuff."

Pam giggled.

Alan polished off another beer. "What's your secret for staying single?"

"It's easy," she said. Leaning forward, she whispered, "Don't close your eyes."

"What?"

"When you kiss—don't close your eyes."

He looked dubious. "That's your secret weapon?"

She nodded emphatically, and noticed the room still bounced slightly even when she stopped. "When you close your eyes during a kiss, your mind starts playing all kinds of games. You start to imagine a make-believe world where love conquers all. And you forget that most marriages end in divorce—or worse."

"My parents seem pretty happy," he said.

"That's nice," she said, and meant it. "My dad split when we were little, so I barely remember my folks together."

"I'm sorry."

She smiled sadly. "Me, too. That's why I'd rather stay single and childless than risk dragging kids through a mess."

"I'm for the childless part," Alan noted wryly. "A toast," he said, lifting his cup to hers, "to keeping your eyes open."

"Hear, hear," she agreed, touching her cup to his, then giggled when beer sloshed over the side. A gust of cold air blew over them and Pam shivered. Dusk was approaching, and the temperature had dropped dramatically. "I think I'll go back to the room and change."

Alan climbed down from the stool slowly. "I need to check in with my secretary and see if she found us a room. I'm not anxious to spend another night in Hotel Hell.''

''It's not so bad,'' she said as they walked, picking their way carefully back down the unlit path. The clear night and bright moon made the going easier, and the now-deserted white beach stretched below them like a wide satin ribbon. ''Ooh, look at all the stars,'' she said, waving her hand overhead. ''Let's go for a walk.''

''Anything to avoid going back to the room,'' he agreed, falling in step behind her.

She pulled loose pants from her canvas bag and stepped into them, then decided to carry her sandals. ''The sand looks like snow,'' she said, digging in her toes. The tide was coming in, eating away at the beach and forcing them to choose a higher path. The air felt cool and invigorating and Pam tried hard to focus on anything but the romantic atmosphere as they headed down the beach toward their hotel. Millions of stars twinkled overhead and, as always, simply thinking about the distances their mere existence represented left her breathless. And coupled with the sight of Alan's handsome face silhouetted in the moonlight, she was left downright light-headed. ''Alan, do you really think there's life on other planets?''

''Sure,'' he said without hesitation. ''I think it's pretty arrogant to think the entire universe was created just for us.''

She tingled in appreciation of his honesty—she could never broach this subject with any of the men she dated. ''I agree—but it's a little scary, don't you think?''

He shook his head. ''Nah, if they were going to harm us, they would have done it by now.'' Then he grinned.

"Besides, with all our societal and environmental problems, Earth is probably the laughingstock of the universe."

"What you're telling me," she said with a chuckle, "is that I clawed my way out of one slum simply to exist in a larger one?"

"In a manner of speaking," he conceded with a laugh.

"Okay, the 'P' stands for 'pessimistic,' right?"

He laughed again, something she was beginning to look forward to. "So I'm not the most upbeat person, especially this week." He brushed against her accidentally and her arm burned from the contact. They walked past several tall dunes, which cast tall shadows over them, throwing them into almost complete darkness.

"What doesn't kill you will make you stronger," she said, wondering for whose benefit she was speaking— Alan's or hers? She stumbled on a clump of grass and yelped, grabbing Alan's arm on the way down. But she caught him off guard and he fell with her. Pam grunted when she landed, then was struck with the thought that being horizontal felt pretty good. She gingerly lifted her head and saw Alan sprawling face first next to her. When he raised onto his elbows, his face was covered with a layer of white sand. Pam burst out laughing.

"You," he said with mock fierceness, "are dead meat."

She shrieked and tried to scramble to her feet, but he grabbed her bare ankle and yanked her down to the sand. Weak with laughter, she tried to crawl away from him, but he dragged her back and rolled her over, pinning her arms down.

Her laughter petered out at the closeness of his face

to hers in the darkness, and a warning siren screamed in her head. He lay half on top of her, his chest against hers. His T-shirt had worked up and she felt the warm skin of his stomach through the flimsy cover-up she wore. Every muscle in her body tensed and her pulse pounded in her ears. "Alan—" she said in a shaky voice.

"Pam," he cut in with a hoarse whisper, his breath fanning her lips. "Please don't tell me to stop, because then I'll have to."

She couldn't see his eyes, but she could hear the loneliness, the desperation in his voice. "Alan," she croaked with as much strength as she could muster.

He sighed slowly and lifted his head a few inches in resignation. "What?"

Seconds stretched into a minute as the waves crashed behind them and the love scene in *From Here To Eternity* passed before her eyes. God, Alan was so sexy and so…so…so *here*. Who cared about eternity? "Kiss me," she said breathlessly.

For a while, he was completely still, and she wondered if perhaps he hadn't heard her. But then he lowered his mouth with such sweet slowness, she was able to anticipate the feel of his lips on hers and ready herself for his taste. His lips were like velvet, she thought, as her mouth opened for his. When his mouth met hers, Pam moaned at the surge of desire that swelled in her chest. If she had expected tentativeness, those expectations were banished immediately. It was as if his lips knew hers, as if they had explored the surface and depths of her mouth many times. His tongue boldly tangled with hers in a slashing, grinding dance and he shuddered, offering a deep groan that echoed down her throat.

The urgency of their kiss increased and he released her arms to seek out more forbidden areas. He caressed her collarbone, then blazed a trail south to cup her breast and thumb the beaded nipple, practically the only skin her bathing-suit top covered. She arched her body into him, and slid her hands under his shirt to feel the hard wall of muscle across his back. He kneed her legs open, then shifted to lie cradled between her thighs.

Longing pulsed through her body and moisture gathered at her core where he pressed the hard ridge of his erection against her. Slipping her hands below his waistband, she gripped the smooth rounds of his hard buttocks, her mind spinning with the responses he evoked from her body. He lifted his head and gasped, "Not here. Someone might—"

She cut him off with a deep kiss, then whispered, "The beach is deserted, no one will see us. Besides," she murmured, yanking his T-shirt over his head, "I think it's kind of exciting."

In a flurry of sand, she pushed down his trunks and dragged them off with her feet. He lay naked on top of her, kissing her deeply and kneading her covered breasts with a slow intensity that told her he planned to take his time undressing her, enjoying her. She writhed beneath him, urging him on with her wandering hands, anxious to explore his body.

Then a blinding light flashed over his shoulder, directly in Pam's eyes. "Hold it right there, mister," said a gruff male voice.

Alan stiffened, then lifted his head and swung to

look over his shoulder. He raised his arm to shield his eyes. "What the hell?"

"Police," the man boomed, thumping his badge unnecessarily since the uniform said it all. "Stand up slowly and put your hands in the air."

Alan scoffed. "You can't be serious—"

"I said, on your feet!"

Pam's heart pounded in her chest and she squeezed her eyes shut, unable to watch. When she finally chanced a glance, Alan stood squinting into the cop's light with his arms in the air, hosting a monster erection.

"God," the cop said, wincing.

"I hope that means you'll let me find my pants," Alan snapped, outraged.

"Make it quick," the officer said. "I'd hate to haul you in naked."

"What?" Alan barked. Pam sprang up, her heart in her throat.

The cop gave him a sneering smile and pulled out a pair of handcuffs. "This is a family beach, you pervert. You're under arrest for indecent exposure."

8

"I'VE NEVER BEEN so humiliated in my life," Alan declared as he followed Pam out of the city jail and squinted into the late-afternoon sun. She looked chipper in her crisp white shorts and red silk blouse. He, on the other hand, still sported the sand-crusted swimming trunks and T-shirt he'd been wearing last night when the cop hauled him into jail like a common criminal. Between the cot he'd slept on and the realization that he and Pamela Kaminski had been minutes away from sharing carnal knowledge, he hadn't slept a wink.

"No one will find out," Pam said in a soothing voice.

"Oh, really?" he asked. "Is that like, 'It's deserted, no one will see us'?"

She frowned. "I said I was sorry a hundred times—didn't you hear me?"

"One hundred thirty-six times," he corrected. "I heard you during the entire walk to the squad car last night, *and* as you ran alongside the police car when we drove away, *and* this morning in the courtroom while the judge was lecturing me—" He stopped and stared toward the street in disbelief, then pressed his palms against his temples. "Pam, are you nuts?"

"What?" She pushed the cheap sunglasses high on

her forehead and unlocked the door to the powder blue limo.

"You left this pimpmobile parked in a fire zone in *front* of the jail for two hours?"

She shrugged her lovely shoulders. "I turned on the hazard lights."

"Oh, well," he said with as much sarcasm as he could muster. "I didn't realize you'd turned on the *hazard* lights." He summoned a dry laugh. "After all, everyone knows that hazard lights cancel out every broken law. Mow down a pedestrian? No problem, just turn on your hazards."

"Well, it's still here, isn't it?" she demanded hotly.

"Who the hell else would want it?" he cried, feeling on the verge of hysteria.

She pointed to the passenger side. "Just get in, will you?"

"Oh, no," he said, holding out his hand for the keys. "You are *not* driving."

"I drove here without any problems!"

"Oh, really?" Alan crossed his arms, then nodded toward the front fender. "And I suppose that telephone pole–size dent just appeared from nowhere?"

She bit her bottom lip, and handed over the keys in silence.

"Thank you," he said, then opened the driver-side door just as a police car pulled up behind the limo with its siren silent but flashing. When the young cop stepped out, he had already begun writing the ticket.

"Sir," he said in a pleasant voice. "Do you have any idea what the fine is for parking in a fire lane in front of a government building?" Alan closed his eyes and counted to ten.

A few minutes later, Pam studied the pink carbon copy the police officer had given him and whistled low. "A hundred and forty-five dollars?"

"Do me a favor," he said calmly, gripping the steering wheel so hard his hands hurt. "Just sit over there and don't talk."

"Look, Alan, I know you're upset—"

"Upset?" he crowed. "Just because I'm now considered a sex offender? Why would that upset me?"

"It's not as bad as you make it sound."

"Before yesterday, I'd never even received a speeding ticket."

Pam lay her head back. "Do you realize you can rearrange the letters in your name to spell 'anal'?"

He scowled in her direction. "I'm not going to apologize for being a law-abiding citizen."

"Your secretary called last night."

His stomach twisted. "You talked to Linda?"

"Relax, I told her I worked for the hotel and all your calls were being routed to me. She found you a room."

"Finally, some good news," he said, his shoulders dropping in relief.

"I told her you changed your mind."

He weaved over the centerline. "What?"

"She needed an answer immediately, and I didn't know how long you'd be in jail..." Her voice trailed off and she raised her hands in a helpless gesture. Her manicured nails had gone from peach to bright red during his incarceration.

"I'll call her later to see if the room is still available," he said. "Right now, even the broken couch in Hotel Hell sounds good." Then the thought struck him that Pam might think they'd be sharing the same bed, after what nearly transpired last night. Except now that he'd had a few idle hours to ponder their lapse, he realized what a huge mistake it would have been. No matter how much he *wanted* to sleep with Pam, only a jerk would have rebound sex with his ex-fiancée's best friend. Besides, he admitted begrudgingly, as infuriating as she could be, Pam was starting to grow on him, and he didn't want to tread on their burgeoning friendship, didn't want to be relegated to her bottomless dating pool. "I'll call and see if the pullout bed can be fixed."

"Done," Pam said with a little smile. "This morning I slipped the maintenance man a twenty and he fixed it in no time."

"Great," Alan said, nodding.

"Yeah," she said.

After a pregnant pause, they both spoke at the same time.

"About last night—" she said.

"I want to apologize—" he said, then stopped and they both looked away and laughed awkwardly.

"It was the moon and the stars—"

"—and the beer and the ocean," she added.

"I was still feeling a little rejected over the wedding—"

"—and I was feeling lonely."

"What a big mistake it would have been," he said, attempting a casual laugh.

"Huge," she agreed.

"Gigantic—"

"Colossal—"

"What with you being Jo's best friend—"

"—and you being Jo's ex-fiancé."

Feeling relieved, Alan inhaled deeply. "So we're in agreement." Then he glanced over and realized with a sinking feeling that despite his new resolve, he still wasn't immune to her remarkable beauty.

"Completely in agreement," she assured him with a bright smile.

SHE HAD DONE a lot of stupid things in her relatively short life, Pam decided the next day as she lay in a rental chaise on the beach and watched a kidney-shaped cloud move across the otherwise clear sky. But all of them rolled into one wouldn't have compared to the absolute brainlessness she would have exhibited if that cop hadn't shown up the night before last.

Luckily, Alan seemed to agree with her and they had touched on, danced around and sidestepped the issue of their sexual attraction while somehow agreeing that the sex act itself would have been a grievous error. The logical side of her brain had no problem going along with that argument, but the emotional side of her brain kept remembering the feelings raging through her that night when Alan kissed her—after all her bragging, she had actually closed her eyes! And though she had definitely responded to him on a physical level, he had also stirred something deep inside her. Alan had accidentally managed to blaze a trail where no man had gone before, and the realization saddened her because a relationship between them was impossible. Unthinkable. Inconceivable.

He was still in love with her best friend, for God's sake. And she wasn't about to return to Savannah arm in arm with Alan and have Jo think they had been carrying on behind her back all these years. Besides,

Alan P. Parish came from Savannah's most prosperous family, while she came from Savannah's most prose-*cuted* family. He wouldn't be interested in anything other than a sexual relationship with her. Typically, such a revelation wouldn't bother her, but she was starting to feel a weird sort of affection for the man, striking a memory chord from when she'd first known him in high school. Warning bells chimed in her head and some untapped part of her soul telegraphed increasingly urgent distress signals.

SUBJECT IS DANGEROUS STOP HEART IN JEOPARDY STOP PROCEED WITH CAUTION STOP

"Our paths keep crossing." Enrico's undulating voice wafted above her. Pam opened her eyes to see him standing over her, surveying her new red two-piece suit with open admiration. He wore a straw hat and snug little bikini swim trunks that Europeans seemed fond of wearing. Pam pressed her lips together in amusement at the recollection of Alan's scoffing reference to the shiny, elastic garments as "nut-huggers."

"It must be destiny," the dark-skinned man continued with a charming grin.

"Or just a small beach," she offered, making no movement to encourage him to stay. She had enough on her mind, and she felt her patience dwindling.

"Could I interest you in dinner tonight?" he asked. "I know a restaurant where the lobster is fresh and the drinks are strong." He wagged his dark eyebrows and Pam wondered where he or any other man had gotten the idea that women found the gesture provocative.

"I already have dinner plans," she lied. "Thanks anyway."

Enrico's expression grew sultry as he dipped his head. "And do you also have plans for dessert?" he asked, his meaning clear in the husky timbre of his voice.

"I'm on a diet," she said, smiling tightly. "Thanks anyway." Then she retrieved a book from her canvas bag and opened it.

"That man in the bar yesterday, he is your boy-friend?" Enrico pressed.

Pam glanced up from the book, suddenly at the end of her fuse. "No," she said with quiet authority. "He's my husband."

"Oh?" He looked surprised, then pulled a sad face. "And he has left you alone yet again."

"I wore him out," she said evenly, then looked back to her book.

Enrico must have taken the hint because he moved away after a tongue-rolling farewell, but she felt his dark gaze linger over her and shivered.

The book was one that Alan had purchased, one she'd devoured years ago, but it was worth another read. Especially if it took her mind off Alan, who lay spread-eagle on the water bed where he'd slept since returning from jail yesterday afternoon. She had eaten dinner alone last night and crawled into the lumpy pull-out bed where she'd lain awake for hours thinking about the man only a few feet away.

She sighed and immersed herself in a world of fantasy and science fiction, caught up in interstellar wars, life and romance in the next millennium.

In the early afternoon, she gave in to hunger pangs and walked up the path to the grill. After ordering a messy hot dog, she sat down at a table overlooking the beach to sort through the last few days' disturbing turn of events.

The crowds had thinned a bit since the locals had resumed their midweek work schedules, leaving behind vacationers and snowbirds who seemed to group almost exclusively by twos. With a start, she remembered that today was Valentine's Day, so no wonder everyone was paired off—lots of folks were probably here for their anniversary since February fourteenth seemed to be a popular date for weddings. The bartender confirmed her theory by announcing a couples' sand castle-building contest for the remainder of the afternoon, with the winning pair to receive a romantic dinner at a local seafood restaurant.

Her mind wandered to Alan and she hoped he was resting. As if on cue, he emerged from the trees that hid the pebbly path below their balcony. To her dismay, her pulse kicked up as she watched him move with natural athleticism down the slight incline and out onto the white sand. A towel lay around his wide shoulders, and he carried a small gym bag, which she surmised was full of books. His head pivoted as he scanned the area. Was he looking for her? she wondered with a little smile. Then he waved to someone farther down the beach and Pam forgot to chew the food in her mouth as she spotted Robin the Computer Lady and her big floppy hat.

Swallowing painfully, she watched as Robin stopped and waited for Alan to walk to her, which he seemed eager to do, she noted wryly. Today Robin wore a high-necked tank suit of boring brown, but Pam conceded her legs were long and slim. From a distance, the woman's resemblance to Jo was uncanny. She held on to her hat with one hand as she tilted her head back to smile up at Alan. Pam stabbed her chili dog with enough force to snap the plastic fork.

And Alan seemed to have recovered from his ill mood, she noticed as he offered the woman a broad smile. Robin gestured in the direction from which she'd come and Alan nodded happily, seemingly anxious to follow her…where? To her blanket? Pam sank her teeth into her bottom lip. To lunch? She shredded the paper napkin in her lap. To her room? Pam felt something akin to gas pain in her stomach. At least if he had a fling with Robin, she reasoned, the sexual tension hanging between herself and Alan would be relieved. And maybe they'd be able to get through the rest of the week and arrive back in Savannah with all friendships intact.

The computer couple stopped after a few steps and Robin squirmed, pointing to her shoulder. Alan stopped, investigated and brushed away the offending object. *Oh, brother—the old "something's on me, will you get it off, you big strong he-man" trick.* Pam rolled her eyes. *Amateur.*

But Alan must have been convinced because he inched closer to Robin as they strolled away. When Pam could no longer see them from her chair, she stood up. When they disappeared past tiptoe level, she walked to the corner of the deck. "Go for it, Alan," she muttered as she hung out over the edge with her back foot hooked around the railing to keep from falling. "I couldn't care less."

THE POOL AT THE RESORT where Robin was staying glimmered blue and white, interrupted only by a few adults who lounged in one corner, with firm grips around their drinks. Alan sat next to Robin, bored with shoptalk and hoping something conversational would pop into his head. Accepting her invitation to join her at the pool had seemed like a good idea an hour ago, but now he was feeling restless. For some maddening reason, Alan couldn't keep his mind off where and with whom Pam had found entertainment for the afternoon.

"What's wrong?" Robin asked cheerfully.

"Nothing," he assured her. She was very attractive, and had pulled her chair so close to his she'd pinched her fingers between the two arms. And if he had any doubts she was interested in him physically, they were banished when he felt her bare foot caress his leg from calf to ankle. Startled, he stiffened.

She flashed him a flirty smile. "Want to take a swim? The pool is heated."

"Sure," he said, pushing back from the table, suddenly wanting to escape. He followed her into the shallow end, then swam the length of the pool, not at all surprised when she surfaced near him at the other end. With the concrete wall at his back, he closed his eyes and raised his face to the sun.

"Great day," she said, allowing her body to graze his beneath the water.

"Mmm." He really should find Pamela and apologize for being so cross yesterday.

"I always stay in this resort when I'm in town," she continued.

"Nice," he murmured.

"My room has a fabulous view," Robin said near his ear, and several seconds passed before her meaning sank in. She rubbed her breast against his arm and his eyes popped open.

Her mouth curved provocatively. "Want to go up for a look?"

Alan glanced at her and realized with a sinking feeling that she reminded him of Jo—in more ways than one. Although Jo had never been as forward as Robin, he experienced the same mild stirring of sexual interest when he looked at the slim woman in her sensible brown bathing suit. All the time he had dated Jo, he'd hoped their relationship would become more sensual, but now he had to admit that their chemistry had never been quite right. And while he had loved Jo from the beginning, he had never been *in* love with her...had never craved her company so much that he experienced physical pain when he was away from her...had never been tempted to get naked with her on a dark beach.

"Alan?" Robin whispered, moving in for a kiss. Her mouth shifted against his pleasantly and Alan tried to conjure up some level of desire, especially in light of his new revelation. He absolutely couldn't be falling for Pam....

Robin's mouth became more insistent and Alan awkwardly pulled her against him, running his hands over her slight curves and waiting for his body to respond.

She lifted her head, breathing heavily. "How about that view?"

Alan's mind raced. *Do it, Parish. Get Pam out of your head and out of your system.* "Um, sorry," he said, withdrawing and pushing himself up and out of the pool. "I promised Pam I'd...take her shopping."

Robin stared at him from the water. "You'd rather go shopping with your sister?"

"No," he said hurriedly, grabbing his towel and gym bag. "It's just that I promised...I'll see you later, Robin."

"Count on it," she said pointedly, as if next time he would not get away so easily.

Alan trotted off in relief, then slowed to a walk when he reached the beach. He made his way back up the shore, keeping an eye on the horizon for a Wave Runner rider in an overflowing neon pink wet suit and wrestling with the bombshell of the feelings he harbored for his ex-fiancée's best friend.

Along the way, he noticed several sand castles, some simple, some intricate, and realized a contest was under way. A few hundred yards later, he noticed a loose knot of men had gathered to watch a work in progress. But as he approached, he recognized the fake flower tattoo on the firm hip of Pamela Kaminski. She crawled on all fours and stretched to add yet another tower to the elaborate castle she had created. He smiled wryly at the realization that although her sand fortress was by far the most impressive he'd seen, *Pam's* turrets were gaining far more attention than her castle's.

Seemingly oblivious to the attention, her head was bent in concentration, although she kept brushing back a strand of golden hair that had escaped the high ponytail. The red bikini was a masterpiece, he acknowledged, marveling at the way she filled it to bursting yet managed to keep everything safely in place as she moved around. His body began to harden at the memory of her lying beneath him in the sand. But knowing that train of thought led to a dead end, he forced himself to squash the provocative vision. Uncomfortable with the thought of being a part of the ogling crowd, he stepped forward and announced, "There you are!" in a loud voice.

Pam glanced up and smiled, then sat back on her heels, offering a mouth-drying view of her cleavage. Her breasts were confined by two tiny triangles of cloth that had to be much stronger than they looked. "Hi," she said, and Alan could almost hear the groans of dismay as the men realized their up-close perusal had come to an end. One by one, they drifted away.

"Are you alone?" she asked, peering around him.

"Yeah," he said, suddenly wondering how he could have been so angry with her yesterday.

She turned her attention back to the sand castle. "Have you been in bed all this time?"

"Pretty much," he said, shrugging. "But I feel much better."

"That's nice," she said tightly, but she didn't look up.

She was probably still miffed at him for the way he'd behaved yesterday afternoon, he reasoned. "I'm sorry I was so grouchy when you came to pick me up," he said, not sure why he felt the need to get back into her good graces. "I did appreciate it."

"It's okay," she said in a tone that didn't sound okay. Then she glanced over her shoulder. "You got it all out of your system, right?"

"Right," he said, hoping he looked properly contrite. "Truce?"

"Truce," she said with a suddenly cheerful smile, then stood and dusted sand from her knees.

"Hey," he said, studying her design. "You need a moat." He took one of the buckets she'd been using as a mold and filled it with water, then fed the small channel she'd dug around the perimeter of the castle. After several trips, the moat was filled, and she nodded, satisfied with his contribution.

"That's quite a spread, little lady," the bartender from the grill said as he made his way toward them. "Nice castle, too," he muttered to Alan with an envious wink as he walked by. The chubby fellow shook her hand and gave her an envelope. "The best sand castle by far—you two have a real nice Valentine's Day dinner." Then his expression turned serious. "Be careful after dark, though—I hear we have a pervert on the loose, some naked guy scaring women and little kids."

Alan frowned, but at least Pam managed to restrain herself until the man had walked away. "Pervert?" She threw her head back and laughed. "Is that what the 'P' stands for?"

"Ha, ha, very funny."

"Here," she said, handing him the envelope and wiping her eyes. "You and Robin have a nice evening."

"Robin?" He shook his head. "I've spent all the time with her today that I want to. What about Enrico?"

"Somehow I don't think he'd be much of a dinner companion," she said, and Alan got her meaning loud and clear: the man was a lover, not a talker. He tried to stem the jealousy that flooded his chest, but the thought of Pam with another man was crushing. Had she rendezvoused with the hairy horndog last night or this morning—or both?

"Looks like we're stuck with each other, then," he

said with a casual shrug that belied the emotions raging through him.

"Looks like it," she said, falling a little short of looking happy at the prospect herself.

PIER TWENTY-EIGHT was bustling with couples celebrating Valentine's Day. Boasting a large bar, a roving Italian quartet and a great oceanside view, Pam could see why. As they waited at the bar for their table, she noticed Alan's gaze lingering on her again. Although she had hoped his little diversion with Robin would ease the situation, she had felt more on edge than ever while they were getting ready for dinner.

Just to be safe, she had emerged from the bathroom already dressed in a simple deep pink sleeveless sheath, but she'd felt him watching her while she piled her hair on her head with various combs. And she had to admit she struggled to keep her attention elsewhere while he applied lotion to his reddish shoulders before donning a dress shirt.

He did look fabulous, she decided, and allowed herself a bit of pride to be on his arm tonight. When they had attended functions together in Savannah, it had been different—everyone knew he was devoted to Jo, so Pam had never entertained thoughts of what kind of couple she and Alan might make. But now she knew they were garnering a fair share of attention, and she conceded they looked like a classic "match": tall with blond hair and glowing tans. But looks could be deceiving, she noted with a little twist of her heart.

"Well, if it isn't the newlyweds," a man's voice said behind her. Pam registered Alan's slight frown before she turned to see Cheek and Lila, the senior-citizen couple who, thankfully, they hadn't seen naked in a while.

"Cheek," Lila said with a motherly smile. "They're not married, remember? They're just friends, right?"

"Right," Alan and Pam said in unison.

"Wasn't it a lovely day?" Lila continued, waving vaguely toward the beach.

"Great dress," Cheek said bluntly, talking to Pam's breasts.

"Er, thanks," Pam said as Alan cleared his throat.

"You're getting a nice tan," Lila commented.

"I was on the beach all day," Pam told her.

"This beach?" Cheek asked in amazement. He leaned forward then glanced around as if he were about to divulge military secrets. "There's a nude beach about twenty miles away," he said in a conspiratorial tone. "It's five bucks a head, but it's worth it," he finished with an emphatic curt nod.

"We'll keep that in mind," Alan said tightly.

The man turned to Pam and said, "If you decide to go, we'd be glad to give you a ride."

"I said," Alan said, his tone louder and his expression harder, "we'll keep it in mind."

"Great," Cheek said, completely missing the rebuff. "You want to see if we can get a table for four?"

"No!" Pam and Alan nearly shouted together.

"Uh, it's a very special occasion for us," she said with a smile, leaning into Alan.

He put his arm around her waist and nodded. "We really wanted to be alone tonight."

"Oohhhhhhh," Lila sang, her eyes twinkling and her finger wagging. "Friends indeed! Do I hear wedding bells?"

Pam scrambled for something to say to get rid of the couple without embarrassing Alan further. "I guess you could say it was the idea of wedding bells that brought us to Fort Myers, right, Alan?"

He hesitated only a few seconds. "Oh...right."

Lila laughed delightedly. "Dingdong, dingdong." Her head bounced left, then right.

Pam tingled at the intimacy and awkwardness of the conversation. Thankfully, their name was called and they said a hasty goodbye.

"*Talk* about dingdongs," Alan muttered as they followed a waiter to their table.

"They're harmless," she said, waving off his concern.

"They should be somewhere playing shuffleboard instead of scaring up entertainment for a nude-beach matinee," he said as he held out her chair.

The waiter handed them their menus, took their wine order and left.

Pam laughed and opened her menu. "Percy," she said.

"What?"

"Your middle name—Percy?"

He scoffed and rolled his eyes. "No."

"Pendleton?"

"No."

"Pernicious?"

He laughed. "No. Forget it—I'm not telling you."

"Will you tell me if I guess it?"

He dropped his gaze to his menu. "Sure, because you'll never guess it."

"Pembroke?"

"No—and that's enough."

"Who knows it?"

"Only my parents and siblings—and they're sworn to secrecy."

"Jo doesn't even know?"

"Nope. What looks good?"

Pam bit her tongue to keep from saying that he looked mighty tasty. "Probably the orange roughy."

"Fried, of course."

"Of course."

"How about lobster?"

Pam winced at the price. "I don't think the gift certificate will cover lobster."

"Screw the certificate—last night I slept through dinner, and the night before I had a roll of breath mints in jail." He folded the menu and gave it a light smack. "I'm having lobster."

She watched as Alan craned his neck, looking all around. "Our waiter said he'd be right back," she reminded him.

"I know—I'm making sure they didn't seat us near a bunch of kids. I specifically asked for no kids."

"Relax—I don't see any kids."

"They can hide," he assured her, lifting the tablecloth for a peek.

"The 'P' stands for 'paranoid,'" she declared.

"Would you stop with the 'P' stuff already?"

"Alan, kids have to eat, too."

"Fine—as long as they're not sitting near me. Nearly every time Jo and I—" He stopped and a strange look came over his face. "There I go again."

Pam's heart twisted at the hurt that flashed in his eyes. "Alan, you have a lot of history with Jo—you can talk about her. Nearly every time you and Jo what?'' Jo had divulged that her and Alan's sex life had been practically nonexistent, so she was relatively sure he wasn't going to say something too personal. Because of Jo's comments, Pam had always labeled Alan as a wet fish, but now she was doubting her best friend's judgment.

He straightened, but his cheer seemed forced. ''Nearly every time Jo and I ate out, it seemed like some spoiled kid would ruin it—screaming, throwing food.'' He passed his hand over his face and a dry laugh escaped his mouth. ''Now I'm wondering if things were going sour between us, and I was simply looking for any excuse to explain the awkwardness.''

''What's so bad about kids anyway?'' she asked.

He opened his mouth to answer, then looked puzzled. ''I don't know—they're loud—''

''I'm loud.''

''And messy—''

''I'm messy.''

''And the diapers—''

''Okay, you got me there,'' she said with a grin.

''Do you like kids?'' he asked, his eyebrows raised in surprise.

Pam shrugged. ''I practically raised my kid sister.''

''I didn't know you had a kid sister.''

Pride swelled in her chest every time she thought of Dinah. ''She's ten years younger—twenty-two. I sent her to *your* high school, except I made sure she finished,'' she added with a laugh.

''Where is she now?''

''Finishing up at Notre Dame,'' she said with satisfaction. ''But she'll probably start law school this fall.''

Alan whistled low. ''Not bad.''

"Well, I wanted to make sure one of the Kaminskis ended up successful and on the right side of the law," she said, thinking about her thuggy brothers.

"You're doing all right for yourself," Alan said. "Top sales producer for the largest realty company in Savannah."

Pam tingled under his praise, but knew that no matter what her achievements, she was, and would always be, a Kaminski. Dinah had informed her she would not be coming back to Savannah to practice, and Pam suspected the blight on the family name had influenced her decision. Looking across the table at a man whose name alone put him out of her reach, Pam suddenly felt queasy.

"Will you order for me?" she asked, then excused herself to the ladies' room, telling herself she had to banish the ridiculous thoughts that galloped through her head every time she looked at Alan.

In the rest room, she splashed cold water on her neck, then pondered the wisdom of leaving Alan in Fort Myers and returning to Savannah early. Once she was back in her normal surroundings, these crazy feelings for Alan would evaporate. She could fabricate something about being needed at her office, and make her getaway. The fact that she didn't want to leave him was frightening enough to cinch her decision. She left the ladies' room feeling sad but resolute.

On the way back to the table, a male voice stopped her. "We *must* stop meeting like this, Pamela."

She turned to find Enrico dressed in black slacks and a shiny red shirt. Annoyance fueled her temper. "I can't stop to chat—I need to get back to my table."

His smile was slow and syrupy as he fell in step

beside her. "Did your husband bring you or has he abandoned you once again?"

"No," Pam said through clenched teeth as she walked. "We're having a quiet, romantic dinner." But he followed her around the corner, where she came up short.

Alan stood by their table, sharing a deep kiss with Robin the computer lady.

9

SEVERAL SECONDS PASSED before Alan registered the fact that Robin, who had appeared from nowhere, was kissing him very hard and very invasively. After he managed to untangle his tongue from hers, he clasped her arms and gently pushed her away. Her eyes held the slight glaze of drunkenness. "Robin," he said with a little laugh, "I don't think this is the place."

"Oh? Then how about here?" she slurred, yanking his waistband hard. The button on his fly popped off and flipped up in the air.

A gasp sounded behind him. "Alan, how could you?" He wheeled to see Lila and Cheek standing near him, being led to a table. Lila stood with her hand over her heart. "I thought you were going to propose to Pamela tonight."

"P*rrrr*opose?"

Alan turned the opposite direction, toward Enrico's rolling voice. The dark-haired man stood just a few steps away, with a possessive hand on Pamela's waist. Alan frowned. Where had *he* come from?

Enrico's expression was black as he stared at Pam. "I thought the two of you were already married!" Pam looked at Alan. Her mouth opened and closed, but no sound came out.

"Married?" Robin yelped, jerking his attention back to her. "I thought she was your sister!"

"Sister?" Lila shrieked, and he swung his head back to see the older woman's face twisted in distaste. "That's disgusting."

Cheek appeared slightly less distraught. "Well, it's illegal anyway."

Everyone started talking at once, and Robin advanced on him, her eyes narrowed, and her steps wobbly. "Alan, what the hell is going on?"

Alan held up his hands. "Wait a minute. *Wait a minute!*" The group quieted. He took a deep breath and a step backward, then fell over a potted fern, landing on his tailbone hard enough to set his glasses askew. The waiter hurried over to help him up, but Alan, clawing the air in frustration, brushed him off. He scrambled to his feet, straightened his clothes, then made chopping motions in the air to punctuate his point.

"Look...you...you *people!* Pamela and I came to have a nice, quiet Valentine's Day dinner." He felt a vein bulging at his temple. "The nature of our relationship is nobody's business!" He yanked up his pants by his sagging waistband. "Now, I'll thank everyone to move along!"

Lila and Cheek were the first to bustle away, then Robin and Enrico slipped off in the same direction. Alan had the brief thought that the two of them should get together, then he looked at Pam and swept an arm awkwardly toward the table. "Shall we?"

She nodded, then stooped and picked up his wayward button. She handed it to him, then moved stiffly to her place at the table. After pulling out her chair, Alan reclaimed his seat, snapping the napkin before settling it over his lap. For several long minutes, they toyed with their wineglasses and fingered the silverware.

Although he couldn't fathom why, Alan felt as if he owed Pam an explanation. When he could stand the silence no longer, he cleared his throat. "I wasn't kissing her, you know."

"Not that it matters," she said, sipping the wine that had been served in her absence. "But the lipstick on your mouth, nose, ear and eyelid proves otherwise."

He swiped the napkin across his face, frowning at the reddish stain that transferred. "I mean I wasn't kissing her *back*."

"Like I said, it doesn't matter."

"I guess not," he conceded with a wave, "since you were skulking in the hall with your Latin lover."

She frowned. "My lover? Where on earth did you get that idea?"

His heart lifted a notch. "You haven't been messing around with him?"

Pam rolled her eyes. "If I wanted to mess around with him, why would I have told him you and I were married?"

Unexplained relief flooded through him. "And he believed it?"

"Crazy, huh?" she asked with a little laugh. "That someone would think we were husband and wife?"

"Yeah," he said, joining her laughter. "Ridiculous."

"I mean, you and me—" Pam's giggles escalated.

"Right," he said, laughing harder. *"Mr. and Mrs. Alan Parish."*

She roared. *"P-Pamela P-Parish!"*

Alan wiped his eyes and took a big gulp of wine. "The way the last couple of days have been going, I suppose anything seems possible."

"It's been an adventure," she agreed.

He sighed and glanced across the table, struck anew by her glowing beauty. Pam looked like a movie star, her hair and skin wrought with gold, her mouth wide, her eyes shining. Her gaze met his and Alan's ears started ringing. He felt as if he were teetering on the edge of a precipice, in danger of falling into a pit so deep he might never return. The notion skating through his mind, the emotion blooming in his chest was nothing short of insanity. He was falling for Pamela Kaminski.

Pam's smile evaporated and she squirmed in her chair. Looking into her glass, she said, "I was thinking about leaving tomorrow."

Alan stopped and choked on the wine in his throat. "Leaving? You mean, going back to Savannah?"

She nodded.

He experienced the panicky feeling that something wonderful was about to slip through his fingers. "B-but why?"

Pam abandoned her glass and rolled her eyes heavenward, counting on her beautifully manicured fingers. "A bad flight, a flat tire, a dilapidated hotel, a powder blue limo, a police record..." Her voice trailed off. "You came to the beach for a week of R&R," she said. "And so far it's been more like a week of S&M."

"Well, it hasn't been your fault," he offered generously.

But she simply smirked.

"Not totally," he added weakly.

"Lying is not one of your talents."

Spotting an opening, he leaned forward with eyebrows raised. "Is that a concession that I have talents elsewhere?"

"No."

Deflated, he sat back. "Oh."

Surprised at the wounded look on his face, Pam scrambled to soothe his hurt feelings. "I mean, I wouldn't know if you had talents elsewhere…" She swallowed and searched for firmer footing. "It's not like Jo and I ever discussed your, uh…anything."

He shifted in his seat. "Well, I should hope not."

"Oh, no," she assured him hurriedly. "Jo and I never talked about what you and she did—or *didn't* do."

Alan pursed his lips. "Didn't do?"

A flush burned her neck on its way up. "I didn't say 'didn't.'"

"Yes, you did."

Panic fluttered in her stomach. "Well, I didn't *mean* 'didn't.' I meant…oh, damn."

He closed his eyes and downed the rest of his wine. After setting his empty glass on the table with a thunk, he inhaled deeply. "So, Jo wasn't happy with our sex life."

Pam shook her head. "She *never* said that."

He flagged the waiter for more wine, then gave her a dry laugh. "Well, I have to admit we didn't exactly keep the sheets ablaze."

She held up her hands. "I don't want to hear this."

"I can't explain it. Jo is a beautiful woman, but when it came to—"

Pam put her hands over her ears and started to hum,

but she could still read his lips, and what she saw made her squeeze her eyes shut. "I'm not listening," she sang. "I'm noooooooooooooot liiiiiisssstennnnnniiiiing. I'm noooooooooooooot liiiiiiissstennnnniiiiing. I'm noooooooooooooot liiiiiiissstennnnnniiiiing." When she opened her eyes, Alan sat staring at her, along with two waiters who stood by the table, their arms loaded with trays. She smiled sheepishly, straightened her napkin, then gestured for them to serve.

During dinner, neither she nor Alan mentioned the subject of her returning to Savannah early. They talked about their respective jobs, mutual acquaintances and state politics. They talked about the Braves and the Hawks and the Falcons and the Thrashers, one advantage of having sports-minded brothers, she noted. They laughed and argued and laughed some more, and Pam hated to see the pleasant meal come to an end.

For dessert, they decided to split a rich, velvety cheesecake with cinnamon topping, which reminded Pam of the unused bottle of body liqueur in their room.

She picked up her utensil and with every luscious bite, she imagined devouring him—biting, licking and swallowing him whole. She savored every succulent bite, allowing the sweetness to melt on her tongue before letting it slide down her throat. The more she ate, the more moist her flimsy panties grew until she nearly moaned aloud. At the sound of Alan's chuckle, she glanced up, afraid she had. Instead, he was simply watching her.

"Was it good?"

"Wonderful," she said, smiling to herself.

"You're killing me," he said, shifting in his seat.

She frowned. "What do you mean?"

"Pam," he said, leaning close and lowering his voice. "Do you always eat dessert with a knife?"

With a start, she stared at the huge, blunt dinner knife in her hand. She glanced up with a sheepish smile, enormously relieved to see the roving Italian musicians were approaching their table.

The men were dressed in brilliant costumes of red, black and gold, with snow-white shirts. The violinist nodded to Alan and kissed Pam's hand, then put his instrument to his shoulder and began to play a sweet, haunting melody, accompanied by the other musicians.

It was almost too much for her—the great food, the good wine, the beautiful music...and Alan's company. She glanced over at him and inhaled sharply at the desire she saw in his blue eyes. He abandoned his napkin, stood and swept his hand toward the tiny vacant area by their table. "May I have this dance?" Then he leaned forward and whispered conspiratorially, "Of course, I'll have to hold you close to keep my pants up."

She grinned, then accepted his hand and allowed him to pull her into his arms for a slow waltz. He was a surprisingly good dancer, with natural rhythm and perfect form. It was a good thing he could lead, she decided with her chin resting on his shoulder, because she was too weak-kneed to do little more than follow. He smelled wonderfully spicy and she ached to taste the skin on his neck. He melded her body to his until she felt every muscle beneath his clothing. They might have been the only two people in the universe. When the music ended, she sensed his reluctance to part was as strong as hers, but with an audience, they had little choice. While the other diners applauded, Alan raised her hand and kissed her fingertips.

"Happy Valentine's Day," he whispered.

Later, on the way back to the hotel, Pam was quiet, consumed by raging desire for the man next to her, yet lamenting the ramifications of her actions. Conversely, Alan seemed downright cheerful, whistling tunelessly under his breath and fidgeting with all the gadgets on the limousine panel until she was ready to scream. The walk from the parking lot to their door seemed interminably long to her.

"Couldn't get that room Linda had reserved, huh?" Pam said, laughing to hide her nervousness as she stepped through the door onto the familiar shag carpet.

"Actually," Alan said with a smile, "I told her I'd changed my mind since we only have two more nights. Want to go down to the beach for a walk?"

Remembering the disastrous results of their last moonlit stroll, she shook her head.

"How about the hot tub?" he asked.

"I'm not fainthearted, Alan, but even *I* am not brave enough to climb into that algae-infested wading pool. Besides, Cheek might be in it, naked."

"Which could account for the algae," he said. "Then let's make our own hot tub."

She laughed. "What?"

He gestured toward the bathroom. "That ridiculous tub in there—it's plenty big enough if we fill it up with hot water."

Amazed at the change in his demeanor, she reached up and lifted his glasses. "Who are you and what have you done with Alan P.—the-'P'-stands-for-tight-as-a-pin—Parish?"

His mouth quirked to the side. "You better get your bathing suit before he comes back."

Pam looked into his blue eyes and studied his boyish face. He was so incredibly handsome...and had turned into such a surprise. Ignoring the warning flags that sprang up en masse at the periphery of her brain, she grinned and said, "I'll meet you in the deep end."

She grabbed her suit, went into the bathroom, then turned on the hot water, unable to ignore the pounding of her heart. Biting her lip hard, she stared at herself in the mirror as she tucked her curves into the gold bikini that had sparked a light in Alan's eyes at the department store. Beneath the harsh illumination of the bare bulb in the room, she looked raw and vulnerable. Her eyes stung from indecision. She wanted Alan so much her chest hurt. "If this is wrong," she whispered, "send me a sign."

The bulb popped, then went dark with a sizzling sound.

She stood in the dark for several seconds, then said, "I need to be really, really sure. Would you mind sending another sign?"

"Pam?" Alan knocked lightly on the door. "Who are you talking to?"

"Uh, no one," she yelled. "The light went out."

His chuckle reverberated through the door. "I'll get the Elvis candles you bought."

Pam looked heavenward. "I gave it my best shot."

He was back within a few seconds, wearing trunks and bearing matches. She placed "Love Me Tender" candles around the room strategically, growing increasingly alarmed at the romantic atmosphere they were creating. She lowered herself into the hot water just as Alan reappeared with a bottle. "Ta-dah!"

"Champagne?"

He uncorked the bottle, spilling foam on the pink tile. "Since I didn't get a drop at the wedding reception, I gave Twiggy fifty bucks to find a bottle of my favorite. Happy Valentine's Day." Alan handed her a full glass, then stepped into the water, only to jump back out. "Good Lord, Pam! Are you cooking shrimp in there?"

Already light-headed at the sight of the candlelight dancing on his sleek, muscled chest, she sipped the champagne and giggled as the bubbles went up her nose. "Ease in, Alan, you'll get used to it."

He tried again, gasping and wincing, sending her into fits of laughter as he squatted into the water inch by inch. "It's a good thing I don't like kids," he muttered as he settled in up to his armpits. "Because my sperm have been parboiled."

"Is that what the 'P' stands for?"

"Cute, real cute."

"Is it 'Parker'?"

"No."

"Preston?"

"No."

"Palmer?"

"No! Enough already. Either turn on the cold water or the egg timer because I'll be done in a few minutes."

Pam turned on the cold water to let it drip. "What's the big deal about your middle name?" She started as his leg brushed against hers beneath the water.

"It's private," he said with a smile. His leg brushed

hers again, and she nearly groaned with the desire that welled within her. "Don't you have something private, something you don't share with everyone?"

She manufactured a laugh. "Private? You forget who you're talking to. My life has been public property in Savannah since I was sixteen. Don't tell me you haven't heard the stories."

"I have," he admitted, raking his gaze over her. "But I'm not sure how many of the stories are true and how many of them are pure fantasy on the part of the men who told them."

Her neck felt rubbery, so she laid her head back and looked at him through slitted eyelids. "Alan, have *you* ever fantasized about me?"

His eyes widened and he cleared his throat, then drained his champagne glass. Pam's skin tingled in anticipation.

"I've always thought you were beautiful, Pam," he said finally, moving lower in the water and settling his leg against the length of hers. "But I've never fantasized about you."

She pressed her lips together in disappointment. He wasn't attracted to her, after all. The sexual current she'd felt between them had been a figment of her teenage imagination, dating back to the time when she'd dreamed that Alan P. Parish would notice her, ask her out, take her to his fine home—

"Until this week," he added quietly.

Pam lifted her head.

"I know what you think of me, Pam—that I'm an automaton, a computer geek—"

"A tight-ass," she added with a smile.

He smirked. "Thanks." Then he moved closer, and

set her glass aside with his. He floated inches over her in the water before lowering himself against her, setting the warm water into motion. "But I'm not a machine, Pam."

His face was only inches from hers, and she felt his breath fan her cheek. The water lapped around them, warming her skin, then falling away to leave her covered with goose bumps. Her nipples hardened. His proximity crowded her senses and she had never felt so close to losing control. "Are you sure? Because I— I can certainly feel your hard drive."

"I want you."

Pam closed her eyes, trying to recall any shred of relief she had felt the morning after their near lapse on the beach, any rationalization that she shouldn't be feeling like this. But now his hands on her obliterated all doubts, negated all concerns, neutralized all complications. And her hands moved of their own volition to the nape of her neck to loosen the ties of her bikini top. She allowed the water to float the material away from her breasts, and Alan crushed her against him, claiming her mouth in a plundering kiss.

Pam raised her body to meet his and he clasped her urgently, squeezing her hips against his, whispering her name into her throat. After a thorough exploration of her mouth, he set aside his fogged glasses and drew back to view her breasts.

"You are magnificent." The sheer wonder in his voice sent waves of desire flooding her limbs. He dragged her breath from her lungs by pulling a puckered nipple into his mouth.

"Oh, Alan." She pushed her fingers through his hair and arched into him, urging him to take as much of her into his mouth as possible. His erection strained against her thigh, and she ran her hands down his neck, over his muscled back, and under the waistband of his trunks.

Their moans echoed off the walls of the small room and Pam had never felt so aroused. The combination of the heated water, the candlelight and the man were incredibly erotic. Every nerve ending, every muscle, every sense burned and throbbed with raw desire and she raked her hands over his body. His name emerged from her throat over and over, as if some part of her suspected their time together was short and she wanted to experience as much of him as possible.

He devoured her, drawing on her breasts one at a time, rolling her sensitized nipples between his finger and thumb. His hands skated over her body, assuming the rhythm of the water until their movements became so frenzied, the now-lukewarm water splashed over the edges and onto the tile.

Alan felt his body growing more engorged, yearning for release. The feelings she had unleashed in him were so staggering, he prayed he could maintain control long enough to please her. ''Let's go to bed,'' he said thickly against her neck and she moaned her agreement.

He drew back and tried to stand, fell, and succeeded in dunking them both before they gained their footing. Pam stopped long enough to grab a towel for her sopping hair. The sight of her standing bare-breasted was enough to make him grit his teeth.

''We'd better hurry,'' he said, tugging on her hand.

They slipped and slid across the tiled floor, laughing and cursing until they crossed the threshold of the bedroom. They tumbled onto the bed, launching a small tidal wave. Alan kicked off his trunks and rolled down her bikini bottoms, groaning when he uncovered the nest of wet blond curls between her firm, tanned thighs. He raised himself above her, pushing her wet hair back from her face. "You are so beautiful," he whispered hoarsely. "I need to make love to you now—are you protected?"

She nodded, her blue eyes luminous, her luscious upside-down mouth soft and swollen. With utmost restraint, he lowered himself, rubbing his straining shaft against her. Oh so carefully, he probed her wetness, then sank inside her slowly, capturing her mouth with his and absorbing her gasps as their bodies melded.

Heaven. She felt like pure heaven around him, pulsing, kneading, drawing his life fluid to the surface much too quickly. He slowed and clenched his teeth, wanting their lovemaking to last, postponing the moment she would pull away from him. For now he wanted to be inside her, wrapped around her, smelling her, tasting her. When he found a slow rhythm, she began to pant beneath him, clawing as his back. He was so stunned at the level of her response, he was momentarily distracted from his own building release and concentrated on making her climax powerful.

He laved her earlobe and whispered erotic words he'd never uttered before, phrases loosened from his tongue by the fantasy woman writhing beneath him. He moved with her, responding to every moan and gasp with more intense probing until her cries escalated and she climaxed around him, her contracting muscles finally breaking his restraint and unleashing the most intense orgasm he'd ever experienced. They rode out the vestiges of their explosive pleasure, slowing to a languid grind. At last they stilled, but the water mattress bumped them against each other, eliciting gasps as their tender flesh met.

He gingerly lifted himself from her and rolled to spoon her against him, half to hold her close for a while longer, half to avoid facing her until he had time to sort out a few things for himself. The regrets, the remorse, the self-recrimination had not yet set in, and for the time being, he simply wanted to enjoy the intimacy of lying with this wonderful creature, however fleeting the time might be.

Alan sighed and closed his eyes, pushing his nose into her damp hair, inhaling her scent. He couldn't remember feeling more content, but he blamed his thoughts of spending the rest of his nights like this on the fog of sleep that ebbed over him. His dreams were restless, fraught with stress-packed, nerve-shattering days of living with Pamela Kaminski.

10

WHEN PAM'S EYES popped open, the first light of dawn had found its way between the heavy opaque curtains over the window and sliding glass door. Despite the sunny warmth, a cold blanket of dread descended over her. She craned her neck slowly toward the mirrored ceiling, muttering words of denial until she was faced with the naked truth.

"Oh…my…God," she murmured, groaning at the tangle of bare tanned arms and legs they presented. They'd *done* it—the deed, the wild thing, the horizontal bop—they'd had *sex*. She and Alan. Her and her best friend's ex. Panic ballooned in her chest and she pushed herself up, frantically whispering, "Oh my God, oh my God, oh my God."

Alan stirred and rolled to his back, displaying a puptent erection beneath the thin sheet. She averted her eyes, cursed the erotic scenes that kept replaying in her head and began to extricate herself from his grasp as gently as possible.

"Hey," he mumbled in complaint, pulling her against him.

She punched his arm. "Let me go," she protested, scrambling to get out of the rolling bed.

"You really should work on that morning disposition," he muttered with a yawn.

She bent and scooped a towel from the floor, which she wrapped around herself. Astounded at his nonchalance, she bounced a pillow off his face. "Get up! Can't you see we're in big trouble here?"

He blinked and sat up, shaking his head as if to clear it, then swung his feet to the floor. "Excuse me?"

"Alan, we had sex last night."

"I was there—or don't you remember?" he asked wryly, standing for a full-body stretch.

That was the problem—she remembered his mind-blowing participation all too well. Pam glanced down at his raging morning erection, then expelled an explosive sigh. "Put a towel on that rack, would you?"

She tossed him a pillowcase they had somehow managed to work free during their lovemaking, then jammed her hands on her hips. "*What* are we going to do now?"

Holding the crumpled cloth over his privates, Alan scrubbed his hand over his face, then ventured, "Go to Walt Disney World?"

"That's not even remotely funny."

"Could I have a few seconds to wake up? And maybe relieve myself?"

It had meant nothing to him, she realized with a jolt. And why should it? He wasn't the one who would have to face Jo on a regular basis when they returned home. In fact, from a man's point of view, sleeping with the best friend of the woman who had ditched him at the altar was probably the most perfect revenge he could exact. Hurt stabbed her deep, and she felt like a fool for not seeing the situation so clearly last night. Pam swept her hand toward the bathroom. "Be my guest," she said with as much indifference as she could muster.

When he had closed the door, she strode to the closet, yanked out her large canvas beach bag and started stuffing her personal articles inside. Most of the clothes she could leave here, she decided—since Alan had bought them, he could dispose of them however he wished.

Not relishing another plane ride so soon after their turbulent experience a few days ago, she decided that the bus sounded like the best alternative home—even if it took two days, which she presumed it would. Today was Thursday, so she'd still be back in Savannah by late Friday, or Saturday at the latest. Which would give her plenty of time to decide what—or if—she was going to tell Jo.

She jammed her Elvis paraphernalia into the bag and practiced her speech. "Gee, Jo, you were finished with him and he was just so darned sexy. No, I promise we weren't sleeping together behind your back while you and Alan were an item."

"Pam."

Alan's voice sounded behind her, jangling her already clanging nerves so badly she dropped the bag, and her towel with it. Yanking the towel back in place, she wheeled to find Alan leaning on the doorjamb.

"What are you doing?" he asked quietly.

She retrieved the bag and continued rooting through the tiny closet. "What does it look like I'm doing? I'm packing."

"To go home? Why?"

She turned and leveled her gaze on him.

He did, at least, have the grace to blush. "I mean, I can guess why, but I don't think this is the best way to handle what just happened, do you?"

"You have a better plan?"

Alan shrugged. "Try not to blow it out of proportion. I was lonely, you were lonely. We had a romantic evening—everyone treated us as a couple. We drank half a bottle of wine, then topped it off with good champagne." He looked contrite. "I owe you an apology—I feel guilty as hell for dragging you down here, and now…"

"Now look at the fine mess we've made," she finished for him, ending with a sigh. "There's no need to apologize, Alan. You didn't exactly hold a gun to my head."

He pressed his lips together in a tight line. "Sleeping together wasn't particularly smart, considering the touchy circumstances, but we're adults and surely we can exercise enough control to make sure it doesn't happen again."

"Oh, it can *never* happen again," she said emphatically.

"Agreed," he said, walking to stop an arm's length away from her. "Since we have that settled, now you can stay."

"It's not settled, Alan," she said, dropping her gaze. "What am I going to tell Jo?"

"*We,*" he said firmly, "aren't going to tell Jo anything. She's married, Pam. She doesn't care about my sex life—or yours. And even if she did, it's none of her business."

"But how will I face her?"

"As if nothing happened," he said simply, affirming her earlier suspicion that their lovemaking had shaken her far more than it had affected him.

"But I can't lie to her, Alan. She's my best friend."

He lifted his hands. "Fine—if we get home and Jo asks you, 'Pam, did you and Alan sleep together?,' you can say, 'Yes, as a matter of fact, Jo, we did.'"

"It would never occur to Jo to ask," Pam said with a wry smile.

"My point exactly," he said. "But you might arouse her curiosity if you went scurrying home early." He gave her a lopsided smile. "So put down your bag and I promise to stay out of your way until Saturday. Hopefully we can still go home as friends."

He made it sound so simple—they had made a mistake, and they wouldn't do it again. Period. That was Alan—Mr. Practical. She lifted a corner of her mouth. Maybe that's what the 'P' stood for. Even though he obviously wasn't wrestling with the same troubling issues their lovemaking had unearthed in her psyche, perhaps he was right. Maybe they needed a couple of days to get back on a casual footing. Although she would never look at Alan in quite the same way, it would be a shame to lose his friendship because she simply couldn't cope with their lapse.

"I'll stay," she said lightly. "And of course we'll go home as friends." She dropped the bag and gave him her brightest smile. "I'll go shopping today, and do some sight-seeing."

"And I'll find something to do," he said. "And if you're out late—"

"—or if you're out late…"

"—we'll see each other…"

"—tomorrow," she finished.

He nodded. "Fine."

She nodded. "Fine."

"Do you want to shower first?"

Stephanie Bond

"Sure," she said, and walked past him. The pink-tiled room did not seem nearly so electric this morning, although the vestiges of their interlude were scattered throughout: her bikini top, the burnt-down candles, the half-empty bottle of champagne. She closed her eyes for a few seconds and squashed the mushrooming regret when it threatened to overwhelm her.

"By the way," Alan said behind her.

She whirled to see him squinting at her from the open doorway, just as something crunched under her foot.

"Have you seen my glasses?"

Pam looked down, picked up her foot, then winced and nodded.

ALAN PUSHED his glasses higher on his nose, frowning when he encountered the bulky piece of masking tape that held the broken bridge of his frames together. He sank lower in the upholstered seat of the nearly empty movie theater and smirked at the corny previews. With a sigh he glanced at the vacant seat next to him and imagined Pam sitting there, munching popcorn and giggling like a teenager.

It was funny how much his perception of her had changed in the last few days. She was still the sexy bombshell who made him a little nervous, but now...now he had glimpsed the warm, funny, smart woman who lurked beneath the showy facade. Sure, her showy side inflamed his baser needs, but it was her squeal of laughter when they'd ridden the Wave Runner and her shining face when he'd filled the moat of her sand castle that stayed with him every waking minute.

The ear-numbing, teeth-jarring, bone-melting, mind-blowing sex was simply a bonus.

He smiled a slow, lazy grin. The sex was a big, fat cherry on top of a sundae more delectable than any he could have imagined as a kid. Which presented an interesting paradox, he noted as the main feature bounced onto the screen. If Pamela Kaminski was such a catch, what was keeping him from pursuing her with gusto?

He imagined Pam counting off the reasons on her brightly colored fingernails. "Because my friendship with your ex-fiancée means more to me than any relationship we could ever have, Alan. Because I have dozens of men waiting for my return, Alan. And most important, because you're not the kind of guy I'd settle for, Alan."

The flick started, a splashy good-guys bad-guys film with several gorgeous women and just enough one-liners to make it amusing. But his mind wandered from the movie plot to Pamela so often, he lost track of which double agent crossed which federal bureau so when the movie credits rolled, he wasn't quite sure what had happened or who had gotten the girl. But he had the sinking feeling it wouldn't be him.

He sat through another matinee he couldn't follow, at the end of which he had to admit that for the first time in his thirty-odd years, he was completely consumed with, distracted by and besotted over a woman. A woman who was beyond his reach.

When he walked outside, he squinted into the light, even though dusk was already falling. Oh well, he thought as he joined the mingling crowd on the sidewalk, things would be different when they got back to Savannah. He would return to his demanding job running his consulting business, and she would return to the frantic pace of real-estate sales, along with her bottomless pool of boyfriends. They would probably see each other occasionally at charity functions. He would wave and she would smile, and no one would ever know they had made passionate love in a gaudy room in Fort Myers on Valentine's Day.

Determined to stay away from the beachfront area to avoid running into Robin, Alan strolled along the retail district, browsing in music and electronics stores. He wandered by a jewelry-store window and stopped when he spotted a gold sand-castle pendant. He desperately wanted to give Pam something to remember him by, and the pendant seemed to call him. He walked inside and left fifteen minutes later with the pendant and a matching gold chain. He wasn't sure when or if he'd give it to her, but for now, buying the pendant seemed like the right thing to do.

He bought a couple of CD's by local artists, then stopped at a sports bar and ordered a sandwich and a beer. The ponytailed bartender who served him found a Georgia State basketball game on one of the many TV screens and made small talk while he washed glass mugs.

The barkeep wore a tight T-shirt with the sleeves ripped off to show his many tattoos to their best advantage. Alan tried not to stare, but he must have failed because the guy quirked a bushy eyebrow and asked, "You ever had a tattoo?"

Alan shook his head and pointed to one on the man's arm, squinting. "Is that an ad?"

"Yep—best tattoo parlor in town is just down the street. I get a discount for wearing the ad."

"Human billboards," Alan acknowledged with a tip of his bottle. "Now *there's* an untapped industry." He figured he must be getting a buzz because the idea of someone selling their skin to advertisers, inch by inch, actually sounded plausible. In which case, Pam's body would be worth a fortune, he noted dryly, wondering how much her cleavage would command on the open market. *Location, location, location.*

The bartender leaned on the bar and asked, "Hey, man, are you busy later tonight?"

Alan frowned and deepened his voice. "You're barking up the wrong tree, fella."

"Huh?" The bartender pulled back, then scoffed. "Nah, man, my girlfriend's swinging by and bringing a friend with her. You like redheads?"

"Sure, but—"

"Great! Her name's Pru."

"Thanks anyway, but I'm really not—"

"Saaaaaaaaay." Something past Alan's shoulder had obviously claimed the man's attention. "I could go for some of that," the bartender whispered in a husky voice.

Alan turned on his stool to see Pamela walking toward the bar wearing an outfit of walking shorts and sleeveless sweater that would have been unremarkable on ninety-nine percent of the female population. She seemed intent on finding something in her purse and hadn't spotted him yet. If Alan had been quick—and motivated—he could have thrown some cash on the bar and left. But his reflexes were a little delayed, he conceded, and the sheer pleasure of seeing her after spending the day apart disintegrated his thoughts of leaving.

When she looked up, she did a double take and

stopped midstride, then approached him with a wary expression on her face. "Small world," he offered along with a smile. He patted the stool next to him. "Have a seat—I'll buy you a beer."

She leaned one firm hip against the stool and gestured vaguely. "Thanks anyway—I actually came in to find a pay phone. My cell-phone battery died in the middle of a conversation with Mrs. Wingate."

"Is she ready to buy the Sheridan house?"

"Not yet—she's got a priest over there now consecrating the flower beds."

"Don't let me keep you."

"That's all right," she said with a wave. "She probably took getting cut off as some kind of omen and might not come to the phone anyway." Pam glanced at the bartender. "Nice artwork," she said, nodding toward his colorful arms.

Wearing a wolfish grin, the man flexed his biceps and leaned toward Pam. "Thanks."

Jealousy barbed through Alan and he glared at the beefy man. "Pam, what did you do all day?"

She told him about her day of sight-seeing. "There are some beautiful homes here and over on Sanibel Island," she declared. "The real-estate market seems to be very strong—lots of money to be made."

He bit the inside of his cheek as a disturbing thought struck him. "You're not thinking about moving?"

"Not here," she said. "Even though I like it. I always thought Atlanta would be nice—I have lots of friends there."

So she had lovers all over the state, he mused. "Atlanta's a fun city."

She nodded and brushed a lock of hair behind her

ear—the ear in which he'd murmured unmentionables only last night. "As long as my mother is alive, I guess I'll stay in Savannah."

"I can't imagine the state my mother will be in by the time I return," Alan said with a wry grin.

"She liked Jo, didn't she?"

He nodded and peeled off the curling corner of the label on his beer bottle. "She thought Jo would make an excellent wife and hostess, an asset to my career."

"She doesn't want grandchildren?"

"My sister has two kids, and my mother thinks that's plenty enough people in this world to call her Granny."

Pam giggled. "Mom doesn't have grandkids—that we know of. Of course, knowing my brothers, who knows how many Kaminskis could be running around."

Alan laughed and tipped his bottle for another drink. Every family, rich or poor, had its dysfunction. "Have you had dinner?"

"I'm not really very hungry," she said, dropping her gaze again. "Thanks anyway. I'm tired—I think I'll get back to the hotel and turn in early."

Their eyes met and the reason behind her fatigue hung in the air between them. Alan gripped the bottle hard to keep from reaching for her. "Ah, come on," he said. "Why don't you stay for a beer—what's one beer between friends?"

The corners of her uneven mouth turned up slowly, then she relented with a nod. "Okay, one beer."

ALAN STARTED AWAKE, then winced at the sour taste in his mouth. But the movement of his facial muscles sent an explosion of pain to his temples and he groaned aloud, which sounded like a gong in his ears. He closed his eyes and waited until most of the pain and noise subsided before attempting to put two thoughts together.

He was in the hotel room, and he could hear Pam's snore beside him, so it appeared they had slept in the same bed. Straining, he remembered they had consumed large quantities of beer and had left the sports bar, but that's when his memory failed him. Had they gone directly back to the room? And then what?

He opened his eyes one at a time in the early-morning light and gingerly reached up to adjust his broken glasses, which were somehow still on his face. He moved his head to see the reflection in the ceiling. Another gonging groan escaped him when he saw they were indeed naked and intimately entwined.

Not again.

Pam lay on her stomach and the sheet had fallen down to expose the rub-on rose tattoo on her tanned hip. When his scrutiny triggered inappropriate responses beneath his half of the sheet, he pulled himself up a millimeter at a time and stumbled to the bathroom in search of a glass of water.

His hip ached from the unaccustomed lusty exercise, and he rubbed it as he downed the water. But at the sharp tenderness of his skin, he turned to glance in the mirror and smiled dryly. He must have been blitzed because he'd allowed Pam to rub one of her fake tattoos on *his* hip. A wet washcloth and a little soap would take care of it, he figured. Except when he scrubbed at the tattoo, the pain increased and the stubborn design refused to budge. ''I must be allergic to the dye," he muttered, and scrubbed harder. But minutes later when he lifted the cloth and saw the tattoo still had not faded, terror twisted his stomach.

"No," he said frantically. "It can't be real!"

He backed up to the mirror for a better look, but he couldn't make out the tattoo. Letters of some kind? It was backward in the reflection, so he snatched up Pam's hand mirror and positioned it to read the reflected word. His eyes widened and his hands started to shake.

"Paaaaaaaaaaaaaaaaaammmmmmmmmm!"

Pamela jerked awake, unable to pinpoint the origin of the invasion into her peaceful sleep. She swallowed painfully and lifted her head. The sound of breaking glass from the bathroom made her sit up. "Alan," she called, holding her head. "Are you okay?"

The door swung open and he emerged naked, his face puckered and red. "No, I am not okay. In fact, I'm about as far from okay as I've ever been!"

Pam rubbed her tender hip and grimaced. "Don't make me play twenty questions, Alan. It hurts to talk."

"You!" he bellowed, shaking his finger at her. "You talked me into it!"

She sighed. "Did we do it again?"

"Yes!" he roared. "But that's not what I'm talking about."

Her frustration peaked. "Then what *are* you talking about?"

"This!" he yelled, then turned around and pointed to his bare hip.

She leaned forward and squinted. "A tattoo? You got a tattoo?" Laughter erupted from the back of her throat. "You got a tattoo!" Then she stood, twisted to look at her own hip and squealed in delight. "No—we both got tattoos! A rose! Isn't it great?" She strode over to him and glanced down. "What does yours say?" Then she stopped and stumbled backward at the sight of the name etched on Alan's skin, enclosed in a red heart. "P-Pam's?" She covered her mouth with both hands and lifted her gaze to his.

"THERE ARE ALL KINDS of new laser procedures to remove tattoos," she assured him as they moved down the path toward the beach. Alan walked woodenly beside her, occasionally stabbing at his taped glasses.

"But I think we're skirting the bigger issue here," she continued, trotting to keep up with him, even though he was limping slightly, favoring his tender hip. "What happened last night absolutely *cannot* happen again."

"I agree," he said curtly, staring straight ahead.

"We've only got one more day and one more night, so we should be able to stay sober and keep our hands to ourselves."

"Right."

"Let's try to enjoy the time we have left," she said amiably as they stepped onto the warm white sand.

He stopped and turned to her. "How about 'Let's just try to make it through tomorrow with as few calamities as possible'?"

Pam swallowed and smiled weakly. "That's fine, too."

They rented chaise lounges and Pam couldn't help noticing that Alan waited until she had hers situated, then planted his several feet away. "Safety precaution,'' he said flatly, then snapped open the newspaper he'd brought to read.

Frowning, Pam turned to her own reading material and tried to blot the disturbing thoughts of Alan from her mind. She had missed him yesterday, and the realization had shaken her badly. So when she'd stumbled across him in the sports bar, she had allowed herself to be persuaded to stay for a drink because she simply wanted to spend time with him. And although the rest of the night remained fuzzy, some incidents she recalled rather clearly.

Such as the fact that she *had* been the one who suggested they get tattoos, inspired, possibly, by the bartender's impressive collection. And Alan had been hesitant, but she had dragged him down the street, and sent him into one booth while she entered another one for her design of choice. Where he'd gotten ''Pam's'' was less clear to her, and the fact that they'd made whoopee again last night only added to the confusion.

Her heart lay heavy in her chest and she tried to convince herself that things would be better once they returned to Savannah. For one thing, she would rarely see him, if at all, since their connection to each other— Jo—no longer existed. It was for the best, she knew, because she didn't want to be running into him at every turn…didn't want to be reminded of the few days they were together when names, backgrounds and at-risk relationships were irrelevant and all that mattered was the powerful sexual chemistry between them.

''Hello.''

Pam looked up and smothered a cringe when she saw Enrico standing over her chair, his lips curved into a sultry smile. Resplendent in orange nut-huggers, the man nodded toward Alan who was still hidden behind a newspaper. "I see your man is neglecting you once again." He wagged his eyebrows. "Perhaps I can remedy that situation."

Annoyed, Pam began rummaging in her bag. "I doubt it."

"Could I interest you in a walk up the beach?"

She jammed on her sunglasses. "No."

"How about a drink?"

She lay her head back. "No."

He leaned close to her and the stench of alcohol rolled off his breath. "You like to tease, no?"

"No," Alan said behind him.

Pam lifted her head and looked up at Alan who stood with his paper under his arm, glaring at Enrico. How like a man to ignore a woman until someone else comes sniffing around. She smiled tightly. "I can handle this, Alan."

His gaze darted to her, then he lifted his hands in retreat and reclaimed his chair.

But Enrico folded his arms and followed him back to his chair. "She is not worth fighting for, *señor*?"

"That is enough," Pam declared, sitting up. "I think you'd better leave, Enrico."

Enrico stood over Alan, taking advantage of the situation. "She is too much woman for you, eh?"

Pam's patience snapped and she scrambled to her feet. "Leave, Enrico!"

He sneered and jerked a thumb toward Alan, who had risen to his feet. "Perhaps your man is weak?" Just as he lunged for Alan, Pam launched herself at the man with an angry growl, climbing his hairy back. She propelled him into Alan and they all went down in the sand. Once the breath returned to her lungs, Pam pummeled the man's back.

Sand flew as they rolled around, scrambling for leverage. Alan splayed his hand over Enrico's face and pushed him back, trying to avoid the man's swinging arms. Pam yelped, clawing the grit out of her eyes while showering Enrico with the blinding stuff. Alan rolled behind the man and grabbed him in a chokehold. The man grabbed handfuls of sand and threw them in the air.

Somewhere in the background she heard a voice yell for the police. Incensed, she wanted to land one good jab while Alan held him. Pam made a fist, drew back and threw the hardest punch she could through the swirling sand, eliciting a dull groan when she made contact with skin and bone.

She stepped back to blink her eyes clear. But when she massaged her throbbing knuckles in satisfaction, she saw Enrico several yards down the beach, jogging away, and he appeared unfazed by Pam's right hook.

When she glanced back to the site of the scuffle, her stomach twisted. Alan sat in the sand, glaring at her, holding his hand over his right eye.

Whatever apology she might have conjured up was cut short by the arrival of a uniformed officer. "Hello," the cop said, standing over Alan with a tight smile. "Again."

"WELL, look on the bright side," Pam said as she led the way to the double-parked limo the following morning.

Numb from another night in jail and a head full of

contradicting thoughts, Alan gingerly touched his swollen right eye and asked, "And that would be?"

"We didn't have sex last night," she said brightly.

Which would have been the only redeeming event of the past twenty-four hours, Alan thought miserably.

"And we're leaving today," she sang, obviously anxious to return home. "I checked us out of the hotel—Twiggy said goodbye. I bought a suitcase and packed your things—they're in the car."

He stopped and stared at two new dents and the Kaminiskiesque parking job that left only two tires of the pimpmobile on the street, but he didn't say anything. Instead, he opened the back door of the limo and climbed in, banging the door closed behind him.

"You're letting me drive to the airport?" Pam yelled from the driver's seat after she buzzed down the divider panel.

Alan clicked his seat belt into place, pulled the strap tight and laid his head back. "Your definition of driving is a loose interpretation, but I'm too drained to argue."

"Okay," she said excitedly, revving the engine. "I'm starved—do you mind if we stop and get something to eat on the way? We've got plenty of time before the flight."

"Go for it," he said, removing his broken glasses so he couldn't witness the driving event.

Of course, he hadn't anticipated she would attempt to take the limo through a drive-through window—they were stuck in a tight curve by a squawking monitor for forty-five minutes. No longer surprised by any stunt she pulled, Alan ordered an ice-cream sandwich to hold against his puffy eye and munched a hamburger in the back seat during the melee. When the scraping sounds became too unbearable, he turned up the TV and watched a rerun of "Laugh-In" until she finally eased the car by the metal posts and the high curbs.

She buzzed down the panel when they were on the expressway again. "We still have over an hour," she yelled cheerfully. "We'll make it."

He buzzed up the panel and unwrapped the ice-cream sandwich.

Five minutes later they were at a dead standstill. She buzzed down the panel. "It's a freaking parking lot out here—the radio says there's a tractor-trailer overturned and we won't move for at least an hour. Don't worry—we'll still make it." She smiled, then buzzed up the panel.

Alan sighed and picked up the remote control. Then a thought struck him and he buzzed down the panel. "Hey, Kaminski?"

She twisted in her seat. "Yeah?"

"Have you ever gotten naked in a limo?"

Her smile was slow in coming, but broad and mischievous. "No."

"Want to?"

In answer, she buzzed up the panel. Alan sighed again and laid his head back. "Can't blame a guy for asking," he muttered. Especially since she'd go back to her stud stable once they returned to Savannah.

Suddenly the door opened and she bounded inside, toppling over him, laughing like a teenager. She straddled him and kissed him hard, then asked, "Do you think an hour is enough time?"

"We'll have to hit the highlights," he whispered, locking the door.

"What about the lowlights?" she said, pouting.

"In the interest of time," he murmured, pulling at her waistband, "I'll have to give them a lick and a promise."

RUNNING THROUGH the parking lot of the car-rental return, Pam yelled, "That can't *ever* happen again."

"Right," Alan yelled back. "Never."

They rushed into the building. Alan forked over an obscene deposit to a pinched-nose man in case his insurance company wouldn't cover the various damages to the limo, then they sprinted through the airport as fast as his still-aching hip would allow. When they dropped into their seats on the plane, he found it unbelievable that only a few days had passed since they'd left Savannah. It seemed like a lifetime ago—not to mention a small fortune ago, he noted wryly.

After takeoff, he donned a set of headphones, not to ignore Pam, but hoping to put some perspective on the week before they reached Savannah. Indeed, the more distant the Fort Myers skyline became, the more painfully clear the answers seemed.

Instead of trying to dissect the roller coaster of emotions she had evoked in him this week, he simply needed to consider the facts: he had been vulnerable, she had been eager to comfort a friend. Besides, even if the circumstances were ideal—which they weren't— and even if he had the intention of taking a wife— which he didn't—he couldn't imagine any woman more unsuited to marriage than Pamela Kaminski.

Thankfully, their flight was uneventful—the little mishap when Pam sent an entire overhead bin of luggage pounding down on two passengers didn't even merit an eye twitch on his new scale of relativity. Rankling him further, she seemed oblivious to his brooding, chatting with the flight attendants and somehow managing to paint her toenails during the flight.

It was only when they were landing and he glanced over to see her death grip on the padded arms of her seat that he conceded to himself how extremely fond of her he'd become. Alan reached over to squeeze her hand, and the grateful smile she gave him made his heart lurch crazily. He knew in that moment that even if his eye healed, the tattoo was safely removed, the charges were dropped and his car insurance wasn't canceled, he still might never fully recover from his week with Pamela.

She was her usual cheery self through baggage claim and on their way back to her car, reinforcing Alan's suspicion that, for Pam, the week had simply been a casual romp—the woman had no earth-shattering revelations weighing her down. And despite the trouble that seemed to follow her around, he was going to miss her. Perhaps, he decided, after a few weeks had passed and he had shaken this somber, life-evaluating mood, he'd call her, just to see how she was doing.

He offered to call a cab, but she insisted on driving him home, saying she needed to check on some new home listings in his neighborhood, anyway. On the way, she ran two red lights, but stopped traffic on the bypass to let a mother duck and her ducklings cross.

When she pulled onto the long driveway, Alan stared at his imposing home and realized with a jolt that only one week ago, he had anticipated returning to carry his bride, Jo Montgomery, across the threshold. Now he felt almost giddy with relief at the change in circumstances. He and Jo would have been content, but not entirely happy. She had never looked at him the way she looked at John Sterling. And he owed it to himself to find a woman he could care about that much.

"Are you okay?" Pam asked, jarring him out of his reverie.

"Uh, yeah," he said, realizing she was waiting for him to get out. But when he grasped the handle, she stopped him with a hand on his arm.

"Alan," she said softly.

"Yeah," he said, his heart thudding against his chest.

"I'm sorry."

"Sorry?"

"For breaking your glasses and denting the limo and getting the ticket and having you tattooed and blacking your eye and getting you arrested."

"Twice," he amended.

"Twice," she agreed.

Her blue eyes were wide, and her upside-down mouth trembled. She was so beautiful, she was impossible to resist. He inhaled deeply and gave her a wry smile. "Forget it." Her happy grin was worth every misery he'd experienced over the week.

He opened the door and retrieved the dark suitcase she had purchased and packed for him. When he walked around to the driver's side, his mind racing for something to say, he suddenly remembered the pendant he had bought for her. "Oh, I almost forgot," he said, rooting through his gym bag until he came up with the black box. "For you."

"For me?" she asked quietly, taking her lower lip in her teeth. She slowly lifted the lid and stared at the gold sand castle, then ran her finger over the surface. "It's beautiful," she whispered, then raised shining eyes. "But why?"

Because I want you to remember me, to remember us. "Because," he said with a shrug, "I wanted to thank you for keeping me company. It was fun," he lied. It wasn't fun—it was surprising, disturbing, stimulating, stressful and amazing, but it wasn't fun.

"I love it."

She pulled the necklace from the box and fastened the clasp around her neck. The pendant disappeared into her cleavage and Alan swallowed hard.

"Thank you, Alan."

"I'll see you…" His voice trailed off because he didn't want to appear as desperately hopeful as he felt.

"Sometime," she finished for him.

"Right," he said with a nod.

"Fine," she said with a nod.

Alan watched as she rolled up the window, backed over several hundred dollars' worth of landscaping and pulled onto the road directly in the path of a luxury car whose owner stood on the brake to avoid a collision. Then, with a fluttery wave and a grind of stripped gears, she was gone.

11

PAM SLAPPED HER KNEE and laughed uproariously. "That's the best April Fool's gag I've heard today, Dr. Campbell."

Eleanor Campbell pursed her lips and steepled her fingers together over her desk. "It's no joke, Pamela. You're pregnant."

Shock, alarm and stark terror washed over her. Her throat closed and her fingers went numb. "H-how is that possible?"

Dr. Campbell smiled. "Do you want layman's terms or the scientific version?"

"Whichever will make it less true," Pam whispered. "I take my birth control pills faithfully."

"But if you had read the warning brochure for the antibiotics I prescribed for that ear infection a couple of months ago," she said sternly, "you would have known the medication can reduce the effectiveness of birth control pills." She sighed and gave Pam a sad smile. "I take it this is not a happy occasion for you and the father."

Pam closed her eyes and swallowed. "When did it happen?"

"According to the information you gave me regarding your last cycle, I'd guess on or about Valentine's Day."

If she didn't open her eyes, she decided, she wouldn't have to face it. Wouldn't have to face the fact that she was living up to the tainted Kaminski name by conceiving an illegitimate child. Wouldn't have to face the fact that life as she knew it was over. Wouldn't have to face the fact that Alan, whom she'd not seen or spoken to since returning to Savannah—and who *hated* kids—was the father of the baby growing inside her.

"MR. PARISH?" Alan's secretary's voice echoed over the speakerphone.

Alan left what had become his favorite post, the high-backed chair by the window, to push a button on his desk panel. "Yes?"

"I'm sorry, sir. Tickets to the scholarship social are sold out."

He cursed under his breath safely out of range of the microphone. "How about the hospital golf benefit?"

"Sold out."

"The lighthouse-preservation dinner?"

"Gone. The only tickets I could find for this weekend were for the podiatrists' political-action campaign dinner and the bird-watchers' society all-night skate at the roller rink."

Alan frowned. Feet or feathers—not much of a choice. "Get me two of each," he said. He dropped into his leather chair, then flipped to Pam's business card in his Rolodex—as if he hadn't memorized it. Hell, he'd dialed it twenty-eight times in the weeks since they'd returned to Savannah, but he'd always hung up before the first ring. Now he had a good excuse.

Well, maybe not good—but reasonable.

He sighed. Okay, it wasn't even reasonable, but he prayed his ploy didn't come across as desperation…even though it was.

After punching in her number, he cleared his voice, fully expecting to have to leave a message on her voice mail, but to his surprise, Pam's voice came on the line. "Hello, this is Pamela. How can I help you?"

"Uh, hi, Pam. This is Alan…Parish."

A few seconds of silence passed. "Hi, Alan. What's up?"

"Oh, not much," he said, summoning a nervous laugh. "I just called to wish you a happy April Fool's Day."

More silence, then, "That's nice."

He picked up a pen and started doodling on a pad of paper. "So, how have you been?"

"Fine, I guess," she said. "How's your eye?"

"It healed."

"And, uh, the other end?"

"Well," he said, shifting in his seat, "it's a delicate operation—I'm still trying to choose the best doctor."

"Jo told me the two of you talked things through."

"That's right." Not that there were any unresolved issues in his mind. But he knew it had made Jo feel better to explain why she had canceled their wedding.

"She seems really happy being a mom," Pam said.

He tried to concentrate on what she was saying, but he kept picturing her nude in the limo. "Yeah, can you imagine taking care of three kids?"

"Um, no, I can't."

And her breasts—God, he shuddered just thinking

about them. "Just the thought sends chills up my spine."

"I remember your view on kids, Alan."

Funny, but right now he could legitimately say the most difficult part about having a baby would be sharing his wife—emotionally and physically. Pam was the kind of woman that made a man selfish. Alan shook his head to clear it. Pam, a wife? What was he thinking?

"Alan, are you still there?"

"What? Sure, I'm here." He cleared his throat. "Say, Pam, are you free this weekend to attend a business function?"

During her few seconds of hesitation, he died a thousand times. "What kind of business function?"

His mind raced—what the devil had Linda said? "Uh, there's a feet convention at the skating rink."

"Excuse me?"

"I mean, a political fund-raiser for birds."

"What?"

Where was his brain? "Forget business—can we have dinner tonight at the River Plaza Hotel?"

"Is something wrong, Alan?"

She obviously thought the idea of them having a date was so far-fetched there had to be some other compelling reason for them to get together. "I need to talk to you...about Jo," he said, wincing at his choice of subject matter, but it was too late.

"Jo?" she asked.

"Yeah," he said, rushing ahead. "I'm having trouble working through some things and I hoped you could help me."

The silence stretched on.

"Pam?" he urged.

"Sure," she said softly. "What are friends for?"

His heart jumped for joy. "Really? I mean—" he swallowed "—that's great. Uh, seven o'clock?"

"Seven sounds fine."

She didn't sound too happy about it, but he didn't care. He just wanted to see her again. Alan's mind raced for another topic to prolong the conversation. "Have you sold the Sheridan house?"

"Not yet—Mrs. Wingate hired a poltergeist-detection team to spend the night there. We're waiting on the results. Listen, Alan, I really need to run."

"Oh, sure," he said, fighting to keep the disappointment out of his voice. "I'll see you tonight." He hung up the phone slowly, trying to be optimistic, but he'd heard the distance in her voice. Alan looked down at the pad of paper he'd been doodling on and stopped, then jammed his fingers through his hair and sighed.

He'd drawn the outline of a heart and inside, in slanting letters, he'd written the word *Pam's.*

PAM SETTLED the phone in its cradle and blinked back hot tears. How ironic that after all these weeks, he had chosen today to call. Today, when she was wrestling with how to break the news to him that he had fathered a child while on a fake honeymoon with his ex-fiancée's best friend.

How could she face him? How could she present him with the news of a child he did not want by a woman he did not want? Wouldn't the Parish family be proud. She could hear the whispers now, see the sneers on her brothers' faces.

She dropped her head into her hands. How could she

face Jo? Since Pam's return, her friend had thanked her profusely for offering Alan a comforting hand during a very trying period in his life. Only it would soon become clear that she had offered Alan more than her hand.

How could she face her child? How could she tell her child that he or she was conceived in lust by a father who had just been jilted and by a mother whose dreams were too outlandish to be realized?

And how could she face herself? She had been careless with her heart, and careless with her body. She had known Alan was in love with her best friend. He'd used her to get over the hurt, and she had let him. She had let him on the slimmest hope that the man who represented everything she wanted in a partner—security, integrity, heritage and nobility—would recognize in her what no man had ever seen and fall in love with her.

Perhaps she had loved him ever since he'd hauled her off Mary Jane Cunningham's back in high school. He had taken up for her, but she'd given him a shin-shiner because she didn't know how else to react to someone in his social class. She couldn't very well act as though she *liked* him.

Since that day, she had found it easier to make fun of him rather than admit he had something she envied. And when their paths had crossed again as adults, she had simply picked up where she'd left off. Only in the wee hours of the morning when she was alone with her thoughts and fears and dreams had she been honest with herself. Only then had she admitted that Alan was the man she wanted but knew she'd never have, so she'd filled her dance card with has-beens and wannabes and never-would-bes.

Just like Alan had filled his dance card with her in the wake of Jo's rejection.

She shoved her hands into her hair. Now what? Pam wiped her eyes and pulled her address book from a desk drawer. After dialing an Atlanta extension, she sniffed mightily, feeling better just at the anticipation of hearing the voice of a dear old friend. Someone with a little objective distance. Someone she could trust to set her straight. Someone with big, broad, undemanding shoulders.

"Hello?"

"Manny? It's Pamela."

"Well, hello, baby doll!" He clucked. "You'd better have a good excuse why I haven't heard from you lately."

She smiled at the laughter in his voice. "Would you settle for a good excuse for calling now?" As much as she tried to maintain control, she could not keep her voice from breaking on the last word.

"What's wrong?" he asked, immediately serious. "Oh, God, it's a man, isn't it?" He sighed dramatically. "The straight ones all seem programmed to seek and destroy."

"I need to get away for a few days," she whispered.

"I'll alert the pedestrians of Atlanta that you're on your way."

ALAN CHECKED his watch for the twentieth time. Where was she? Pam was only a few minutes late, but after he'd talked to her, the rest of the afternoon had crawled. He was impatient to see her, to talk to her. He drummed on the surface of the hotel bar, feeling ready to come out of his skin with anticipation. The bartender slid a shot of whiskey across the bar and he downed it, hoping it would give him the courage he needed.

He loved her. It sounded ridiculous and she'd probably laugh in his face, but he didn't care. The week in Fort Myers, although admittedly fraught with disaster, had given him a taste of her spice for life, and he had become addicted. Every day since returning home, he had told himself the restlessness would pass, that they had simply been caught up in the romance of a beach fling. But he finally had to admit to himself that he wanted Pamela, that he *needed* Pamela in his life.

And he refused to share her with other men—he wanted a commitment. Marriage seemed a bit ludicrous considering he had been standing at the altar with another woman just a few weeks ago. Besides, Pam had made it perfectly clear that she wasn't looking to become anyone's wife. But he hoped she would at least move in with him, a public declaration that they were a couple. Then perhaps someday they would both be ready for marriage…and a family.

Alan stopped and shook his head. He still had to get through tonight—he'd worry about the heavy stuff later. His imminent concern was the risk of her choking from laughing too hard. In his mind he reviewed the Heimlich maneuver, then checked his watch again. She was worth waiting for.

AROUND EIGHT O'CLOCK Pam found a parking place a half block from Manny's apartment building. Her back ached and her feet were swollen from the five-hour drive, an omen of the months to come, she knew. She'd cried off her makeup by the time she'd reached Macon, but Manny wouldn't mind. City sounds greeted her when she opened the door and lifted herself out of the car. Little Five Points was one of her favorite areas in Atlanta, and ablaze with crimson, pink and white azaleas, it was certainly one of the prettiest this time of year.

She rolled her shoulders and stretched her legs, then grabbed her bag. Although it was only a short walk to Manny's building, followed by a brief flight of stairs, her feet felt as though they were made of concrete by the time she arrived at her friend's apartment. He swung open the door before she'd finished knocking and swept her into a huge hug.

When he set her on her feet, he chucked her lightly under the chin. "Pam, one of these days you simply must begin to age."

Pam smiled at the tall, fair-haired man she'd met at a club several years ago. They'd hit it off and had maintained contact over the years, visiting at every chance. Manny Oliver was a confirmed homosexual and a world-class good guy. Pam looked at his dancing eyes and sighed. "Manny, if you ever decide to jump ship, I want to be the first to know."

"Darling, you and Ellie would be the only women in my lifeboat."

"How is Ellie?" Pam asked, referring to his former roommate.

"Disgustingly happy," he said, rolling his eyes. "Married less than a year and she and Mark are already expecting a baby." He shuddered. "I ask you—what woman could possibly endure those hideous maternity fashions?"

Pam pursed her lips and dropped her gaze. "Got any dos and don'ts for me?"

"Oh, no," he murmured, sinking into a chair. "Not you, too."

She nodded, her eyes welling with tears.

He simply opened his arms and shooed her inside, then rocked her through another crying jag. Only after she'd blown her nose twice and gotten over the hiccups did he question her.

"Who is the proud papa?"

"His name is Alan Parish."

"Does he know?"

She shook her head.

"Are you going to tell him?"

Pam nodded.

"*Tell* me this guy is husband material."

She laughed dryly. "He had a wedding in February."

"Pam," he chided. "Even *I* don't mess around with married men."

"No, he was marrying my best friend, but she called off the wedding at the last minute."

"Ah. And you picked up the pieces?"

"Something like that. But I don't think he's ready to make another trip to the altar." She laughed softly, then added, "Not with me anyway."

"How do you think he will react to the news?"

She bit her bottom lip to stem another flood of tears. "He hates kids."

Manny frowned. "Well, if that's the case, he should keep his pants zipped."

"It's my fault—my pills failed."

"That's a moot point. Now you have to make plans

for this baby. Are you going to keep it or give it up for adoption?''

''I'm keeping it.''

''And can you expect any help from this Parish guy?''

''I'm not sure.''

Manny squinted and angled his head. ''Pam, is there something you're not telling me?''

''I'm in love with him.''

''The plot thickens. And his feelings for you?''

''Zilch.''

''Not true—he got naked with you, didn't he?''

''Okay, I suppose he's physically attracted to me.''

''It's a start.''

''But he's still in love with my best friend.''

''He told you this?''

''No, but he hasn't called since we were together— until today when he asked me to meet so we could talk about his feelings for her.''

''Sounds like a jerk to me.''

''Oh, no—he's really a great guy. In fact, one of the reasons I admire him so much is that he was so committed to my friend.''

''If the man doesn't scoop you up and count his blessings, he's obtuse,'' Manny insisted.

''He's a little uptight,'' Pam admitted, smiling fondly. ''But when he lets go, he can be very endearing.''

Manny handed her a cup of tea and lifted one eyebrow. ''And good in bed, I certainly hope.''

She nodded miserably.

He sighed. ''Promise me you won't wear stripes in the last trimester.''

ALAN STRUGGLED to keep his voice calm. "But you don't understand," he explained to the receptionist at Pam's office. "I *have* left voice-mail messages. I've left *fourteen* voice-mail messages."

"Perhaps her cellular phone—".

"She's not answering. Pam was supposed to meet me last night and she didn't show. I'm worried about her."

The receptionist didn't seem particularly sympathetic that he'd been stood up. "Sir, all I can tell you is that Ms. Kaminski said she'd be out of the office for a few days. I can give you her pager number—"

"I called her pager number—she's not answering!"

"Then I'll transfer you to her voice mail."

"Wait—" he yelled, but he heard a click and Pam's voice message, which he'd now memorized. Alan slammed down the phone and cursed. He reared back and kicked his desk as hard as he could, bellowing when the pain shot up his leg.

"Mr. Parish," Linda said, sticking her head through his doorway. "Are you okay?"

Alan inhaled deeply. "I'm fine, Linda." Then he limped to his valet and yanked on his jacket. "Cancel my appointments for the rest of the afternoon."

PAMELA LIVED IN a neat little town house in an artsy part of town—Alan suspected she'd made a good investment, considering her line of work. He had been there only twice to pick her up for some event they had attended together, but he hadn't gone inside. The tiny driveway was vacant, and the shades were drawn. The outside light glowed weakly in the bright midmorning sun, as if to fool someone into thinking she was home.

He walked up the steps and retrieved her untouched morning paper, then knocked on her front door several times before going around to the back and doing the same. After ten minutes, Alan climbed back into his car and pounded his steering wheel in frustration. ''Pam, where are you?'' he shouted into the cab of his car. *''Where are you?''*

He laid his head back and exhaled, then straightened and turned the key. Within minutes, he was heading toward Jo Montgomery's office, not sure what he was going to tell her, but absolutely certain that he had to find Pam.

As luck would have it, Jo was in a deep embrace with her new husband, John Sterling, when Alan knocked and stuck his head through her open doorway. They quickly parted, although John kept a possessive arm around Jo's waist while she straightened her clothing.

''Alan,'' she gasped. ''What a nice surprise.''

''We didn't hear you come in,'' John said with a tight smile.

''I wonder why,'' Alan said dryly. ''Jo, could I have a word with you?''

''Of course,'' she said quickly, then glanced at her husband, who wore a wary frown.

''It's about Pam,'' Alan informed him impatiently.

''Jo, I'll see you at home,'' John said, dropping a quick kiss on her mouth. He nodded curtly to Alan as he left.

''Do you want some coffee?'' Jo asked politely.

Alan shook his head. "I'm looking for Pam and I thought you might know where she is."

Jo averted her gaze and relief swept through him. Jo knew, which meant at least Pam was okay.

"Did you leave her a voice message?" she asked.

"Sure did."

"Maybe she hasn't had a chance to return calls."

"Where is she?"

"Alan—"

"I have to see her, Jo. It's important."

"She asked me not to tell anyone—"

"Jo, there's something you should know."

Jo frowned. "Alan, what's wrong?"

He exhaled noisily, suddenly unsure of himself. "Something happened when Pam and I were in Fort Myers."

"Alan, I don't think this is any of my—"

"I fell in love with her."

Her eyes widened slightly, and a slow smile climbed her face. "What?"

"I fell in love with her." He raised his hands in the air. "Jo, I swear to you on everything I hold sacred that nothing ever went on between us when you and I were together." He pursed his lips and gritted his teeth before continuing. "But when we were in Fort Myers, I saw Pam in a new light. She's warm and funny and smart—" He broke off and shrugged helplessly. "She makes me happy, Jo, and when I'm with her, I understand what you must feel when you're with John."

Jo's eyes were full of unshed tears. "Alan, nothing would make me happier than to see the two of you together."

"I have to find her, Jo, and tell her how I feel. Even

if she doesn't love me, I can't go another day with this on my heart.''

She smiled, displaying a dimple. "How about five hours?''

"Five hours?''

"She's in Atlanta, staying with a friend for a few days.''

Alan frowned. "A male friend?''

She nodded, and hurt stabbed him hard in the chest. He laughed softly and shook his head. "What's the point if she's with another man?''

Jo walked over to him and touched his arm. "It's a good thing John didn't let that stop him," she said quietly. "For both our sakes.''

12

AFTER A MORNING of hugging the toilet, Pam napped away the afternoon, then dragged herself toward the tub. A shower, she'd discovered, was a heartbroken, pregnant woman's solace because there she could cry freely and it didn't matter.

Not that she didn't cry everywhere else anyway. Throughout the day, Manny pampered her with cool cloths for her forehead, warm cloths for her neck, pillows for her feet, pillows for her back, the latest magazines and nice, bland food when her stomach could stand it. She felt lumpy and frumpy in one of Manny's old sweat suits, but being enveloped in his big, masculine clothes gave her comfort.

When dusk began to fall, he dragged a cushiony chair out onto the fire escape and planted her there while he brushed her hair. The spring breeze was unusually balmy, inspiring Pam to inhale great lungfuls of fresh air. A zillion stars glittered overhead, triggering memories of the night she and Alan strolled along the moonlit beach and the passion that had swept them away.

Well, actually, Alan had been swept away to jail, but that night had been an awakening for her, and she would never forget it. She toyed with the sand-castle pendant that hung around her neck, where it had been since the day they'd returned to Savannah.

"Maybe I need a change of scenery," she said, sipping the cup of peppermint tea Manny had prepared for her.

"You're welcome to this apartment," he offered. "But in a couple of months you'll have to find another roommate."

She twisted in her chair. "You're moving?"

"To San Francisco, in June."

"Why didn't you say something?" Pam demanded.

"Darlin', you've got enough on your mind." He clucked. "I was planning to send you a change-of-address card."

"What's in San Francisco?"

"A career path," he said flatly. "On New Year's I took a glimpse into my future, and believe me, there's nothing pretty about a senior-citizen drag-queen performer."

Pam laughed—Manny hadn't yet seen his fortieth birthday and was an exceptionally handsome guy. "What will you do?"

He bowed. "Concierge at the Chandelier House, at your service, madam."

"Manny, that's wonderful—you'll be a big hit!" Then she made a face. "I'll miss you though."

"You and the *bébé* will have to come out for a visit."

"We will," she declared, grinning at him in the mirror.

Manny cocked his ear toward the apartment and held up a finger. "I think I heard a knock, I'll be right back."

Pam sank deeper into the seat and wrapped her hands over her stomach. *Imagine,* she thought with a little smile, *Alan's baby growing inside me.* And although she wasn't foolish enough to believe raising a child on her own would be easy, she would do what she had done all her life—make the best of her circumstances. This child would be loved, if by no one else, then by her.

"Pam," Manny said from the doorway, "you have a visitor."

She jerked her head around in surprise, then gasped when she saw Alan standing in the living room, his suit jacket over his shoulder and his face grim. To see him after so many weeks was a shock to her senses, and she couldn't fathom why he was here. Standing on wobbly legs, she stepped into the doorway, aware that Manny hovered an arm's length behind her.

Alan straightened when Pam stepped into view. His heart slammed against his chest painfully. She looked beautiful, but different. Softer, perhaps, with no makeup and her hair loose around her shoulders. Wearing her lover's clothes, she looked dewy-eyed and vulnerable. Jealousy ripped through him and he tried not to think about the rumpled covers and pillows on the couch. Seeing their recent sex venue only strengthened his resolve that under no circumstances would he share her with another man.

"Alan, this is my friend Manny—"

"We already met, sweetheart," Manny assured her, but his eyes never left Alan.

Alan's hands twitched at the casual term of endearment, but he tried to focus on the reason he'd come.

"Alan," Pam asked, taking another step toward him. "What are you doing here?"

"Looking for you."

Her smile was shaky. "Obviously, but why?"

Alan glanced to her tall boyfriend, but the man wasn't about to budge from the room. "Would you excuse us, um, Manny?"

The guy poked his tongue into his cheek, then glanced to Pam with raised eyebrows for confirmation. She nodded.

"I'll be in the bedroom," the man said, glaring at Alan. "Yell if you need me, Pam."

"Thanks, Manny."

Alan waited until he heard the bedroom door close before speaking, and then he didn't know where to start. "I waited for you the other night."

"Something came up—I should have called."

"I was worried."

"I'm fine," she said with a nervous laugh. "How did you know where to find me?"

"Jo."

She nodded, lowering her gaze.

"Look, Pam," he said, stepping closer but maintaining a safe distance. "I didn't mean to embarrass you in front of your boyfriend, but—"

"He's not my boyfriend. Manny's gay."

Relief swept through him. "Really? Hey, that's great—I say a man's got to do what a man's got to do, and if that means marching—"

"Alan, what do you want?"

He mentally went down the list he'd made and left in the car. "I didn't mean to embarrass you in front of your boyfriend—"

''You said that already,'' she said, lifting a corner of her mouth. ''Don't tell me you've got a script.''

Panic flooded his vocal cords. ''I love you, dammit!''

She stood stock-still while he hung out swinging in the breeze, waiting for her answer. Seconds ticked by.

''Say something,'' he said.

''I'm pregnant with your baby.''

He froze and glanced around the room, absorbing her words, but finding them too unbelievable to comprehend. ''Come again?''

''I'm pregnant with your baby.''

Strange, but the words sounded exactly the same the second time. Alan felt his jaw drop, close, then drop again. Intelligent words to combine into an appropriate response had to reside somewhere deep in his brain, but they didn't seem to be forthcoming.

She waited.

His mind raced. Men became fathers every day— coming up with a reply for the woman he loved couldn't be that hard.

''Gee,'' he said with a shaky laugh, then felt the room close in around him. ''I think I'm going to pass out.'' But even though the trip to the floor seemed to be in slow motion, the thump of his head against the wood revived him somewhat.

Alan heard Pam scream for Manny, then heard the man tell her to get a pitcher of water from the refrigerator.

Manny slapped him lightly on the cheeks, then a stinging blast of ice water hit his face, taking his breath. His temple throbbed with a new pain.

His eyes popped open and through his water-speckled lenses, he saw Pam standing over him holding a glass pitcher.

"Uh—Pam," Manny said. "You could have taken out the ice first." He handed her a chunk as large as a man's fist, tinged with blood. "He might have a concussion."

"I'm fine," Alan mumbled. "Help me up."

Manny helped him to the couch then gave him a cloth to hold to his bleeding temple. "You're going to have a heck of a goose egg, man."

Alan smiled and shrugged, looking at Pam. "It comes with the territory."

"I hope your insurance is paid up," Manny muttered on his way out of the room.

"Sounds like I'm going to need the family plan," Alan said, locking gazes with Pam.

"Alan—"

"Why didn't you tell me about the baby?" He clasped her by the upper arms. "I've missed you like crazy these past few weeks, and I was nearly insane wondering what happened to you last night."

"When you called, I was trying to decide how to break the news, then you said you wanted to talk about your feelings for Jo—"

"It was an excuse—I didn't think you'd meet me otherwise."

She blinked. "That was dumb."

"I was desperate!"

Pam winced. "How much does Jo know?"

"Everything."

"Oh no."

"And she said she couldn't be happier. In fact, she

encouraged me to come after you.'' His Adam's apple bobbed. "Pamela Kaminski, will you marry me?''

Her eyes widened. "M-marry?''

"You know—you'd be the wife, I'd be the husband.''

"Wife?'' she whispered, then smiled tremulously. "I hadn't planned on ever being anyone's wife.'' Then she laughed, her eyes filling with tears. "But I hadn't planned on ever being anyone's mother, either.''

He grinned. "I've noticed lately that life is full of surprises.''

"Alan, I know you don't like kids—''

"Unless they're mine,'' he corrected.

"But kids are loud…''

"So are you.''

"—and messy…''

"So are you.''

"—and the diapers…''

He winced. "You got me there.''

"It won't be easy.''

Alan curled his fingers around her neck and pulled her face close to his. "Is that a yes?''

Her eyes were luminous as she studied his face, then she dabbed at the blood on his temple. "That's a yes,'' she whispered, then added, "The 'P' stands for 'papa.'''

THE CHURCH WAS somewhat less crowded this time, Alan noticed from his view at the altar. Which was fine with him, as long as the people who mattered were there.

His parents sat on the front pew, crying happy tears because Pam had enchanted them as much as she had enchanted him. Pam's mother sat on the opposite side, dabbing her eyes. Her two brothers stood next to him, fingering their tight collars, waiting for Pam to make her entrance. Her older brother, Roy, pointed to Alan's bandaged hand. "What happened?"

"A little mishap when we tried on rings," Alan explained with a shrug.

"Sounds like Pam," Roy affirmed with a nod. "You'd better lower your deductible. By the way, where the devil is she?"

Alan tried not to betray the nervousness that wallowed in his stomach. "She must be here, or the director wouldn't have let them start the music."

"They've played that song so many times, I know it by heart," Roy whispered hoarsely.

"Maybe she had a sudden case of morning sickness," Alan said, trying to squelch humiliating flashbacks from the last time he stood at the altar.

"It's two in the afternoon."

"Well, you know women's bodies can be...unpredictable."

Roy grinned. "Not the word I would have used, but whatever."

After another five minutes of "O Promise Me," Alan glanced at Jo, who stood an arm's length away in a simple bridesmaid dress. She chewed on her lower lip and shrugged slightly, then mouthed, "Want me to go check?"

Alan sighed, feeling sick to his stomach. If Pam had changed her mind about becoming his wife, he wanted to be the one to know. He walked down the aisle, trying to block out the concerned murmur that swept through the guests, then marched through the back doors of the chapel.

His hand shook as he opened the door to the bride's waiting room, and his heart pounded when he saw it was empty. He checked the bathroom, but found it abandoned, as well. With a sinking heart, he realized she must have changed her mind. He gritted his teeth, then laughed bitterly. He was zero for two.

His eyes stung with emotion as he walked back toward the chapel once again to tell everyone to go home, but as he walked past the open doors of the church entrance, he heard a familiar beeping horn. He glanced outside in time to see Pam's Volvo jump the curb and come to a screeching halt, mere inches from a stone statue of some important-looking saint.

Dressed in full bridal regalia, with a voluminous veil and enormous train, she took quite a while to extricate herself from the car. When she did, she gathered the skirt in her arms, hiking it up to her thighs to run across the churchyard in bare feet. Carrying her shoes in one hand, she waved when she saw him in the doorway. "I'm coming!" she yelled. "I'm coming!"

"Where have you been?" he demanded when she came to a halt in front of him. God, she was gorgeous, especially with her slightly rounded tummy.

"Mrs. Wingate paged me," she said breathlessly. "Her head psychic told her she had a one-hour window of safety to buy the Sheridan house." She panted for air. "I was already dressed, and I figured I could leave and get the papers signed before anyone missed me." She smiled happily, her chest heaving. "Did anyone miss me?"

He sighed, wanting to shake her. "You scared me to death—I thought you had changed your mind."

She looped her arms around his neck. "Not on your life—you're stuck with me, Mr. Alan P. Parish." She pulled his mouth to hers for a deep kiss.

He raised his head, then bent down and lifted her into his arms. "Let's go make you my wife before anything else happens." Then he turned, carried her toward the chapel and whispered, "I have a confession to make."

"What?"

"I told the guy at the tattoo parlor that the 'P' stands for 'Pam's.'"

Epilogue

ALAN RAISED his hands. "Pam," he said in a soothing voice. "Put down the nail file."

"You!" she yelled at him from the hospital bed. "You did this to me!"

"Honey," he said, "don't you think it was a combined effort?"

He ducked as the vase of flowers flew past his head and crashed against the wall at his back.

"You're right!" he affirmed hurriedly, raising his arms in surrender. He put on a mournful expression and gestured vaguely toward her huge stomach. "It's all my fault—I did this to you and I am the lowest scum on the face of the earth."

Her face contorted with pain and Alan's heart twisted in agony. His beautiful wife was lying in abject misery, and he couldn't even get close enough to the hospital bed to practice the Lamaze they had learned together.

"Do you have your focus point, sweetie?" he called, inching closer.

She lay back, panting, then pinned him with a deadly look. "I'm focusing on a life of celibacy!"

"Honey, you don't mean that," he said in his most cajoling voice, but stopped when she held up the makeshift dagger. "Celibacy is good," he assured her with a nervous laugh. "We can make it work." Alan retreated the few inches he'd advanced. "How about an ice chip?" he asked.

"How about I chip your tooth?" she offered, smiling sweetly.

The door swung open and Dr. Campbell strode in with a smile. "How're we doing?"

Alan, weak with relief to have an ally, smiled broadly. "Just great," he said, then glanced at Pam's murderous expression. "I mean, not very well at all."

"Let's see where you are, Pam." To Alan's alarm, the doctor eased Pam's swollen feet and ankles into the stirrups, giving him a bird's-eye view beneath her hospital gown.

He swallowed and cleared his throat. "I think I'll wait outside."

"Oh no you don't," Pam said, ominously. "You're not going anywhere."

Alan nodded obediently and wiped his sweaty hands on his slacks. "Right—wild horses couldn't drag me out of here."

The doctor glanced at the monitor. "Here comes another contraction, Pam. Just try to relax."

"Remember to breathe, sweetie," Alan called. "Hee-hee—"

"Shut up!" she shouted.

"I'm shutting up," he said, nodding vigorously.

"If the pain's getting to be too much," the doctor said to Pam, "I can go ahead and give you an epidural."

"Thanks anyway, Dr. Campbell," Alan said from the wall. "We decided from the beginning to go for natural childbir—"

"Give me the needle, Dr. C.," Pam cut in, "and I'll give it to myself."

"Oh my," the doctor said, moving her hands beneath the gown.

Alan glanced over, then squeezed his eyes shut, muttering thanks to the heavens for the thousandth time today that he was not a woman.

"Forget the epidural," the doctor said, depressing the nurse call button with her elbow. "You're ready to start pushing."

Alan's eyes popped open. "Already?"

"Already?" Pam shrieked. "It's been nine hours!"

But I'm not ready, I'm not wise enough yet to be a father. Perspiration popped out on his hairline and panic rose in his chest, suffocating him.

The nurses rushed in and dressed him in sanitary garb as if he were a kid going out in the snow. He was relegated, happily, to a corner as they prepared Pam for the final stages of labor. Alan had never felt so guilty and helpless in his life. She agonized through two more contractions before the doctor said, "Daddy, you come jump in anytime."

Alan glanced to Pam for affirmation, but her eyes were squeezed shut to ward off the pain. Her hands were on the bed railing, so at least her weapon had been confiscated.

"Pam?" he said weakly, stepping closer. "Sweetie?"

She didn't open her eyes, but she lifted a hand toward him, and he went to her side with relief.

"Alan," she whispered, lolling her head toward him.

"Yes, dear?"

"What does the 'P' stand for?"

"Pam, now doesn't seem like the time—"

She twisted a handful of his shirt and pulled him close to her. "I said, what does the 'P' stand for?"

"Pam, you need to push," Dr. Campbell said. "On the count of three."

"Alan—" Pam said through clenched teeth.

"One—"

"—what does—" Her face reddened.

"—two—"

"—the 'P' stand for?"

"—three—push!"

Her face contorted in pain and she screamed. Alan, scared half out of his wits, yelled, "Presley! The 'P' stands for 'Presley!'"

She grunted, bearing down for several seconds, then relaxed on the pillow and opened her eyes. "Presley?" she panted.

He nodded miserably. "My mom was a huge fan."

She laughed between gasping for air, readying herself for another push at the doctor's urging. He held her hand tight and whispered loving words in her ear.

"Here comes the head," said the doctor.

She bore down and squeezed his hand until he was sure she'd broken several bones. His heart thrashed in his chest and he looked around to see what he would hit when he passed out.

"One more push, Pam," the doctor urged.

She took a deep breath and screamed loud enough to rattle the windows. Alan held on, wondering if his hearing would return.

"Here we are," the doctor said triumphantly. "It's a big boy."

Relief and elation flooded his chest and he kissed Pam's face, whispering, "It's a boy. It's a boy."

Pam, exhausted but beaming, held her hands out to accept the wrinkled, outraged infant. Alan's heart filled to bursting as he looked down at his son, whose lusty cries filled the air.

"Do you have a name?" the doctor asked.

"Not yet—" he said.

"Of course we do," Pam said as she raised her moist gaze to her husband. "Our beautiful son's name is Presley."

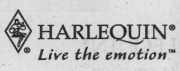

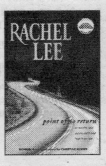
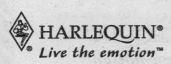

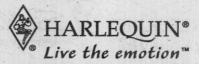